Masquerade

CLARISSA ROSS

CRIMSON
ROMANCE

F+W Media, Inc.

This edition published by
Crimson Romance
an imprint of F+W Media, Inc.
10151 Carver Road, Suite 200
Blue Ash, Ohio 45242
www.crimsonromance.com

ISBN 10: 1-4405-7287-9
ISBN 13: 978-1-4405-7287-6
eISBN 10: 1-4405-7288-7
eISBN 13: 978-1-4405-7288-3

Cover art © iStockphoto.com/mammuth

1

Lady Enid Blair, a young, sloe-eyed beauty with golden tresses and soft, creamy skin, understood that any shocking thing was possible in the city of Paris in 1789. But this wedding dinner a few short hours after her marriage to Lord Andrew Blair far exceeded anything she or any other good English virgin could have imagined. It was the climax of a series of unsettling events that had occurred ever since she had agreed to marry the dashing but dissolute young nobleman two months ago.

"La-di-da sort of fellow," her father, Lord Alfred Henson, had commented weakly from his sickbed. Then his eyes—plum-colored like Enid's—had met hers in a look of appeal. "Because of my illness and a slump in my business interests, we are nearly destitute. Lord Andrew has offered to extend unlimited credit to me, and your marriage to him would be provident, indeed."

Enid had had no deep love for Andrew, but she had known that he moved in the highest social circles of London, was much admired by some for his reckless behavior, and was enormously wealthy. She had felt obliged to agree to the match for the sake of her parents, and when Andrew had made his proposal, she had accepted, but with a chill in her heart. She had sensed that even if she strove to be a good and faithful wife, the marriage was in some way doomed.

This had not been the best of circumstances in which to consent to become a bride, but worse had followed. Not only had Andrew insisted that Enid give up her religion for him, he had also demanded—as a firm provision of their agreement—that they be married in Paris at the chateau of his good friend Vicomte Claude Robert.

On the long journey to France, Enid had been chaperoned by her elderly nurse, Mrs. Giddings, but this morning, before the wedding ceremony, Lord Andrew had dismissed the kindly woman and sent her back to England.

Plump Mrs. Giddings had come to Enid's chamber in tears. "I must leave you now, dear child," she said. "May the good Lord watch over you!"

Enid had risen from her dressing table in astonishment. "He is sending you back before the wedding?"

Mrs. Giddings had nodded, her sallow face reflecting her misery. "It was always my hope to see you take your vows on your wedding day, but as things are, I'm just as well pleased not to be here. To see you married to the likes of him is too distressing!"

Enid had embraced her nurse, saying tearfully, "I shall miss you so, but you must not worry."

"Worry, indeed!" Mrs. Giddings had declared indignantly. "What else can I do? That young rake is not marrying you out of affection but to suit his own convenience. Don't you realize that?"

"Mrs. Giddings!"

"It's true!" the woman had persisted. "You know the things that have been said about him in England. And now he's the guest of his good friend the vicomte! Did you note their greeting when they met the other day? Kissed each other on the lips in full view of everyone!"

"The French have different ways," Enid had murmured, though the incident had shocked her also.

"*This* Frenchman has different ways," Mrs. Giddings had sniffed. "And so has your husband-to-be, if I may make so bold."

"I'm sure it is not as you think," Enid had protested.

Mrs. Giddings had eyed her with great concern. "You have always been my girl, a good Christian lady. You are doing this for your father and mother, I know it all too well. But I pray you will not be crushed by this atmosphere of sinfulness—that you will rise above it. I pray you will!"

Enid had embraced the woman again. "Thank you, dear Mrs. Giddings. Your words give me comfort and cheer. I wish you a safe and pleasant voyage home. And when you see my parents, please give them my love and say I shall write them each day."

With Mrs. Giddings gone, Enid had felt miserably alone. The French maids assigned to her were attentive enough, but she could not understand all that they said; besides, she had had the uneasy feeling that at times they were making fun of her. After completing her toilette, she had donned a pale blue gown and gone downstairs for luncheon.

The vicomte, who was to be best man at the wedding, the Duchess d'Orleans, whom the vicomte had selected as Enid's matron of honor, and Lord Andrew had been standing together at the foot of the stairs, indulging in a rather excited conversation when she joined them. The vicomte, a young, effeminate man in a white wig and a dark blue velvet jacket, was good-looking in a fine-featured sort of way. He had kissed Enid's hand and introduced her to the duchess, a somewhat mannish woman in looks and gestures, but who spoke in a soft, deep-throated voice.

"What a lovely bride you will make," the duchess had remarked, studying Enid through a jewel-studded lorgnette.

Andrew had given the vicomte a smiling glance from his dark, hooded eyes and added, "And how kind of Claude to allow us the use of his private chapel!"

This statement had surprised Enid. "I had no idea…I assumed we would be married in some lovely cathedral."

The vicomte had laughed softly. "You will find our family chapel as impressive as any church in Paris. Petite perhaps, but in excellent taste."

"And so appropriate, since the wedding is to be an intimate one," the duchess had commented.

"I'm sure Enid will be delighted with the wisdom of your choice," Andrew had said. "Is that not so, my dear?"

"As you've made all the other arrangements, I must leave this to your judgment as well," she had replied.

Claude had been quick to reassure her. "You will not be let down, dear lady. The personal confessor to our family, Cardinal Léger, has consented to perform the ceremony. He will arrive in the late afternoon."

So she had sat down to luncheon in a small anteroom adjacent to the dining salon, which was being prepared for the elaborate wedding dinner. Much of the time the others had spoken in French, in which Enid was not too proficient. She could follow only part of what was being said, and thus she could not help but feel left out of the conversation. Her companions had paid her scant attention as they laughed and talked among themselves. Enid had comforted herself with the thought that later, when they were alone, Andrew would lavish all his love on her.

Nothing had happened at the luncheon to upset her, but shortly afterward an incident had occurred that had sent Enid into a flurry of doubts about the advisability of this marriage to which she had agreed.

She had decided to question Andrew further about the details of the wedding ceremony, and had been making her way from her bedchamber along the wide, shadowed corridor when she had suddenly come upon the Duchess d'Orleans, some twenty feet away. The duchess had been standing at one of the many full-length mirrors that adorned the corridor walls, carefully studying her tall frame. While Enid had watched from the protecting shadows, the woman had reached up and removed her wig, revealing the head of a man with short-cropped hair. Enid had almost cried out her shock at this unbelievable sight. Then the duchess had replaced the wig, and Enid had again seen the image of a titled noblewoman. But there had been no doubt in her mind that for some unaccountable reason this person was a man posing as a woman—a woman who would be her matron of honor!

The duchess had walked away and entered a room that apparently was hers. Enid had waited a moment, then, with her heart pounding, had sped to Andrew's chamber and knocked on the door.

A young valet had answered, eyeing her impudently. Andrew, who had been standing before a pier glass powdering his wig, had come forward to greet her, his handsome face breaking out in a welcoming smile.

"Andrew, I must speak to you alone," Enid had whispered in a quavering voice.

He had nodded to the valet, who departed immediately. After she had entered, Andrew had closed the door and taken her in his arms. She could smell his perfume and powder. He had kissed her gently and murmured, "Why is my tiny sparrow trembling so?"

Close to tears, she had replied, "I do not like any of it—being so far from home, having my wedding here rather than in a church. And I do not like your friend Claude—he always seems to be mocking me!"

"That is ridiculous! I'm afraid you are being childish, my sweet."

"There is something else," she added. "The duchess is a man! I saw her remove her wig, and I'm certain she is a man!"

Andrew had frowned for a moment and then laughed good-humoredly. "You have discovered a secret, it is true. But not the one you think. The duchess is simply one of those unfortunate women who are afflicted with baldness. She cut her hair short as a remedy and in the meanwhile wears the best of wigs."

Enid had realized he might be telling the truth, though she had still entertained doubts. "There are other things about the duchess which suggest she is a male…her voice and her mannerisms."

Andrew had begun to lose some of his cheerfulness. "This is not the time or place to discuss the poor woman. We are to be wed within the hour. It would be more seemly if you devoted your time to readying yourself for the ceremony."

Enid had been party to his bad humors before and knew that nothing would be gained by further argument. She could only hope that he had told her the truth and all would be well.

He had kissed her again and smiled as he saw her to the door. "Try to look happier. After all, this is to be the most important day in your life."

"I'm sorry. It's just that I'm so far from home and my parents."

"Your father is bedridden and your mother is his nurse," her husband-to-be reminded her. "They could not have attended any public ceremony had we been married in London."

"We could just as well have been married in my father's house in Surrey as here in the house of the vicomte!"

"To be married in the chapel of a vicomte's house, and by a cardinal, is an honor. You must not show yourself to be ungrateful."

"I have no wish to be, but I'm very confused by all I find around me."

Andrew had laughed softly. "That is the proper state of mind for any young bride-to-be. Off to your room and dress, now!"

She had obeyed him. The two chittering little French maids had dressed her in a gown of bridal-white satin adorned with a flowing lace veil. Just before she had left the room the duchess had appeared, wearing a formal gown of purple silk with a lavish diamond pendant at her throat. In that strange voice the duchess had trilled, "Such a dear bride! I'm so delighted!"

The noblewoman had escorted Enid downstairs and then to a distant wing in which the chapel was located. The chapel was small, but, as the vicomte had promised, it was very beautifully decorated. The stained-glass windows behind the rosewood altar depicted scenes of Christ's journeyings. The highly polished oaken communion table was intricately sculptured with a fine eye to detail. Tiny candles flickered in several niches, their light bathing the sanctuary in a warm glow.

After a few moments the cadaverous-looking cardinal had appeared, clad in heavy crimson robes. He had bowed to them and taken his place before the altar. Then Andrew and Claude had arrived, Andrew in a handsome gold velvet waistcoat embroidered in white and matching breeches, and the vicomte in a red brocade waistcoat, also embroidered in white, and dark red breeches.

Andrew had stood beside Enid and whispered, "How lovely you look, dearest."

She had given him a tiny smile, thinking wistfully of her parents and Mrs. Giddings. Then the ceremony had begun, and within a short period of time they had been proclaimed husband and wife. The cardinal had remained only long enough to bow gravely to each of them and shake their hands.

"Lady Blair!" In his mocking fashion the vicomte had addressed Enid by her new title. "What a stunning pair you and Andrew make!"

"Thank you," she had said. And to the duchess, "I appreciate your part in the ceremony."

The duchess had purred her pleasure. "This is my first experience as a matron of honor, and I shall treasure it."

"And now for the high point of it all," Claude had announced with simpering smugness. "The wedding dinner, to which I have given my greatest attention."

Andrew had cast a knowing glance at him. "I'm sure we all shall be delighted by it! It is bound to be an unusual surprise for my new wife."

"What a divine notion!" the duchess had exclaimed with matronly approval.

"So let us proceed to the dining hall!" The vicomte and the duchess had led the way, and Enid had followed on Andrew's arm. For a brief while she had felt that perhaps the marriage would turn out better than she had expected. Andrew appeared to show a sincere affection for her, and even though his friends were strange, they had gone to a great deal of trouble to make the wedding a success. So it would be on to the wedding dinner and then to that blissful wedding night when she and Andrew would be one. Afterward, she would be closer to him than anyone, and she would sway him from his gambling, his drinking, and his odd choice of friends.

The dining hall was large, high-ceilinged, and almost completely draped in green velvet curtains. The table for their wedding feast had been set for four, with Enid and Andrew at opposite ends of the white damask tablecloth. The gleaming silver, sparkling cut-glass crystal, and gold plate almost took Enid's breath away. She had rarely seen such opulence. The silver candelabra with its lighted white tapers offered the only illumination.

"It is magnificent!" she had found herself exclaiming.

The vicomte, seated to her right, but midway down the length of the table, had smiled and assured her, "It is only the start, Lady Blair!"

"I'm sure the food and wine will equal the splendor of our surroundings," the duchess had proclaimed.

"I have no fear of that," Andrew had chuckled, apparently enjoying a private joke with Claude and the duchess. "I have sampled Claude's hospitality before."

"I trust this dinner will not disappoint you," the vicomte had said with a smile for both Enid and Andrew. He had seemed so very pleasant she had reproved herself for having been suspicious of him.

He had rung a bell placed beside his wine glass, the signal that eventually caused Enid to allow that any shocking event was now possible in Paris. The bell signaled the entrance of a Nubian bearing a silver pitcher of amber wine. The huge black man came directly to her side and poured the liquid into her wine glass.

It was not his actions that startled her but his lurid appearance. Except for the golden cloth turban wound about his head and a gold chain at his neck, the man was completely naked. Despite her modesty, she could not ignore the fact that he was more than adequately endowed. Enid was a twenty-year-old virgin who had never seen a naked man before, and the sight of the giant black servant whose body was so totally exposed caused her cheeks to burn and her breath to come out in little gasps. From the others at the table she heard unsympathetic titters.

But this was to be only the beginning. Other young male servants, some no more than mere boys, appeared to serve the dishes of food and the decanters of wine. All of them were naked except for the elaborate gold jewelry about their throats. This endless display of male nudity so upset and confused Enid that she was barely able to raise her eyes from her plate as the feast proceeded.

It was almost a relief when equally naked young women came to remove the glasses and dishes. However, lithe females with full, round bosoms and curving bodies were in the minority. It was evident that male servants were the main attraction.

Andrew and his friends talked among themselves in French and largely ignored Enid, except to turn to her occasionally and raise their glasses in leering toasts. Enid was overwhelmed with embarrassment and confusion; her most urgent impulse was to flee from the scene before her. But she did not know what sort of response this would elicit from her new husband. She was certain that, no matter how vicious his behavior, he would be firmly of the opinion that she should remain all through their wedding feast.

The sight of the massive male organ had at first aroused her slightly, but now she felt repulsed by the smirking young servants as they waited on her. With each passing moment she thought she was in the middle of a wild nightmare.

"To my wife!" Andrew slurred in English, and rose to offer her another toast. The other two joined in with drunken glee. The wig of the duchess was now slightly awry, and the grand dame looked more like a man than ever. The vicomte spent much of his time stroking the buttocks of the youthful male servants.

Enid saw the wine dribble down the front of her husband's ruffled shirt as one of the serving boys placed yet another course in front of her. She jumped up from the table.

"You must excuse me!" she cried. "I have a dreadful headache!" She turned, and lifting her skirts slightly, ran from the room. Jeering laughter followed her exit and echoed in her ears as she raced through the corridors and up the endless stairways of the great gray stone chateau. When she reached her own room, she threw herself on the wide bed and sobbed with despair. She had not expected the wedding dinner to be a paragon of perfection, but she had not dreamed it would turn into an exhibitionist orgy.

After a little while she recovered somewhat and saw that her nightgown and robe had been carefully laid out on the bed. Slowly she began preparations for the arrival of Andrew. She bathed and perfumed her body and stood before the long mirror, inspecting herself critically. Could she match the beautiful women whom she had seen below in the dining hall?

As she gazed at her naked reflection she could not help but feel pride in her slender, curvaceous body. Her breasts were firm and uplifted, her long golden curls were repeated in miniature in the thick mound between her legs, and her hips and thighs flowed in a slim, provocative line. Surely she could offer Andrew enough to turn him from his promiscuous ways. With a sigh, she reached for her thin silk nightdress.

Before she could slip it on, the door to her room was thrown open and an irate and besotted Andrew staggered in. Seeing her naked, he sneered, "Were you in such a hurry for the bed, then?"

Holding the gown protectively before her, she replied, "It wasn't that! I could no longer endure the dreadful things going on down there!"

"All that was for you!" Andrew gasped, swaying toward her. "Claude put on the show for you!"

"Then he needn't have bothered!" she retorted bitterly.

Andrew moved toward her, taking off his jacket as he moved and throwing it on the stone floor. He seized her by the arms and tore the nightdress from her. Then he pressed her naked body to him and began kissing her on the mouth while his hands explored her roughly.

She tried to resist his violent attempts at lovemaking, but he had thrown her onto the bed and was feverishly undoing his breeches. His angry, sneering face loomed above her as he thrust his hard, erect member into her and began to pummel her insides. The direct attack brought such a sharp pain that she cried out repeatedly. Her moans only urged him on, and within a matter of minutes he had expended himself and withdrawn from her.

While he busied himself with buttoning his breeches, he said, "That fulfills my obligation, I trust. I hope you have not been disappointed." With that he lurched away, managed to pick up his waistcoat, and left the chamber, slamming the door behind him.

Enid lay there, completely miserable and humiliated. She had never felt so abused in her entire life. She tried to summon a logical reason for his unforgivable treatment of her on their wedding night, but the best she could do was to come up with only a shadow of an explanation that excused Andrew in his state of disgusting drunkenness.

2

After a tormented sleep in which the naked young males of the dining salon flitted in and out of her dreams, Enid awakened to a sun-filled morning. She felt disgraced and very much alone. A maid brought her breakfast on a tray, but she could eat only a small portion. She dressed hastily in a new yellow cambric gown chosen for the honeymoon and went downstairs in search of her husband.

The first person she met was the young vicomte. He offered her a simpering smile. "I trust you enjoyed a pleasant wedding night?"

She did not reply directly but asked instead, "Where is my husband?"

"Andrew has gone out for a short while," his friend said. "He will be back soon."

"I see," she replied tautly.

"He has many friends in Paris."

"Really?"

"And he likes to gamble," Claude added. "You will soon discover that."

"I know it already," she said in a quiet voice. "You have no knowledge of where he has gone?"

"None at all." The effeminate nobleman appeared to be enjoying her plight. "The duchess has also left and sends her love to you."

"How kind," she responded in the same low tone.

His pale eyes held a mocking light as he went on. "You are annoyed at my party for you last night?"

She looked down at her slippers. "Let us say I did not understand it."

"You will," he assured her. "After you spend some time here, you will begin to understand the ways of my house."

"I would hope that we would leave here shortly," she countered bravely.

His fine-featured face registered surprise. "But why? I offer you my home as your own. You must feel free to use it as such."

"Your offer is most generous, truly, but I feel it is unfair to begin married life under that kind of condition."

The vicomte was amused. "But of course, you are still a little country girl. You would do well to broaden your outlook and become more a woman of the world."

"I have no wish to change!"

"Andrew may have some ideas about that. I know he plans to remain here. There are so many things we both enjoy together. He likes the gaming table, and so do I. He has a fondness for beauty such as Paris offers, and so do I."

"Was last night a sample of what you choose to call beauty?" Enid demanded.

"I suppose you could say that," the vicomte replied, toying with a lace handkerchief.

"You are a single man entitled to your preferences. But Andrew has married me, and he must consider me in these matters."

Her husband's friend gave a small, brittle laugh. "I fear you know much less about Andrew than I."

"That doesn't surprise me at all," she replied, and spun around angrily toward the stairs.

Enid remained in her room, seated by the window, until the late afternoon, when Andrew appeared. He was wearing a brown linen waistcoat and fawn breeches; his eyes were bloodshot and his face was bloated.

His opening remark was curt. "I understand you have been unpleasant with Claude."

She rose from her chair. "That isn't true. I told him I was unhappy here and that I wished to spend my honeymoon somewhere else."

Andrew's handsome face became mottled. "How dare you say such a thing when he has been so generous to us?"

"I do not care for his generosity," she returned sharply. Then she gave her husband a pleading look. "If you love me, Andrew, take me away from here. I want to forget this place and the ugliness of last night. There is an unhealthy atmosphere here!"

He eyed her coldly. "I suppose, in the ugliness of last night, you wish to include my lovemaking."

"If you care to call your rape of me by that name!" she flared.

He nodded as if he had expected this reply. "Let me put your mind at ease so that you may enjoy your sojourn here. I shall not inflict my crudeness on you again."

Enid believed he was making an apology. She touched his arm and said in a more pleasant fashion, "I do not blame you. You were in a drunken state and suffering from the unfortunate influence of your friends. Another time it will be different, I'm sure."

Andrew moved away and stood with his back to her. When he spoke again, his voice held a note of shocking finality. "There will be no other time."

She stared at his back and gasped, "I'm not sure I understand."

He turned to her, his weakly handsome face white and grim. "I know that you don't, but it is better that you do. I propose that we be man and wife in name only. That we present a happy facade for the world but otherwise live as single people."

"You are saying this because I protested about last night?"

"No. I'm saying it because it was my original intent. Only one as naive as yourself wouldn't have guessed it long ago."

"Our marriage is to be a charade?"

"If you wish to call it that."

"But why?"

"Dammit, woman, must I be brutally frank? I married you for respectability, and it will be your duty to fulfill that task, and to give my name a proper tone. I do not ask for or expect an heir. I simply want you to serve me on public and social occasions, and in return I shall take care of your parents and keep you in the best of circumstances."

She stared at him as the truth slowly dawned on her. "Our marriage is a sham—a kind of unpleasant joke!"

"Yes, I suppose it is," he agreed.

"Your friends think so! That is why they staged that dreadful display last night!"

Andrew said wearily, "You are a most tiresome jade. Let me say it bluntly. Both Claude and I have a definite preference for young men. Do you understand me now?"

She shook her head, dazed by his brazen declaration. "I heard such gossip in London and closed my ears to it. I would not believe it!"

"That is why I have married you. Simply to put such rumors to rest. And for that you are ideal."

"You scoundrel! I suppose you and the vicomte are lovers?"

"We are at times," he admitted with a smile. "That shouldn't shock you. He is a very pretty fellow, don't you think?"

Tears brimmed in her sloe eyes. "I hate you! You are loathsome! I can never forgive you for degrading me!"

"Be grateful for our marriage agreement," he sighed. "Your parents need worry no more. And you can become a great lady of London and the Continent."

"A great lady whose husband despises and mocks her?"

"Not at all," Andrew said, less hostile now that he had made his confession. "You are perfectly fine in your own way. I certainly could have chosen another young woman, but I was taken by you. And if you were a lad, you'd have no trouble keeping me faithful to you!"

"I suggest you married me because Lord Alfred Henson, even though ill and destitute, possesses a more honorable name than you do. You chose me carefully so there would be no scandal against us. My father's name would ensure that his friends give at least a token respect to what they must know is an obscene marriage!"

"You are sharp," he acknowledged. "I was aware of that on our first meeting."

"How you must hate me to do this to me!"

"Don't be tiresome, my dear. After I left you last night I joined the duchess in a round of Parisian night spots, and I'm very weary today."

"Debauchery!"

He shrugged. "Call it that, if you like. And by the way, you were right—the duchess *is* a man."

"A witness at our wedding!" she gasped with horror.

"I'm sure that makes it legal nonetheless," Andrew told her. "He long ago assumed a feminine identity and a suitable name. So, you see, it takes all kinds to make up our world."

Afraid she might faint, Enid closed her eyes and took several deep breaths. "Am I to understand that you refuse to take me away from here?" she asked.

"I will not leave here, but if you wish, I can have you moved to a hotel for the rest of the time we're in Paris. I can visit and dine with you a few times for appearance sake."

"You would dare suggest such a thing?"

"I'm only trying to make things as pleasant for you as I can under the circumstances. Really, Enid, I'm not a cad. I will always look out for you."

"You are not a cad but a fiend!" she shot back.

"Whatever," he said with a sigh. "Tell me, don't you have a married friend who lives near Versailles? I believe you spoke of visiting her while we were here. You could do that on your own."

Enid shuddered. "I would be ashamed to have Lucinda know what I have come to!"

"But she need not know! Surely you can be discreet." Andrew warmed up to the idea. "Explain that I'm kept in Paris by a series of business problems and that you wished to see her for a few days."

"I could not face her! How am I to face anyone?" Enid cried in despair.

"I'm certain you will accommodate yourself to the situation in time," her new husband said, moving toward the door. "Since you probably don't wish to come down for dinner, I shall have a tray sent up to you. I beg you to think about all we have discussed and to try to work out a sensible plan. If you choose to be foolish about yourself, at least think of your parents and their welfare." With that, Andrew turned and left the room.

Enid was a proud, spirited girl who had bent herself to her husband's rakehell behavior in order to win him over. But his blunt revelations left her with no hope. Only someone who had no intention of changing his ways would so openly flaunt his sexual proclivities.

She was beyond tears. Pride and anger replaced her former desolation. She went to the window and gazed out at the chestnut trees swaying slightly in the spring breezes. Andrew had been right about one thing at least. She had been incredibly naive to enter into this marriage. Now she was a partner in the charade from which she must somehow extricate herself as best she could. The major weakness in any line of battle she might evolve was her parents. They needed her husband's financial support and had no conception of the depths of his perfidy. If they had known, they would never have allowed the marriage to take place.

Enid's mind slid back to that last discussion at her parents' home in distant Surrey. The picturesque old country house on the vast Henson estate seemed very dear to her now. And so did her parents.

She had stood by her father's bedside, opposite her mother, who had sat holding Lord Alfred's hand. Lady Caroline, an older edition of Enid, was still a beauty in middle age. Her dark blue eyes had showed concern as she had asked Enid, "Are you completely certain about this marriage, my dear?"

"Yes, I am," Enid had replied quietly.

Her father, prematurely aged by the stroke that had disabled his left side, had murmured, "You must not do it for our sake, though Andrew has been quite generous to us."

"The young man has more money than he knows what to do with," Lady Caroline had told her husband. "And remember, you and Andrew's father were close friends. If his father were alive today, he would gladly tide you over this difficult time."

Lord Alfred had sighed. "If I could regain my strength, I might be able to recoup some of the losses I incurred from the latest South Seas venture. I fear we have another South Sea Bubble on our hands—nearly seventy years after the original!" He had laughed without humor. "My problem is to delay disaster until I have a chance to gather something out of the rubble."

Enid had known that the doctor had only the faintest hope for her father's recovery. "You must not worry," she had said. "I like Andrew well enough. He is not my ideal, but he is attractive and popular, and he seems to like me. I could wait a long time and not make as good a match."

"That is very sensible thinking," her father had agreed.

"Besides, I have more than reached a marriageable age. Am I not already twenty years old?"

"It is my opinion that marriage should be entered into only for love," Lady Caroline had demurred wistfully.

Enid had smiled wryly. "I haven't said I don't love him, Mother."

"I see it in your face, child."

To this her father had added his concern. "You must be frank with us, my dear. You are more important to us than anything else.

Even if we had to sell this place and live in one of the cottages, it would be preferable to your making an unhappy match."

Enid had given him a determined look. "I'm sure I can make Andrew happy and all will be well."

Lady Caroline had risen and kissed her. "You have always been a dutiful daughter and a comfort to us."

Enid had smiled at her mother and kissed her father on the forehead. "Neither of you must worry. I think it best that we follow Andrew's plan that he and I be married in Paris. It will save you both concern and expense."

"But to be married in a foreign city without anyone there of your own!" Lady Caroline had lamented.

"I shall have Lucinda stand up for me. We were the best of friends before she married Duke d'Orsay and went to live in Versailles."

"I had forgotten about Lucinda," her mother had said, looking less upset. "She would be an excellent choice, of course, and in a way would represent your family and your English friends."

"I shall write her." But Enid never had. Andrew had protested the idea immediately. He had insisted that the vicomte, who was giving them his house, make all the wedding arrangements. And because of her blind faith in him, she had agreed, not realizing what lay ahead of her. But she had been optimistic about so many things in those days.

She shook herself out of her reverie when a maid arrived with a tray of savory food and drink and placed it on a small oak table. Enid felt little like eating, but she forced herself to partake of some nourishment. At the same time she tried to determine how best to deal with her plight. She came to a rather surprising conclusion.

Perhaps if she ignored her husband's failing and showed faith in him, in time he would reconsider his unhappy way of life and turn to her as he should have from the beginning. The more she pondered this, the more it seemed to make sense. Patience, she told herself, is a necessity now.

When she had finished the meal, she decided to tell Andrew that she would try to make the best of things if, in his turn, he would promise to give her some consideration. She fixed her hair, arranged her yellow gown to its most becoming state, and left her chamber.

In the hallway she met the vicomte, who bowed and said, "I trust you are feeling better, Lady Enid."

"Much better," she replied. "I'm on my way to tell my husband I no longer object to remaining here for a while."

Claude looked uneasy. "I'm most pleased to hear this. But perhaps it would be better to wait until later to discuss this with Andrew."

"I think it best to get it over with at once," she told the slender young nobleman. "We parted earlier with bitter words."

The vicomte continued to appear uncomfortable. "I strongly advise that you let it go until the morning, Lady Enid."

Enid shook her head. "My mind is made up. I must speak to him now. The longer the harsh words remain between us, the more harm will be done."

Claude shrugged. "Then you must do as you wish."

She thought his manner strange, but then, he was a rather peculiar individual. She moved on until she reached the door to Andrew's room. She knocked on it gently and then, with a smile on her lovely face, opened it.

What she saw made her smile swiftly change into a look of horror. On her husband's bed were Andrew and one of the male servants. Both were nude, locked in a sexual embrace. They did not even seem aware of her, so deeply involved were they in their amorous bout. Enid quickly closed the door and stood outside it for a moment, stunned beyond belief.

She understood now why Claude had been so unwilling for her to intrude on her husband. He had known! Until this moment she had thought she could accept the lifestyle of the man she had married, but now that she had confronted it, she realized she could never condone what was to her an ugly, sordid business.

Her one driving thought was to escape from the chateau and all that it symbolized. She returned to her room and wrote Andrew a lengthy note outlining her feelings. Then she set about packing one of her large valises. This done, she went downstairs to seek out the vicomte. She found him reclining on a mauve silk divan in the drawing room, holding the hand of one of the younger and more attractive servant boys.

"May I intrude?" she asked.

The vicomte rose hastily, and the youth immediately departed.

"Yes, dear lady?" the vicomte said.

"I understand now why you wished me to delay talking to Andrew."

He sighed. "I tried to prevent your coming upon him."

"I appreciate that. But I believe it is better that I discover the truth bluntly. Therefore, I cannot remain here after all."

"Where will you go?"

"Andrew suggested a hotel or a visit to my friend in Versailles. I have decided on the latter. While she is not expecting me, I know she will welcome me for a short visit. By that time Andrew will no doubt be ready to return to England, and he can escort me back to London."

"You do not plan to break with him completely?"

She hesitated a moment. "I dare not as yet. My parents need his help, so I will play the role of his wife as he wishes. But I won't remain here to witness his antics."

"You will be faced with the same problem back in London," the vicomte warned her.

"I will count on his being more discreet in England," she replied. "At any rate, that is something I will deal with later. In the meantime, will you please give him this envelope with my note enclosed?"

"Gladly."

"One thing more. I will need a carriage to take me to Versailles."

Claude nodded. "I can manage that easily, though it will take a little time to arrange. Let me caution you that making the journey by night could be dangerous."

"I shall risk it."

"Very well. I will have the carriage ready in an hour, and a driver whom I trust to look after you. But you must allow several hours for the trip, especially at night. You won't arrive there until dawn."

"As long as I am on my way," Enid told him firmly.

"It would be wiser to leave at dawn than to ride through the night," he advised.

"I prefer to take the risk to remaining here."

He shrugged. "Well, you know best. I shall look after the carriage at once."

An hour later Enid returned downstairs, dressed in a gray cloak with a silver fox hood, and carrying her valise. Claude was waiting for her in the reception hall. There was no sign of Andrew, who she assumed was still in bed with the male servant.

"I planned to send someone up to get your bag," the vicomte said.

"I'm quite capable of carrying it, thank you anyway." Enid tossed her gold curls. "I was brought up on a country estate and have led an outdoor life."

"I can see that," the nobleman remarked. "So now you will visit the town where our king has his palace. Louis and Marie Antoinette have resided in Versailles all through their reign."

"I am aware of that. Is my carriage outside?"

"It will be in a moment," he said. "Are you sure you won't reconsider this step?"

She gave him a sharp look. "I do not see my husband here to argue with me."

"He does not know of your plan to depart. I didn't dare to intrude on him."

"I understand. And I'm fully determined to do as I told you earlier."

"I will deliver your note," he promised. After a moment's pause he went on. "I have been at the court in Versailles and have talked with the king and his Marie."

"Indeed?"

"I'm a friend of Louis's cousin Philippe d'Orléans...Who is the lady you intend to visit?"

"She is the wife of Duke Victor d'Orsay."

"Ah, yes." The vicomte nodded. "They have a fine estate not far from the palace. The d'Orsays are an old family with a great deal of money. True aristocrats!"

"So I have heard."

The vicomte sighed. "But time may be running short for us aristocrats. The common people are in a turmoil. The American Revolution has offered a dangerous precedent. There is growing talk of a revolution in France, and if all goes well with the American Colonies, I fully believe the idea of rising against the French government will become a reality."

"I did not know there was so much unrest here."

"Nations, like individuals, have their problems," Claude pointed out sagely. "Accordingly, I hope you will accept my apologies for last night. I felt it was what Andrew wanted."

"Do you always obey his wishes?"

Red tints darkened the cheeks of the young nobleman. "Your husband is very close to me," he admitted.

"So he informed me," Enid said coldly.

The sound of neighing horses reached their ears, and Claude appeared vastly relieved. "That will be your carriage," he told her.

"Then I shall bid you farewell."

He hesitated by the door. "Let me warn you once again that you are embarking on an imprudent course. The roads at night are beset by highwaymen, so I have instructed the driver to carry a musket for protection. I wish you a safe journey."

"Thank you."

The vicomte took her valise and opened the door for her to precede him down the stone steps. The closed black carriage waiting in the circular drive was trimmed with elegant brass fittings and drawn by two sturdy-looking roans.

The driver, a stalwart middle-aged man, gave Enid a glance of sheer curiosity as she nodded to him and entered the vehicle. He took the bag from the vicomte and placed it on the floor by her feet.

"If the lady wishes anything or wants to speak to me during the journey," the driver told her, "there is a small window hatch which opens directly behind my seat above."

"I shall remember that," she said, looking out at him. "Are you familiar with the road to Versailles?"

"Yes, madam," he replied. "Though I would just as soon travel it by daylight."

She raised an eyebrow. "Are you also afraid of footpads?"

"There are many about, madam."

"Tonight we shall hope to elude them."

"Yes, madam."

The vicomte stepped forward. "Good luck!"

"Thank you," she said.

The spring night air held a slight drizzle as the carriage headed down the long path to the main road. Enid sat back as the heavy wheels clattered over the cobblestones of Paris. After a long while they reached the open country.

She was beyond any feeling of grief. Her one desire was to hold on until she reached a safe haven in Lucinda's home. Huddled in a corner, her mind full of desolate thoughts, she was gradually lulled into a light sleep.

Only moments later a rapping sound awakened her, and it took her a full minute to realize that the driver was knocking on the rain-spattered hatch from the outside. She quickly opened the small pane and asked, "What is it?"

"Trouble, madam," was his reply. "We are being trailed by a horseman."

"A single horseman?"

"Yes. A highwayman, no doubt." The driver's voice was tense. "And I thought you should know he is gaining on us."

"What will you do?"

"Deal with him as best I can. Lash the horses on, for a start. Sit back in your seat, madam!"

"I will," she promised. A small clutch of panic rose in her throat as the driver urged the horses on and the carriage rumbled forward at a reckless speed. The vicomte had warned her, and she had refused to listen!

3

Enid crouched in the corner of the dark coach. She could hear the angry urgings of the driver as he repeatedly lashed the horses, and several times she was certain that the careening carriage would topple to the ground. She saw now that the vicomte had been right about her traveling at night. To succeed in eluding the highwayman would be a matter of sheer luck.

She became aware of the rider's approach and heard a shouted exchange between him and the driver. Then the carriage slowed and she braced herself for the confrontation. She had no idea what to do or say. Her French was not very good, a fact she deeply regretted, but at this point it seemed a minor concern.

The carriage came to a halt, and a moment later the door was opened by a tall man wearing a hooded raincape. He spoke to her in slightly accented English. "You are traveling to Versailles, madam?"

"Yes," she replied in a trembling voice.

"There has been a misunderstanding," he went on to explain. "Your driver took me for a highwayman, but I am only a traveler, like yourself, who wished to ride along with you for mutual protection."

Her fear drained away slowly and her breathing grew more regular. "I also was of the opinion you meant to rob us."

"Well, now you know better. I understand you are going to the chateau of Duke Victor d'Orsay. By an odd coincidence, that is my destination, too. So we shall be fellow house guests."

"The Duchess d'Orsay is an old friend of mine," Enid told him.

The man nodded. "Of course; she is English."

Enid wished she could see his face, but it was in shadow. His speech sounded like that of a gentleman and his voice was deep and warm.

"We are almost halfway there," he said. "Please allow me to introduce myself. I am Count Armand Beaufaire."

"And I am Lady Enid Blair."

"My pleasure, your ladyship."

"You are welcome to ride in the carriage with me," Enid offered.

"Couldn't you tie your horse to the rear?"

"I think not. In any case, my purpose is to provide you with protection, and I can do that better by riding alongside the coach in the manner of a guard."

Having said this, the count closed the carriage door and spoke briefly to the driver before remounting. Then the carriage began to move through the dismal night at a proper pace.

Now that Enid could relax again, she found it interesting, even exciting, that this courteous nobleman was going to the same place as she. No doubt Lucinda knew him well and could tell her more about him. She wondered how her childhood friend would react to her surprising visit and the events surrounding it, and she hoped that Lucinda would be sympathetic and would remember one of their last conversations together.

Lucinda's father was a titled gentleman, and he and his family had lived on a nearby estate. They had moved to London when Lucinda was sixteen, and she had been launched into society there. At a brilliant affair during one winter season she had met the older Duke d'Orsay, who had promptly fallen in love with her. Lucinda, on her part, had soon found him her ideal.

She had spent a week in the country with Enid before embarking on the final wedding preparations. They had strolled in the woods together, hand in hand, as in the old days. The pretty, black-haired girl had insisted that they always remain friends.

"Even with the English Channel between us?" Enid had murmured.

"I will be far away," Lucinda had admitted. "But we can write. And if one of us ever needs the other, we must not hesitate to give our help."

Enid had smiled sadly. "You will never need my help now that you are marrying a rich and titled man."

"Sometimes life plays strange tricks," her friend had pointed out. "I just ask that we stay friends and keep in contact."

"That is not a difficult promise. I shall miss you terribly."

"And I shall miss you. But that is the way of life. Soon you will marry, too."

"I cannot see matrimony in my future as yet," Enid had said. But that had been long before she had met Lord Andrew Blair. Now she was indeed married, as well as in grave trouble, so she felt justified in seeking out her friend.

The rain was still lashing the countryside when the carriage reached what Enid assumed was the d'Orsay chateau. The driver and Count Beaufaire approached the door and pounded on it. Several long minutes elapsed before it was opened rather timorously by a thin, elderly servant wearing a nightcap and a white nightshirt and holding a candle. He recognized the count immediately, became very apologetic, and opened the door wide. Then he vanished into the shadows of the hall to summon others.

Beaufaire approached the coach and opened the door for Enid. "You may enter the chateau now," he said. "I have explained to old Simon that you are a guest of the duchess's."

"Thank you," Enid murmured gratefully as she stepped down. "I had no idea how I might gain entry."

"People are wary at this hour of the night," he remarked as he escorted her through the rain into the reception hall of the imposing mansion.

The driver followed with her bag. A stablehand came to take the horses and the carriage, and another led the count's steed away.

"What about the driver?" she fretted. "He will need to rest."

"I have arranged that with Simon," the nobleman told her. "He will be given a bed in the stablehands' quarters. He can sleep there tonight and return to Paris in the morning."

Enid was now able to see Armand Beaufaire's face clearly. Its features were strong and firmly etched; his even white teeth contrasted sharply with his dark complexion. His black eyes held a glint of amusement, but his expression was stern. He looked to be about twenty-six or so, but he carried himself with the dignity of an older man.

As they waited for the servant to return, he stared at her with interest. "May I inquire what drove you to make a dangerous journey on such a bad night?"

She felt her tenseness return. "I know it was foolish of me. My host in Paris warned me of the risks, but I foolishly did not listen to him."

"I *could* have been a highwayman," he reminded her dryly.

"And I could have been robbed or even killed."

"That is true," he agreed.

"May I ask why you made the journey under the same conditions?"

It was his turn to hesitate. When he replied, his tone was wary. "I had an urgent matter to discuss with the duke, and as I did not wish to attract attention to my visit, it seemed a good idea to arrive in darkness."

She listened with growing curiosity. So this fine-looking man had his secrets also. She smiled and said, "Well, it turned out well for both of us. Your idea that we join forces was an excellent one."

Their conversation was interrupted by the servant's return. He had pulled his breeches up over his nightshirt, revealing his thin shanks. He still held a lighted candle, which he used to lead them up one curving stairway and then another. After they reached the upper floor, he assigned Enid to a room and continued along the corridor with the count.

A wood fire had been started in Enid's room. She stood before the hearth for a few moments to warm her chilled body. Then she removed her damp clothing and began to prepare for bed.

In her haste she had brought along only one extra gown, but she did have undergarments and a nightdress. She could tell nothing about the room from the glow in the hearth or from the light of the single candle Simon had left for her. However, she saw that the bed was large and had a canopy. After donning her nightdress, she slid between the cool sheets and soon was asleep.

Once again her repose was interrupted by nightmares. This time she dreamed of the naked young men at the vicomte's, as well as her moments of terror in the onrushing carriage. Several times she wakened in near hysteria, to fall back into a fitful slumber.

She was aroused in the sunlit morning by the door to her room being thrown open. Lucinda, still in a dressing robe, her dark hair tumbled pleasantly about her shoulders, ran into the room and over to her bedside.

"Dear Enid!" she cried, and kissed her on the cheek.

Enid smiled and returned her friend's greeting. "I made myself your guest," she said. "I trust I am not an unwelcome one!"

"Unwelcome in my house? You know that will never be! But what are you doing in France? Tell me everything!"

"I came here on my honeymoon."

Bewildered, Lucinda sat down on the bed. "Then where, pray, is your husband?"

"In Paris."

"In Paris," the dark-haired girl repeated. "And pray, why have you separated?"

"That is a rather long story," Enid replied wryly. "I would have sent you word of my marriage at the time it was planned, but Andrew objected."

Lucinda's eyebrows lifted. "This Andrew of yours sounds stranger by the moment! Who is he, anyway?"

Enid took her friend's hands in hers and spoke in a troubled voice. "I have come to you in desperate need, Lucinda. My marriage is really a sham, a fiasco. I had to have someone to talk to and somewhere to rest and think things out."

"You have picked the best possible place," Lucinda declared firmly.

"I shall leave as soon as I have decided what to do."

"Talking of going—and you have barely arrived! Nonsense! You must stay a while and get to know Victor, my husband."

Enid smiled sadly. "I will stay as long as time allows. I expect to hear from my husband when he is ready to return to London."

"Now I simply must know what is behind all this!"

"Promise you will never tell anyone except your husband, and that you will bind him to silence."

"Whatever you ask. Just tell me."

Haltingly, Enid told her story. When she had finished, she said, "So now you know the terrible predicament I'm in."

"You entered into a loveless marriage for your parents' sake—if only you hadn't!" Lucinda cried, then embraced her.

"I did not guess Andrew's vice," Enid sighed. "I have been so sheltered all my life."

Lucinda looked grim. "We know about such things here in France. Sodomy seems to be the fashionable vice, together with lesbianism! It is no wonder your debauch of a husband wanted to spend his honeymoon in Paris—and no mystery that he didn't wish to spend it with you!"

Enid eyed her friend incredulously. "You mean that such corruption is prevalent over here?"

"Very! The king was forced to dismiss several members of his court who were caught in a flagrant situation. There are whispers of a seraglio of sodomites in Versailles. The king fears to take the offenders to public trial because of the dishonor it would bring to many fine old families and because that kind of publicity might increase people's desire to experience those very same sins."

"How horrible!"

"The king had to dismiss one of the worst offenders, the queen's head of household who had perverted one of her Hungarian subalterns."

"What are things coming to?" Enid shuddered in dismay.

"I dare not think," Lucinda told her. "The entire country seems to be eaten away at the core with rottenness. There is a great deal of poverty and discontent, and even talk of a revolution."

"Surely people like you will not be touched by such happenings."

"I hope not." Lucinda frowned. "My husband is most generous with the peasants who work the estate, and he is kind to the servants. But should the dam burst, I doubt that any of his good deeds would be remembered."

"I find it all too frightening!"

Lucinda smiled brightly and placed an arm around her. "Let's not dwell any longer on these ugly thoughts! We are together again, and that is what is important now. I had lost hope of ever seeing you here."

"And I of coming, but fate has worked it out in a strange fashion."

"You shall enjoy every moment of your stay," Lucinda promised. "We will talk of England—all the things we loved there—and go for rides in the country. You shall see the palace and maybe even get a glimpse of King Louis and Queen Marie Antoinette. The king loves the theater, and whenever a Molière play is performed on an afternoon, he is almost sure to attend."

"To be so near the royal palace! It does sound exciting!"

"And it also increases our danger. For if and when there is an uprising, it is claimed that the king and queen will be the first seized."

"Is nothing being done to cope with this problem?"

Lucinda nodded. "Yes. We Royalists have our own secret organization. We spy on the meetings of the would-be revolutionists and try to minimize their potential. It is on such business that Count Armand Beaufaire is here to see Victor."

"The man who met my carriage on the road last night?"

"Yes. You were fortunate it was he and not some roguish highwayman. The roads are full of them. In Armand you had the best of guards. He has been active in the army despite his high title, and he is an expert fencer as well as a crack shot. He has also made his name in the boudoirs of our land, since his reputation as a ladies' man follows him everywhere."

"Indeed! After what I have been through, it is a relief to hear that some still exist!"

"You may be sure about Armand Beaufaire."

"Is he a bachelor?"

"A widower. His wife died in childbirth, and it is said this tragedy broke his heart. He has time to woo many women, but no inclination to marry any of them."

"What about yourself? Do you have children?"

"Alas, no," Lucinda said. "My husband is more than twice my age. But I do not blame it on that. I fear the truth is I'm barren, for it is well known he has several bastards among the women on the estate."

Enid blushed. "Lucinda!"

Her friend laughed. "I'm being honest with you, as you have been with me. But do not get the wrong idea. Victor is a good husband. Those incidents happened before our marriage, and truly, I could not ask for more devotion."

"I'm glad!"

"And with all the trouble lurking in the background I'm thankful we have no children. It's difficult enough for us to be caught up in a wave of national madness without having young ones to suffer along with us."

"I shall never have any children," Enid said sorrowfully. "How can I? I do not even have a proper husband!"

"Will you stay with Andrew?"

"I must, at least for a little while," Enid replied. "Back in England, with my friends to keep me company, I may be able to close my mind to what is going on. But I couldn't remain in that wretched chateau with him—I had to get away!"

"And he told you that you should come here alone?"

"Yes. He doesn't care what I do as long as I don't bother him."

"Then I should lose no time in finding a lover for myself," Lucinda stated.

"How can you say such a thing?" Enid cried in dismay.

"I'm telling you what you should do."

Enid shook her head. "I know there are wives who do such things, but I never hoped to be one of them."

"Remember, you didn't know what your marriage would be like."

"That is the truth, but I'm not prepared to have an affair."

Lucinda rose from the bed. "In time," she said. "Now I must go and dress. Please join us for the morning meal."

"I will, but I must warn you that I brought only one dress with me, a rather plain one. My mind was in a state of havoc when I decided to come here."

"Not to worry. You and I wear the same size, and I have many outfits I'll be glad to let you borrow. I shall send in a maid with several you can choose from."

Enid was delighted to find her friend so unchanged by marriage and the exalted social position she now held. After the maid had brought in half a dozen gowns, Enid dressed carefully in a sea-green linen morning dress and did her hair in the upsweep that was so popular in England. Then she made her way to the cheerful yellow breakfast room.

4

Lucinda and her husband, along with Count Armand Beaufaire, were already seated at the table. The men rose, and Duke Victor took her hand and kissed it, saying, "Welcome to our house."

"Thank you," she replied. She noticed that the duke walked with a slight limp and was quite overweight. He had a vast protruding stomach and heavy jowls. But his face was pleasant, and the wrinkles at the corners of his blue eyes were obviously the result of his long years of observing life with good humor.

"You have met Count Armand," he said.

"Yes. He kindly assisted me last night." She graced the stern-faced count with a smile.

His stern expression melted into one of pleasure as she joined them at the table. "Madam is a brave young woman. I know of few who would have ventured out on the highway at such an hour, and on a stormy night as well."

"Put it down to stupidity, Count Beaufaire," Enid laughed. "I have learned my lesson. When I travel next, it shall be by daylight."

"That would be advisable," Luanda's husband agreed.

"I do so want to show Enid around," Lucinda told him.

Victor beamed at her over his breakfast plate. "Then by all means, do so. I have to lock myself up with Armand for the morning. We have much to discuss. Why don't you two take the pony cart and ride about for a while?"

"That is an excellent idea," Lucinda declared happily. "I can handle the pony, but some of the horses scare me!"

After breakfast the men retreated to the duke's study while Enid and Lucinda prepared to go for their ride. Enid wore a large green hat with a matching scarf tied over it and gathered under her chin to keep the bonnet in place. Lucinda, in a similar bonnet of blue, took her out to the front steps. The groom brought around the good-sized pony cart and they drove away.

Enid was impressed by the well-kept grounds. "What lovely trees and hedges! And the grass is so perfect. You must have excellent gardeners."

"My husband takes an interest in the landscaping," Lucinda said proudly. "But, as I recall, Henson House always had the best grounds in the country."

"Not any longer," Enid sighed. "Since my father's loss of his fortune and his illness, little has been done to maintain the estate."

"A pity! Perhaps you should interest yourself in it."

"I may. At least it would keep me busy and would put to good use some of my husband's money."

After Lucinda had finished showing Enid her own estate, she took her farther abroad to see something of the town and the grounds of the palace.

As they drove along, Enid asked, "What story did you tell the duke about me?"

"I was most discreet," Lucinda assured her. "I told him you were married, but I didn't let him know you were a new bride. I gave him the impression you had been married for some time and that your husband was detained in Paris on business matters."

"Thank you. Now I won't feel so awkward."

Lucinda glanced at her. "I think you ought to cultivate Armand's friendship. I could tell at the breakfast table that he was quite interested in you."

Enid blushed. "I'm sure you imagined it."

"No, I think it's the truth. You could do worse than to have a friend like Armand."

"You are a matchmaker—or worse!" Enid protested. "You must remember I'm a married woman!"

"And such a marriage!" Lucinda said, rolling her dark eyes.

They next ventured close to the royal palace. Enid was enthralled by the sight of the great edifice extending over so much ground. The walls enclosing it, as well as the grilled entry gates, were guarded by soldiers. Lucinda pointed out various sections of the palace: the chapel, the Hall of Mirrors, the Hall of Battles, the Peace and War salons.

She indicated another area, at the far end of the north wing. "There is the Opera, a fine theater in miniature. I shall try to have us invited to one of the performances. That would be a special treat, I promise you!"

"Such magnificence!" Enid marveled. "I am overwhelmed!"

"Do not be deceived," her friend warned. "We have come upon a time of poverty. The king is weak, though pleasant, and is overshadowed by his pleasure-seeking Hapsburg wife. The court is beset with financial problems. My husband calls it a gilded slum!"

"A gilded slum!" Enid echoed as she gazed at the glory before her.

"Victor means that money is almost always short there. The king's grandfather spent so much on his mistresses, it is said the salaries of servants, including the present king's tutors, remained unpaid for years. Victor says that when Louis was five, he saw the royal plate melted down for coinage."

"That is hard to believe!"

"Much of what goes on now *is* hard to believe." Lucinda jiggled the reins of the pony, and the cart moved forward. "An American, Benjamin Franklin, wrote a report on Versailles, claiming that its waterworks were out of repair and that a great part of the front of the building had shabby brick walls and broken windows. It caused a scandal."

"Was it true?"

"I fear so. This Franklin came here to gain support for the American Revolution. He was a sensation among the court people. The king unbalanced his finances even more to help Franklin's cause. Mobs have come, crying out their hunger at the palace gates, and it is said that when Marie Antoinette was told they were behaving in this fashion because they had no bread, she suggested, 'Let them eat cake.' Whether that is true or not, it has now made her the most hated woman in all of France."

As they drove back onto the grounds of the d'Orsay estate, the gardeners and the women bearing baskets of produce stopped and bowed to them. It was hard for Enid to believe there could be so much unrest in this land. Then she remembered that Lucinda had explained that the duke had been especially considerate of his people, even though he was surely a Royalist.

Enid also began to understand that this was a country of excesses. That would account in part for what had gone on at the vicomte's chateau on her wedding night. And Andrew fitted in with this atmosphere of degeneration. He was at home in a nation on the brink of moral and financial disaster. She prayed that such conditions would never reach England.

She and Lucinda rested after luncheon. They dressed for dinner and went down to the drawing room to join the men for a glass of wine before proceeding to the dining salon. Both Victor and Armand were attired in elegant velvet, Victor in dark blue and Armand in white. Enid was grateful to Lucinda for her rich purple silk gown. She thought she noted a slight expression of surprise on the duke's face when he first saw her, and she assumed he had recognized his wife's dress.

Lucinda, with her usual poise, set the situation aright by telling her husband, "Would you believe it, sir? Lady Enid has a gown exactly like mine!"

"So I see, and charming also," he said gallantly.

Lucinda gave Enid a knowing smile. "I promise you I will not wear mine during all the time you are here. We will not be seen dressed alike!"

The large drawing room was paneled in walnut and adorned with ornately framed portraits. Heavy crimson drapes flanked the broad windows overlooking the garden. The furniture was the best, and so were the dark red carpets. Enid thought she had never seen a more tasteful or richly decorated chamber.

Armand offered her a glass of wine from his hand. "I prefer to serve you rather than to call on a servant," he said.

"And I prefer receiving my wine from you directly," she responded with a smile.

"Were you impressed with Versailles?" he asked.

"Extremely so, though I am alarmed to learn there is so much unrest in the country."

The stern look returned to Armand's handsome face. "There are grave problems, a major one being wheat. Bread is a staple of our people. Actually, we don't have a shortage of grain, but a surplus of fear. So we have bread riots! Everyone is convinced there will be shortages or the price will rise too high. The situation is not dangerous at the moment, since the price of bread has fallen by a sou."

Enid sipped her wine. "We do not live in an easy age. I know from my own experience in England that poachers of deer are sent to the gallows."

"It is the same here," Armand said with a scowl. "People are arrested, and some are given the death sentence for relatively small thefts."

"What can be done?" she asked.

"The people must be taxed less and treated more kindly," he replied. "The American Revolution has shown the way."

"Do you believe such a revolution will take place here?"

"I pray not, but those of us at the top must learn to be temperate. Otherwise we may be overwhelmed."

She gave him a searching glance. "You sound extremely concerned."

"I am."

"But you are one of those at the top!"

"And true to my group," the count said proudly. "But I see the wrongs even while I fight to subdue those who would start a revolution."

"Is that why you are here?"

"Yes. It can do no harm to tell you, since you are English."

"And my French is so lamentable as to be of little use to me in communicating anything!'

He smiled. "Basically, you speak fairly well. Some added time and practice, and you should have no problems."

"Thank you."

"I came here to warn the duke that soon there will be an assault on the royal palace. And that great care must be taken to defeat the uprising. Should the king and queen be captured by these revolutionists, it could set the whole nation aflame."

"I can understand that your burden of duty is great," Enid said softly. "I admire you for being true to your class while accepting its weaknesses. Your struggle to prevent your country from being torn by dissent is an honorable one."

Victor and Lucinda had been standing a little distance away. Now they drew nearer. The duke pointed an accusing finger at Armand. "You were looking far too serious, my friend. I fear you bore our English guest with our problems."

Enid protested. "No, Duke. I'm most interested in all that the count has told me."

"Ah!" Victor's blue eyes twinkled. "So you have made another conquest, Armand!"

"If I have done that by quoting dull political facts, I'm surely worthy of being assigned to the royal court." Armand offered one of his warmest smiles with this remark.

Lucinda said, "I have told Victor of your interest in the theater, Enid, and he thinks he can arrange for us to attend a performance at the palace."

"That would be exciting beyond anything I could imagine!" Enid cried.

The duke tapped the side of his nose. "I have certain friends at court who are usually willing to do me a favor."

Armand's gaze was fixed on Enid as he remarked, "You have such a rare English beauty, my lady, that I wonder you have not been taken for an actress."

"Thank you." Enid smiled and blushed.

"In our section of England a daughter of the gentry would be considered disgraced if she set foot on the stage," Lucinda explained. "That is suitable only for women of a certain type."

"My favorite kind of women, my dear," her husband laughed, and they all joined in.

The group moved on to the dining room, elegant with its crystal chandelier, mahogany appointments, and sparkling tableware; yet the feeling was one of warmth. The conversation was pleasant and the food excellent. Enid could not help comparing this dinner with the sorry orgy of her wedding night. A shadow crept over her as she realized that this was only an interim period, that eventually she would have to return to Andrew.

Count Armand had noticed her change of mood. Later, in the drawing room again, he said to her, "I watched you at dinner, Lady Enid. There was a moment when you were suddenly sad."

They were seated on a gold brocade loveseat. Lucinda had gone off to tend to some household affair, and Victor had left to seek several sketches of himself and Lucinda that a visiting artist had drawn during the previous summer.

Enid stared at the nobleman. "You are most perceptive."

"So you did feel sad?"

"Yes."

"May I ask why?"

She hesitated. "I may as well be truthful. My marriage has turned out to be something very ugly."

"I'm sorry."

"So am I."

"Have you left your husband?"

"Only temporarily. There are important reasons why I must remain with him."

"I see," he said quietly.

She turned away from his intent gaze. "Perhaps one day I shall be able to be free."

"If freedom is what you wish, I most fervently hope the time will come soon."

Enid faced him again. "You are a most considerate man."

"I do not think so. Not more than the average."

"I disagree," she said. "Perhaps that is your secret."

His dark eyebrows lifted. "My secret?"

"Yes. I have heard that you are a man of many conquests among my sex."

His smile was thin. "Someone has been grossly exaggerating."

"I wonder."

"It is true I have a natural fondness for women," he was ready to admit, "so I count quite a few among my friends."

"That is good."

He gave her another searching glance. "I trust that you may be one of them," he said earnestly.

"I would be honored by your friendship," she replied simply.

Their exchange ended as the duke appeared with the artist's sketches. He offered them to Enid for her inspection. "I think they are excellent. Most lifelike. Don't you agree?"

"I do," she said, examining the various studies in pen and ink.

"The man is an excellent artist, but addicted to the grape," Victor confided. "If he returns to our part of the country this year, I shall commission him to do portraits of Lucinda and me."

"And keep him away from spirits while he is working," Enid advised with a smile as she returned the sketches to him.

Lucinda came into the room and joined them. "Have you and Armand run out of conversation yet?" she asked Enid.

Enid laughed. "I doubt that we ever shall. I find him most interesting."

Armand demurred. "It is Lady Enid who is the brilliant one when it comes to words. I have seldom met so sharp-witted a woman."

"And you are truly a judge of that," Lucinda teased.

The duke snorted. "That is a compliment for him and a warning for you, Lady Enid. Your husband might not remain in Paris if he knew who your companion was here in the country."

"I do not think my husband is given to such worries about me," Enid said.

"I'm sure you've offered him no cause," d'Orsay was quick to interject. "And I must also add that Armand's conquests have been given too much weight."

"Thank you," the handsome count said. "I think I have already explained that to Lady Enid's satisfaction." He glanced at Enid as if for confirmation, and she gave him a warm look.

Lucinda moved toward the gilt-edged ebony card table near the fireplace. "In that case, let us sit down and play a game of cards. Armand and Enid can be partners."

5

Several days later the duke announced that they had all been invited to Versailles to attend a performance of Molière's *Tartuffe*. Enid was thrilled by the news, as was everyone else. D'Orsay's contact at the palace had not let him down.

Meanwhile, Enid and Armand had become close friends. They had exchanged their ideas about philosophy, history and the arts, and had gone for long walks on the grounds of the estate. The more she learned about him, the more she liked him. Though Armand was a man of title and wealth, he was sincerely concerned about the common people, and this quality endeared him to Enid.

She told Lucinda, "If your husband and Armand are good examples of the French nobility, I must regard that group as a very special one."

"They are among the best," her friend agreed, "but believe me they are in the minority. Do not forget your Vicomte Robert in Paris. There are many others like him, some even worse. The nobility is not noted for having a high moral consciousness, I assure you."

The afternoon on which they were to attend the play arrived, and the duke arranged for their departure in a large open carriage. Everyone was in a relaxed, jolly mood, and for a little while Enid forgot Paris and the travesty that was her marriage.

Along the way the two men debated the merits of Molière's plays. "My favorite is *The Imaginary Invalid,*" the duke insisted. "I cannot forget the line 'Nearly all men die of their remedies, and not of their illnesses.' I consider it a classic!"

Armand laughed along with the others and said, "We mustn't forget *The Misanthrope,* or this saying from it: 'The more we love our friends, the less we flatter them. It is by excusing nothing that pure love shows itself.' There is much truth in that."

Enid spoke up. "Don't underestimate today's play. I have seen it done in an English translation and I think it's a fine comedy."

"The clergy still doesn't like it too well," Lucinda remarked. "The study of the mock pious priest is very damaging."

"I understand it's the king's favorite play," Victor offered with a chuckle.

As they rolled through the countryside on this pleasant May afternoon, they made an attractive foursome. Enid had borrowed a dark pink silk dress with lace trim from Lucinda, who looked lovely in a crimson silk gown embroidered in gold. Armand and Victor were garbed, respectively, in blue and green jackets and matching breeches.

The guards at the main palace gate challenged them, then let them pass when the duke presented a written note from his friend. Enid's heart began to beat faster as the group left the carriage and Armand escorted her inside. They made their way along a broad corridor, at the end of which an elderly servant greeted them and said, "To the left for the play, your lordship."

Armand thanked him, and they proceeded to the entrance of the small but magnificent theater. The oval-shaped room was already nearly filled with people both seated and standing. Enid thought the profusion before her of gilt, marble, sky-blue velvet, and fine chandeliers the most breathtaking display of opulence she had thus far seen.

"This is called the Royal Opera," Armand said in a low voice.

The duke and Lucinda had come up beside them. Victor murmured, "Down front and center. The king and queen are in the large chairs. They use their royal box only in the evenings."

Enid stood on tiptoe and caught a brief glimpse of a rather stout, good-looking man, in a white jacket rich with decorations and embroidery, and a pleasant-looking woman with light brown hair, wearing a dress of royal purple, cut very low. The two were smiling and exchanging small talk with people who were clearly ladies and gentlemen of the court.

"I fear we shall have to stand in order to have any view of the stage," the duke whispered.

"I do not mind," Enid whispered back.

Lucinda smiled and nodded her agreement. Armand stationed himself just inside the doorway, and Enid and the d'Orsays stood beside him. The play began and a hush fell over the audience. Once the comedy was under way, there was almost continuous merriment from the assembly. The actor playing the priest gave a convincing caricature of all the hypocrites of the world. Enid thought he was excellent.

The other members of the cast were equally talented. The famous lines came brilliantly, especially "Those whose conduct gives room for attack are always the first to attack their neighbors," "She is laughing in her sleeve at you," and "The beautiful eyes of my cash-box!" It was an unparalleled treat, and Enid had no awareness of the passage of time. Even with her limited French, her knowledge of the play allowed her to enjoy it thoroughly.

At the play's end the actors came forth to take their bows. There was generous applause, and a loud comment of praise from King Louis. Then the audience stood politely to one side to allow the monarch and his wife to exit from the theater. The royal couple passed so close to Enid that, had she wished to, she could have touched the king's sleeve.

Louis was a man of medium height and had the prominent Bourbon nose. Marie Antoinette was regal and tiny, very much a Hapsburg. As Louis walked by Enid he deigned to offer her the slightest of friendly smiles.

After the royal group had moved away, Lucinda could not contain her excitement. "I saw it, Enid!" she cried. "I could hardly believe it! He actually smiled at you!"

Her husband laughed. "The king has an eye for pretty faces."

Armand agreed. "And in Lady Enid he most assuredly saw one."

Enid blushed. "You make too much of it. He was merely being polite to us onlookers." But she was secretly delighted and knew this was a moment she would long remember.

Lucinda sighed. "At least he's much more attractive than that addled German we have on the throne in England."

"You must not say spiteful things about King George," the duke admonished her. "It is not becoming in a wife of mine."

"He helped England lose the Colonies," Lucinda reminded her husband. "Many cannot forgive him for that."

Enid gave Armand a knowing glance. "Taxes again, I fear!"

They left Versailles and headed back to the estate in a happy frame of mind. Armand was in excellent form and regaled Enid with tales of the history of the palace and how it had come to be built. She listened avidly, interjecting some thoughts of her own, and in a short time they were back at the chateau.

When she came down for dinner a little later, she found Lucinda waiting for her in the reception hall. By the look on her friend's face, Enid knew that she bore unpleasant news.

"A letter arrived from Paris while we were out," Lucinda said. "It is addressed to you—and sent by your husband."

Enid took the envelope from her. "I knew it would be coming soon." She quickly scanned the short note. Then, with a look of sadness, she told her friend, "I fear I must leave tomorrow. Andrew requests that I depart in the morning so we can proceed to England the next morning."

"I don't want you to go—it's much too soon!"

"Not really." Enid folded the note and put it back in the envelope. "Our honeymoon wasn't meant to last more than a week or so, anyway."

"Honeymoon!" Lucinda exclaimed scornfully. "How can you dare to call it that?"

Enid shrugged. "That is what I must pretend it has been."

"I think it's unfair, terribly unfair, and I fear we may never meet again!" Luanda's voice shook with the weight of her emotions.

"But of course we shall," Enid insisted, then placed an arm around her good friend. "I'll plan to visit you regularly."

Lucinda brightened at once. "Do you mean that?"

"Certainly. I'm sure that once we get back to England, I'll be able to make definite arrangements with Andrew and will be free to travel about from time to time. He'll be glad to have me out of the way as much as possible."

"But how can you accept such a future?" Lucinda demanded.

"I can because I must," Enid said firmly. "Now, let's not mention my departure until after dinner. I don't want to spoil everyone else's good mood."

"Whatever you say," Lucinda agreed.

Dinner was a most pleasant affair of duck à l'orange and a casserole of spring vegetables in a cream sauce. Afterward they moved to the drawing room; the men had cognac, the women port. Then Lucinda complained of weariness, and she and the duke retired early. Enid realized her friend had acted discreetly in order to leave her alone with Armand on her last night at the chateau.

After a moment or two of silence Armand said, "The shadow has fallen once again. I noticed it during dinner."

Enid smiled wryly. "I can have no secrets from you, it seems."

"What is wrong?"

"I must leave in the morning. My husband wishes me to join him so that we can return to England the following morning."

"Are you going?"

"Yes."

Armand searched her face intently, his black eyes very serious. "You once told me you did not love him—that you planned to separate from him."

"That is impossible for the present."

His eyes met hers and held them. "You have a good reason to leave him."

Startled, she asked, "How do you know?"

"You told me he is staying at the house of Vicomte Claude Robert. All Paris knows him to be a pederast. The facts speak for themselves."

She lowered her gaze and murmured, "I suppose they do."

"It is a tragic thing for a woman to be wasted in this way."

"Yes," she whispered.

"And so beautiful a woman, too," Armand added in the same grave tone. He paused a moment, then said, "There is a moon tonight. Why don't we go outside and observe it?"

She allowed him to take her hand and lead her out the doors at one end of the room that gave access to the garden. The air was fragrant with the scent of roses and the moon was bright and full. Its silver magic gave the garden an other-world quality.

Armand took her by the arm and turned her toward him. At the burning look in his eyes Enid felt a wild current course through her body. Then he began to speak. "I have no right to say what is in my heart. My country is on the brink of great danger and I live constantly under the threat of violent death. But, heaven forgive me, I have fallen in love with you and can no longer remain silent."

She smiled through sudden tears. "I wanted to hear you say just that."

"It is madness for us to fall in love!"

She laughed softly. "That is the marvelous thing about love. There is no logic to it."

"My little English philosopher." His voice had grown husky. "I can only pray your wit and courage will protect you until I can properly claim you for my own!"

"I hope so, too, but I am afraid that we will never see each other again."

He drew her closer to him.

"Nevertheless, I shall always love you, deep in my heart," she vowed.

"And I you," he whispered, crushing her to him in a fierce embrace and searing her lips with ardent kisses. His tongue sought hers, delicately at first, then with insistence, while his fingers gently explored the soft flesh of her bosom swelling above her low-cut gown.

Enid responded to his caresses with an abandon uncharacteristic of one so inexperienced in the art of love. But Armand's deft touch had aroused her dormant passions into full flower. As she felt her gown slip off her shoulders and drop to her feet, she trembled with eager anticipation. A moment later he had cast aside his own clothing and lowered her to the bed of grass.

She clung to him, delighting in the feel of his well-muscled body atop hers. He brought his lips to her breasts and nibbled at their taut rose peaks, then lowered his head to her smooth stomach. She heard herself moan in a frenzy of joy and agony. Then, just as she thought the universe would explode into myriad silver particles of moonlight, he entered her moist flesh and began a series of slow, unbearably sweet thrusts that gradually elevated her to a rarefied atmosphere.

Eons later, after reaching the zenith of their desires in a final rapturous outpouring of love, they lay spent and happy in each other's arms.

6

On the drive back to Paris, Enid thought about her change of attitude since the rainy night she had traveled to Versailles. Now she had Armand Beaufaire and his declared love to console her. She was still tingling from their night of passion. She had never met anyone who had appealed to her so strongly, and she knew she would never forget him.

She also knew she had to be sensible. The chances of her meeting Armand again were slim, despite her promises to Lucinda to return to Versailles. Because of the impending revolution, travel might come to a halt at any time. To add to the hazards, Armand was working actively for the Royalist cause as an agent against the revolutionists. In this role he was constantly under threat of death.

With her usual courage, Enid refused to consider the darker aspects of the situation. She was aware of the difficulties she and Armand might face before coming together again, but she would go on hoping it would happen. In the meanwhile, she would try to make the best of her mock marriage to the dissolute young nobleman.

When she arrived at the vicomte's chateau, Andrew was waiting for her in her bedroom. Elegantly attired in a yellow coat and blue breeches, he nevertheless looked more worn and pale than when he had first arrived in Paris. Evidently the round of orgies had taken its toll on him. And on his temper.

He greeted her coldly. "Well, madam, you are most rosy-cheeked and cheerful after your stay in the country."

"I had a pleasant visit with Lucinda," she said.

"No doubt." He could barely conceal a sneer. He clasped his hands behind his back and continued. "I did not care for the way you left here. It was abrupt and foolhardy."

"I'm sorry, but I felt I had to get away at once."

"So Claude told me. Please bear in mind that I will tolerate no such behavior in the future. I insist that I be informed of your comings and goings."

"You were so occupied with your own affairs, it hardly seemed to matter."

"My affairs are my business," Andrew snapped. "At any rate, we shall be leaving in the morning, and when we reach my home in London, I will expect you to conduct yourself in a more proper fashion."

Enid stared at him. "You dare to say that, after all *you* have done?"

"You are my wife, dear lady, not my governess. Keep to your position."

"Am I to have no freedom in exchange for what you ask?" she demanded.

"Within reason," he replied evenly. "We must conserve our money for a time. The gambling table has not been kind to me here."

"Then you would do well to curb your gambling in London!"

He shrugged. "I will decide that for myself."

"And *I* shall expect the generous expense account you promised me." Enid whirled about and began to rearrange her long curls at the dressing table.

"You are bolder now than when you left, I realize. Has Lucinda instilled this rebellious spirit in you? Or is it merely that you had more interesting companionship in Versailles? Wait—is it possible you had a dalliance with a man?"

She turned around and eyed him with scorn. "You are the expert when it comes to male dalliance!"

"A sharp tongue will never endear you to me, sweet Enid."

"I do not expect endearment," she countered. "I only ask for respect."

Lord Andrew made no reply to this. After a tense moment he said, "The vicomte requests that you join us downstairs for dinner."

"Thank you, but I would prefer to have my meals up here until I leave."

Her husband smiled sourly. "You will not be missed at the dining table, I can assure you. However, I will see that trays are sent up to you."

She saw nothing of him or the vicomte until the next morning when she stood in the entry hall, waiting for the coach that would take her and Andrew to the Channel boat.

Claude came forward and kissed her hand as Andrew went out to check the luggage. "I trust that when you return we shall enjoy more of your company."

"Thank you," she said. "However, I doubt that I will be back in the near future."

"Lord Andrew visits Paris at least two or three times a year."

"I am sure he will continue his visits, but those will be by himself. This was a rather special one, you will recall. Our honeymoon."

The vicomte's smile was weak. "Yes, of course. A most special occasion."

So she said goodbye to France, at least for a while. Throughout the crossing she was preoccupied with her own thoughts and Andrew grew increasingly annoyed with her. He was convinced that her aloofness was a result of her visit to Versailles, but she refused to enlighten him with an explanation. Her brief romance with Armand was her prized secret.

• • •

The London town house off Regent's Park was large and gloomy; it felt empty with only herself, Andrew, and the servants. All immediate relatives were dead, so he had been living there by himself.

Enid could only speculate as to the type of excesses that had gone on there, and she noticed that the servants viewed her as an object of interest.

Andrew had been discreet enough to see that they had adjoining rooms, but the connecting door was kept locked most of the time. They made public appearances together, attending elegant parties and the theater. He went to the gaming houses alone and often returned with a male companion.

Those were difficult nights for Enid. Despite the thick walls, she was frequently able to hear their laughter and talk. The sounds of passion between her husband and another man continued to shock her.

The one bright thing about her return to London was the news from Surrey that her father's health was gradually improving and that he was again applying himself to his many investments.

Enid wrote her parents of her life in London, making it appear happy and carefree, and promised to visit them soon. She also wrote to Lucinda, and after a few weeks she received a reply. Things had grown worse in France, but the duke would not think of leaving his estate. Armand was still valiantly combating the revolutionist underground and had vanished somewhere in the environs of Paris.

Enid knew she could not bear the boredom of her existence without some outside interests, so she appealed for help to a lawyer who looked after much of her father's business. Edward Minchy was a small man with sharp black eyes who always wore his white wig too far back on his head and was usually attired in black. He was considered one of the wisest solicitors in all of London.

As she sat by the roll-top desk in his rather shabby London office, he studied her and rubbed his chin. "So you married young Lord Blair, did you?"

"Yes."

"Not a notable love match, I assume. I'm familiar with his reputation."

Her cheeks crimsoned. "I fear that I knew nothing until I became his wife."

Mr. Minchy eyed her shrewdly. "But he has made it clear to you now?"

"All too clear," she replied shamefacedly.

The lawyer coughed. "Well, I doubt that you'll be bothered by having children, if the London gossips have it right."

"They are all too correct, Mr. Minchy."

"Are your parents aware of this situation?"

"They have no idea of the depths of his perfidy. Nor do I want them to."

"Your father is a just man and a righteous one. If he knew the truth, I doubt that he would allow you to live under the same roof as Andrew Blair."

"My father and mother would be shocked," she agreed. "But father has been ill, and I don't want him bothered with this."

"Ah," Mr. Minchy sighed. "Well, there are signs of his improving. Perhaps you can discuss it with him later."

"Perhaps."

"In the meantime, what can I do for you?"

"I need to fill in my time," she said. "And I would like to improve my French so that I could speak and interpret it like a native."

"An odd wish," the solicitor told her. "We English are proud of our language, and it serves us comfortably wherever we may go."

"Perhaps, but my desire is to better my French as a personal accomplishment."

"Well, in that case you need a first-rate instructor."

"Someone reliable. I hoped you could make some suggestions."

The little man looked happier. "As a matter of fact, I can. I know a fellow who translated some papers for me. He has also translated a good deal of plays for the theater people. His name is Gustav Brideau, and he has rooms not far from here."

"I would like you to send him a message, telling him I want to hire him for a few half-days a week as a private instructor."

"Very well, I shall do it," Mr. Minchy promised. Then he paused and said, "Do you think your husband will allow this?"

"Why shouldn't he?"

"Gustav Brideau is young and charming. I understand he performed romantic roles in Paris."

"That should make no difference to my husband."

"I'm merely warning you in advance. This man is most attractive."

"Send him to my house tomorrow morning if he is available," she told Mr. Minchy, and bade him farewell.

The next morning the young Frenchman arrived, and more than verified the lawyer's description of him. Gustav Brideau was tall and slender, with broad shoulders, a distinguished manner, and fine features crowned by dark, curly hair. That he did not wear a wig, like most of the men of fashion Enid knew, impressed her at once.

"You have no wig, Monsieur Brideau!"

"No, I don't," he said in perfect English. "I have plenty of hair of my own, so why should I wear one?"

She smiled. "It is the style, you know."

"I am not a slave to style, dear Lady Blair."

"That is refreshing. And you speak English like a native!"

The dashing fellow bowed. "Thank you for the compliment, my lady, but I assure you I am a born Frenchman."

Enid sat back in her chair and studied him. He was taller than either her husband or Armand, and more youthful in appearance than they. She could not help but think, wryly, that Gustav Brideau, with his good looks and curly hair, would be the sort of man to quickly turn her husband's eye.

Certainly he appealed to her, though not in the same way as Armand. She had fallen completely in love with the dignity and fine nature of the count. "I understand that you are often engaged in translation work," she said.

"I do a fair amount of it, my lady."

"For business and also for the theater?"

"That is true."

"I'm mostly interested in improving my handling and understanding of the spoken word," she explained. "I write your language well enough."

"That gives you a sound foundation, my lady," Brideau assured her. "We should have no trouble at all."

"Then I would like you to come two mornings and two afternoons a week."

He bowed. "That can be arranged. May I mention that I also give lessons in fencing?"

"Fencing?" She laughed. "What would a young lady do with fencing?"

"Some ladies in the theater have need of that skill," he replied. "Also, they have found that this type of training has increased their gracefulness and slimmed their figures."

Enid lifted her eyebrows. "These side benefits had not occurred to me," she admitted.

"You might consider trying the sport," he went on. "I think it could be useful for protection in these dark days of violent crime. I give lessons in my attic flat, which has a good deal of room since the roof is high and peaked. I suggest you come one day when I have a female student so you can decide if fencing interests you."

"Thank you. I shall look forward to it."

Thus began Enid's association with Gustav Brideau.

After a few French lessons he made a suggestion. "Why must we be so confined on these pleasant summer days? Couldn't we go for a walk in the streets, or even riding, and carry on our conversation exercises while we take in various surroundings?"

"What an excellent idea!" Enid exclaimed.

The next day when he called, she went out with him to tour the shopping district nearby. This gave her a chance to use a different assortment of words.

"You are becoming very proficient," Gustav assured her.

"I'm doing better," she agreed, "but I want my French to be perfect."

It was inevitable that their walks should lead to their going riding together. There were several fine horses idle in the Blair stable, so Enid ordered two of them saddled and she and Gustav cantered into the park, conversing happily in French.

A few nights later, at a ball given by a married couple whom Enid and Andrew knew, the dowager Lady Stubbs came up to them and peered at Andrew through her lorgnette "It was *not* you I saw riding with your wife in the park the other day," she declared. "It was a dark young man!"

Andrew's expression grew grim. "Madam, you must be in error. My wife does not go riding, and certainly not with gentlemen other than myself."

"But I saw her!" the elderly woman protested. "Didn't I?" She put the question directly to Enid.

Enid blushed and replied, "It's possible. I have ridden in the park several times lately."

"Who was the man?" her ladyship demanded.

Enid wanted to send her packing but decided to be polite. "The gentleman you refer to is my French instructor."

"Indeed!" Lady Stubbs sniffed, and tottered off.

Andrew gave Enid an ugly look. "We will go into this matter later."

He waited until they had returned to the town house before he lashed out at her. "You are making a laughingstock out of me! I caught two of the servant girls joking about your French teacher the other day! What is going on here?"

Enid removed her black taffeta cape to reveal bare shoulders and low-cut turquoise evening gown. Holding the cloak loosely in her hands, she said wearily, "And don't you know they also joke about you and the men you bring here?"

"I have heard nothing about that!" he snapped.

"They take care that you don't. But behind your back they call you a sodomist."

"Don't try to draw attention away from your own deeds by putting me in the wrong," he retorted sharply. "I was content to let that fellow come here for your French lessons. But I didn't give you permission to go out with him, let alone to raid my stables and take him riding with you!"

"The horses needed exercise!" she protested feebly.

"It seems to be the tongues of our friends that are getting the most exercise from your indiscretions!" he stormed.

"You know there was no harm in any of it!"

"I would like to believe that, but in this day and age in London, I very much doubt it."

She tossed her head angrily. "You judge me on the basis of your own disgraceful conduct!"

"I forbid you to go riding with that man again or to walk the streets with him!"

"May I continue to take my lessons here?"

"Yes, if you must." Andrew sighed heavily. "Though I confess I'm suspicious of your sudden ardor for the French tongue. I have an idea it stems from your trip to Versailles. You have been most secretive since you were there."

'That is sheer nonsense!" She turned and went up the broad stairway to her bedroom, leaving him standing below glaring after her.

It was then that she made the decision to visit Gustav's attic studio. Since she was forbidden to be seen with him in public, she would meet him there. That would be her way of defying her husband.

• • •

Two mornings later she appeared in the doorway of Gustav's attic flat. He was fencing with a pretty young girl whose face was hidden behind a wire mask. The girl was wearing a skirt that had been divided in the center and sewn down to form makeshift pantaloons. Only when she moved about was it clear that she was not wearing a short skirt.

The parries were brisk, and for a few minutes Gustav didn't notice Enid's presence. Then he called a halt to the fencing, and, mopping his brow with a white handkerchief, crossed the room to greet her.

"Lady Blair! I was not certain you would keep your promise."

"I never break one if I can help it," Enid told him, smiling warmly. "Who is the young lady?"

"Her name is Susan—Susan Smith. Surely that is English enough for you!"

The girl had taken off her mask, and Enid saw that she was extremely pretty, with flowing auburn hair and clear green eyes.

Holding out her hand in a manlike fashion, Susan said, "Call me Susie!"

Enid shook hands with her. "Are you in the theater, Susie?"

"I am at that," she said proudly. "I'm at Drury Lane. One of the company headed by John Philip Kemble."

Enid shook her head in bewilderment. "I do not get to the theater too often."

"He's the brother of Sarah Siddons. You must have heard of her!"

"Yes. I have seen her on the stage," Enid said.

"John is her younger brother. There are two other brothers, but Stephen is a year older than he, fat, and a bad actor to boot. And Charles is only thirteen or so. We sometimes use him in plays where a boy is needed."

Gustav placed an arm around the actress and gave her a knowing smile. "Susie is the leading lady of the company. She is my leading lady as well!"

Susie smiled up at him and exclaimed, "You are a one! What will Lady Blair think? It's bad enough to find us fencing and me wearing this strange outfit!"

"I think your outfit is very practical," Enid told her. "And I see no harm in your caring for each other. I think it's delightful."

"I would like to be married, Lady Blair, as you are," the attractive young woman said in her vivacious way.

Enid hesitated. "You should take care. Marriage is not always what it seems."

"That's what my mother says," Susie agreed. "She married a traveling actor and has never had a decent dress to call her own. All because my poor pa's talent is no match for his thirst for gin!"

"So you are a child of the theater?"

Susie laughed. "I've been called that, and I love it. It's the only way of life I know. Kemble says I have a future, though it's hard to tell with him, he's such a moody fellow."

"Is he of a melancholy nature?" Enid asked.

"Very much so," Gustav answered. "He even plays his light romantic roles with a grim intensity. And his Hamlet is the most melancholy of those I have seen in both France and England."

"I shall have to see him perform," Enid said. "And you as well, Susie."

"Thank you, my lady." The young actress studied Enid with bright green eyes. "Most great ladies are old or ugly. You are young *and* beautiful."

"That compliment is surely pay enough for my visit. I fear I must return to my carriage now."

Gustav offered to see her down the stairs.

At the entrance door Enid turned to him and said, "I like your friend Susie. She is charming."

"She is very talented, too," the Frenchman agreed.

"I'm sure of it."

"Have you thought about taking up fencing?"

"Perhaps I shall try it," she replied. "But first I'm going down to Surrey to see my family. I have been away a while now, and since summer is here I feel the moment is right."

Gustav looked forlorn. "How long will you be gone?"

"A month, maybe less."

"You will lose much of your proficiency in French if you do not keep at it," he cautioned her.

"My father speaks French fairly well, so I plan to have test conversations with him."

"It won't be the same," Gustav said unhappily. "At least not for me."

She smiled and touched his arm. "I will return as soon as I can, and we shall resume our lessons. And fencing, too. In the meantime, have a nice summer with your Susie Smith."

He frowned. "She does not mean that much to me."

"I'm sure you get on well together."

"We do, but so do you and I."

It was on the tip of her tongue to tell him their relationship was very different, but she thought better of it. "I must go."

Gustav stepped out on the pavement and helped her into the carriage. "I may wish to write. Where will you be?" he asked.

"Write me a letter in French," she said, excited at the idea. "And I shall write a reply for you to judge. It will be a sort of exercise. I shall be in Hensworth, Surrey. My father is Lord Alfred Henson, and you can send your letters in care of him."

"Excellent!" The handsome Frenchman's hazel eyes were beaming with happiness.

As the carriage moved away and she waved to him in farewell, she had a momentary qualm that Gustav Brideau was becoming much too fond of her. While she was physically attracted to him and often ached for fulfillment as a woman, she did not want to have an affair with him. For one thing, there were echoes of Armand in his manner, and she had no intention of sullying the memory of her brief, but beautiful, romance with the nobleman. For another, she was loath to give herself cheaply. She had no wish to match her husband's excesses in another direction. Although Andrew continued to bring his boys home and to make life generally uncomfortable for her, she would not lower herself by seeking out affairs simply to punish him. Thus, she would strive to keep Gustav as a friend and a teacher and hoped he would respect her wishes.

Andrew was strangely amenable to the idea of her visiting her parents for a month. His attitude puzzled her momentarily, but the truth soon came out.

"It will be rather convenient, as a matter of fact," he said. "Vicomte Claude Robert is coming to spend a week or two as my guest. I know you don't like him, so it's better that you're going away."

"I wouldn't care to be in his company," she agreed.

Andrew looked piqued. "You ask me to accept *your* friends, but you refuse to be civil to *mine.*"

"Yours are often so much more than friends," she reminded him.

He crimsoned. "We have an understanding, do we not?"

"Yes," she said quietly. "But since you are so worried about the servants' tongues wagging, I trust you will be discreet in your carryings-on with the vicomte. No dinner parties with naked young male servants!"

"You will never forgive me for that little joke, will you?"

"I doubt that I ever could."

7

Enid stood in the summerhouse on the rear lawn and gazed out at the vine-covered, old brick mansion, at the great elms sheltering it, and at the apple trees in the orchard. She could hear voices and the whinnying of horses from the stables beyond. This was her home, the place where she had grown up and which she loved more than any other. It was the preservation of Henson House and all that it meant to Enid and her parents that had been the true reason behind her marriage to Andrew. Oddly enough, she needn't have been so quick to marry him after all, since her father was now well enough to look after his affairs again.

She had been heartened the moment she had seen him. Despite Lord Alfred's use of a walking stick and his loss of weight, much of his old spirit was restored, and his voice was firm and strong. Her mother also looked less ravaged. Lady Caroline's middle-aged beauty was almost in full bloom again, and she was planning several social events while Enid was at home.

One of the first things Enid's father had done was to take her into his study for a private talk. In that book-lined room which she had always regarded with awe, he had studied her with troubled eyes and asked, "What about your marriage?"

She had been on guard at once. "I don't understand your question, Father."

"I think you do."

"Father!" she had protested weakly.

"Let us speak freely, my daughter. I am no longer a sick man."

"For which I'm grateful."

"And I," he had agreed. "The Lord has been good. But I was struck down at an unhappy time in my fortunes."

"That was unavoidable."

66

"I am now recovering some of my losses, and, with luck, I shall soon be back to where I was before my illness. You will never again have to worry about my ability to keep this place and take care of your mother."

"That is the best possible news! I am so happy!"

He had sighed. "But I fear that, in the interim, you have suffered the most because of my situation. You are the one who saved me and thereby paid a great price."

"What are you saying?" Fear had risen in her throat. Had he heard some wicked gossip?

"We are not so isolated here in Surrey," he had told her. "Word does get down from London, you know. And the news about your husband and his actions is not what I would wish to hear."

She had glanced away. "Gossips make much of little."

"I did not care much for the fellow when we first met," her father had continued, "but you seemed taken with him. And when he most generously offered to back any overdraft at my bank, I began to think that he was, after all, a sound fellow. It was only his manner that was annoying. In any event, I have cost him nothing. All has been paid back, and I am not beholden to him any more."

"That he did not tell me."

"It is something I felt you should know." He had paused, then said, "I do not wish your mother to hear any of this, since it might throw her into despair, but rumor has it that you have wed a foul man—a sodomist!"

Enid had not been able to look at her father. "It wasn't your fault, nor mine. Neither of us had any idea at all."

Lord Alfred's voice had threatened to crack. "I should have trusted my instincts about him! I should not have let him blind me with his offers of money!"

"It is done now, Father. Please don't berate yourself."

"That is why you are here alone, with no husband by your side—why you are so clearly unhappy. My poor dear girl, what is to become of you?"

Her courage had slowly come back now that the worst had been spoken. She had glanced at her father's sorrowful face and replied, "I shall make a life for myself."

"How?"

"I'm not sure just yet. But I shall. And one day I hope to win my freedom from Andrew."

"He wants you as a facade and will not make it easy for you to leave him. I fear he could be most dangerous!"

"I know all that," she had admitted.

Lord Alfred had leaned forward in his chair, his arms on his cane. "Does the cad have any love for you at all?"

"Not as we understand love. He has a cold nature but a devouring passion. And that passion is not for women."

"So you have nothing between you!"

"Little. He regards me as an acceptable decoration for his house, as a suitable companion for social events. He has a possessiveness about everything he owns, and I expect he considers me a possession as well."

"Never!" her father had exclaimed. "Oh, dear Lord, I literally sold you to this fellow in exchange for my own security!"

"*I* made the decision. You urged me to be sure of what I was doing—even up to the moment I left for Paris."

"The Paris wedding!" he had cried. "That alone ought to have warned me!"

"Going to France turned out to be a very important thing for me."

Lord Alfred had frowned. "What do you mean?"

"You remember Lucinda?"

"Of course. She lives in Versailles with her husband."

"I went to visit them. They were most kind to me after Andrew had abused me. I met a man there…a friend of theirs. His name is Armand Beaufaire…and I fell in love with him."

"Does your husband know about this?"

"I think he suspects something, but he has no way of truly knowing."

"It is unfortunate you didn't meet this man earlier."

"I agree. He is a French count, and since things are very bad over there now, I am forced to realize that I may never see him again."

"Do you plan to continue a loveless marriage with Blair?"

"For the moment. To pass my time better, I have been taking French lessons, and have become much more proficient in the language than I was. I'm even thinking of taking up fencing."

Her father had looked astounded. "Is that a woman's sport?"

"Some of the actresses in London are trying it. I thought I might, too."

Lord Alfred Henson had stared at his daughter and then spoken. "Well, it seems I will have to let you make your own decisions. I am sure you are capable. I do not know what this Frenchman is like, but surely he must be a better man than Andrew Blair."

"I can promise you that!"

"If you truly love each other, I trust the time will come when you may marry honorably. Though at the moment there are notable barriers to that."

"I don't think Andrew would be sympathetic to the idea of my leaving him."

"Obviously not. He is using you as a front. But whatever you do, know that I will help you in any way possible."

Now, gazing about her at the lush summer verdancy of the country estate, Enid found her father's words reassuring. That he was financially independent again was a great relief to her. The house was a much happier place with Lord Alfred up and about.

• • •

A few days later, after one of her mother's wonderful dinner parties, Enid received a rather disturbing letter from Lucinda. Matters in France had worsened. There was considerable unemployment, and the commercial treaty with England had resulted in a flood of superior as well as poorly made English exports. In Carcassonne alone a thousand workmen had been laid off, and elsewhere workers had smashed English machinery in the belief that such equipment was costing them their jobs.

Lucinda went on to say that the many uprisings had frightened off travelers from England and other countries. Half the laborers in Paris were unemployed. There was far less court spending, and one result of this was the recent bankruptcy of the queen's personal dressmaker, Rose Bertin. A few weeks earlier a freak hailstorm had swept the Paris region and wreaked much damage. Grain was in short supply and the price of bread had soared, causing women and children to stand in endlessly long lines before bake shops.

Despite all this gloomy news, Lucinda claimed that she and her husband were happy. The duke would not think of leaving his estate, so they would remain in France and weather the darkening clouds. The most exciting tidbit for Enid was the brief mention that Armand Beaufaire was planning a trip to England.

Enid's pleasant holiday took a different turn soon afterward with the arrival of Gustav Brideau one fine morning. The young Frenchman rode up on a black mare while she was standing by the rosebushes talking to the gardener. Wearing a light blue summer dress and a large bonnet to shield her face from the sun, she looked very much the country lady.

At first she could not believe her eyes. However, when Gustav turned his mount over to a stableboy and came striding toward her, she no longer had any doubts. In a white shirt open at the neck, a blue vest, and navy blue breeches, with his dark hair wind-tousled and his hazel eyes full of merriment, he emanated charm and romance.

"You!" she exclaimed as they met on the lawn.

"Yes, it is indeed I! I hired a horse in the village and found my way here." He was bursting with vitality.

"If I had known you were planning a visit, I would have arranged for a carriage to meet you," she said, flustered.

He laughed. "No need. I enjoyed the ride. I wanted to see you in your native surroundings." He looked about approvingly. "It is lovely here. Magnificent. And you are truly deserving of it."

"Will you be able to stay a few days?"

His eyes twinkled. "If I'm invited."

"Of course you are. I'll speak to my mother and father. They will place a room at your disposal."

"London is very dull without you," he remarked.

"What about all your theater friends?" she asked as she took his arm and led him toward the house.

"Most of them are also in the country. The summer season in London is very quiet. But when you return, there is one actor I want you to meet. John Philip Kemble."

"Susie Smith's leading man!"

He smiled. "Only on stage. He lives a solitary life away from his work. But I think he's interesting, and I believe you would feel the same."

"I shall look forward to the meeting," she said.

"And will you begin fencing lessons when you return?"

"As soon as you like. I'm excited about doing it. Now, let me introduce you to my parents."

Lord and Lady Henson were pleased to meet Enid's good-looking friend, who had an easy knack of fitting in with people. Before long they felt completely relaxed with Gustav, as if they had always known him. Lord Alfred spoke with him about hunting, showed him his prized gun collection, and promised to see him ride to hounds one day soon. Lady Caroline was equally captivated by the high-spirited Gustav.

For Enid, Gustav's visit held a mixed blessing. She enjoyed his company but feared her husband would hear of his arrival in Surrey and spitefully make the most of it.

She did her best to maintain a polite barrier between herself and the young man. They worked at her French lessons, went riding through the countryside, and often spent hours talking. Enid was impressed with his agile mind.

One warm, starlit night they strolled out to the summerhouse before retiring. Dinner had been exceptionally good, and her father had fallen into a nostalgic mood, recalling his younger days in London, to everyone's delight.

When Enid and Gustav reached the summerhouse, he surprised her by sweeping her into his arms and kissing her ardently.

She pulled back from him in alarm. "You take liberties!" she protested.

"Didn't you want me to kiss you?" he asked. "Surely this is the right setting."

"I wish for us to remain friends."

"And I would like to see us *better* friends," he declared, ready to embrace her again.

"No," she said gently. "You must not spoil things, Gustav. I'm very fond of you, and perhaps I *would* enjoy your embraces, but it would be the end for us. I am a married woman; you must remember that."

A look of scorn crossed his face. "Your husband is a libertine who does not appreciate you!"

"But he is also intensely jealous of me and insists that I avoid any hint of scandal."

"He provides quite enough of that with his lads!"

"Maybe so, but I do my best to make our marriage seem like a normal one so that our position in society is preserved."

"Position be damned! I'm fond of you, and you need a man!"

Enid recognized the pulsing forces within her that had been brought to the surface by his embrace. Wryly, she said, "I wish I could deny that, but I truly can't!"

"Leave your husband and come live with me," Gustav implored her. "I could make you happy."

"You could, and thank you, but I do not feel the match is right."

"There is someone else?"

"Yes."

"Who?"

"You don't know him. He doesn't live in London, nor even in this country."

Gustav groaned in dismay. "How can I be expected to compete with some unknown man?"

"You cannot," she said, lightly tapping his hand with her fan. "We will continue to be close friends, better friends than we would be if we allowed our passions full rein. And you will make me an expert in fencing as you have in French!"

"That's not my ambition where you are concerned. I had other hopes."

"For the time being, you must be content with these things," she told him.

"All right, if you insist. But I refuse to give up hope."

After this conversation with Gustav, she felt less tension between them. He remained at her father's estate for a few more days and then returned to London. When she was certain that the vicomte had left for Paris, she packed her belongings, kissed her parents goodbye, and rejoined her husband.

Lord Andrew was cool in his greeting of her. Shortly after she was reinstalled in the London town house, Enid learned of his excesses in gambling. Whispers came to her of his huge losses in many of the gaming houses, as well as in the homes of the socially elite. She also discovered that Andrew's almost constant companion at the gaming houses was the Duke of Bridge-water, a half-mad nobleman, who talked of nothing but canals, had destroyed all the gardens around his home, and would not allow any woman servant in his employ.

Enid went to Gustav's studio for her first fencing lesson. She found that Susie Smith had abandoned her acting career and had moved in with Gustav. Some claimed this had happened because of a falling-out between Susie and Kemble, who had wanted her to assume more minor parts in his company so that he could advance the talents of another actress to play opposite him.

Whatever the reason, it was a fact that Susie had become Gustav's mistress. She seemed to be quite happy with the gallant Frenchman.

As soon as Enid became proficient enough, she and Susie began to fence together. One afternoon, after they had indulged in an especially lively match, Susie threw down her mask and said, "You have a natural ability at this. I declare you are already my superior!"

"But you have been fencing so much longer," Enid protested.

"No matter. You have caught on very fast, and you are taller and stronger than I."

Gustav was of the same opinion, and when Enid came for her fencing lesson the next afternoon, he told her, "I want you to take part in a little game."

She stared at him. "What sort of game?"

"A practical joke I wish to play on someone. Susie suggested it to me."

Enid smiled. "Your Susie is too often given to mischief. Just what is this joke?"

"Remember my speaking of the actor Kemble?"

"Yes. You promised I would meet him."

"I still want you to. I think you'd like him, and he couldn't help but be enchanted by you. Now, let me explain. Kemble thinks most seriously of himself. It is his one fault. He has been acclaimed the finest actor in all of England, and perhaps he is. He also considers himself the best swordsman in London, and in that he is surely wrong."

"So?"

"I propose to set up a match pitting Kemble against an unknown young man of great fencing skill. I am positive that Kemble will be defeated."

"What part am I supposed to play in this?"

He laughed. "You, my dear Enid, will be the young man!"

"You're mad!"

"Not at all. I swear you can defeat him in a fencing match."

"I very much doubt it—and in any case, I'm not a young man!"

"We can manage that," he went on quickly. "Your figure is relatively slender. With the proper clothing, a wire mask, and your hair tied securely under a bandana, who would guess?"

"It's preposterous!" she exclaimed.

"At least let Susie fix you up in the disguise. If you are not satisfied, there will be no need to go ahead with it."

She hesitated. "Suppose I can make myself look like a young man and deceive Kemble. What is the point to my defeating him at fencing?"

"To take him down a trifle," Gustav said. "He is a good fellow, but he has grown too full of himself. This little trick would be just the thing for him."

"And if he surpasses me with the blade and inflicts a serious wound on me, what then?"

"I will tell him you are a novice." Gustav rubbed his hands together, enjoying himself hugely at the prospect. "He is not a vicious type who would be liable to lose his temper."

"It is I who would have to risk that!"

"I swear it is worth doing," he urged. "And I shall be on the sidelines to call the match to a halt if it goes against you."

"I fear I sense the purpose behind all this," Enid remarked wryly. "Susie is still suffering from his treatment of her and wishes to see him humiliated."

"That's part of it," Gustav allowed. "You wouldn't rob her of this chance to even a score, would you? It is only fair that you ladies stand by each other!"

"Let me think about it," Enid said.

8

A week later Enid found herself disguised as a young man, masked, and with sword in hand, facing a tall, courtly man who studied her with a patronizing air. In the background stood Susie Smith and Gustav. The match had been artfully arranged by them, and Enid, against her better judgment, was a willing party to the conspiracy.

"Begin, gentlemen!" Gustav commanded, stopwatch in hand.

"En garde!" John Philip Kemble declared dramatically.

Enid took what she hoped was a manly stance, and the struggle between them began. She soon realized why she need not fear the distinguished actor. He was much larger-boned than she, of course, and not nearly so agile. His style of fencing was as deliberate and heavy as his style of acting. He was good enough, but simply not as quick-footed or as quick-thinking as she.

Their swords clashed, and although his thrusts were skillful, Enid always wound up besting him. After several minutes she saw that the struggle of combat was taking its toll on him. As he darted back and forth, trying to get in closer to her or to force her sword from her hand, he began to breathe heavily, and perspiration lined his cheeks. Enid remained cool and alert.

Kemble grew more frantic in his efforts as he became wearier. Enid parried her weapon with his and continued to outfence him. Then, at last, he let himself get into a position that allowed her to give his blade a vicious twist and tear it from his hand.

"Enough!" Gustav cried. "I declare the mystery youth the winner!"

Kemble mopped his brow with a white silk handkerchief. "I'm not sorry the match is at an end," he sighed. "I bow in defeat to a better man."

Gustav laughed. "Not exactly!"

Kemble frowned. "What do you mean?"

"You lost to a woman!" Susie exulted as she came forward.

Kemble's face turned ashen. "You're jesting!"

Gustav crossed over to Enid and removed the mask and the bandana covering her hair. Enid found herself blushing prettily as her blonde curls tumbled down her back.

The actor stared at her in shock. "I cannot believe it!"

"You had better," Susie told him dryly.

Awed, Kemble moved closer to Enid. "You truly *are* a woman!" he exclaimed.

"Yes," she said quietly. "Please forgive my deception."

Kemble turned to the other two. "I know who must have conceived this dubious jest. Suppose I had seriously harmed this lady?"

Gustav laughed. "I would have stopped you. Take it in good stride, friend Kemble, and meet Lady Enid Blair!"

The actor bowed. "My great honor, madam. You are expert at fencing."

"Never so expert as you are on the stage," Enid replied charmingly. "I have much admired your Hamlet, and wished to meet you to tell you so." A little fib, nothing more.

Her ready compliment overcame his bad humor. At once he looked less sullen, and he even managed to smile at her. "You are something of an actress yourself. I vow I would not have taken you for anything but an agile lad."

Susie put an arm around Enid. "We'll go into the other room, and in a few minutes you'll see what a fine lady she is."

Gustav told the actor, "You refresh yourself, John. And then we'll join the ladies for a hearty luncheon with plenty of excellent red wine!"

As Susie was helping Enid into her regular clothes in the bedchamber, she cried, "He's taken with you! Not that I'm surprised! So is Gustav! But Kemble doesn't show interest so easily in a lady."

Enid laughed. "I don't want him to become too obsessed with me. I have, as you know, a jealous husband."

"So you do," Susie agreed. "But what do you think of our Kemble?"

Enid sat before the mirror hanging above Susie's dressing table. She smiled at her reflection as she began to arrange her hair. "I think he is a nice, rather somber man. Perhaps a little too concerned with his own importance."

"You have hit it exactly," Susie said. "But do not think lightly of him. He is something of a genius, and in the parts where his melancholy style is called for, he excels."

Enid gave the former actress a searching glance. "Have you quite forgiven him for his slight of you?"

"Probably not," Susie was quick to admit. "But if he hadn't encouraged me to leave his company—and his attentions—I wouldn't have fallen in with Gustav so soon. And I'm deeply in love with that Frenchman."

"Enough to marry him?"

"If he will have me."

Enid rose and placed an arm around her friend. "I predict that one day soon he will. I think he fears you will return to the stage."

"I might do that, but I wouldn't leave Gustav. Many actresses have happy family lives outside the theater. When their confinement time comes they leave, but some of them return to the boards."

"I think I can understand why," Enid said. "It's a wonderful world of make-believe, so different from mundane reality."

Susie smiled. "At least all events are ordered. And when your time on the stage is over, you don't really mind coming back to reality."

They went out into the main room, which served as the living area, library, and dining room of the cramped lodgings. Gustav had set out plates of food and a decanter of red wine.

Kemble's liquid brown eyes widened when he saw Enid. "You are right!" he exclaimed. "She is a most beautiful maid! Fairer than I have seen for many a day!"

Enid allowed the actor to seat her next to him. She laughed and said, "That sounds suspiciously like a quotation from a play."

"It is," Susie told her, and they all laughed. "I have heard John speak those very lines onstage."

Kemble looked a little guilty. "You ought not to give away the secrets of a fellow professional."

"But I'm no longer in the profession!" Susie protested.

"You will be," he said. "If you would forget your pique, I could use you at Drury Lane again."

"Don't attempt to lure her back!" Gustav growled, pouring wine for everyone.

"No harm would come of it, Brideau. You may be sure of that. She is a fine soubrette, and as such I would like to hire her again."

Susie looked up from her plate to ask him, "Doesn't Lady Blair make a better boy than your sister, Mrs. Siddons, did when she played in *As You Like It?*"

Kemble nodded. "Lady Blair would make an excellent Rosalind. My blessed sister refused to wear proper male attire when she masqueraded as a boy and the result was a strange hodgepodge. That harmed the play."

"You are having a successful season at Drury Lane with your own company," Enid observed.

"My public is loyal," Kemble told her.

"Perceptive of talent," Gustav amended. "And John is an innovator when it comes to scenery and costumes. He has brought forth many new ideas in staging."

Kemble could not take his eyes off Enid. "You are the wife of Lord Andrew Blair, isn't that so?"

"Yes," she replied in a small voice.

"I have met him and some of his companions," Kemble said, running a hand through his dark chestnut hair. "They gamble at a club I frequent on occasion."

She smiled grimly. "I understand it is rumored that my husband's gambling losses amount to nearly the same sum as our national debt."

The actor laughed. "Judging by the wild plunges I have seen him indulge in, that could be true."

No more was said about Andrew, and the talk turned back to the theater. Enid learned that John's younger brother Stephen was a member of his company, a man addicted to overeating. It also came out that John and his famous sister, Mrs. Siddons, did not get along very well. John thought she was both arrogant and avaricious. She was known to be mean in her payment of the actors in her company and to be continually battling with the managers of the theaters where she played. Enid was thrilled by all the inside chatter of the theater world, and the discovery that even the idols of the West End had their share of human foibles was a revelation to her.

After lunch, Kemble insisted on taking Enid home in his open carriage. As they drove through the sunny streets, she blushed at the knowledge that many people recognized the famous actor by her side and were unquestionably trying to guess who his latest conquest might be.

As they approached the turn into Regent Street, Kemble said abruptly, "I want to see you again."

"I will visit the theater some evening."

He frowned. "No. I meant I want to spend time with you and get to know you better."

Enid gave him a warning look. "You forget my husband."

Brown eyes met those of sloe. "Why can't you forget him? For at least a little while."

She glanced at the red brick houses and the great, full-leaved trees lining the street. "I realize you are aware of his reputation… his great weaknesses."

"Yes."

"However, I have a pact with him that I'm loath to break. At least for now."

"I'm merely asking that we meet away from the theater, though of course I would like you to see my Hamlet again, and my Brutus, too. But I think it's more important that we become friends."

"You are well known," she reminded him. "Many questioning eyes have focused on this carriage ever since we left Gustav's."

"I cannot help being a public figure."

"But I can help being seen in public with you," she countered.

"Then let us meet privately," he urged. "I like to dine in my lodgings after the performances. Will you join me there?"

She hesitated. "To what purpose?"

"I admire you greatly and I would like to have you for a friend."

"I wish it could be so," she said.

"Do I interest you at all?" he asked her gravely.

She felt her cheeks flush. "It may be that you interest me too much."

"That could not be." He smiled ruefully. "Pray think over what I have said. I will send you a message shortly, inviting you to dine with me. I trust you will accept."

She made no reply. The striking-looking actor was unlike anyone she had ever met before. He lacked the aristocracy and French charm of Armand, but he possessed other qualities that made her regard him with admiring eyes. He was an artist, with an artist's sensitivity. She was certain that he approached each of his roles with an intellectual interest. He was not a shallow fop, like so many of the males she had met in London society and, indeed, like a goodly number of the theater's leading men.

Kemble saw her to the door and kissed her hand. Once more he promised, "You shall hear from me."

Enid did not expect to see him again very soon.

Several nights later Andrew informed her they were to attend a house party hosted by Sir James and Lady Evelyn Drake. Enid knew her husband would insist on her accompanying him, so she didn't protest. Besides, he had been in a bad mood lately, as the gaming tables had continued to go against him, and she was especially anxious not to cross him.

She chose a new rose satin gown for the affair and dressed her hair with rose and white silk ribbons. A vibrant emerald necklace and a matching pair of earrings completed her ensemble.

Sir James and Lady Drake represented the younger social set, and their party offered a healthy sprinkling of the city's young bloods and their ladies, as well as many notables from the worlds of politics and the arts. In the crowded drawing room of the large Regent Street mansion, it was not surprising that Enid should find herself face to face with John Philip Kemble, resplendent in a formal gold jacket and fawn breeches, a white wig covering his chestnut hair.

The actor instantly looked less bored and hastened to bring her a glass of wine. Then he began to speak earnestly. "I have done little but think about you since our meeting."

She smiled. "Did you think of the boy who bested you at fencing or the girl who refused your invitation to dine?"

He arched an eyebrow. "I do not recall your declining my invitation, only showing a certain hesitation in accepting it."

"That almost amounts to the same thing."

"I have not given up hope. You know I lead a very solitary life."

"What about the lady who took Susie's place in your heart—or should I say bed?"

"You have the sting of a wasp!"

"I like to speak frankly."

"That is frank enough for anyone." Kemble shuddered. "The truth is, the lady in question proved to be a worthless actress, a baggage who gave me no pleasure—in bed or out of it."

"But you would like Susie back in your company."

"I need her in my company. But that is all I want from her."

"From what she said to me, I think she may be ready to return to the stage."

"Good. I'm happy to hear that. Susie is a talented young miss, but not as adept at fencing as you."

"I fear that is a small talent."

"Your beauty alone would be enough," John complimented her with his usual gallantry.

"Thank you." Then she noticed that Andrew, who was standing a little distance away with an unhealthy-looking, spindle-shanked young fop, was watching her out of the corner of his eye.

Kemble noted the same thing. "Your husband has found a crony," he remarked.

"That is a simple accomplishment."

Their eyes met and locked. Enid looked away first.

"I've been working on some new set designs for my next production of *Hamlet*," Kemble said, his voice suddenly husky. "My sister thinks I'm spending far too much on staging the play, and I'd welcome your opinion."

"But I know nothing about staging plays!" Enid protested.

"You have exquisite taste and good judgment. They are all that is required. Would you look at my sketches for the designs and the costumes?"

"If you'd like," she said softly.

His smile lit his face from within. "Just your saying that has given me added interest in the project!"

Soon Enid moved on to talk with some of the other guests, but she was conscious of Kemble's presence all the while. He seemed to be everyone's favorite.

On the drive home, Andrew sat beside her in sullen silence and tugged abstractedly at his white brocade evening jacket. Then he glanced at her and demanded sourly, "Why did you decide to make me look ridiculous at the party?"

She gave him a puzzled look. "I don't understand."

"You spent so much of your time with that actor Kemble!"

"Surely there was nothing wrong in that," she said. "I met him at my fencing instructor's studio."

"Most people would think, from your actions, that you'd been gracing his bed!" Andrew snapped.

"Don't judge me by your habits!"

"Come to think of it, you may have been doing just that," he went on. "You certainly acted as if you'd met before. Touchingly intimate!"

"I've just told you, we did meet before!"

"So you did. Well, I will depend on you not to sully my name by giving him your simpering attentions again!"

Enid flashed him a hateful look. "How dare you, sir!"

"The man is not a proper person for you to associate with. The Drakes shouldn't have had him at their party. He is not of society."

"I disagree with you! You are sorely mistaken!"

"The facts speak for themselves. The man is an actor!"

"And why aren't actors suited to society?"

"They are buffoons, itinerant entertainers, paupers with nothing more than an elegant facade!"

"I prefer an elegant facade to a rotting interior." Enid turned her back on her husband and ended the conversation.

• • •

Two days later, when she went to Gustav's for her fencing practice, she found him alone in his lodgings.

"Susie isn't here," he announced. "She's gone back to Kemble."

"Only to his company. You can't hope to keep her off the stage with her talent."

Gustav agreed cheerfully. "She should do what she enjoys. And now Kemble has eyes for no female but you, so she is safe from him."

Enid stared at him in disbelief. "You're jesting!"

"No, it's the truth. Kemble is like a lovesick calf. It's amusing, really. I think it's because you whipped him at fencing."

"It must be," she mused, "for I have never given him the slightest bit of encouragement. At least I don't think I have."

"I know that. But John Kemble is a moody fellow, and you've apparently pulled him out of his doldrums. You could do him a great deal of good."

"I wonder."

"I'm sure of it. Besides, it seems my own cause is lost, so I may as well plead his."

She laughed. "Silly! You know that I'm deterred by the same problems in both instances. I am a married woman."

"I think it's the other man, the one you were so mysterious about. He is the one who must be exorcised from your mind before you can be free to love properly."

"I'm resigned to never seeing him again," she sighed. "He is caught up in the French troubles."

"The Bastille has already fallen, and God knows what will happen next." Gustav shook his head. "I'm glad I chose to live in England."

Enid eyed him worriedly. "Will it be much worse?"

"Heads will topple like rotten apples falling from the trees in late autumn."

She sighed again. "Ours was only a brief acquaintance, but I believe I loved that man at first sight. I think we could have been very happy." Enid's expression was wistful. Then, as if in an effort to cast out unhappy thoughts, she straightened her shoulders and flashed a warm smile at Gustav. "It is in the past now. Perhaps I am lucky to have Kemble in love with me."

"Have you ever seen him play Romeo?" Gustav asked.

"No. I've never seen him perform at all."

"I'll take you this afternoon," the Frenchman promised. "Susie is doing Juliet. It is a part she has always played well. And I think seeing Kemble in the role of Romeo will give you a glimpse into his soul. You'll appreciate what a tender, romantic fellow he is."

"I have found him gentle of nature thus far."

"He will never disappoint you," Gustav promised.

Drury Lane was crowded that afternoon. On the way inside, Gustav nodded to a bewigged, full-faced gentleman who was talking with several companions in the lobby. "That is the very eminent playwright Richard Sheridan," Gustav whispered to Enid. "I'm sorry to say he and Kemble have very different ideas about how Drury Lane should be operated. Sheridan is part owner of the theater, while Kemble is only the manager."

"What is the problem, then?"

"Gossip has it that Sheridan is going to send Kemble and his sister, Mrs. Siddons, packing as soon as their lease is up. Mark my words, that would be a real pity."

The theater was almost filled by the time they took their places in the dress circle. After a moment Gustav whispered to her, "Glance over at the dress box on the lower right level and you will see Prince George the Fourth."

She looked in the direction Gustav had indicated and saw a handsome man talking to a group of four equally well-dressed people, two ladies and two gentlemen. He was poised and elegant, very much a member of the British royal family.

"At least he appears in control of all his faculties," she remarked, "unlike what we hear about the king."

"You can be assured of that," Gustav agreed.

The curtain rose on the great Shakespearean play, and Enid, along with the rest of the audience, found herself enthralled throughout.

When the curtain came down for the last time, she knew herself to be one of Kemble's most dedicated admirers. The solemn actor had given the best performance of the romantic tragedy that she had ever witnessed. It appeared that many people in the audience felt the same. There were numerous curtain calls, and at the final one Kemble led Susie out with great dignity. The crowd went wild, and Enid could see that Susie was crying with joy.

Enid and Gustav went backstage to visit Susie in her tiny dressing room. The actress ran to Gustav and threw her arms around him.

"Thank you for allowing me to return to the stage!" she exulted, her tears still flowing. "Did you hear the cheers and the applause?"

The Frenchman kissed her soundly. "I felt I was sharing it with you!"

"You were!" she exclaimed. "You made it possible for me! Now you must go and speak with John while I change my clothes."

Enid and Gustav proceeded down the dimly lit corridor to Kemble's larger quarters. A dozen or so fans were milling about, congratulating the actor and getting his autograph. Not until they had departed and Kemble was about to disappear behind a screen to shed his costume did he notice Enid's presence.

His soulful brown eyes were full of joy as he came forward and grasped her hands. "Dear Lady Blair," he said huskily. "You did come to see me after all."

"And I am the richer for it," she told him.

Her hands lingered in his for a long moment, and their eyes met and held, as they had at the Drakes' party. Later, Enid was to remember this silent gaze and consider it the beginning of their real intimacy.

He ended the magic moment by saying, "I'm having a light supper at my place—you must join me! There'll be just the four of us and my servants."

Enid made a feeble protest, but Gustav overwhelmed her with his insistence that she join the party.

So it was that not too long afterward she found herself seated at the round oak table in the actor's modest lodgings. Kemble made a charming host, and the roast mutton was the best she had ever tasted. Gustav and Susie were in a happy, romantic mood, holding hands and exchanging kisses as if they had just discovered each other.

Kemble leaned toward Enid and said with a smile, "I swear they indeed have a love match."

"Did you doubt it?"

"I did at the start," he admitted. "I found Susie much more rewarding as a stage love."

"You were not the right man for her," Enid ventured.

"I know that now." His eyes sought hers as he added, "Since I have met the woman who I am confident can completely fulfill me."

Enid felt her cheeks burn and quickly turned her attention to her wine glass. Then Gustav and Susie announced that they were leaving. Enid was about to rise from the table when Kemble stopped her.

"I shall see you home later," he said. "I wish to show you those sketches of my proposed new production of *Hamlet*. This is an ideal time."

"Very well," she agreed a trifle nervously.

They saw the couple off, and then Kemble led her into a candlelit room that served as his den. From a sheaf of papers he withdrew several sketches of stage settings and costumes.

"My idea is to do the play in its own period," he explained. "The current trend is to do it as a story of our time, which spares the cost of scenery and costumes. But I'm sure this production will be more authentic for capturing the right atmosphere."

Enid sat on a small divan with him, going over the drawings he had placed on her lap. "They are excellent!" she declared.

He brought her another glass of red wine and held it between them, his serious face brightening with a smile. "To the success of the project!" He sipped from the glass and then handed it to her. She sipped some wine as well and placed the glass aside to meet his impassioned embrace.

Enid was never clear afterward as to what had actually happened in those first frantic moments of realized love. She remembered his warm lips on hers, the caresses of his gentle hands on her shoulders and bosom, then being lifted up as effortlessly as if she were a snowflake and carried into his bedchamber.

Slowly, with infinite care, he removed her clothing until she stood before him naked, bathed in a golden glow from the lamplight. She felt no shame, only a deep hunger to be possessed by him. Kemble divested himself of his own garments, revealing a compact, lithe body, and crushed her to him. Enid trembled at the feel of his throbbing maleness and clung to him as he placed her on the bed.

To each caress, to each flick of his tongue over every inch of her body, she responded with soft moans, writhing in an almost unbearable state of desire. She lost all sense of time and space, conscious only of the delicious, incredible sensations coursing through her. At long last, Kemble arched his flanks and penetrated her moist flesh, driving slowly at first and then harder, bringing them both to a peak of rapture that exploded again and again until they were enveloped in a glow of peacefulness.

John caressed her brow and sought her lips once more. Enid returned his kiss feverishly, wrapping her arms around him as if she feared losing him.

"You know this had to be, my dearest," he murmured.

"Yes," she whispered.

"I love you as I have loved no one before."

"And in you I have found the perfect lover."

His smile was melancholy. "My only fear is that what we have is too good. It is a thing apart. A precious union like ours could not withstand the tests of an ordinary mating!"

"What do you mean?"

"I mean that you are wed to a jealous, cruel man who will not let you go because he needs you to protect his appetites. And I am wed to my profession to such an extent that I could never be a satisfactory husband. I could never give myself wholly to a woman, even to one I love as deeply as you."

Inexplicably, Enid knew he was right. Their passionate melding was a delicate flame. And, like a delicate flame, it could be quickly snuffed out by the buffeting winds of the everyday world.

"What are we to do?" she wondered.

Kemble stroked her breast and felt the pink tip grow taut beneath his fingers. "We must be thankful for what we have. We must cling to it, knowing full well that it must remain a thing apart."

"And will you forbid me your bed one day, as you have done with others?"

"Never," he vowed.

"I want your love always!" Enid declared unabashedly.

His lips nuzzled the warm hollow of her throat. "And you shall have it, dearest. From this day on, no one will love you as I do."

"And if we part?"

"We shall part," he said sadly. "That is why our being together now has a special meaning. We know it may be of a short duration, but it is very important to us. And whether you break off with me first or I with you, we will always have this link between us. You will live forever with the memory of our union, as will I."

These words, declaimed with deep sincerity by the emotional actor, could not fail to affect her greatly. They seemed burned into her mind. She accepted their inherent truth, just as she accepted the fact that in Kemble she had found what she desperately needed at the moment.

• • •

Their trysts continued, requiring little strategy on Enid's part since Andrew had a new lad in whom he was seriously interested. Graham Farnsworth had come to the house as a page and soon found himself in her husband's bed.

Andrew now referred to Graham as his private secretary, and the youth accompanied him everywhere. They had attended a party given by Prince George, who, it was claimed, had twitted Andrew heartily about his "son." Andrew had brazened out the awkward moment by stating that he was indeed considering adopting the lad.

Kemble continued to draw large audiences to Drury Lane despite his quarrels with Sheridan. Susie was once more a favorite among his leading ladies. Gustav and Enid often attended the theater together, after which the four of them would seek out a small tavern or enjoy a repast at Kemble's flat.

It was now openly understood among their intimates that Enid and Kemble were lovers. She was able to spend many a late afternoon and evening with him because Andrew was so enthralled with his latest discovery. She no longer cared what her dissolute husband did, or with whom, except that she worried about his incessant gambling.

Reports of Andrew's profligateness had reached even her father's ears. And when he and her mother came up to London for a few days in mid-November, Lord Alfred approached his daughter in a concerned fashion. "Do you know all you should about your husband's finances?"

"Not nearly enough," Enid admitted.

She and her father were seated opposite each other in the sitting room of the suite he had engaged for his stay in London, located above the Swan Tavern.

"What I have heard is most disquieting!" he told her, leaning forward and tapping his walking stick impatiently.

Enid looked down at the worn green carpet. "There is much gossip about Andrew and his new boy."

"It was for that very reason that I refused your hospitality," Lord Alfred stated. "I will not sleep under the same roof with someone who abuses my daughter by openly proclaiming to all that he is a lover of boys!"

"I have grown used to it, Father."

"More's the pity," he retorted angrily. "I speak so frankly because your mother is out to tea with her old friend Mrs. Deacon. If I were you, I would immediately dismiss this Graham from the household staff."

"He is my husband's employee, and even if I should force Andrew to release the youth, he'd replace him with someone similarly oriented. Graham, at least, tries to be agreeable to me."

"I owe nothing to your husband now," her father growled. "I hate myself that I ever did."

"You mustn't feel that way."

"I do. It was to make my debt to him easier that you were given to him in marriage."

"I made the decision, remember?"

Lord Alfred studied her sadly. "You went through with it because I was ill and in financial trouble. And you doomed yourself to a life devoid of love."

"I have found love outside my marriage," Enid said quietly.

"The Frenchman? I thought you hadn't heard from him—that he was caught up in the revolution over there."

"He is. I was not referring to him, but to another man, here in London."

Her father's face paled. "I trust you have not become one of those socialite baggages who allow themselves to be laid behind every screen and in every secret corner!"

Enid blushed fiercely. "I have not become promiscuous, Father!"

"I sincerely hope not! Don't destroy our name because Andrew Blair has seen fit to let his own grind into the dust!"

"There is only this one man. We shall never marry and we may not be lovers for very long, but right now I'm grateful for him, and he seems thankful for my love. And when we part, it will be as friends."

Lord Alfred stared at her. "You are saying some very strange things, my daughter. Are you sure this man is not merely using you for his own purposes?"

"I am quite sure."

"And what about this other fellow—your Frenchman?"

"He is different. I would marry him and live with him all my life if I could. But, alas, that is not likely to be. I have given up all hope of ever seeing him again."

Her father nodded. "With things so calamitous in France, you are wise to resign yourself to that."

"So, for the time being, I have the love of an honorable man."

"Do I know him?"

"I think not. He is not of society, but of the arts."

"A painter?"

"I would rather not divulge his name," Enid said, "but I know you would approve of him if I did."

Lord Alfred shook his head. "A sorry age we live in! I wish you had a proper husband, a home, and children!"

Enid attempted to change the subject. "You mentioned my husband's finances, Father. What have you heard?"

"My banker tells me Andrew is slowly selling off his assets and gambling the proceeds away. His house in the country is already gone, as well as his Arabian horses and prize Guernseys. When he runs short of cash again, it will have to be the London town house. And then what?"

"Perhaps then I may safely leave him," Enid concluded.

"I hope so," her father said fervently. "You can return to us any time you wish."

"Of course. I know that."

He sighed deeply. "Do not let that villain of a husband sink you into the mire of his companions. Save yourself from that, I beg you."

"Have no fear," she assured him.

• • •

Later that evening, basking in the afterglow of Kemble's glorious lovemaking, Enid related the conversation with her father. "I didn't tell him who my lover was," she added.

"I shall go to him and reveal myself if you wish," John offered.

She smiled up at him and shook her head. "No. That would not be in keeping with your character. A husband-to-be might do that, but not a lover."

Kemble stroked her full breasts gently. "Never doubt my love," he murmured.

Once more their passions were aroused, and this time they made love slowly, savoring every kiss, every caress. Their desire for each other was pure, their union approaching the sublime. Enid moved under Kemble as a petal opens itself to the sun, and he filled her with rays of heat that consumed them both in an explosion of white-hot light. Gradually they descended to a more earthly plane and rested contentedly in the warmth of each other's arms.

9

A few days later, Enid went to visit Gustav and Susie and found her fencing instructor in an agitated state. He began to talk excitedly as soon as she entered their lodgings.

"France is truly aflame! The mob has marched on Versailles! Only by chance was Lafayette able to save the lives of the king and queen and transfer them to the Tuileries. They are virtually prisoners there!"

"What more can happen?" Enid murmured worriedly. She was thinking of Armand, Lucinda, and the amiable Victor.

"Chaos! Anarchy!" Gustav stormed as he marched back and forth. "They are talking of liberty, equality, fraternity. I fear that may simply mean the collapse of France as a nation!"

Susie appealed to Enid. "Listen to him! He's angry enough to want to go over there!"

Gustav halted his pacing. "I might be able to do something, to help somehow. Instead, I remain here on the sidelines!"

"This is your home now," Enid pointed out.

"I'm still a Frenchman!" he declared.

"What about Susie?" Enid asked.

The young actress's green eyes were filled with tears. "He thinks more of his blessed France than he does of me!"

"Not so!" Gustav denied, his mood suddenly changing. He dropped to his knees at Susie's feet. "We shall be married! That settles it!"

"Is that your price for leaving me?" Susie asked brokenly.

"No. It is to prove my love…and to have something to come back to here if I should go to France."

Susie put her arms around him. "I don't want you to go. You will surely be killed in all that madness!"

He said no more.

The news from France grew more ominous daily. The new group of so-called citizens had begun listing Royalists, subjecting them to brusque trials, and quickly sentencing them to the guillotine. The flower of the French nobility was losing its head to the blade, and all the while the extremist demagogues seemed constantly to shriek still louder for bloodthirsty revenge.

One late December morning Gustav and Susie were married in a small London chapel. Enid and Kemble stood up for them, and Enid could not help but recall her own wedding ceremony in France and what had followed afterward.

• • •

Two months later Enid and Andrew were invited to Sir Drake's home again. When Enid came downstairs, she found her husband waiting for her in a brown dress jacket with gold embroidery. Graham, standing next to him, was wearing a white-powdered wig and the identical jacket. The outrageous goings-on of Andrew and Graham had reached new heights. The youth was no longer treated as Andrew's servant; there was no need to continue that mockery.

Andrew took a healthy swig of his drink. "Do Graham and I not look a picture?" he asked tipsily. "We are dressed like twins."

"So I see," Enid remarked. "Is Graham accompanying us tonight?"

"Certainly," Andrew said. "I allow you free choice of *your* companions. I'm told you're seen in Kemble's company often enough."

"But I don't bring him along when we are invited to private parties," she replied with dignity.

Andrew chuckled. "No need to. He is usually already there."

Graham apologized to her with a wave of his long fingers. "I have no wish to be the cause of controversy. I can easily remain at home tonight."

Andrew faced him belligerently. "No, I will not have that!"

The boyish, small-featured lad looked unhappy. "I think Lady Blair is right. You will do well tonight to confine yourself to her company alone."

"And have her desert me for Kemble or that fencing master the minute we get to the party?" Andrew complained peevishly. "I know what the gossips of London are saying!"

"And I do not care!" she said.

Andrew placed an arm around Graham's shoulders. "This is my good friend, and he shall be at my side."

"Which will surprise no one!" she said, drawing on her white gloves and adjusting the folds of her pink brocade gown.

Andrew chuckled again. "Would you like to join us at a party in the morning?" he asked her.

"What sort of party?"

It was Graham who replied. "There's to be a hanging at Tyburn!"

"A hanging!" she repeated, aghast.

"Yes," the effeminate youth continued. "A group of us is planning to attend the affair. There'll be plenty of spirits and food, and it'll be truly jolly all around."

Andrew commented dryly, "You would be the only female among us. This wench poisoned her husband, and so there is a lot of popular feeling against her. It will be a delight to see her spindly neck stretched!"

Enid looked at and listened to the two of them, and felt she might be ill. Fighting her nausea and repulsion, she replied, "I have not come so low as that. I certainly do not wish to be a witness at the execution of a fellow human."

"You would not do well in France," young Graham warned her. "We hear there are executions there every day."

"Let us not worry about the Frenchies, but get along to our party," Andrew suggested. "The carriage is waiting."

Enid was glad for an excuse to end the distasteful talk. On the way to the Drakes' her husband and the youth sat side by side, touching each other and whispering endearments. She felt like a complete outsider, which, in fact, she was.

It was little better at the party. She had hoped that Kemble would be there, but he wasn't. Many of the guests were strangers to her.

Lady Drake approached her soon after she had arrived and asked in an anxious tone, "You speak French like a native, don't you?"

Enid hesitated. "I manage quite well."

"Thank goodness!" the fashionable lady beamed with relief. "I need you to help me entertain some guests."

"Oh?"

"The refugees who were fortunate enough to make an early escape are beginning to arrive from France, and so few of our people can converse with them."

"I see."

"You must come and meet some of them," Lady Evelyn urged.

Enid followed her hostess through the crowded drawing room. The orchestra was playing in the adjacent ballroom, and already many couples had begun to dance. Lady Drake, regal in an ice-blue silk gown, made her way to a less congested section of the room. As she passed the buffet table, Enid heard her husband regaling a group of men with the amusements in store for them at the hanging on the morrow.

She tried to put this unpleasant subject from her mind and hastened after Lady Drake, who had paused next to a man dressed all in white, standing rather stiffly by a wall. As Enid drew nearer, she had to stop herself from gasping aloud.

Lady Drake smiled and said, "Count Beaufaire, this is Lady Blair. The count has just arrived on our shores."

Armand discreetly gave no sign of recognizing Enid. He bowed deeply to her. "My great pleasure!"

Lady Drake tapped Enid on the arm with her fan. "I'm sure I can leave the count safely in your hands, Lady Blair."

As soon as she was out of earshot, Enid cried, "Armand!"

"My darling Enid," he choked, his voice full of emotion.

"I was certain something had happened to you," she whispered, drinking in the sight of his handsome face, his hard-muscled body. Then she glanced hastily around to see if they were being spied on.

"Where can we go to be alone?" he asked.

"I don't know the house too well, but there is a small conservatory off the main corridor. We could go there."

A moment later they had left the crowd behind and were inside the cool, glass-enclosed room that was brimming with rows of brightly colored plants and flowers. As soon as they were safely hidden in the shadows, Armand clasped her to him in a passionate embrace.

She rested her head against his shoulder. "I have dreamed of you so often," she whispered.

"And I of you." Gently he stroked her golden hair.

"I was certain you were dead. I had no news of you, not even a letter from Lucinda. And the reports from France have been terrifying!"

Armand's black eyes flashed dangerously. "They have not been exaggerated. Everywhere there is bedlam. The whole nation has become a chaotic madhouse!"

"But you escaped safely, thank God." She pressed herself against him, still unable to believe he was actually there with her. "What about Lucinda and the duke?"

"Both are dead," he said quietly. "Killed by the same mob that attacked Versailles."

"Oh, no!" she gasped, then began to shake uncontrollably. He held her close and kissed her wet cheeks, offering her words of comfort.

She was still in his arms when the door to the conservatory was thrown open, and the light streaming in from the corridor revealed the figures of Sir Drake and her husband.

An enraged Lord Andrew snarled, "So it has come to this! My wife has lost all manner of respectability!"

Armand released Enid and turned to Andrew, saying in English, "But you do not understand, my lord. I have brought your wife bad news."

"I saw what was going on!" Andrew bellowed.

Sir James, aware that other ears were straining in their direction, spoke up quickly. "It would be better to settle this later!"

"No, I will have my say!" Andrew declared stubbornly.

Enid went over to him and pleaded, "Please do not make a scene. Count Beaufaire has brought me word of Lucinda's death. She and the duke were killed by the mob that attacked Versailles."

The irate Andrew pushed her roughly aside. "I want to hear nothing of that," he snapped. "I simply wish satisfaction from this man!"

Sir Drake took him by the arm. "Later!" he urged.

"Now!" Andrew insisted, freeing himself from his host's grip.

Armand was studying Andrew's antics with cool disdain. "Very well," he said. "You found your wife with me in a compromising circumstance. You ask for satisfaction. I shall be happy to oblige you."

"No duels!" Sir James protested.

There was a murmuring from the shocked crowd that had gathered at the conservatory door. Then one of the men shouted drunkenly, "Why not a duel, Andrew? Since you are the most profligate of gamblers, make it a duel with cards!"

Enid was outraged by the jeering laughter that followed this sally. She tugged at Andrew's arm. "Please, let us leave now!"

"No!" He glared at her. To the count he said, "Very well. Let us make it a duel with cards."

"Whatever you wish," Armand returned coldly. "And what are the stakes to be?"

Andrew gave Enid a sneering smile and then told the distinguished Frenchman, "Let us make it easy. The winner shall have the key to my wife's bedchamber!"

Armand objected. "I think that is insulting to her ladyship!"

"That is what you want," Andrew said nastily, "so why be hypocritical about it? If you lose, you are never to see or speak to my wife again."

"When is the contest to take place?" Armand asked.

"Here and now," Andrew declared, elated at getting his way. "We'll go directly to the card room."

Armand hesitated, then turned to Enid. "What shall I do?"

"Play with him," she said bitterly. "He will only devise some other torture for me if you don't."

"Very well," the Frenchman agreed. "Lead the way."

Sir James continued to protest as the two men and Enid headed toward the card room, which was on the other side of the ballroom. Word of the unusual duel quickly made the rounds of the party. Soon the room was filled with curious onlookers.

The youthful Graham came over to Enid and asked in a low voice, "Do you wish me to get your carriage?"

"Please," she replied.

Graham nodded. "I begged him not to make a scene, but he wouldn't listen." With that he pushed his way through the crowd and vanished.

Enid remained close to the card table with Sir James and Lady Evelyn. Her host and hostess were appalled at the scandalous turn of events, which would be the talk of London the following morning.

The two combatants faced each other, Armand pale and calm, Andrew red-faced and gulping down whiskey after whiskey. One of the servants brought a fresh pack of cards and placed it on the table.

The cards were cut and Armand had the first deal. From the start it was clear that he was more coolheaded and a better player than Andrew. The crowd gasped as he won hand after hand. Andrew became angrier with each loss and made repeated blunders, indicating to Enid that the duel was near an end.

Armand revealed his final hand, which outclassed Andrew's. Andrew uttered an oath and threw down his cards. Then from his pocket he produced a ring of keys. With great deliberation he detached one of them and tossed it across the table in a contemptuous gesture.

"There is your prize!" he cried. "And let me assure you that you rob me of nothing!"

Armand picked up the key and rose from his seat. "If this were my own country, I would have killed you!"

There was a ripple of concern from the assembled guests. Enid's eyes filled with tears of humiliation. She felt a hand touch her arm and saw that it was Graham. He nodded to signify that the carriage was waiting, and she allowed him to escort her to the front door and down the marble steps.

"Don't worry about Andrew," the youth advised. "I'll keep him here until he is too drunk to do anything but fall into a hotel bed somewhere."

"Thank you, Graham," she said with sincerity, holding back her sobs until she could release them in the solitude of the coach.

"I'm afraid you have nothing to thank me for," Graham stated grimly. "Without wishing to be, I have been cast in the role of your adversary." He shrugged and saw her on her way.

Enid wondered what the aftermath of the card game had produced. Both men had been on their feet, glaring at each other, when she had left. She was fairly certain that the Drakes would prevent the outbreak of any real violence. Nevertheless, the episode had been disgraceful. Andrew's repute was considered low in London society; now it would be as nothing. She would also be an object of scorn, and probably Armand as well. That would not matter to him, however, since he was in London only temporarily. She thought about Kemble and wondered what he would have to say when he heard about the debacle.

By the time she had reached the town house she shared with Andrew, she was exhausted from her tears and in a strange state of mind. Armand had honorably won the key to her bedchamber. She could do no less than make good his winnings, even though the circumstances held no happiness for her. What happened afterward she would leave to fate.

The news of the murder of Lucinda and her husband had so unnerved Enid that she was prepared for almost anything. It seemed as if her familiar world was coming to an end. In its place would be a new, more savage, and immoral plane of existence.

Deliberately, she shed her clothing and stood naked by the window, waiting for Armand's carriage to arrive. She did not have long to wait. Within a matter of minutes a coach appeared along the cobblestones, and she saw Armand jump out and hurry to the front entrance.

She left the window and turned to face the door. The candlelight in the chamber cast a warm glow over her creamy body, highlighting her round breasts and the rosy peaks already growing taut. Her blonde hair cascaded over her shoulders and flowed in rippling waves to the top of her shapely hips.

There were sounds of approaching footsteps on the stairway, and then a key turned in the lock. Armand threw the door open and stood there staring at her, an expression of mild surprise on his face at the sight of her awaiting him in the nude.

Enid broke the silence between them. "My husband has lost, so I'm ready to pay the debt of honor!"

The surprised look on his face became one of open delight. He crossed the room and took her in his arms, exclaiming, "You English women!"

"Don't French women pay their honorable debts?"

"The odds were set by your husband, not by me, and their purpose was to humiliate you," Armand reminded her.

"You are entitled to your winnings, and you know I would not object to your claiming them."

His arms still around her, he murmured, "This is not the way I planned our first meeting after all these months, and I shall not ravish your body because I won a bet from a drunken pervert."

"Who happens to be my husband and who set the terms of your gamble!"

"Never mind, *chérie,*" Armand soothed. "I love you deeply and truly, and I will await a more suitable time and place for our reunion." With that he kissed her gently and made his way out of the chamber and down the stairs.

She went to the window again and saw him enter his carriage and drive off. Only then did she succumb to her second desperate sobbing of the night, flinging her naked body across the bed and giving free rein to her grief.

After a half hour's time she donned her nightdress and attempted to sleep. She left the candle burning for company, and so was able to note Andrew's rumpled condition when he awakened her much later by his clumsy entrance. She had never seen him so consumed with spirits, yet he managed to stagger awkwardly about.

He came to the foot of her bed and snarled, "Slut!"

"Please go to your own room!" she begged him. "Where is Graham?"

"On the street where he belongs!" Andrew gloated. "I picked the little swine up out of the gutter and I tossed him back there tonight!"

"Why?"

"Because he showed himself to be on your side! A pretty picture, isn't it? *My* little bedmate helping *you!*"

It was all too plain that Graham had tried, albeit ineffectually, to plead her case and had been discarded by Andrew because of it. She felt sorry for the lad, despite his attachment to her husband. "You owed him more than that. He was only trying to spare us more shame!"

"I will judge what he did on my own terms," Andrew flared, still in an ugly mood. "Tell me, did you enjoy your bedding down with that Frenchman?" he leered. "They are considered most expert!"

She edged across the bed as he approached her menacingly. Then she cast aside the covers and leaped toward the door, but he adroitly blocked her way.

"Count Beaufaire came and left at once!" she cried. "He didn't touch me!"

"A likely story!" Andrew jeered, attempting to seize her.

"It is true!"

"I'll bet he admired your lovely, creamy skin." Andrew growled low in his throat and reached out for her. "I'll make it black-and-blue for the next time!"

"Please!" she sobbed, backing away from him toward the bedside table and the candle in its heavy brass candleholder.

Andrew lunged at her, and reacting instinctively, she grasped the candlestick and struck him on the temple and across the cheek. At the same time the candle fell to the floor and went out, and the room was left in shadows.

Andrew lay stretched out in an ugly sprawl, completely unconscious. Still sobbing, Enid began to dress quickly and thrust a few things into a portmanteau. Then she raced down the stairs and halted in surprise at the sight of Graham standing there.

"I followed him home," the youth said.

"He said he has finished with you!"

Graham smiled grimly. "He went through all the motions, but I vow he'll change his mind in the morning!"

"I struck him with the candleholder—he may be dead!" she told Graham in a choked voice.

He took her by the arm as she began to sway back and forth. "It would take more than that to kill him, I assure you!"

"I must leave here at once," she wailed.

"I have a carriage waiting outside. Take it. I will stay here and see that he is all right."

"Please let me know his condition—I am so afraid!"

"Where will you be?"

She gave him Kemble's address and then he saw her to the carriage. Once inside its dark interior, she wondered if the events of this night had truly happened or if they had been a ghastly nightmare. She knew only too well that they were real and ugly.

Kemble was still up and reading a playscript when Enid burst in on him. He received her with his usual consideration. After drinking some brandy and unburdening herself to him as she sat before the fire, she felt more in control of herself.

"I can never go back to Andrew," she declared with a shudder.

"That is a sensible decision," the actor agreed.

She gave him a frightened glance. "If Andrew is still alive, that is."

"Who knows about your striking him?"

"Graham."

"His boy?"

"Yes. I sent him up to see how badly I had hurt Andrew."

"But you didn't wait to find out if he was dead?"

"No."

"So Graham could testify against you if you really killed Andrew."

"I suppose so, though I doubt if he would. He has been on my side in this."

"Strange," the actor said thoughtfully as he bent over the hearth to stir the glowing embers.

"He is not a bad young man. I am saddened that Andrew has corrupted him so."

"Perhaps this will turn out to be a changing point in his life," Kemble suggested.

"I hope so. In any event, I shall always be grateful to him."

"What do you plan to do?" Kemble asked, rising to his feet and picking up his brandy glass.

"If there are no complications, I shall go down to Surrey and stay with my parents. They will welcome me. My father has never been happy about my marriage."

"That I can understand. But what about us?" His voice tensed slightly.

"I cannot stay here," she said. "It would spoil things. You would be touched by the scandal."

He laughed. "Most theater people thrive on scandal."

"And my being here would make us behave like man and wife. That would be fatal to our relationship!"

Kemble's large brown eyes searched her face. "This Frenchman, Count Beaufaire, who has suddenly turned up in London—he's my phantom rival, isn't he?"

"Yes," she confessed.

"I suspected as much. Do you still love him?"

"More than I had imagined." Now that the question had been asked of her, she realized the depth of her feeling for Armand.

"Will he remain in London?"

She shrugged. "I do not know. I had very little time to talk with him."

"I wonder that he did not claim his winnings," Kemble could not refrain from musing.

"He is too much the gentleman," Enid said softly.

Kemble sighed. "I have no doubt that you will hear from him again."

"I hope so. He brought me word of the death of my best friend and her husband. We spoke of little else before Andrew broke in on us."

The actor put down his brandy glass and asked, "Do you think you'll be able to sleep now?"

"I'm surely weary enough."

"Then let me see you safely to bed."

She rose slowly, staring at him. "What about you?"

"This is not a night for us. I shall make myself comfortable on the divan here."

"That doesn't seem right!" she protested.

"It is exactly right," Kemble said, putting an arm around her. He saw her to his bedchamber, kissed her good night, and closed the door gently behind him.

10

When Enid appeared in the sitting room the next morning, Kemble had already made a pot of tea and set out plates of bread, cheese, and smoked fish. He kissed her tenderly and said, "I insist you eat a good breakfast."

She sat down at the oak table. "You should have waited and let me prepare it."

He laughed. "We actors are used to making our own meals. Don't forget I toured for some years and lived in the meanest of lodgings. One is forced to become self-sufficient under those conditions." He poured a cup of tea for her and then filled his own.

"I had a few bad dreams last night, John," she said.

"You were fortunate to sleep at all after such an experience."

They had barely begun to eat when a knock sounded at the door. Kemble opened it, to reveal Graham standing there.

"May I speak with Lady Blair?" he asked.

"Certainly," Kemble said. "You must be Graham."

"Yes, sir." The lad crossed the threshold almost shyly, looking younger than usual, and bowed when he saw Enid. "Good morning to you, Lady Blair."

Enid rose quickly. "Thank you for coming, Graham. What news do you bring?"

"All is well. You did not kill Lord Andrew."

"Thank goodness!" she gasped, a wave òf relief washing over her.

"How much harm was done him?" Kemble asked.

"He received an injured temple and had a good chunk of flesh torn from his cheek," Graham replied. "He will bear a scar to his dying day."

Enid shuddered. "He is so vain, he will never forgive me for that! What about you, Graham? How did he behave to you this morning?"

The youth looked forlorn. "He gave me no thanks for calling a doctor and seeing him safely to bed."

"He is most unfair!"

"He blamed me for helping you get away, and he called me a number of unpleasant things." Graham's face turned crimson. "Many of which happen to be true."

"So you cannot go back to him," Enid said.

"No, I can't."

Kemble spoke up. "I think you should be grateful for that. There is nothing but a sorry end for most sexual deviants. And if you chose to stay with him, you would be forced to continue along the same perverse path."

Graham eyed the actor earnestly. "I have given that some thought, sir. I haven't always lived Lord Andrew's way. Not long ago I even courted a girl."

"You would do well to return to that time," Kemble advised.

"I agree," Enid declared firmly. "If Andrew would take you back, or if you were to have an alliance with some other man, it would surely work against you. Save yourself while there is still a chance."

"Thank you, Lady Blair." Graham smiled, then he turned to Kemble. "If I had employment of some sort, things might go better for me. I have always had a yearning for the stage."

Kemble studied him with a professional eye. "Your face is pleasant enough, and you have a good figure. Your speech is that of the upper class. If you could subdue your somewhat effeminate mannerisms, I think I could try you out in a few minor parts."

Graham nearly burst with excitement. "Would you sir? Truly?"

"Why not? You showed Lady Blair exceptional kindness. I can do no less for you. But remember, there are no sexual misfits in my company. I allow none of that."

"I wish to get away from it, I swear!" the youth cried.

Kemble nodded. "Very well. Go to Drury Lane and ask for Mallory, my stage manager. Tell him you're to play the walk-on parts in the new production. He'll give you instructions, and you'll have a chance to apprentice yourself to the theater."

"Thank you, sir, thank you!"

"The pay is small," Kemble warned him. "Only ten shillings a month."

"I can manage," the youth assured him. "Thank you both!" And with a low bow he hurried out.

When he had gone, Enid asked Kemble, "Do you really think he will reform?"

"It is hard to say. I'd be willing to wager there is hope for him, and I'll see he gets every encouragement. With his sensitive mien he could go far."

Enid and Kemble seated themselves at the table again, and John poured fresh tea. While she sipped at hers, Enid thought about her decision to go to her parents. She didn't want to leave London without first trying to contact Armand. She also wanted some of her clothing.

After the breakfast dishes were cleared away, she sent a messenger to the Blair mansion, asking the housemaid to pack several gowns and a few personal articles and have them delivered to Kemble's flat.

Then she had an inspiration. "John, I think I will spend a few days with Gustav and Susie. I'm sure they can put me up."

"Why not remain here?" he asked in surprise.

She blushed. "You know why."

His facial muscles tightened. "You can think of no one but the Frenchman."

She made no reply.

"All right," he said with a sigh. "I shall not push my luck. I'll see you to the studio. And when your luggage arrives, I'll bring it over there."

Susie was alone when Kemble dropped Enid off later on his way to rehearsal at Drury Lane. The auburn-haired actress was delighted to hear that Enid wished to remain with her and Gustav for a while.

"I'm thrilled to have you!" Susie bubbled. "Gustav is out now on some business involving the refugees from across the Channel, but I know he'll feel the same."

Enid told Susie what had happened the night before and ended with, "It is my hope that Gustav can locate the count for me before I leave London."

"There is every chance he can, since he is in close touch with all the refugees," his new wife said. "And you were right to leave that wretched Andrew!"

"I hope so."

Susie gathered up her bonnet and shawl. "I really must go. I shall be late for the rehearsal. You rest, and when Gustav gets back, I'm sure he can help you."

Enid remained alone in the studio for what seemed endless minutes. Then she heard someone knocking on the door. She opened it to a short man with thick white hair and a haunted look on his lined face. He was dressed shabbily and appeared nervous.

"I am Duval," he told her in French. "I was to meet Gustav and I missed him."

"I'm sorry," she said. "He has gone out and won't be back for a while."

The man twisted his black, three-cornered hat in his hands. "May I wait for him?"

Enid hesitated. "Are you a friend?"

"A friend from France. I escaped only a week ago. Gustav is helping me and my family get settled here in London."

Enid relented at once. "Then do come in and sit down."

He obeyed her, all the while watching her warily. At last he broke the silence by asking, "Are you Madam Brideau?"

"No," Enid replied with a small smile. "I'm a friend of Gustav and his wife."

"I see." Duval again lapsed into silence.

She decided to try to question him a little. "Did you see the revolution start?"

"I was there when it began," he replied. "When they stormed the Bastille."

"Tell me about it."

"No one believed it was possible. The rabble stole nearly twenty-eight thousand muskets and cannons, and then they stormed the Bastille. I was on duty there, under General Besenval, and by doing my duty as a military officer, I became an enemy of the people!" He shook his head sadly.

"Go on," she urged.

"The general had plenty of troops to guard the fortress, and the governor of the Bastille—De Launay—was a good-enough man. He had inherited the post from his father. He wasn't a soldier, mind you; he wore a gray frock coat. Well, at noon on July fourteenth the mob demanded that he remove the artillery from the eight round towers. De Launay warned them that he would resist any attack until death. But he finally agreed to do their bidding when they said they would disperse."

"And did they?"

"No. As soon as the cannons were removed, they demolished the first of two drawbridges and brought their guns into position against the second. The officer in charge of our troops suggested we surrender, but De Launay said he would rather blow up the Bastille. Our commander decided to act on his own and sent out a note, offering to surrender if the mob would spare the garrison."

"Did that work out?"

"Not at all," Duval said bitterly. "One of the rabble, an ex-soldier, accepted the note and took it to the others. Then he came back with the word that they would agree to the commander's terms.

That was the beginning of the slaughter. Without permission from De Launay, the commander lowered the drawbridge and the throng rushed in, murdering everyone in sight. I made myself scarce in the dungeons until I had a chance to escape."

"What about the others?"

"It was bedlam! The insurgents went about smashing the windows and the furniture, releasing the prison's few convicted men. De Launay was seized by the crowd. Some tore out his hair—others jabbed him with swords. Finally a cook named Denot cut off his head with a butcher's knife! He later boasted of the deed and demanded a medal for it. The dripping head was skewered on a pike, and this poor man, who had only done his duty, was described on a placard as a disloyal, treacherous enemy of the people!"

"Everyone must have gone mad!"

"It is the time of madmen! I heard someone with a foot long beard proclaim that he was God and must slaughter all of us."

"You were indeed fortunate to have escaped," Enid murmured.

"And to have brought my wife and children with me," Duval added. "We traveled north and remained hidden near Calais for days, until a boat came late one night and took us and other refugees aboard. From there it was an easy journey to London."

"Aren't there people trying to help the so-called enemies of the people to flee the country?"

Duval nodded. "There is an underground here, led mostly by Frenchmen who had already emigrated to England. Gustav is one of many who have helped save lives."

"I knew he was deeply concerned about the plight of the Royalists."

"He is directing things here in London," the white-haired man told her. "But I'm sure he would rather cross the Channel and fight the rebels who are bent on destroying France."

"We know that the king and queen have been uprooted from Versailles."

"They are in grave danger."

"Friends of mine…the Duke and Duchess d'Orsay…lived near the palace and were murdered by the rioters."

"Many of the Royalists have suffered the same fate."

"Have you heard of a nobleman by the name of Beaufaire?" she ventured.

Duval's worn face lit up. "He is a hero among us. He was fighting for the cause even before the revolution broke out into the open."

Just then Gustav arrived. He saw Enid first, then Duval, and his face registered surprise. "What's going on here?" he demanded.

"I will tell you about myself later," Enid answered. "But Monsieur Duval has been waiting to talk with you."

Gustav frowned and then turned to his countryman. "If you will come this way."

She waited while the two men went into the kitchen area and had a rather lengthy discussion behind a closed door. After they came out, Duval hurried away and Gustav turned his attention to her.

Enid said, "Susie is at a rehearsal."

"And you?"

"It is a long story, so we had best be seated." They sat down on the studio cot and she told him all that had happened, finishing with her wish to stay with him and Susie until she had contacted Armand.

"I know this Armand," Gustav said. "I spoke with him only yesterday. He is a count."

"Yes, he is. Do you think you can take a message to him?"

"I suppose so. He is staying in London for a little while." The young Frenchman paused. "I'm glad you're breaking away from that swine of an Andrew."

"It is a permanent move," she assured him. "I shall not go back to him."

"And Kemble?"

"Will remain very close to me. But it is Armand whom I love, and he alone."

"Your love is living a dangerous life."

"I am well aware of that."

Gustav eyed her closely. "Are you sure of your feelings about him?"

"More sure than I am about anything else."

"I believe you. And I will try to find him for you."

"If only you could!"

"I may meet him tonight," Gustav said. "There is to be a conference about some new arrivals. We have to be wary. Would you believe that the mob already has spies here in London? They report what they can learn about our activities, and when our agents return to France, they are often picked up and sometimes convicted on the word of these spies. Not a few of us have been beheaded!"

"Don't tell me about it!" she begged him.

His tone was grave. "If you give your heart to the count, you must be prepared to have it broken at any time. He could be executed on his return to France. He needs the luck of the very devil to escape that fate."

"He is doing noble work. Let us trust that Heaven will protect him!"

"Too often Heaven seems unaware of what is happening down here," the fencing master said bitterly. "I want to take the same risks as Beaufaire. I intend to go over there."

"What about Susie?"

"Better that she be a widow than married to a coward."

"She might prefer the latter."

A half hour later Susie and Kemble returned from their rehearsal, and it was like old times at the studio. Fresh bread, ripe cheddar cheese, cold meat, and a tawny port wine were brought out for feasting. Kemble was in one of his better moods; having Enid near him always lifted his spirits.

He told her, "The boy, Graham, did quite well at the rehearsal. He is green, of course, but he is sound of purpose, and I think we can make an actor of him."

"Just save him from Andrew," she begged.

Since Kemble had picked up her luggage at his flat before coming to the studio, Enid was able to freshen up and don a more suitable dress. When she presented herself again, Gustav had left for his meeting and Susie had crossed the road to visit a sick friend, leaving Enid and Kemble alone.

"Are you still determined to make contact with Beaufaire?" Kemble asked.

"Yes," Enid said. "I'm sure Gustav will find him."

"That's very likely. They are both working for the same organization." The actor looked concerned as he went on. "London is full of gossip today. The card game between your husband and your lover is on the lips of every tattletale."

"I wish them joy with it," she said with disgust.

Kemble began to pace and then turned to her abruptly. "I do not want to lose you!" he cried.

"You never will. I shall always remember you," she said softly.

"But are you ready to embrace this Frenchman?"

"He was my lover before I gave myself to you. And we had our terms."

"I'm willing to forego them," Kemble said in a rush. "You have the grounds to free yourself of Blair. I want you to be my wife."

"But you were the one who claimed marriage would spoil our romance!"

"I was wrong," he argued. "That wouldn't happen, I swear it. Not in our case."

Enid smiled, and rising, went to him and put her arms around him. "You must not renege on our agreement. I need you for a friend. I count on you!"

He grasped her by the shoulders and gazed down at her, his expression bitter. "You expect me to encourage you to carry on your romance with this count?"

"Yes, if you truly love me."

"That's nonsense. Ridiculous! You cannot expect it of a man. Perhaps in some stage comedy, but never in life. I want you for myself!"

She raised her lips to his and kissed him. "You are second in my heart."

"That is simply not good enough, my dearest."

"You must be content, John. Please. I cannot change my feelings."

He held her tight. "Then I shall pray that fate will bring you back to me, that events will reverse themselves and you will be mine again."

Enid was relieved when Susie returned from her visit and eased the tension. Kemble remained only a short time longer and then left. Enid knew he was upset and preferred to avoid a possible meeting with Armand.

Susie had also noticed this. With a wise smile she remarked, "John Philip is in a melancholy mood."

"I know."

"Because of the appearance of the count in London?"

"Yes. But we had agreed that our love affair was not to be binding."

"And now?"

"He wants to go back on his promise and he expects me not to honor mine. He wants to marry me!"

"You could do worse," Susie observed wryly.

"I have given my heart to Armand. That's not something I take lightly, despite my feelings for John."

"After last night Armand may feel differently about you."

"He was a gentleman. He didn't even try to make love to me, though my husband had wantonly gambled my virtue and lost to him."

"That's what you might have expected from someone like Andrew."

"He has been paid for it," Enid sighed. "I have been told that I scarred his pretty face."

"He will hate you for that!" Susie warned her.

Enid shrugged. "He hates me in any case, and I cannot undo what is done."

Gustav was late in returning. When he finally did arrive, Enid knew at once that something was wrong. "What has happened?" she asked.

He studied her grimly. "Your friend has had a change of luck."

"Armand?"

"Yes."

"What has happened?" she repeated imploringly.

"It is bad news. He has been captured by one of the top agents of the revolutionists. A vicious man named Louis Esmond."

"He is here in London?"

"Yes, along with some of his cohorts. They're seeking out information on Royalists like Count Armand who are helping some of the nobility escape from France."

"You say he has been captured. Do you have any idea where he is?"

"Just one clue," Gustav said. "The revolutionist group has been storing supplies here in London. They're using a large warehouse near a dock. My guess is that somewhere in that warehouse is their headquarters and that Armand has been taken a prisoner there."

"Is there no one to help him?" Susie asked.

"It is very difficult to organize a rescue group," Gustav replied. "I have returned for my sword. Then I'm going down there to see what I can find out."

"Do not go alone!" Susie begged her husband. "You'll be killed!"

He put a comforting arm around her. "Believe me, my chances are better alone than in a group. Perhaps I can slip into the warehouse unnoticed and, when the opportunity presents itself, somehow rescue the count."

"I will go with you!" Enid cried.

Both Gustav and Susie stared at her in amazement. Then Gustav shook his head. "No. It's too risky for a woman."

"I can protect myself, at least with a sword. You know that," Enid reminded him.

He hesitated. "I don't see how you can help me."

"You should both give up the idea. It is too foolhardy a mission!" Susie protested.

"The chances might be better than you think," Gustav said.

"I can at least act as a lookout—someone to warn you of any movement," Enid insisted.

Gustav eyed her with uncertainty. "You might be useful in that way."

"I want to help Armand! Please let me!"

He nodded. "All right. I have a tiny pistol here that you can carry easily. It is not a formidable weapon, but it might come to your aid in a difficult situation." He went into the next room to get the weapon.

Susie was distraught. "I say you're both mad!"

"We must try to rescue Armand," Enid told her friend. "So many other lives depend on him. And we can't let Gustav go by himself. It is better that I join him."

Gustav reappeared with the pistol and his sword. He handed the pistol to Enid and showed her how to use it. Then he buckled his sword onto a belt encircling his hips.

"How far is it to the warehouse and the dock?" she asked.

"A ten-minute walk. Perhaps a little more on a dark, cold night like this."

She put on her cloak and drew the hood over her long blonde hair. "I'll keep close to you in case we meet up with thieves."

"The area between here and there is filled with predators of the night, and we must take great care to elude them." Gustav tossed a flowing crimson cloak over his shoulders, amply concealing the sword beneath it. His wide-brimmed hat with its feather of gray might have belonged to any young merchant out on the town for the night.

"I shall share the danger with you," Enid said firmly. "It is only right."

Gustav smiled at her. "You're a game little creature! I'll play the role of a merchant who's slightly fuddled with wine, and you'll be the wench I picked up in the tavern!"

Susie continued to protest. "This is not a children's game! How can you be so foolhardy?"

Gustav embraced his wife. "I take few risks. I remain here in London rather than travel to France because of you. I must do what I can for Count Armand. Otherwise I would feel I had to give up the work altogether."

"Perhaps you should do that," Susie said tearfully. "You owe France nothing. This is your country now!"

"No matter," he told her. "I cannot stand by and see such grave injustices carried out." He moved to the door.

Enid hastily kissed her friend on the cheek and whispered, "Do not worry—I shall protect him!" This was a bluff to make Susie feel less apprehensive, but at the same time it helped bolster her own courage.

11

Enid followed Gustav down the stairs and clung to his arm as they emerged into the fog-ridden night. The few people they encountered along the narrow back streets and mean alleys were either wandering drunks or elusive night denizens searching for likely prey.

Once they passed a girl huddled in a dark doorway. She came out with a querulous "Looking for a good time, sir?" and then when she saw Enid, she moved silently back into the shadows.

A sailor singing loudly and off-key staggered by and uttered some silly compliment to them. After he had disappeared, they passed another man, silent and sinister, who eyed them warily.

To quell her nervousness, Enid began to speak softly to Gustav. "You mentioned this man Louis Esmond, an agent of the revolutionists. What does he look like? I should at least have a description of him."

"He's past middle age," Gustav said, ambling in a tipsy fashion along the dark lane. "He is totally bald and doesn't wear a wig."

"That alone should make him easy to spot."

"Also, he wears a black eye patch over his left eye. He served in the army long ago and was badly injured. He walks with a slight limp."

"He sounds more like an invalid than a dangerous foe."

"Do not underestimate him," Gustav warned her. "He is one of the true mad dogs of the revolution. He hates the nobility because he blames his injuries on an officer of noble blood who was in command of his regiment. Also, he is drunk with power and aiming for a top post in the tribunal of the revolutionists."

"The more I hear, the more I fear him!"

"Be sure that you do." Gustav's voice was tense. "To be alarmed is to be prepared. And about the pistol—use it only if you must."

"Please explain."

"It will make a noise, not a loud one, but enough to warn our opponents. Let me try to settle things with my sword. Use the pistol only as a last resort."

"I wish I had a sword," Enid complained. "I would be able to use it well!"

"I know that, but it wouldn't be seemly for a woman to be wandering about the streets with a sword!"

"It isn't seemly for me to be out on such a night and at such an hour either," she pointed out.

"Blame that on your romance with Count Armand, not on me," he countered.

She gave a nervous laugh. "I'm not concerned about where to place the blame. I only wish to help Armand."

At that point a watchman of the night strode by, ringing a bell and crying out in melancholy tones, "Eleven o'clock and all is well!" He kept repeating this as he moved away from them, his words echoing in their ears.

All at once Gustav came to a halt and whispered, "The large building directly ahead is the warehouse."

Enid peered through the yellowish fog and made out a dark, two-story structure. "What now?" she asked.

"We must be very careful. It fronts on the dock, where the main entrance is."

"And?"

"We dare not try that," he told her. "We must seek out a window or door on this side of the building through which we can make our entry. If I find a suitable place, I shall have you stand guard outside it."

"Where do you think they may have hidden him?"

"Probably on the upper floor. That would give them a better chance to defend their position in case of attack."

"So shall we go on?"

"Yes," he said. "All seems quiet thus far."

He moved cautiously toward the warehouse and then inched his way alongside it, checking the windows in the hope of finding an open one. Enid silently matched his steps, her heart beating faster, her nerves stretched taut. And then she experienced a thrill of fear as she heard the unmistakable sound of a footstep behind her. She had barely enough time to whisper the single word "Danger!"

Gustav whirled around, his sword drawn and ready beneath his flowing cloak. And not a moment too soon, either, as two men, also armed with swords, sprang out of the darkness at them. Enid cringed against the brick wall of the warehouse and watched her companion bravely defend himself against the accomplished pair.

The clash of metal filled the silent air as blades locked, and locked again. Gustav was a master swordsman, and despite the odds against him, he managed to keep the two attackers at bay. They cursed in French and lunged at him fiercely, yet each time, by some miracle, he was able to withdraw and then return to the fray.

Enid held the pistol outside her cloak now, ready to use it if the struggle clearly went against Gustav. And with each passing it seemed as if it would. But he had warned her not to fire the weapon unless it was absolutely necessary.

The three men parried back and forth in the fog. Once Gustav fell to one knee, but even in that endangered position he held off his opponents. Moments later he found an opening in the defense of one of the men and plunged his blade into him. The man cried out and stumbled backward as Gustav freed his sword to fight off the second attacker. The wounded man fell face downward on the cobblestones, his own weapon clattering as it rolled from his limp hand.

Enid seized this moment to rush forward and retrieve the sword, as well as one of his pistols. Then, with a purposeful look on her lovely face, she gave her attention to helping Gustav, who had almost lost his weapon to his opponent and had staggered slightly as he fought to regain his balance. Enid was certain the second man was about to finish her friend, so she lunged forward and thrust the sword deep into his side.

The bearded man turned to her, his face revealing his shock, and then he toppled down beside his companion. She picked up his sword and went over to Gustav, handing him the gun she had retrieved.

"He almost had me! You saved my life!" Gustav panted, smiling at her with effort.

"Please don't think about it."

"Let's continue," he said, still gasping for breath.

She glanced at the two fallen men. "What about them?"

"They'll give us no trouble for a while," he said grimly. "They'll either live or die. This is war, you must understand."

Gustav took the initiative again and began searching for an entrance to the warehouse. Enid followed close on his heels, the sword in her hand and his pistol beneath her cloak. He halted by a window and then turned to her and whispered, "This one will give us entry!"

She waited while he raised it carefully and climbed inside. Then he helped her over the sill. They stood for a moment in the dank darkness of the old warehouse, listening for some signs of life. After a few moments they heard footsteps moving above them and the low murmur of male voices, the words undistinguishable.

"My guess was right," Gustav whispered. "They are on the level above us."

"What do we do now?" she asked.

"We must find a stairway and try to get up there without their knowing it. Do you want to wait by the window?"

She shook her head. "You may need me and my sword."

"If we have to attack, use the pistol as well this time," he advised. "There will be no need for silence now."

She nodded. "I understand."

Their eyes having become more adjusted to the darkness, they began to explore the lower region of the warehouse. In one area there were stacks of wooden cases.

Gustav tapped one of the cases and whispered, "Weapons and ammunition!"

"They are setting up their own army!" Enid gasped.

"Yes," he agreed grimly.

Then they found the stairway. Gustav motioned for her to let him go first. He climbed almost all the way up before he gave her the signal to follow.

The upper floor of the warehouse had been partitioned off to provide office space as well as more room for storage. With Gustav leading the way, they crept across the dark area at the head of the stairs toward the direction from which the voices were coming. Every so often he turned and smiled at her encouragingly.

They reached a wall with a single door in it that Enid decided must lead to some sort of office. It was from behind this door that the voices were coming. As they neared it she felt her pulse quicken, for she saw that it was ajar several inches. Both she and Gustav could see clearly inside.

The small room was lit by a single candle resting on a table. Armand was sitting in a chair, bound to it with strong rope. Standing over him was the man whom Gustav had described to Enid. The bald head, eye patch, and harsh, smiling face could belong only to the infamous agent of the revolutionists. He was flanked by two mustached, villainous-looking men armed with swords and pistols.

Louis Esmond was speaking softly to Armand. "I require only the names I have requested. That is all I ask, just the names."

Armand, tied tightly to the chair, looked more stern than ever, and his face bore the lines of strain and weariness. "I have nothing to say to you," he replied.

The bald man turned to his two companions and asked mockingly, "Did you hear that, good citizens? Surely he must know we cannot miss this opportunity."

The older of the two henchmen growled, "Get at him! Have it done with!"

Esmond turned back to Armand with a cruel smile. "You heard him, Count. He is an impatient fellow! Not at all like me."

"I have nothing to tell you," Armand repeated doggedly.

"But of course you will talk," Louis Esmond said smoothly. "A certain application in the proper places to stimulate you may be required. You have heard of torture, I am sure."

"Your infamous methods are a disgrace to France," Armand retorted, straining at his bonds without result.

"At least it is known that I'm not one to be taken lightly," the bald man countered.

The older henchman asked, "Shall I warm the poker?"

Esmond nodded. "Yes. Bring it to me when it is ready."

The man vanished from sight. Gustav's warning glance told Enid that it was not yet time to move or make any sound.

Esmond regarded Armand once more. "Why must you be so tedious? I very much dislike having to use strong methods of persuasion."

The count eyed him with disgust. "I have heard that you enjoy administering torture—especially to women and children!"

The agent's purring manner abruptly deserted him. He slapped Armand hard across the face and shrieked, "I will not have you saying such things! I was a soldier in the king's army! I served well and honorably! I bear the wounds of battle in the service of my country!"

"And now you despoil the country you once defended," Armand sneered.

Esmond whirled away from him in anger. "What is the use of wasting talk on you? You are like the others—too arrogant and stupid to realize a new day has dawned for France! You cannot hope to stay the tide!"

The other associate of Esmond's shuffled his feet impatiently. "What about Gaston?" he asked gruffly. "He and Marcel should have returned by now."

Esmond scowled at him. Then he said, "You'd better find out where they are and what's keeping them."

"Will you be safe?" the man asked.

"Yes," Esmond said. "It is more important that we know they are all right and guarding this place."

"I'll go search for them," the rough fellow promised, and he headed for the open doorway.

It was a moment of unrelieved tension for Enid and Gustav. They huddled in the shadows, away from the room, and hoped they wouldn't be seen. The ruffian clumped down the stairs, unaware of their presence.

Esmond was talking smoothly to Armand again. "The poker is ready, Count, and I shall begin with your left eye. That is the one I lost for France. You shall lose yours for stubbornness."

"In a worthy cause," Armand said in a low voice.

The older henchman now approached with the poker, white-hot at its point. Esmond grasped it by the handle and held it close to Armand's eye. "I shall count to ten, and if you do not reply by then, darkness will descend—most painfully, I fear—on the vision of your left eye."

Gustav nodded to Enid that this was the moment for action. He sprang out of the shadows with his sword drawn and burst through the doorway to stand before an astonished Esmond, the weapon pointed directly at the bald man's throat.

"Release the count," he ordered Enid.

She moved quickly to do his bidding. The henchman, as stunned as Esmond, nevertheless attempted to draw his gun. But Gustav was too quick for him. The pistol belonging to the fallen swordsman was now in his free hand, and he fired a fatal shot.

By this time Enid had almost freed Armand, who was shouting encouragements to her. Esmond stood glaring helplessly at the three of them. His associate who had gone outside to search for the guards returned, halting in the doorway at the sight before him, and then came at Gustav with his sword.

Enid stopped her efforts to release Armand, whipped out her pistol, and aimed it at the newcomer, sending a bullet into him. He dropped to the floor at the same moment that Esmond let out a howl of rage and risked a lunge at Gustav.

Gustav was momentarily caught off guard, and the bald man sped past him and out into the darkness beyond. Gustav ran after him, sword in hand.

Enid quickly finished untying Armand, and he stood up stiffly, rubbing his wrists and ankles.

"I'll be able to move in a moment or so," he promised her.

"Are there any others?" she asked.

"There were five," he said, "including Esmond."

"We took care of two outside. And these two as well!" She glanced grimly at the prostrate forms on the wooden floor.

"Then Esmond is the only one left!" Armand cried.

"We'd best get out of here," she urged him.

"Yes. I can manage now."

They had reached the head of the stairs when Gustav came racing up to them. He was breathless and pale. "Esmond got away!" he groaned. "The slimy vermin escaped!"

"It cannot be helped," Armand said, "and we must make ourselves scarce. He may return with reinforcements at any moment."

"We have one last task before we leave here."

Armand nodded. "I understand."

Enid did not know what they were talking about. But when they reached the lower level, she realized what it was. The two men quickly splintered one of the stacked boxes and hunted for sacks to place among the kindling. Then Gustav found a taper and some matches, and after lighting the candle, he flung it on the sackcloth. When the blaze was under way, they hurried from the building.

In an alley nearby they sought out a hiding place from which they could gaze through the fog at the warehouse. Within a comparatively short time they heard a loud explosion from within. The windows were shattered and they could see flames blazing. It would not be long before the entire structure was completely destroyed.

The glow from the fire reached as far as the alley, and Enid could see the triumphant expressions on the perspiring, weary faces of the two men beside her. She had no idea what she looked like, but she didn't care. She was filled with a strong feeling of elation.

Then there were shouts in the streets. She was positive she saw Esmond lead three or four men up to the blazing building and then fall back in chagrin as another explosion occurred and flames shot up through the roof of the warehouse. More onlookers appeared out of the fog, and there were cries of excitement and glee from some of the drunken observers.

"Time to be gone from here!" Gustav said tautly.

"A night's work well done," the count commended him. "And you, Enid, have taken more risk than you should have!"

"I wanted to be here," she said simply.

He kept a comforting arm around her as they made their way back to Gustav's studio. When they finally arrived, they found Susie in a dreadful state of alarm. As soon as she saw them she recovered from her fright, and even found it possible to laugh at them.

"You look like three scarecrows!" she teased.

And it was true! Perspiration, soot, and grime had combined to give them a very strange appearance. After some scrubbing they more closely resembled themselves, although their clothing still reeked of smoke. Susie prepared a late-night meal, and Gustav told her of the events of the past few hours.

Susie listened grimly, and when he had finished, she said, "The truth is, four men are dead and any one of you could easily have been added to the list of victims."

"We don't know that they were all fatally wounded," Gustav demurred.

"The ones in the warehouse surely died," Enid said.

Armand sighed. "Violence is always regrettable. But this is now an undeclared war."

Susie was indignant. "Those Frenchies aren't content to destroy their own country. Now they slink over here and kill!"

Her husband patted her hand. "They are concerned mostly with agents for the Royalists. And with the English people who deal with them."

"You are a Royalist agent," she reminded him. "What sort of security do we have now?"

"None," he admitted. "Now that I have shown myself to them, we will be listed among the enemy."

"You had better stay in the shadows for a time," Armand suggested. "Keep them off guard before you take an active part again."

"They will probably still seek him out for vengeance," Susie worried.

Gustav smiled wearily. "That's the price you pay for having a French husband."

"A French husband who is wild and reckless!" Susie cried. Immediately she placed her arms around him and kissed him, saying, "Still, I'm foolish enough to be proud of you!"

Gustav kissed her in return, then turned to Armand. "The big problem now is you, Count Beaufaire."

Armand shrugged. "I must return to France as soon as I can."

"I disagree. They will be on the lookout for you. Their agents will be covering the coast. You must wait a week or two at least."

"But I will be in danger in London. Tonight is an example. There are other agents in the city, and Esmond is still alive and undoubtedly determined to capture me again."

Gustav sighed. "That is all too true. London is almost as unhealthy for you as France."

Enid spoke up. "I think I have the answer. I propose to stay with my father and mother in Surrey for a while. It would be an ideal place for you to rest, Armand."

"An excellent idea!" Gustav cried enthusiastically. "I will find a carriage driver we can trust to take you both down there tomorrow morning."

Armand looked unhappy. "I don't wish to run away and hide."

"It is merely a strategy," Gustav told him. "Better to hide for a short time and then strike back when they don't expect you. That is the way to victory!"

The handsome count's face wore a sad expression. "In such a struggle, is there to be any sort of victory?"

"At least we are saving the lives of a few innocents," Gustav said.

While Susie was making up temporary beds for them, Armand took Enid aside to speak to her privately.

"You have problems enough," he said, stroking her hair gently, "without getting caught up in our fight."

"But I want to help."

"You have left your husband?"

"Yes. After the other night I had no choice."

He nodded gravely. "That is true. He is a strange, perverse man. I fear he will make things difficult for you."

"My parents will protect me, so please don't worry about that."

He smiled. "All right, I won't."

"And you will come back to me one day."

"I hope I'll be able to, but we cannot count on it. In any case, I must return and continue my work in France. For as long as I'm needed there."

"At least we shall have a few days together!" she said brightly.

"A few days," he agreed.

12

They were not able to leave until late the next morning. Gustav had needed that much time to find a suitable driver and carriage to undertake the journey. Shortly before noon, Enid kissed Susie and Gustav goodbye, and she and Armand embarked on their trip to Surrey.

Armand was in a more relaxed mood, and as they left London and began traveling southwest through the early March countryside, she told him of her growing-up days in Henson House. He was much taken with the character of her native heath.

"A dairy region," he said with a smile. "Why did you ever want to leave such a peaceful place?"

"I think everyone should venture forth to explore life elsewhere."

"Well, now that you know what London is like, you should be more appreciative of your Surrey."

"If I were happily married, I would like to live there and raise my children there," she said.

"You must be free of Lord Blair, of course, before you can think of doing that."

"Yes. I will have Father set his lawyers to the task at once."

Armand frowned. "What will your parents think of my descending on them like this? They won't be prepared for my arrival."

"But they will!" she insisted. "I have already told my father about you, and that we are truly in love."

"When was this?"

"When I went home for a visit in the summer," she replied. "So of course they will be glad to meet you."

Armand's face brightened. "It will be good to rest in the country for a few days. I'm looking forward to it."

Enid leaned toward him as the carriage rolled over the rough road. "Armand, let us pretend that you are staying for always."

"Dearest, how can we do that? We know better."

She smiled sadly. "Let us pretend, for a little while at least. It will make things so much easier."

"All right," he agreed, kissing her brow and cheek, and drawing her into a protective embrace.

• • •

It was late in the evening by the time they reached Henson House. Enid's parents were asleep, but she roused one of the servants to prepare a room for Armand and made sure that it was close to hers.

After she had shed her clothing and bathed, she donned a peach silk nightdress and tiptoed along the hall to Armand's room. Even though this was her parents' home, she was determined to spend the night in her beloved's arms.

Armand greeted her eagerly, his long-pent-up emotions free to express themselves at last. With consummate care he divested Enid of her silken garment and gazed adoringly at her creamy skin, her rose-tipped breasts, her slender, inviting thighs, and the golden mound of delight nestling between. Enid took as much pleasure in the sight of his naked, sleekly muscled body, as strong and as beautifully etched as his handsome features.

He caught her to him in an embrace that left her breathless and cast a film over her sloe eyes. His maleness was hard, erect, pulsating, and she could barely restrain her desire to feel him inside her.

They moved as one toward the bed, their arms and legs entwined. Armand stroked Enid's body with his hands, the tips of his fingers, his lips and tongue. Every inch of her flesh responded as the wick to the flame. She clung to him in a frenzy of longing, writhing with joyous abandon, until neither could contain the passions about to explode from within.

She arched her hips to meet his entry, answering each deep thrust with a delicious movement of her own. Through the mists surrounding her she heard Armand gasp, and knew that he was enveloping himself completely in her warm, moist depths. Then she, too, experienced a surge to that unparalleled pinnacle of ecstasy, and slowly, slowly, the poundings ebbed and abated.

Murmuring endearments and promises of undying love, they lay there deeply contented, drifting into a blissful sleep.

• • •

Early the next morning Enid crept back to her own bed before the maid came with her tea. And a little later, at breakfast, she had the pleasure of introducing Armand to her parents. Her mother seemed overwhelmed by the dignified, handsome Frenchman. Her father took to him at once.

"Bad time you fellows are having," Lord Alfred remarked.

"We are fortunate to have some staunch British friends," Armand said with a smile.

Enid's father rested his hand on his cane. "Well, to state it truthfully, the English and the French have not often seen eye to eye, but in the face of villainy and inhumanity they stand together."

"Quite true!" Armand agreed.

"And speaking of villainy," Lord Alfred went on, "I can think of none more offensive than that of the man I'm unfortunate to have as my son-in-law. To think that he would seat himself at a gaming table and calmly wager my daughter's virtue is beyond my understanding!"

"You mustn't excite yourself about it, Alfred," his wife put in. "We have known for some time that Lord Andrew was not a suitable husband for Enid."

"I did not expect him to stoop so low," he said, shaking his head.

Armand gave Lady Caroline a reassuring glance. "I think your daughter managed to withstand his cruelty without too much harm done to her. But I don't think she should be exposed to it any further."

"I'm in full agreement," Lord Alfred declared.

"Surely something can be done," Enid's mother fretted, her still-lovely face not hiding her distress.

"I shall see my lawyers tomorrow and get their advice. It would seem to me that Blair's flagrant display of his preference for men would offer grounds for annulment."

Armand nodded. "That would be the best way."

Lord Henson then changed the subject. "While you are here, Count, I beg you to enjoy yourself. You must be exhausted by the dangers you have gone through."

Enid smiled. "Now is the time for recuperation."

"I consider myself most fortunate indeed," Armand said, recalling last night's impetuous lovemaking.

That afternoon he and Enid went riding through her favorite lanes and woods. They stopped by a brook that had not frozen over and allowed their horses to quench themselves of the bubbling, pure water. Then they rode on to the village, where they were the subject of curious interest to the townsfolk. Armand had a distinctly foreign manner and bearing.

They halted for a short stop at the local tavern and both had a tankard of ale, compliments of the tavern-keeper, a jolly, toothless old man whose wig was a trifle askew and none-too-clean.

" 'Tis good to have you home again," the publican said.

"Thank you, Mr. Root," Enid replied with a smile. "I have missed the quiet of Surrey."

"Aye," the old man said gravely. "I have been to London only once. It is too large and wicked for the likes of me. I took the stage back the morning after I got there."

"You'll get into less trouble here," she teased him.

"True, your ladyship, very true," Mr. Root agreed.

It was all very bucolic and relaxing. In the evening Lord Alfred and Lady Caroline sat by the fire and listened to Armand speak of his experiences in France. His account of the murder of Lucinda and her husband sent chills through Enid. Her parents were also very touched, since they had known Lucinda from the time she was a child. Armand described the pillaging of their fine estate and how the vandals had put a torch to it and reduced it to ashes.

Enid's father sighed heavily. "Then this business in France is as bad or even worse than we supposed it to be."

Armand's eye bore a haunted look. "I will not rest while such inequities continue. Uprisings and burnings are rampant, murders less so. As long as these actions persist, I will work as an agent for the Royalists. I can do no less."

"Do you work in disguise?" Enid asked.

Armand nodded. "Always in disguise. I wear the rough clothes of a peasant and use a compound to darken my skin even more. The danger is always there, but at least my camouflage gives me some measure of protection."

Lord Alfred leaned forward. His face was filled with the depth of his concern. "May God keep you safe, my boy," he said in a trembling voice.

Another happy day passed in the idyllic countryside. Armand knew he would love to see it in summer, when the grass and the leaves would be thick and green, and the flowers bright and abundant.

• • •

Later that night, when the house was silent and bright beams of moonlight cast a silver-blue magic over Enid's room, Armand came to her. He closed the door softly behind him and moved to her bedside like a man in a dream. He dropped his dressing robe and stood naked before her. Her eyes caressed his well-formed, muscular body, and she threw back the covers to reveal her own glowing nudity.

No word was spoken between them as Armand gently lowered himself on top of her. Their bodies merged into a steadily increasing rhythm of rapture. Enid breathed words of endearment to him, hoping that their communion would go on forever. She was lost in a world where only feeling mattered, in which she had never before known such elation, such ecstasy, such release. Then their passions exploded in a final, glorious moment that left them both gasping and not quite able to fathom the bliss they had shared.

Armand touched his lips to hers and said in a low voice, "This is our last night together, my love."

At once she began to protest. "No! How can that be?"

"It has to be. I had hoped for another day, but I must leave tomorrow."

She held him close to her. "I cannot let you go."

"There are to be no tears and no discussion. You must be brave in the way I have seen the noble ladies of France meet their dark destiny."

Tears filled her eyes. "I'll never see you again! I know it!"

"You must not think that!" he rebuked her gently. "You must be hopeful, and so will I. One day it will be my great happiness to return here to your Surrey."

"You really mean that?"

"I swear it."

"And you will be cautious? You will take no more risks than you need to? You have been so reckless in the past!"

His smile was tender. "I had no reason to be otherwise then. Now I have the promise of you."

So the brief halcyon interlude at her parents' country house came to an abrupt end. Armand departed in a carriage early the next morning. He displayed no great show of emotion on leaving, nor did Enid. But the simple exchange of a kiss between them served to seal the pact they had made the night before. He promised to send her word of his doings whenever he could, but he warned her that she might have to wait for long periods without any message from him.

• • •

Life was dull gray for her afterward. She tried to interest herself in the affairs of the estate, and she enjoyed being with her father and mother, but always her thoughts were of Armand in that dangerous country across the Channel.

As the weeks lengthened into months, she had warm notes from both Susie and Gustav. John Philip Kemble wrote her several long letters, begging her to return to London and resume her friendship with him. He promised not to press her to marry him and said he would agree to whatever terms she wanted to establish for a relationship between them.

Enid was determined not to sleep with the actor any more. She had become his mistress when she had assumed she would never see Armand again. But Armand had returned and they had resumed their lovemaking. Now she felt more bound to the French nobleman than ever, and she refused to sully her love for him by continuing what had really been a casual affair with Kemble.

At the same time, she missed the friendship of that soberminded man. He had been both a good adviser and an interesting companion. She wondered if they could forge a new relationship, one without any sexual bonds. Judging from the tone of his letters, she thought it might be possible, and she began to consider the idea of returning to London and the excitement it offered.

One of the things that held her back was the fact that her efforts to free herself from Andrew were not progressing very well. It was now nearly five months since the grim night that she had left him. Her father's lawyers had tried to work out some sort of arrangement with Andrew, but to no avail. He was viciously avoiding taking any step that would give her the freedom she so desired from her year-old marriage.

• • •

One day in late August, Enid received her first word from Armand. He was well but very tired from his efforts. He mentioned some incidents that he had referred to in an earlier letter, one that she had obviously never received, and went on to tell her that France was in an uproar, but he hoped to be able to see her again before too long.

• • •

On a rainy afternoon in October, when Enid was seated in the drawing room reading from the sonnets of Shakespeare to her mother and father, a troubled-looking manservant made his entrance and interrupted her in the midst of her reading.

Lord Alfred leaned forward on his cane and asked irritably, "What is it, Hobbs?"

The elderly servant apologized. "Begging your pardon, my lord, but there is a person outside who demands to be brought in here."

Enid and her father exchanged a meaningful glance. Then she inquired, "Who is it?"

The unhappy Hobbs said, "Lord Andrew Blair, your ladyship."

"Andrew!" she cried, springing to her feet.

Lord Alfred raised himself up with the aid of his cane. "You may allow the fellow to come in."

"Very well, my lord," Hobbs said, and went out.

Enid's mother rose. "Do you wish me to retire, Alfred?"

He halted her with a gesture. "No. I think it is better if you remain here."

He had barely uttered these words when Andrew came striding in, wearing a black wool cape and blue breeches. The first thing Enid noticed was the ugly red scar on his cheek. She had indeed marked him for life. His face was florid, and he had put on more weight since she had last seen him. Excessive drinking, she guessed.

Andrew studied each of them with a sour smirk. "How fortunate! I find you all here together! A touching family study!"

Enid's father took a step toward the younger man and demanded, "Why have you intruded on us in this manner?"

Andrew smiled nastily. "I was never an intruder when I came here to extend you credit."

"You have been repaid with interest," Lord Alfred said sharply.

"So I have," Andrew returned coolly. "But I have not been treated fairly in other respects. I charge you with trying to turn my wife against me and encouraging her to leave me."

"There is no truth in that!" Enid cried. "I left you of my own accord."

"Knowing you had a place to come to," Andrew snapped. "And a place where you could entertain your French lover!"

"We shall have none of that!" Lord Alfred fumed.

Lady Caroline moved toward her husband. "Do not upset yourself so, Alfred. It is not good for you, and this young man is not worthy of even your rage."

"Thank you, Lady Henson." Andrew bowed mockingly. "Very well said." He turned to Enid and announced, "I have come to take you home."

"I refuse to go!" she declared vehemently.

"You are my wife, bound to be obedient to me by the rules of our marriage. Your place is at my side, and I want you to return to London with me."

"Not because you love me," she said unhappily, "but because you wish to abuse me further."

"I don't care to discuss that," he told her airily. "Simply pack your things!"

Her father moved between her and the irate Andrew and said in a calm, icy tone, "She will not go with you."

"Is that your last word?" Andrew asked.

"Yes. She intends to be free of you, and there is no hope of her returning with you."

Andrew stared at him for a moment. "I will make you a promise," he said slowly. "I will never let her go."

"You will have to," Lord Alfred argued. "I'll spend every cent of my fortune on lawyers if necessary."

"My fortune is a good deal larger than yours," the younger man sneered, "and I will fight any action you may bring against me until my dying day. I shall make countercharges against you as well—on the grounds that you have interfered unfairly in my marriage!"

"Go!" Enid's father ordered, pointing to the doorway.

Andrew gave Enid a scathing look. "Remember this! Remember this day when I tried to bring us together! Now I shall fight you all the way!" He turned abruptly and strode out of the room.

Lady Caroline collapsed into the nearest chair. "Why did we ever let you marry that madman?" she sobbed.

Enid went to her mother and knelt by her side. "It will be all right," she promised, though she did not believe what she said. Andrew was venomous in his hatred of her and would spare no effort to make her life a misery. And being bound to him by marriage vows was certainly a repulsive situation.

Her father was trembling with rage, and he used his cane to support himself. "Were I a young and healthy man, I'd have thrashed him," he muttered.

That night Enid could not sleep. Her mind was in a turmoil. Visions of the sneering Andrew and his threats haunted her. She was also filled with fear for Armand. She had heard from him only once since he had left Surrey, and naturally she could not help but worry and wonder. Once again she thought about going back to London, where she might be closer to the events of the day.

But this was not to happen for another sixteen months, during which time Enid received two more letters from Armand as well as additional threats from Andrew. She knew she was safest in the home of her parents.

•••

In January of 1792 a letter arrived from Susie, telling Enid of Kemble's new production of *Hamlet,* that was using the costumes and scenic designs he had shown her so long ago. Susie said she had the role of Queen Gertrude, and dropped a wisp of gossip by mentioning that Kemble was now quite enamored of an actress who was playing Ophelia to him onstage and mistress to him at his lodgings.

Enid read her friend's letter with pleasure and interest. It set her mind at rest on one point. During her extended absence Kemble had found a new bed partner, which meant that it would be much easier for her to resume her friendship with him since he wouldn't be expecting any favors from her. This, along with a desire to be with her friends again, solidified her decision to return to London very soon.

Her father made no objection, but he voiced a warning. "You must not so much as attend the same social gatherings as your husband. I do not trust him within a foot of you."

"I will be living in an entirely different world, so you need not worry," she said.

"And where will that be?" he asked.

"My friend tells me there is a vacant flat on the floor below her husband's studio. I can rent it and I won't be alone there."

Lord Alfred sighed. "I am relieved to hear that, at least. And there is no problem about money. I will make arrangements with my London bank for you to draw funds as you require them."

Enid kissed him on the cheek. "You are much too kind to me, Father."

"Kind?" he repeated with dismay. "Hardly. I let you marry that cad when I was in financial straits. I can never repay you for my allowing that mistake to happen."

"It wasn't your fault that the marriage turned out as it did."

"It was my fault to have allowed it," he insisted. "Now, you must promise me again that you will never meet or talk with him. My lawyers say that would work against the interests of our case, such as they are."

"Yes, Father, I promise."

13

In February, Enid set out for London. It was small wonder that she no longer felt like a naive young girl. She had gone through a great deal since her marriage to Andrew Blair nearly three years ago, more than most women did in a lifetime. She had seen the sordid side of life and its cruelties. And she had found a man she loved dearly and whom she hoped to marry one day. In the meanwhile, she would be in London, and if luck ran with her, perhaps Armand would turn up there on one of his underground missions. This was the underlying reason for her return to the city.

Susie was there to greet her on her early-morning arrival. They embraced fondly amid tears of joy. Then the petite actress took Enid down to the cozy flat one flight below the studio and showed her around her new premises.

"Gustav is out on business," Susie said. "It is always business these days. Between my being at the theater and his being involved with the refugees, I hardly ever see him!"

"What is the latest news?" Enid asked.

"Things are much worse," Susie replied, her pretty face shadowing. "King Louis is under attack for treason. He and the queen will probably be in prison before long."

"It has come to that?"

"No one is safe any more. Everyone fears for his life. The revolutionists are even quarreling among themselves and beheading each other!"

"Perhaps that means the revolution will fail."

Susie shook her head. "Gustav thinks it may go on forever."

"Oh, no!" Enid cried in distress.

"Yes. After all, it will be three years in July!"

Then Enid asked the question she had been wanting to voice ever since she had arrived. "Is there any word at all about Armand? I heard from him only a few times, and his last letter was written in November of last year."

"We have heard nothing, otherwise I would have let you know at once."

Enid sighed. "I'd hoped there would be at least a glimmer of information as to his whereabouts."

"Hardly any news is leaking out to us now," Susie explained, "and the trail of refugees has thinned dreadfully. We aren't saving the numbers we did at the start. Gustav is very upset."

"I can well understand that," Enid sympathized. "Has he been harassed by enemy agents, as he was when Esmond was here?"

"Gustav has to be much more careful now," Susie admitted. "They have at least half a dozen agents over here. And we think they are responsible for some of our best men being captured."

"How long can it go on?"

"Too long, I'm afraid. At least for us. Tell me, have you had any success with your efforts to separate?"

"Andrew is still fighting it, after all this time."

"Why? He hates you," Susie said with annoyance.

Enid smiled ruefully. "I suppose that is why he refuses to grant me my freedom."

Susie gave her a swift hug. "You must not worry! Worry brings wrinkles, and you want to look young and beautiful when Armand returns!"

"Yes," Enid murmured wistfully. "When he returns."

"We are giving a performance today, Enid, and I told Kemble you would come."

"I'm a little weary. Do I really have to attend?"

"You must, or he'll be terribly disappointed. You know how much he has missed you."

"What about this new girl of his?" Enid asked.

"Jenny? Jenny Woods. She is attractive and he seems quite taken with her. Though I must say her talent is for comic roles rather than for tragic. Ophelia is a bit beyond her."

"Is he in love with her?"

"Yes, but he keeps asking for you. And today he plans a welcome-back party for you onstage after the show. He is arranging for the publican next door to provide champagne, ale, and food! It will be an occasion! I've told Gustav to come if he gets back in time."

Enid's eyes widened. "A party for me?"

"Kemble thinks a great deal of you. He says your friendship did a lot for him."

"I do like him," Enid admitted.

"Then you must see him perform as Hamlet," Susie said firmly. "He is very good in the role. He had me play Gertrude rather than Ophelia, as I wrote you, though I don't have the stature for her character. But I try to suggest it."

"I'm sure you're quite perfect."

Later they strolled over to Drury Lane. Enid was thrilled to be back in London, and for the moment she forgot her worries about Armand. London was the center of everything, she decided, as she mingled with the lively crowd in the streets. A hint of spring was in the air today. Wagons and carriages rolled by, and there was much bustle and shouting. This was the city of prizefights and bull and bear baiting, of cock fights, horse racing, theater, and gambling—and, she reminded herself, of the likes of Andrew Blair.

Kemble had reserved one of the dress boxes on the right for her sole use. As the theater began to fill, she sat there in regal splendor, hearing whispers as to her identity and feeling very much the focus of attention. At last the curtain rose and the play began.

When Kemble made his entrance as Hamlet, there was a loud ovation. He ignored the applause and continued in his role. But when he gave his soliloquies, Enid noticed that they seemed to be directed at her.

She enjoyed Polonius and the bearded Horatio, and Susie was more than adequate in the role of the Queen, though her small size unfortunately worked against her. But when Jenny Woods appeared as Ophelia, the play really went downhill. Jenny, like Susie, had auburn hair, limpid green eyes and a pretty, oval face. But, unhappily, her face was devoid of expression and she read her lines in a wooden fashion. The Drury Lane audience jeered at her several times but were kind enough not to boo her off the stage, as they sometimes did with players they didn't like.

By the time the curtain fell, Enid was convinced that, despite the untalented Ophelia, this production of *Hamlet* was very good. The costumes and designs were a complete success. She made her way backstage to convey her impressions to John Philip Kemble.

He was waiting for her in the wings, still wearing his costume and stage makeup. He clasped her in his arms and kissed her soundly. "You've come back, dear Enid!" he cried, not hiding his joy at seeing her.

"The play was fine!" she exclaimed.

"That is high praise from you. I know you're an excellent critic."

"It is good to be back," she told him.

"And to have you back," the actor beamed. "We are going to indulge in a feast of celebration."

"Susie told me. But you ought not to have bothered."

"Why not? It is an occasion!" Kemble declared grandly.

She was vaguely aware of others in the background and then recognized Jenny Woods in her Ophelia dress, standing by rather timidly.

"And this is Jenny." Enid moved toward her. "You are so attractive in your costume!"

"Thank you," the girl replied shyly. She was very pretty and very young.

"Jenny is new to the stage, but she is coming along well," Kemble said with a hint of embarrassment. "Now we must go to our dressing rooms and change. Do wait—we shall be back in a few minutes."

As they left her, the bearded young man who had done so well as Horatio came up and bowed to her. "Your ladyship," he said.

"Horatio!" she replied. "You are a very good actor."

He smiled. "Thanks to you."

"I know you," she said suddenly, and then she gasped. "It is the beard! That is why I didn't recognize you! You are Graham!"

"I am Graham," he acknowledged with a small laugh. "And thanks to you, I am now an accredited member of the company."

"How happy I am for you, Graham!"

"And I shall always owe you a debt of gratitude."

"There are no such things as debts among friends," she told him. "And I think we have earned the right to call ourselves friends."

"Kemble has invited me to attend your party," Graham said, "so I'll go now and change my costume." And with a smile he disappeared behind some stage props.

Enid turned around and headed for the empty stage. Suddenly she was startled to see a figure emerging from the shadows of the opposite wings. The figure was that of a man and he came toward her slowly. He wore a long black cape and his pale face was wreathed in a smile. His left eye was covered with a black patch, and his head was completely bald. Enid almost ceased breathing as she realized that the man approaching her was Louis Esmond.

He limped across the stage and greeted her suavely. "May I inquire if you are a visitor like myself or one of the company?"

Enid fought her sudden attack of nerves and strove to present a calm facade. "I am a visitor and a friend of Mr. Kemble's," she replied.

"Ah, Mr. Kemble," Esmond sighed. "What a delightful actor! So fine as Hamlet!"

"I agree."

The bald man was staring at her. "You know, I have the feeling we have met before."

"I think not," Enid lied, aware that her voice was trembling.

"I'm French, as you perhaps have noticed. Have you traveled in my country? It is possible we may have met there."

"I know little of France, aside from Paris and Versailles."

His single eye gleamed wickedly. "Versailles, once the site of the royal palace."

"I understand the king and queen are no longer there."

"No," he said softly, staring at her as if he had secret thoughts. "You know, you are a remarkably pretty young woman. Are you an actress?"

"I fear not."

"Too bad. You would do well, I should surmise. Ugly as I may seem to you now, I myself was once a leading man on the stage."

"That does not surprise me," Enid told him. "You possess great personal magnetism."

"Thank you." He flashed a broad smile. "That is most kind of you. I would still be in Paris and on the stage but for the grave injuries I suffered in the chaos which has overtaken my poor country."

"I'm sorry to hear that," she said, wondering what he was up to.

He shrugged. "I am of the nobility. You understand, I am sure. It would be worth my life to return there. So now I'm here in your London, a poor exile."

Enid thought she was on to his game. He was shrewdly pretending to be his enemy. The agent of the revolutionists was posing as an exiled aristocrat so that he could mingle with the unsuspecting among the refugees and gain valuable information from them. No wonder he was called the revolution's master spy!

He nodded, keeping his good eye fixed on her. She began to feel that he was boring into her mind with his probing stare.

"Are you also a friend of Kemble's?" she asked.

"Only an acquaintance. I was introduced to him by another friend of mine, and we had a pleasant talk. I promised to see his play and he invited me here today. He is having a party for a Lady Blair."

"I am Lady Blair," Enid said.

"Ah!" Esmond seemed delighted. "Like myself, you are of the nobility."

Just then Kemble appeared in his street clothes and shook hands with Esmond. "So you two have met?" he said.

"I find Lady Blair charming," the Frenchman replied.

Kemble smiled at her. "The vicomte is a member of the French nobility, for which you have so much sympathy. I invited him to your party so you could exchange thoughts with him."

"I'm afraid I have very little to offer," she apologized.

"Nonsense," the actor scoffed. "You have been interested in the refugee cause from the start."

Enid was relieved to see the publican arrive with his helpers, their arms laden with food. They set the delicious-smelling dishes on the long table that had been placed in the center of the stage. The members of the theater company began trickling in, Graham and Susie among them.

Susie came up to her. "Any sign of Gustav?" she asked.

Enid took her aside and said in a low voice, "It will be lucky if he stays away."

"Why do you say that?"

Enid nodded toward Esmond as he stood chatting with John Philip Kemble. "That is the archfiend, the agent of the mob, Louis Esmond!"

"Esmond!" Susie gasped.

"Yes. He somehow contrived to meet Kemble and get an invitation here."

"How can I warn Gustav off?" his wife worried. "He could arrive here any minute!"

"Just pray that he doesn't. Esmond is already trying to place me."

"Oh, no! What shall I do?"

"There's nothing to be done for the moment," Enid told her. "Just pretend to be calm."

"I can't when I'm terrified," Susie said. "You don't seem to be afraid at all!"

"I'm trembling inside."

Kemble stepped to the middle of the stage and called out for silence. Everyone was given a glass of champagne. "We are here today to welcome the return of my dear friend Lady Blair," he said. "I'm sure all of you will happily join me in this toast to her!"

He raised his glass, as did the others. Enid found herself pushed forward to make a reply.

"I'm overcome!" she protested. "You have been too kind!" She was not pretending when she claimed to be overwhelmed by the moment. The presence of the cruel Esmond had done that much for her.

Susie edged her way over to Enid. "Perhaps we should get away from here," she suggested.

"I can't just yet. Kemble would think me ungrateful."

"But it is no longer safe for you here!" Susie objected.

"Esmond can't recall where we met. I'm safe until he does."

The party continued happily, and Enid noticed that Louis Esmond was spending much of his time in the company of Kemble. The two chatted earnestly over glasses of champagne. Then she saw Gustav enter and look about for Susie. She decided to try to send him away before Esmond recognized him. But before she could reach him across the crowded stage, he had spotted Susie and gone straight over to her.

Enid saw a worried Susie give him the warning message, and he turned at once and started out. He hadn't taken more than a few steps, however, when Kemble called out to him.

"Don't run off, Gustav. As Susie's husband, you are one of us and are entitled to be here!"

All eyes were now focused on Gustav, so he could do little but turn back to face Kemble. "I wasn't intending to leave," he said awkwardly.

"Then come and have some champagne," the actor insisted.

Gustav crossed slowly to the table and accepted a glass from him. Then Kemble said, "We are drinking to the return of Lady Blair. I'm sure you'd like to join in."

Gustav raised his glass and bowed to Enid, saying, "I have the highest regard for Lady Blair!" And in one long swallow he downed his champagne.

Louis Esmond had been staring at Gustav, and now he moved toward him and said softly, "We have met before."

"I think not," Gustav replied, ready to turn away.

"I insist that we have," Esmond went on in that soft tone. "And now I remember where."

"Do you?" Gustav said, attempting to meet the uncomfortable moment.

The agent now wore a smile of triumph. "Our last meeting was much more exciting. I shall not soon forget it."

"You are making a mistake, I am sure." Gustav's handsome face was drained of all color. He put down his empty glass as if he were about to flee.

Once more it was Kemble who halted him from leaving by saying, "Gustav is married to one of our finest actresses, the lady who plays the Queen."

Louis Esmond continued to smile. "I'm not at all surprised to find that he is a Royalist. My own tastes, however, lie in other directions."

Several people came up to the table just then to refill their glasses, and Esmond moved away. Susie and Gustav, looking thoroughly unhappy, remained where they were as the crowd swirled around them. The party was a great success.

Enid was about to suggest that it was time for them to go when she heard a voice at her elbow. "Now I know where we met before!"

She turned quickly and saw Esmond standing beside her. She stared at him blankly and said, "I do not understand."

"Don't tell me your memory is failing you," he mocked.

Angered, she lashed out at him. "Sir, I have an excellent memory!"

"Then you must surely remember a warehouse and a villainous crew who attacked it and set it on fire two years ago." Louis Esmond purred, his one good eye burning with hatred.

"You have an actor's imagination, sir. I know nothing about what you are saying. And now perhaps you will excuse me."

She went over to Kemble to say goodbye. The actor turned to her and immediately remarked, "You look filled with ire! Has anyone said something to displease you?"

"No," she replied. "The truth is, I'm weary. I debated whether I should come to the party or not. I didn't wish to disappoint you, so I came. But now I really must leave."

"We shall talk more later. Come to my flat for supper tomorrow evening. Jenny will fix us some fine fare."

"Very well," she agreed.

"You look as lovely as ever, dearest Enid. I have missed you greatly."

"And I have missed you, too. Until tomorrow night, then."

She quickly made her way to Gustav and Susie and the three of them moved toward the exit. Louis Esmond was still engrossed in a conversation with Kemble's overweight brother, Stephen. Enid was sure he was trying to garner as much information about them as he could.

No sooner were they in the street than Gustav exclaimed, "He recognized us! He made that very clear!"

"I made no admission," Enid said. "I'm certain he is suspicious, but how can he be certain?"

"He saw us together," Gustav muttered unhappily. "And then together again tonight. He might have been confused about one of us, but seeing us together did it!"

As they walked toward the studio, Susie murmured, "I was going to stand outside the theater and warn you not to come in, but you arrived before I could do that."

"Where did Kemble pick him up?" Gustav asked.

Susie sighed. "John told me a French actor introduced him as Vicomte Gerard, a noble refugee who had been on the stage in his youth."

"Esmond often assumes different identities," Gustav told her.

"Kemble should be warned about him," Enid pointed out.

"I will do it," Gustav promised. "I will wait until the party is over and then go to his flat and tell him."

Susie gave them a troubled look. "What will happen now? Will Esmond come after us?"

"I doubt it," her husband said. "This is London. But he may set spies to watch us and discover our contacts, the agents who work in France. In that way he could make excellent use of us without any violence."

"He probably thinks we are of more use to him alive than dead," Enid offered hopefully.

Susie shuddered. "I wish I could believe that. I won't be able to close my eyes at night!"

When they arrived at their building, Enid went up to the studio to discuss the matter a little further, and then she walked down to her own flat. She had pretended to believe Gustav when he claimed that Esmond and his men wouldn't try to harm them. But she wasn't by any means convinced that this was true. Esmond knew that she and Gustav had rescued Armand and destroyed Esmond's warehouse filled with firearms. That must have been a major setback for him, and he was not a man to ignore a thirst for revenge.

She carefully bolted her door and hoped for the best. It was comforting to know she had Susie and Gustav for neighbors, and because of her extreme weariness, she slept soundly through the night.

14

In the morning she was awakened by a knocking on her door. She put on a dressing gown and called out, "Who is there?"

"Me," came the reassuringly familiar voice of Gustav.

She unbolted the door and let the fencing master in.

"I thought you should know the news," he said, "so I have come to you early. Did I wake you?"

"It doesn't matter," she replied. "Let me hear what news you bring."

Gustav looked grimly pleased. "You will be surprised to know that Louis Esmond left London last night."

"What brought that about?"

"Troubles within the revolutionist group back in Paris. They needed him, and so presumably he had to forget about us and take care of more urgent business."

"What luck for us!"

"Yes. My contacts inform me that the revolutionists are splitting into rival groups. It is hard to tell who will be the leader or who will lose his head as the days go by. Apparently no one trusts the other."

"That is in our favor," she said, very much relieved. "Did you warn Kemble about Esmond?"

"I did, and he was extremely upset. He vowed not to allow him in the theater again. He learned from his brother that Esmond had asked a number of questions about us. Happily, Stephen didn't have much to tell."

"It doesn't matter now, if Esmond has returned to France."

"He sailed at dawn. But he will be back, unless he is removed from power as head of the spy system. That's when we'll have to be extra careful. On his return, he may decide to deal with us."

"Your own agents should warn you of his coming, shouldn't they?"

"That's true, but there are times when they don't always know everything. Just as the other side doesn't always know."

"How long will this awful state of affairs in France go on?" she asked, thinking of Armand and his danger-filled missions.

"Until there is no more France, it seems," Gustav replied slowly.

"And what of Armand?" She voiced her worry aloud. "What can have happened to him?"

Gustav shook his head. "There has been no word."

Enid studied his uneasy expression and then, in a different tone, she asked, "Are you keeping something from me, my friend?"

The fencing master crimsoned. "You know I would never keep any facts from you!"

She pressed him. "But rumors, perhaps? You might think it wise not to pass on any rumors to me. I beg you to tell me anything you may have heard, however fanciful."

Gustav looked down at the floor. "There may be no truth in it …"

"What did you hear?"

"That they have him in prison. There is a rumor that Beaufaire was recently seized and imprisoned somewhere near Paris."

"Why didn't you tell me before?"

"I didn't want to cause you unnecessary pain. It may not be true, after all."

Enid's eyes blazed. "Don't try to make it easier for me!" she protested. "We both know there has been scant word from him as it is. Something dire must have happened to him!"

"I will keep on trying to learn the truth," he promised.

"If he has been imprisoned, he is likely to be dead by now. Today in France it is a short distance from prison cell to the guillotine!" Her voice cracked with the weight of her despair.

"You must not give up hope!" Gustav begged.

"I dare not," she said dully.

Gustav was embarrassed that she had dragged this sorry news from him, and he left soon after.

When Enid had dressed and taken some breakfast, she went up to speak with Susie but found that the actress had gone out. Perhaps to an early rehearsal. So she decided to pay a visit to her father's bank in order to establish herself for credit.

She went down to the street, hailed a carriage and made the short trip to the bank. After she had chatted with the manager and withdrawn some cash, she stopped by several of the better shops to select a few thing she needed. She especially wanted a beige Irish linen tablecloth and matching napkins.

As she emerged from the last of the shops, her purchases tucked under one arm, she came face to face with a dandy who sported long curls and an extravagant cerise greatcoat. It took her only a moment to realize the man was Vicomte Robert!

He graced her with a low bow. "Dear Lady Blair, I had no idea you were back in London!"

"Nor did I expect to meet *you* here."

He made a foppish gesture with his left hand and declared airily, "I have left France. It is no longer safe for one of noble rank to remain there."

"I see," she said inanely, wishing she had never met him and wondering how she would get away from him.

He smiled mockingly. "I'm living with Andrew. He has been so lonesome without you."

"I would expect the absence of some of his lads would disturb him more. But you must be a great consolation to him." Her tone was grim.

"How kind you are to suggest that." The vicomte paused. "Do you wish to send him any message? He will be interested to know you are here in London."

"I have no message for Andrew other than that I wish my freedom."

"I will tell him that," the nobleman promised with a smile. Then he added, "I trust all goes well with your friend and my countryman Count Beaufaire?"

"I have nothing to tell you," Enid said sharply. "And now, if you will excuse me." She turned and hurried down the street.

The meeting upset her more than it should have. A little while later she took a carriage back to her flat, and all the while she had the feeling that she was being followed. She paused on her doorstep to look up and down the street, but saw no sign of anyone. Nevertheless, her fear was real enough.

In the flat she unwrapped the things she had bought and continued to feel nervous. She wondered if Gustav had been ill-informed about Esmond's leaving London. Whether perhaps the master spy was still about and having her followed as a prelude to taking her prisoner. The possibility of this was chilling. Her depressing thoughts had started with her running into the hateful Vicomte Robert, and she could not seem to shake them.

The hour came for her to keep her supper engagement with John Philip Kemble. And still Susie and Gustav had not returned. She lingered in her flat after she'd changed into a suitable navy wool dress and worried about venturing out alone into the evening to find a carriage. However, her fears were put to rest when a driver appeared at her door and announced he had been sent by Kemble.

The man was known to her, and so she accompanied him with no misgivings. Within a short time she reached the familiar surroundings of the actor's flat. But things had changed. It was Jenny who now resided in Kemble's bed and in his apartment. The red-haired girl greeted Enid warmly and took her in to Kemble, who was seated by the fireplace reading the manuscript of a play.

He rose immediately and gave her a warm kiss. "Sit down, my dear." And then he told Jenny, "Wine for all of us. Bring glasses and a decanter."

"It was good of you to send your carriage for me," Enid said.

"I could do no less."

"I've been nervous ever since I met that French agent Esmond at your party."

The melancholy-faced actor sighed. "I must apologize for that. He took me in completely, though it's easy to understand why. I hear he is a master spy."

"He's head of the revolutionists' spy service."

Jenny returned with the wine and served Enid and Kemble first, then took a glass for herself. She sat down meekly on a stool near them, listening to their talk but adding little to the conversation. Enid smiled at her often and was again impressed by her beauty. A pity the girl doesn't have more intelligence to go with that face, she thought.

Kemble sipped his wine. "The conditions in France are growing much more serious," he said, frowning. "Now that the king and queen are bound to be captives, I am told that the British government is very uneasy. Better to have a Bourbon still on the throne than a tribunal of extremists. Diplomatic relations with the French have been brittle enough when their government was stable, but now there is little or no contact."

"And small hope it will change," Enid added.

"The French leaders are also enraged that we have given haven to so many émigrés," the actor continued. "The underground, of which Gustav and your Count Beaufaire are members, has done a fine and courageous job, but its success has maddened its opposition."

"Only a small percentage of the nobility has actually been saved, and men like Armand and Gustav have risked their lives to accomplish even that."

Kemble sighed. "It is only a matter of time until King Louis and Marie Antoinette will be guillotined, and then Heaven help both France and England!"

Enid thought bleakly of Armand. What are his chances? she wondered for the hundredth time.

"Well, it's a sorry business," Kemble said. "What is the news from the count?"

"There has been no recent word." She did not mention Gustav's report that Armand might be in prison.

"Are you concerned?"

"Very."

Kemble gave her a knowing look. "I offer my sympathy. But perhaps I would be able to offer you more if anything should happen to him."

She gazed at him with fear in her eyes. "Please do not consider that possibility!"

"It is always there," he said gently.

"Yes, I know."

Kemble hesitated. He didn't wish to give Jenny any hint of the meaning behind his and Enid's conversation. He didn't want to upset his lovely protégée. He cleared his throat and said, "We both realize he changed things when he arrived in London."

"He will always have the same place in my heart," Enid vowed.

Kemble raised his eyebrows. "And what about your husband? What about dear Andrew?"

"He continues to try to hold me despite the fact that my father's lawyers have proved he is not fit to be a husband."

"I'm sure Lord Andrew has some friendly ears among those who preside over the courts. His is an old title that carries a great deal of influence."

"I met Vicomte Robert today," Enid said with a shudder of disgust. "The man we visited in Paris on our honeymoon."

Kemble smiled grimly. "When they capped the ceremony with an orgy?"

"I shall never forget it! How I despise them both!"

Jenny rose from her seat. "Perhaps we should have our meal now. I have it warm and ready."

Kemble stood up and placed an arm around her, exclaiming jovially, "Is she not a paragon? She let us talk without once interfering!"

"How could I?" the young actress murmured. "I didn't understand what you were talking about."

"It's just as well," the actor laughed.

They went to the oak table and sat down to a pleasant supper. And to make Jenny happy, Kemble had her declaim some lines from the role of Katherine in *The Taming of the Shrew*. He carelessly fed her cues, and Jenny responded well enough. It was evident that Susie had been right, Enid thought—Jenny was best in comedy.

After this entertainment and some more talk, Kemble called the driver to take Enid home. He kissed her tenderly in farewell, and she knew that he would not linger long over discarding Jenny if she, Enid, showed a willingness to be his mistress again. But she would never do that. Not while there was any hope that Armand was alive. And even if her beloved count were dead, she doubted that she would be faithless to his memory.

At her building, the driver helped her out of the carriage and bade her good night, and she stepped inside the dark front hallway. She was in a somewhat relaxed frame of mind, with Armand's fate the only thing worrying her.

Lost in her thoughts, she started for the stairs. Too late she heard a movement behind her, and in the next instant a hood of some sort was thrown over her head and tied tightly about her throat. She tried to scream, but only a gasp and a choking sound could escape her lips.

At the same time she was taken roughly in hand and shoved back out into the cool night. She felt herself float somewhere between consciousness and oblivion. Her weak struggles made no impression on her captors, who, uttering oaths, tossed her onto the floor of a carriage and held her there as the vehicle rattled over many cobblestoned streets.

Enid no longer struggled as she lay there. Now she merely fought to breathe. Every minute that she was forced to remain smothered by this hood, with its taut cord secured tightly around her neck, was unendurable to her. She moaned a little and prayed that her ordeal would soon be over. Then she reached the brink of her endurance and descended into a void of darkness.

15

Something had changed. Enid slowly opened her eyes and realized the hood was no longer over her head. She could see; she was able to breathe again. She tried to move and discovered that her ankles and wrists were tightly bound. She was in a candlelit room that smelled of dampness, dirt, and gin.

As her senses returned, she raised her head a bit. She was lying on a rough cot in a miserable little hovel. There was only one other piece of furniture in the room: a plain chair on which rested the pewter candleholder. Then she heard the sound of an accordion being played somewhere below and the occasional bursts of drunken male laughter.

She tried to put the pieces of the puzzle together. Tried to think back to what had happened and how she had come to this vile place. The laughter sounded again, intruding on her thoughts. And then she remembered. She had entered the front hall and been attacked and taken prisoner.

Esmond! The master spy had no doubt spread a false rumor of his departure to put them off guard. And now he had taken her as a hostage. He might do anything to her. Surely he would try to balance the debt he felt was owed him! Enid's mind whirled dizzily.

The door of the room creaked open, and a hunched-over, elderly crone peered in. The sunken eyes studied Enid to see if she was awake. The old woman did not attempt to speak, but made a chewing motion with her dried-up mouth. Then she vanished in the same silence with which she had entered.

Enid surmised that the old woman was some derelict who had been given the task of watching her. Her head ached and her ankles and wrists had begun to throb. She had the unhappy conviction that she had run out of luck. That the danger she had managed to elude for so long had finally caught up with her. She asked herself bleakly if this was to be the end of her great romance with Armand. He was either rotting in prison or dead by the guillotine, and she was a prisoner of the master spy, the vilest of all the revolutionists!

The door creaked open again, and this time an enormous woman came in. She wore a bright yellow dress with a dirty white shawl tossed over her shoulders. Her many-chinned face was both cruel and none too clean. Her hair was a dark, frizzled mess. The woman came over and gazed down at Enid with cold venom in her beady eyes.

"So you're a lady!" she sneered. "That's what they tell me!"

"Please!" Enid cried. "I'm in pain! Please free me!"

The fat woman laughed hoarsely. "That's not why I'm here, dearie, not by any chance. Don't snivel at me! I have small use for genteel ladies like you who think you're better than the rest of us. Well, we'll see about that!"

From the folds of her dress she withdrew a half-empty bottle of gin. She pulled out the cork and took a generous swig of the colorless liquid. Then she bent over Enid and forced the mouth of the bottle between her lips.

Enid tried to move her head away, but the woman was surprisingly agile for her size. She managed to keep the bottle in Enid's mouth, allowing the burning gin to pour down her throat and choke her. Only when Enid began to gag did the woman remove the bottle. By that time a goodly quantity of gin had involuntarily been swallowed by the helpless Enid.

"Don't choke on it, dearie!" the fat woman chided her. "The likes of me was brought up on gin. Good for you, it is. Brings out the woman in you. That's what all my girls say, and they should know!"

Enid's throat was afire, and her head was reeling from her fear and from the beginning effects of the liquor. She sobbed, "Don't torture me!"

The woman roared with laughter, every pound of flab jiggling in unison, and applied the bottle once more to Enid's lips. Enid bit the woman's fingers and received a stunning blow for her deed. She had the choice of having her teeth bashed in or accepting the bottle again. She allowed some more gin to enter her mouth and slide down her throat. Again she gagged, and again the bottle was drawn away.

"How do you feel, dearie?" the woman asked.

The room was careening wildly around. Enid gasped, "I'm ill! I'm going to be sick! I'll choke if you don't release me!"

"The gin is beginning to warm you, dearie," the woman gloated. "Time has come to cool you off."

She finished the remaining gin, threw the bottle away, and then began systematically to rip all the clothing from Enid's body. Enid felt her navy wool dress being torn roughly away, then her lace décolletage insert, then her petticoats—until at last she lay there completely naked, totally exposed.

"Well, my lady," the enormous woman cackled, "you look much like the rest of us! Slim enough, to be sure, and good-sized above! You have a pair, no doubt of that!"

As she finished speaking, the door creaked open again. With eyes slightly blurred, Enid turned to see a delighted-looking Andrew and his simpering friend Claude enter the room.

Andrew exclaimed, "Excellent, Mother Mag! Is everything ready?"

The woman turned to him and shook with laughter. "Whenever you like, sir!"

Andrew came over to the cot and bent down close to Enid so that she could clearly see the scar on his face.

"Did you think I'd let you off so easily?" he sneered. "Not bloody likely!"

"You!" she managed thickly. She was sickened by the thought that she had been so wrong. It hadn't been Esmond—it was Andrew!

"Claude had you followed. The rest was easy. And tonight I shall have my revenge. My witnesses will testify that you came to a brothel, got drunk on gin, and indulged in the debauchery to which you are so addicted. We'll see then if the courts will grant you your freedom! Especially when I inform them of my distress and my desire to keep you for my wife and reform you!"

Enid moaned and closed her eyes.

"Did she get plenty of gin?" Andrew asked Mother Mag.

"More than a third of a bottle! She's drunk as a turnip!" The fat woman shook again with cruel glee.

Andrew leaned over Enid and hissed, "You are so anxious for men, I shall stand by and see you supplied with a dozen or so!"

Terror cut through her fuddled brain and she opened her eyes. "No! Please!" she begged him.

"Too late for pleading," he said. "I have neglected my husbandly duties, so you claim. Now I shall have the great delight of standing by and watching you be well served."

The vicomte concurred. "It is the very epitome of justice, dear Andrew!"

"Bring them in!" Andrew told Mother Mag.

She waddled to the door and shouted hoarsely, "Ready, boys? A shilling a turn! Pay as you take your place!"

There was a moment's pause, and then a tall, gaunt man stepped hesitantly into the room, followed by a short oldster in a dirty jacket and breeches and a greasy periwig. Behind him was a young seaman whose vacant face bore a wide grin. The last man to enter was a burly brute with a broad, ugly face.

Mother Mag took a stand at the foot of the bed and crowed. "There she is, boys, and she's ready for you! A real lady! All right, you vagabond, give me your shilling and get to it."

The gaunt man at the head of the line hesitated. "Is there to be no screen? Nothing to make it private?"

"All in the open, that's the way it's to be," Mother Mag told him. "Look at those rosy breasts and the cut of those thighs! Now, enough stalling. Give me the shilling!" She held out her hand.

He passed it to her, and there were titters and some rude jests from the men waiting behind him. Still the gaunt man hesitated. He approached the cot awkwardly and then gave Andrew and the vicomte a worried look.

"Why are they here?" he asked Mother Mag. "Why should they be allowed to watch?"

Andrew spoke up. "It is our wish to see you at your manly work! Get on with it, fellow!" The vicomte giggled and placed a forefinger in his mouth, his eyes greedy for the carnal scene about to be played for them.

At this point, the other men impatiently urged the first one on. Looking unhappy, he began to undo his breeches and dropped them to the floor. Enid caught a glimpse of his enlarged member as he sank slowly on top of her. She closed her eyes and for the first time was grateful for the gin, which would help blot out the pain and the disgrace.

The gaunt man penetrated her and was soon panting with delight. The others waiting their turn cried out encouragements, as they would for two mangy mongrels in the act of coupling. Mother Mag roared with laughter and Andrew and Claude joined her in expressing their own glee. Enid's cries of discomfort and terror only goaded them on.

Enid was once more on the brink of unconsciousness when she heard the sound of a pistol shot from below. It was a signal for the worthy on top of her to jump up and scramble into his breeches. His associates let loose with cries of consternation and fear. Mother Mag cursed loudly, and Andrew began a series of rapid-fire questions about the best way to depart without being seen. The voices ebbed and faded as eventually everyone moved out of the room.

Enid lay there moaning. Then she heard her name being called. She gathered all her strength to cry out in return, "Here! In here!"

Gustav came rushing into the room, pistol at the ready. When he saw the condition she was in, he uttered several French oaths and quickly cut her bonds with his pocketknife. Then he sat her upright on the cot, and removing his jacket, put it on her. He buttoned it up and thus covered her nakedness to her knees.

"You'll be all right," he said as he lifted her in his strong arms and started out of the room.

She had no clear memory of what followed afterward. It was hours before the effects of the gin and her shattering experience wore off. When she came to full awareness, she found herself in Gustav and Susie's small bedchamber, tucked snugly in their bed.

Susie was bending over her. "You poor dear!" she murmured.

Enid stared at her. "Gustav came…he saved me!"

"Don't upset yourself," Susie pleaded. "The doctor said you mustn't. He'll be back later."

"How did you know?" Enid's voice was hoarse, her throat was sore, and her entire body was a throbbing, aching mass.

"I was up here when they took you," Susie exclaimed. "I went downstairs and saw them put you in a carriage. Luckily, at that very moment Gustav arrived in another carriage. We followed the carriage you were in to the brothel on the docks. Then Gustav had to get help to break into the place."

"They humiliated me and intended to degrade me even more," Enid whispered.

"That despicable Lord Andrew!" Susie cried. "When Gustav and his men broke into that awful place, they had to battle their way up to you. That gave Andrew time to get away with that French fop."

"He escaped?"

"Yes. Mother Mag took them up to the roof, and they jumped across to the next building and then to another. By the time Gustav realized what had happened, they were gone."

"Andrew is the most evil of all," Enid murmured.

"He won't get away with this," Susie declared indignantly. "Gustav and his men have gone to Andrew's home now. If he's hiding there, they'll settle with him, and if he hasn't gotten there yet, they'll wait for him. You can be sure he'll pay."

Enid made no reply. A great lassitude had swept through her, and she closed her eyes. Once again she lapsed into a sleep that was not a real sleep.

When she awoke again, Susie had some warm gruel ready for her. Enid ate the gruel and felt somewhat better.

"I hope Gustav doesn't get into any trouble," she worried.

"Don't let that concern you," her friend urged.

"Andrew has many corrupt friends like himself," Enid told Susie. "It is hard to strike back at him."

"I know."

"If my father learns what happened, he will be beside himself with rage," Enid fretted. "And he certainly won't want me to remain in London if he finds out."

"Who will tell him?"

"I don't know, but to be truthful, I don't think I dare remain in the city if Andrew goes free and unpunished."

"Try to rest a while longer," Susie suggested. "I'll let you know when Gustav gets back."

A weary Gustav returned an hour later. He came into the bedchamber and took Enid's hand in his. "Are you all right?"

"I'm much better," she said. "What about him?"

"He's taken cover!" The fencing instructor's face expressed his disgust. "Gone into some hole, like the slimy rat he is!"

"I didn't think he would show up at his house."

"Both he and that Frenchman have vanished. The servants say they don't know where either one is. They may be lying, but I frightened them with every sort of threat. I found out nothing."

"So he is hiding somewhere, safe from punishment," Enid stated calmly.

"I wish I could have gotten my hands around his throat just once!"

"Perhaps it is for the best, Gustav. I would not want you to become a murderer on my account."

"I would gladly have killed him!"

"I know that, and I daren't think of what would have happened to me if you hadn't appeared when you did."

"Not soon enough. I blame myself for that."

"You couldn't tackle all those ruffians without going for help!" she protested. "Anyway, I'm here, and I'll recover. That's the important thing."

"The other important thing is that your husband must be made to pay."

"That can wait, really it can." She sighed softly.

Gustav glanced through the open door to be sure that Susie was out of earshot at the other end of the studio. Then he bent over Enid again and said in a low voice, "I'm afraid it will have to, as far as I'm concerned."

"What do you mean?" she asked.

"I'm leaving tomorrow at dawn. I'm sailing to France."

Enid caught her breath. "*Why?*"

"I must. I can no longer be here on the safe side while others take the worst risks. I have to be there to do my duty—as Armand has done."

"What about Susie? She'll be devastated! She is so fearful for you!"

"She must learn to be brave. I'm a Frenchman and I have a duty to perform. I must save the lives of the innocent."

They were silent for a moment when Gustav said, "You can live here with her. You will be company for each other. Kemble will keep an eye on you."

"After tonight, I'm considering leaving London."

"Then you might miss Armand if he should get back here," Gustav cautioned.

Enid sighed. "That alone would make me risk staying here."

"Rest," he urged, rising. "I'm going to break the news to Susie now."

An hour later Susie came into the bedchamber, her pretty green eyes red-rimmed from tears. In a taut voice she said, "You know!"

"Yes," Enid admitted. "He feels he has to go."

Susie sat down on the bed and laid her head on the pillow next to Enid's. "What are we going to do?" she murmured.

"We'll manage somehow," Enid replied quietly. "Gustav has asked me to stay here with you. I shall."

"I'll be in fear every moment."

"I know."

Susie sat up and looked slightly guilty. "Of course you do! Forgive me! I hope Armand is still alive."

"Why shouldn't he be?" Enid said firmly. But she knew her words had no true meaning. Her show of confidence was a facade to help her friend conquer the fears she felt for her husband's safety. Deep within, Enid was filled with an overpowering sense of despair.

16

John Philip Kemble, resplendent in a purple grogram jacket with white brocade and a pair of yellow breeches, paced back and forth in the studio. He and Jenny had come to call on Susie and Enid, who were sharing the flat together. Six months had passed since Gustav had left to take up more active work in the French underground.

The actor halted by one of the windows and stared out at the street below. "Rain again! And in early September!" he declared with some disgust. "I vow that whenever we have an afternoon performance, the weather works against us!"

Jenny, in a brown morning dress and bonnet, turned in her seat and told him, "You will be playing Hamlet today. That always draws a crowd, rain or shine."

"True," he sighed. "They are faithful! They do come!"

"That is because you give such a fine performance," Enid said. She was wearing a bright blue linen frock which complemented her hair and complexion.

The actor bowed. "Thank you, dear Enid. You have always inspired me to do better things. My Coriolanus was created mostly on your suggestions."

Susie appeared with a tray containing a pot of tea, biscuits, and cups and saucers. The petite actress was making a strong effort to appear brave in the face of her husband's long absence. With a small smile she placed the tray on a nearby table and announced, "Midmorning refreshment for everyone!"

She served the ladies first and then Kemble. He stood with the teacup in his hand and directed his attention to Enid. "How have you been feeling?" he asked.

"Fine, thank you, though I still have monstrous nightmares."

"Small wonder. That bastard of a husband of yours should be put behind bars!"

"I agree," Susie said from the chair she had taken near Enid. "But he has been careful to remain in hiding all this time."

"Sooner or later he will show up," Kemble predicted. "He cannot stay away from London forever."

Enid agreed bitterly. "He'll return when he is good and ready, when he hopes to evade any punishment."

Jenny offered one of her rare utterances. "For such a wicked act he must be made to pay!"

Kemble frowned over his tea. "I have heard—as I'm sure you have, too, Enid—that the brothel in which you were held hostage was closed by the authorities. And Mother Mag disappeared in the same manner as your husband."

"No doubt to continue her infamous career as a madam," Susie said with disgust.

"The studio does not seem the same without Gustav here," the actor remarked. Then he went on quickly, "Let us hope he makes a name for himself in that mad country."

"And returns safely," Susie added quietly.

"Of course." Kemble paused, then turned to Enid again. "What about Count Armand?"

"No word," she replied. "Nothing."

"Strange." Kemble frowned.

"Not really." Enid tried to sound casual though she was feeling sharp stabs of pain. "The rumor we hear is that he was captured and is in prison."

"I hope not!"

"Perhaps we'll hear more news now that Gustav is in the midst of it," Susie suggested.

Kemble put down his empty cup and refused the offer of more tea. He gazed intently at Enid and asked, "Would you come to my flat about this time tomorrow morning? I'm expecting a visitor whom I'd like you to meet."

"Indeed?" she said, wondering who it might be.

"I think it's important for you to be there. That is all I'm free to reveal for the moment."

"Of course I'll come if you wish." She thought it was probably something to do with Andrew.

The actor and Jenny left shortly thereafter and Enid thought no more of it. The day passed uneventfully.

The next morning Susie reminded her of the appointment she had with Kemble. After breakfast, Enid put on a dark green dress and bonnet, along with a warm gray cloak, and hailed a carriage to take her to Kemble's place.

He was alone and waiting for her. After kissing her warmly, he said, "I have sent Jenny out to do some shopping."

"Have you?" she murmured rather tensely as he slipped off her cloak and went to hang it up. She moved to the blazing hearth and warmed her hands. "It is chilly this morning."

"The spring season is upon us." Kemble came close, and taking her gently by the arms, turned her to face him. His smile was sad. "You're not fearing I've trapped you into a rendezvous with me?"

"I don't think you would do that."

"I'm not sure you're convinced of that, but let me put your mind at rest. I do not intend to make any undue advances toward you, much as I might wish to. That is not the purpose of my asking you here."

"Oh?"

"Let me tell you bluntly what I could only hint at when Jenny was present. If Armand does not return, I shall attempt to win you back again. I would like you to be my wife."

"And Jenny?"

"A passing companion. Too young and untalented for me to take seriously. In any event, I do not wish to marry an actress, though you have the looks and talent to be one."

"It is strange," Enid said. "Despite my fondness for the stage, I have never wanted to be part of it."

"Let us be grateful for that, and remember what I have just said. I will not press myself on you while Armand is alive and your heart is pledged to him. But afterward, I make no promises."

"That is fair enough." She smiled up at him. "Since I fully believe that somewhere Armand still lives and that one day he will return to me."

"I envy him," the actor said with some emotion.

The discussion was brought to a close by the sound of the bell over the door fairly rocking as someone impatiently pulled the cord outside. Kemble gave Enid a knowing glance and went to the door and opened it.

An amazing-looking man stepped inside. He was taller than Kemble, who was surely tall enough, and broad of shoulders. Enid could only think of the man as massive. To make him seem even more huge, he had a large stomach that strained to break free of his confining black jacket. In fact, he was dressed completely in black. He removed his long black cape and three-cornered black hat and handed them to Kemble. Then he advanced to where Enid was standing before the fire.

Towering above her, he thrust out his own great hands to be warmed. At the same time he nodded and said, "Good morning to you, Lady Blair!"

She stared at him. "You know my name?"

"I have seen you at many London parties," he told her in a rasping voice. His head and his features were small for one so large, and this incongruity made him seem even more overpowering. He had a low forehead, and his heavy black eyebrows beetled over small, shrewd eyes. His mouth was framed by wrinkles and he wore his graying black hair tied back simply. Enid took him to be perhaps fifty or more.

Kemble joined them with a smile. "May I introduce an old friend and former actor, Sir Harry Standish."

The big man bowed. "A great pleasure, my lady."

"And mine," she said. "I cannot believe I could miss one of your dimensions at a party and not remember you!"

Kemble and Standish exchanged a laugh. Kemble told her, "Sir Harry is rather careful to keep himself in the background at social affairs. It is part of his profession. He is in the diplomatic section of our government."

"I'm also working to establish a proper police in London," Sir Harry barked. "It's past time for it, as is borne out by the sordid happening in which you were the victim."

Her sloe eyes widened. "You heard about that?"

"It is part of what comes across my desk during a day of studying the state of our city," Sir Harry told her, scowling. "What happened to you should not happen in any civilized city."

"I fully agree," Kemble put in.

Sir Harry went on. "Your husband is a criminal and a pervert, Lady Blair. He should not be accepted in London society. And I shall do all I can to bar him from it."

"Thank you," she murmured.

"But that is not the reason for my visit here." Sir Harry turned to Kemble. "What about some tankards of good brown ale and comfortable seats for our discussion?"

"At once," Kemble said, and vanished to get the ale.

Sir Harry gazed down at Enid with appraising eyes.

"You are Alfred Henson's daughter?"

"Yes."

"Your father is a fine man. You should be proud of him."

"I am."

He scowled again. "Too bad you married that sodomist Blair!"

"It has been the major misfortune of my life," she agreed.

"Now that fellow is off somewhere in hiding," Sir Harry fumed, repeating what she already knew. "Well, so it goes!"

Kemble returned with the ale and they seated themselves comfortably before the fire. The glow from the burning logs played over Sir Harry's rather stern face. He fixed his impressed gaze on Enid and cleared his throat. "As Kemble has said, I'm a small wheel in the diplomatic service."

Kemble protested. "A rather large wheel, I should say!"

Sir Harry laughed. "Only if you take my size into account. I weigh more, pound for pound, than any two or three others who serve the Crown."

Kemble turned to Enid to explain. "Sir Harry is looking for an actress to help him, but I told him I thought you were much better suited to his requirements than any actress."

She gave the two men a puzzled look. "Requirements?"

"I'm recruiting these days. The king needs sound people for the diplomatic service," Sir Harry said.

Enid was still puzzled. "I do not see my place in this."

"You will," Kemble promised.

Sir Harry took several sips from his tankard of ale and stared at her. "Kemble assures me you can be trusted."

"I would hope so."

The big man continued to study her in his intent fashion. "I hear that you write and speak French fluently, fence better than most men, and ride a horse well."

"All those things are true, but why do you thus recite my abilities?"

He waved her silent. "Kemble also tells me you have a lover who is a member of the French nobility, a Count Armand Beaufaire. A man who has done worthy work in saving many of the nobility from the revolutionists and the guillotine."

Enid smiled wryly. "It would seem that my friend Kemble has revealed a great deal about me."

"Necessary, my dear," Kemble leaned forward to assure her. "Listen and you will understand."

"Do go on," she told Sir Harry.

"I have explained my interest in police work," he reminded her. She nodded.

"It so happens that the branch of the diplomatic service with which I'm connected is not the one responsible for usual routines of the foreign service. My branch is engaged in secret missions with special objectives. We mingle with the consuls and the ambassadors, but our duties are not confined to signing papers and other office folderol."

Kemble interrupted. "May I say something, Sir Harry?"

"Please do."

"You surely have heard of cloak-and-dagger men?" the actor asked Enid.

She hesitated. "You mean spies such as Louis Esmond, the master spy of the revolutionists in France?"

"Exactly," Kemble said.

Her eyes widened as she looked at Sir Harry again. "I have had the ill fortune to meet Esmond. And so you are his sort?" she gasped.

"Not exactly like Esmond, though I'm well aware of his shifty gentleman's talents. We have crossed paths."

"I should have told Sir Harry about Esmond, and he would have identified him for me before you and your friends did," Kemble told Enid.

"It was a clever move of his to intrude on your party," Sir Harry said. "He was plainly gathering information about Gustav Brideau and Count Armand, among others. Part of his work is to learn who the operators of the underground are and then have them systematically exterminated."

"And your work?" Enid asked.

His smile was grim. "I have many tasks assigned to me. The one at the moment will, I hope, interest you."

"I do not follow you," she said.

"How would you like to do something worthwhile for your country and at the same time help the cause of your Armand?"

Her interest was aroused. She saw that Kemble was listening approvingly. "I would like to hear more," she said.

"And you shall!" Sir Harry promised. "You must know that our government is not at all pleased by what is going on across the Channel."

"I would think not."

"It has been a ruinous time for England," Standish went on. "We have lost the American Colonies, and, mark you, they will prosper. Kemble will be touring there one day."

"I don't think so," Kemble objected. "Too far to venture!"

"Be that as it may," Sir Harry said. "Our country is not desirous of more wars, though they will surely come. But we must do what we can to prevent them." He paused and tapped the side of his nose significantly. "Stability!"

"Stability?" Enid echoed blankly.

"Stability in foreign relations," he explained. "That is the thing. Our nation wants it. And with the French in an upheaval, we cannot have it. Better Bourbon and a Hapsburg on the throne!"

"That is not likely. The king and queen have been imprisoned for several months now, and if rumor is true, they will never be freed. They are doomed to the guillotine."

"You are an intelligent lady," Sir Harry observed. "Our agents report that is exactly what will happen. And we are powerless to interfere. We must stand by and let this atrocity continue."

"The French are even now warring with Austria and Prussia, which support the monarchy."

"Their combined efforts will not conquer France or save the king and queen," Sir Harry replied. "Even if France were defeated, the royal personages would be put to death before they could be rescued."

"Then what can be done?" she asked.

Sir Harry's odd face brightened. "Ah! There you have the question and the answer! The genius of the English is much underrated in the field of diplomatic endeavor. But we have the gift, I swear it. And it is through diplomacy that we hope to save the situation. Aside from the king and queen, the royal family of France consisted of three children. The eldest son is now dead, with the younger lad and the girl remaining."

"They are also in prison," she said. "At least that is what has been reported."

Sir Harry continued as if she had not spoken. "Only one immediate member of the family—the king's brother, the Count of Provence—managed to escape. And he is safe outside the borders, waiting to see which way events will turn."

"I find this most intriguing," Enid said, "but I still don't see how it relates to me."

"In the very likely event of the king's being guillotined, who is now next in succession?" Sir Harry asked her.

"The boy. The younger son."

"You have it!" he exclaimed with excitement. He got to his feet and began to pace slowly back and forth as he talked. "The boy! Louis Charles!"

"But he is in prison," she repeated.

The big man hovered over her, and a gloating smile showed on his face. "You think so?"

Confused, she said, "It is common knowledge!"

Sir Harry roared with laughter. He turned to Kemble and poked him with a forefinger. "You heard that? Common knowledge!"

Enid blushed. "I fail to see the humor in what I said."

"Of course you do, woman! Of course you do!" Sir Harry exclaimed. He hovered over her again and added slowly, in a carefully spaced manner, "Because you do not know!"

"Know what?"

"Our secret!" Sir Harry roared. "The secret of the British government, which I represent here. Louis Charles is no longer a prisoner! Through the efforts of a skilled agent posing as a nun, the little prince is free!"

Kemble was enjoying the full drama of it all. He told her, "I promised you this would be worth your while. Doesn't this recital of events thrill you?"

"It surely does," she admitted, "and I'm happy for the boy, of course. But why am *I* being told this?"

Sir Harry was pacing again. "Do not be impatient," he urged. "You have not heard all the story!"

"There is more?" She was astonished.

"Obviously, or I wouldn't have taken the trouble to tell you what I already have."

"The tale becomes even more dramatic," Kemble warned her.

Sir Harry lowered his huge bulk into the chair opposite her and fixed his burning eyes beneath the jutting brows on her once again. "For what I'm about to tell you, more than one throat has been slit. So it follows that I trust you. Do you understand?"

"Yes," she said in a taut voice, wondering if Kemble had introduced her to a madman. "Though I still see no connection between all this and myself."

"In time, all in good time. The two secret agents of the British government who were successful in this ploy are now both dead. Killed in the line of duty, one might say, though they fell in the back alley of a great city. Now we have lost our contacts. The only thing passed on to us before they were killed was the name of the Austrian priest whom they had entrusted with the lad, who one day will be king of France and a staunch friend of the English who saved him. The name of the priest is Father Hans Braun."

Enid stared at Sir Harry as he finished this long exposition. "You're saying that after your agents rescued the young Louis Charles, they placed him in the hands of this priest for safety? And that shortly after that, they were both killed by the revolutionists?"

"You are correct," the government official agreed. "They were a man and a woman whose names are not important to you, but who were two of our best agents in France. Now everything is in chaos. There are only underlings left, with no direction. The boy is out of our hands and the whole affair may collapse."

"How did they manage to save the young prince?" she asked.

"It was a fantastic plan, worked out in every detail," Sir Harry told her. "A farmer told them about a deaf and dumb lad who was wandering about friendless. They found the boy, fed him, and treated him well. They dyed his hair to match the blond locks of Louis Charles and then paid good British gold sovereigns to two of the prince's jailers to turn him over to them and substitute the deaf mute."

"What happened to the poor afflicted boy?" Enid asked.

"He's still in prison, but being fed a princely fare," Sir Harry said. "The warden of the prison knows the lad is not the prince, but he dares not admit it for fear of reprisals to himself. So it remains an uneasy secret. The boy can tell his captors nothing, even if they torture him. In the end they will somehow contrive for him to escape or will simply release him. In either case, he is no worse off than he was before."

"That remains to be seen," Enid said rather sternly.

Sir Harry shrugged. "In my particular line of work one does some things which one would rather not do. But too often there is no choice. My first allegiance is to my country, and that is good. In the course of events some are bound to suffer."

"What have you in mind for me?" she asked quietly.

"That is a direct question," the big man observed with delight. He turned to Kemble. "You heard her! I liked that! She was most direct. It indicates a sharp mind."

"Please do go on," she begged. She glanced at Kemble and saw that he was amused.

Sir Harry rasped, "You are in love with a Frenchman named Count Armand Beaufaire. He has been active in the Royalist cause, saving noblemen from the executioner's block."

"That is true." She wondered why he was repeating what he had said much earlier.

With a gleam of triumph in his small, sharp eyes, the big man pressed on. "And at the moment Beaufaire is languishing as a prisoner in a jail cell. He was captured in a small town near Calais."

"You're sure?"

"My network rarely makes a mistake," Sir Harry said modestly.

"So he *is* a prisoner!" she cried unhappily. This was something Sir Harry had been obliged to learn for himself, since no one in London had the correct information. Gustav had said that Armand was imprisoned near Paris.

"Do you wish to help him?" Sir Harry asked. "Help him and our own government at the same time?"

"If there is any way I can, yes, I do."

Kemble spoke up. "Good girl! I knew you'd say that."

"You had a friend, Lucinda, married to Duke Victor d'Orsay," Sir Harry continued.

Enid was amazed to hear this. "You know a great deal about me."

"They were killed in the rioting in Versailles."

"Yes."

"Suppose she wasn't killed?"

"But she was!"

"How can you be sure? You weren't there. Reports can often be wrong."

Her eyes widened. "You're saying that Lucinda somehow escaped the massacre and is still alive?"

"Perhaps in hiding, moving from village to village in fear of her life," Sir Harry replied softly. "Would you try to help her?"

"Of course I would. Lucinda was my best friend!"

"Exactly," Sir Harry said with satisfaction.

"Is she alive? Tell me!" she begged him.

"I fear she is truly dead," Sir Harry answered. "But suppose she might be alive and in hiding? And suppose that you, as a friend of this poor English girl who had the misfortune to marry a nobleman but was always on the side of the people, decided to go to France to search for her and bring her back to England?"

"I would do so if she were alive!"

"You and your father pay a visit to France in search of this girl. But your real purpose is to find the Austrian priest and the boy. To bring Louis Charles back to England, where he will remain in seclusion until he can be crowned king of France. Does that not excite you?"

"My father could not entertain such a task. He is too old and unwell," Enid replied.

Sir Harry chuckled. "I realize that. So I will have an actor play the part of your father."

"An actor?" Everything Sir Harry had said began slowly to come together. She turned to see Kemble display one of his rare smiles.

"Yes," the actor said, rising. "Sir Harry has asked me to play the role of your father."

Enid sat there, overcome with incredulity. "But this is not a make-believe business. It has nothing to do with the stage. It is real!"

"Can't you see me as your parent?" Kemble wanted to know, a hurt expression on his face.

"You are too young, and we certainly don't resemble each other in appearance."

Kemble chuckled. "I can whiten my hair and fix lines in my face that look real. As for my not looking like you, many fathers bear no resemblance to their daughters."

Sir Harry was leaning back in his chair watching them. "What do you think?" he asked her.

"I would say you need actors for both roles. I'm not that good at make-believe."

"I came to Kemble looking for an actress, and he assured me you would better fill the role. And after meeting you, I must agree." Sir Harry patted his stomach as if to second his statement.

Enid was stunned by all that she had heard. She turned to Kemble. "How would you get away from Drury Lane?"

"My sister, Sarah, is chafing at the bit for a change of pace."

"You would let her take over the company?" Enid asked in surprise.

He nodded. "At the same time I'll spread a rumor that I'm ill and have to go away to try to regain my health. That should protect my absence."

"I vow you will make the ideal team to temporarily replace the two I have lost," Sir Harry declared, beaming at her. "I ask you only to serve until the boy is safe in our hands in England."

"How long do you think that would take?" she asked.

"A matter of weeks at the most."

"Won't the French authorities also be looking for the prince?"

"Only if the prison warden notifies them of the exchange. And since that could mean his own head, I doubt that he will ever admit it took place."

"They will find out sooner or later."

"There is that risk," the big man agreed.

Kemble interjected, "Sir Harry thinks we have less to fear from the French at the moment than from the Prussians and Austrians."

"How do they enter into this?" she wondered.

"They wish to get the boy," Sir Harry answered. "Whoever manages to capture him first will be in a position later on to control the destiny of France. When the revolution fails, and it is doomed to in the end, the people will want a monarch."

"So the Prussians and the Austrians also have secret agents in the field," Enid mused.

"That is precisely what is making me so uneasy," Sir Harry admitted. "We are falling behind. For all I know, they may have the prince now. Of course, we must determine that. In my opinion, he is still in the care of the good Father Braun."

"The priest is an Austrian. Why did your agents trust him?" she asked.

"He has no ties with his mother country. His family has been in France for two generations. That is why my agents put their full confidence in him."

Kemble approached her. "What do you think?"

She stood up. "You are seriously asking me to consider this?"

He smiled. "I thought it would have a greater appeal to you than it has for me. You have an interest in defeating the republicans that goes beyond mere loyalty to the Crown. There is Armand to think of."

Enid considered this and turned to Sir Harry. "May I make a request?"

"As many as you like," he replied graciously.

"If I agreed to this mission and we should be successful, would you then give me all your support to find the count and win his freedom?"

"Count Beaufaire is a hero. You would have the not-inconsiderable contacts at my disposal in any attempt to save him."

"Would you pursue his rescue with the same diligence you expect from me in an attempt to find the young prince?"

"You have my word," Sir Harry proclaimed earnestly. "And my word is that of the British government."

She sighed. "You offer an attractive bait. But I know the peril would be great and that the prospects of coming out of it alive are slim."

"Think of the glory if you succeed," the big man coaxed. "You and Kemble will have your names in the history books!"

Kemble laughed. "A bit more lasting there than on theater placards. Join with me in this, Enid. And we'll find the prince and save Armand."

She shook her head. "You know it will never be that easy."

"I know. But it offers a chance for adventure, which fascinates me. I need someone to pose as my daughter, and you are the ideal person."

"What names would you suggest we use?" Enid asked Standish.

"It would be better if you used your own name," Sir Harry told her. "And Kemble could temporarily take your father's name. I'm sure there would be no objection on the part of your parent, considering the reason."

"He is in the country," Enid said. "He need not even know about it."

Kemble put his arm around her. "I won't try to make the danger seem less than it probably is. But you have already known some danger here in London. And you will remain in danger as long as you stay here."

"That is only too true," she agreed, the memory of Andrew's cruelty still fresh in her mind.

Sir Harry rose from his chair. "I must go now. I shall not ask for an answer until tomorrow. I regret I cannot wait any longer than that. If you are not able to come to a conclusion, I shall have to look, regrettably, elsewhere. I feel you are the two best suited to serve us."

Kemble brought Sir Harry his cape and hat. "We shall give you a proper answer tomorrow," he promised.

"You know where to reach me," Sir Harry said, tossing the cape over his ample girth. "Send a messenger to my office. If you decide to throw your lot in with me, I shall arrange another meeting." He bowed to Enid. "I thank you, Lady Blair. You understand that all I have told you is of the utmost confidence."

"Of course," she murmured tautly. "I understand completely."

"Very well. I shall be on my way now."

Kemble went to see him out. Enid moved to the window and glanced down at the waiting carriage, whose ebony wood frame and ornate brass fittings glowed in the pale morning light. The driver wore a splendid maroon and gold livery, and the horse stamping its hooves between the shafts of the vehicle was perfectly groomed and had the best of harnesses. Sir Harry emerged onto the street and was helped into the carriage.

As the driver resumed his seat and drove off, Enid let her eyes wander across the road, where they rested on two men in shabby clothing who were standing there. One of them came to the curb and raised a hand. An ordinary carriage with a poorly dressed driver appeared, and the two men bundled themselves into the coach and were driven off in the same direction as Sir Harry. Enid realized at once that these men were his bodyguards; they had waited across the road until he left Kemble's flat and were now following him.

The door opened behind her; Kemble was back again. He came over to her and asked, "Well, what do you think?"

She gave a rueful smile. "I think there are great rogues in high places!"

"Without a doubt. But it takes a kind of rogue to oversee such cloak-and-dagger operations."

Enid moved a few steps away and then turned to the actor. "You know that anyone he manipulates is expendable if it suits his purpose. You and I count for nothing but mere conveniences to him. He does not see us as human beings."

"Come, now, aren't you being too hard on him?"

"I think not. He knows we are vulnerable—I because of Armand and my actual fear of London since Andrew treated me so violently. And he has surmised that you are bored with your success and ready for some sort of adventure to take you out of yourself."

"You may be right in both instances. But does that matter? It is his profession to judge people, to seek out their weaknesses and use them to his advantage."

She gave Kemble a frosty smile. "With all the information he has about us, I'm positive that he knows we have been lovers."

"So?"

"It would be convenient for us to travel together. What a wonderful excuse for us to continue our affair!"

Kemble eyed her in bewilderment. "But you have told me that cannot be. That while Armand lives, you will not offer me your favors."

"And I meant it," she said sharply. "And if we can accept Sir Harry's word, we know that Armand is still alive, though captive."

"I think he told us the truth."

"So if we should be mad enough to go through with this, you must keep your place with me. I will not tolerate any nonsense, John."

He sighed. "Have it your way."

"There is also another hazard," she went on. "One that Sir Harry did not seem to consider."

"What do you mean?"

"Louis Esmond knows who I am—he has recognized me."

"I hadn't thought of that," Kemble admitted. "I should have. I'm sorry."

"I don't blame you. But it is a fact. He knows me."

"There is no reason why you should run into him, if you are lucky," the actor said quickly. "The French, hopefully, are still unaware that the exchange of the lads took place and that the prince is at large."

"I wonder. Sir Harry made the situation sound as good as he dared. But I think he truly misled us. This is a shaky enterprise that has crashed on the rocks of disaster. He hopes that we may be able to piece together the wreckage."

"I say let's do it!" Kemble urged. "It will take me a week to turn the company over to my sister and be free. What about you?"

"I have only Susie to consider. She has counted on my staying with her. She has been in a depressed mood ever since Gustav left, and she fears he may never come back."

"She need not be alone. I'll have Jenny live with her while I'm gone, and I'll close up this place!"

Enid could not hold back her smile. "You have an answer for everything, John."

He closed the distance between them and took her in his arms. "I love you, and yet I may never be able to share the future with you. Let us join in this one great experience together. We may wind up with our names linked in the history books."

She laughed up at him. "I knew that line of Sir Harry's appealed to you. Very well, I'll do it."

He kissed her gently on the lips and murmured, "That was as close to being fatherly as I can manage at the moment."

"You will have to do better than that," she chided with good humor. "I find it hard to picture you with white hair and a wrinkled face!"

"Then you have missed me in one of my greatest performances as the mad King Lear!"

Enid moved out of his embrace, saying, "I must leave before Jenny returns, or you may regret it. How do you manage her so easily? She seems to do your bidding, yet she asks nothing of you."

Kemble shrugged. "I fancy she is in love with me."

Enid slipped on her cloak and went to the door. "You know, you might do worse."

"And I could also do better," he replied.

From his expression and his tone of voice, Enid knew he was referring to her, but she chose to ignore this remark and merely smiled at him in farewell.

17

Once on the street, she decided to walk back to the studio. But a few minutes later she began to regret her decision. The streets of London had taken on a menacing air for her. Even though the night of her kidnapping was long past, she had grown increasingly more nervous when she was out by herself. She was trembling now at the sound of rough, loud voices nearby, and she hesitated at the curb to let the great wagons roll noisily by.

Her unsettled state of mind made her wonder whether she was really fit for the role Sir Harry had in mind. Perhaps a while ago she would have been all right. On the night that she and Gustav had rescued Armand from the warehouse, she had not wanted for courage. She had handled both sword and pistol with skill and accomplishment. Neither had she hesitated to take whatever risk was necessary.

But that had been a different matter entirely. Then she had been eager to help Armand directly. Now she was being asked to take on a formidable task with only a vague promise that she could seek out Armand when her other duties were completed. This mission gave her considerable pause. She was fond of Kemble, and having him at her side would help, but she did not know whether she could stand up to the rigors of the assignment.

She looked about her and saw more than the familiar parade of well-dressed gentlemen and ladies. She saw the pinched faces of the poor as they lounged in dark doorways or scurried about on some errands. She knew now that this London that had so attracted her in earlier days was more than a city where lords and their ladies indulged themselves in all sorts of luxuries and debaucheries. This was a place in which the snobbish one hundred or so families that dominated the city's social life paid no heed to what was going on around them. They ignored those who had left the rural areas and now lived, many of them, in degrading poverty in hovels. Thieves, prostitutes, pimps, pickpockets, and murderers abounded. Did those families care? It seemed appropriate that King George III, who was at the very top of the social hierarchy, should roam about his palace in a purple bathrobe, talking to himself endlessly, though he was both deaf and almost blind.

When Enid entered the studio at last, Susie was there waiting for her. The actress hurried over to her nervously, crying, "You are so late! I was half out of my mind with worry!"

"I walked back," Enid said, taking off her cloak and bonnet.

"You know how I worry when I'm alone," Susie moaned.

Enid smiled at her reassuringly. "You're behaving like a child. You never used to be like this."

"So many terrible things have happened. I was at the window before, and I saw a wicked-looking man standing across the street and staring up here."

"You probably imagined it."

"No, I'm sure I didn't. He watched for a long while and then he vanished. I'm afraid word has gone around that we are alone in the studio. And with your flat empty, the whole building is almost deserted."

"You mustn't dwell on such things," Enid said, quelling her own surge of fear.

"What did Kemble want?" Susie asked as she sat down near the window.

Enid knew she could not tell Susie the truth. Sir Harry had sworn her to secrecy. So she put Susie off by saying, "He talked a lot about new plays and perhaps turning the company over to his sister and taking a holiday."

Susie frowned. "He has spoken of that before. I hope he doesn't. Mrs. Siddons is a skinflint and a hard person to act with. I worked with her in the past."

A knock sounded at the door. Susie answered it and then handed Enid an envelope. "It is a message for you."

Enid took the letter and at once recognized her father's stylish handwriting. She quickly tore open the envelope and read the enclosure. It consisted of just a few words: "I'm staying overnight at the Whyte Hart Inn at Charing Cross Road. Urgent that I talk with you."

Susie watched her with anxious eyes. "What is it?" she asked.

"My father is in the city," Enid explained. "He wants me to visit him."

"I shall be at the theater, so I won't mind. Why don't you meet me there after you see your father? We can walk home together."

"I'll go to Drury Lane as soon as I leave the Whyte Hart Inn," Enid promised.

She changed her clothes and then set out for Charing Cross Road, which she reached on foot within ten minutes. The Whyte Hart Inn was a large establishment whose wide courtyard was bustling with people and with the arrival and departure of stagecoaches.

Enid made inquiries of the landlord and was directed to a front room on the second floor. "First on the left as you reach the landing," was his exact instruction. She found the right door and knocked on it, and a moment later her father stood before her.

He looked older than when she had last seen him, and he was leaning on his cane as usual. His lined face broke into a broad smile at the sight of her, and he cried, "My dear girl! I've been waiting for you!"

She embraced him and then sat down on a plain chair near the small hearth. Lord Alfred lowered himself onto the edge of the divan that would also serve as his bed.

"I didn't expect to see you here in the city," she said. "My solicitors have indicated they would like a meeting with me," he explained.

"Oh?"

"Some business affairs to attend to, and the matter of your annulment, of course."

"Are they making any headway?"

He shook his head. "Very little, I must admit. You know that scoundrel Andrew is off somewhere, hiding."

"Yes, I did hear about that." She was hoping her father hadn't learned the scandalous reason for Andrew's disappearance.

Apparently he hadn't, for he said, "It's a bad business, and now it has come to a halt. And on top of that, the villain has taken to writing threatening letters."

Enid was shocked. "Threatening letters?"

Her father sighed. "He sent them to me in care of my solicitors. I read them today. He had sent three at different intervals. They didn't make pleasant reading, I can tell you that!"

"What did he say?"

Lord Alfred hesitated before replying, "They were mostly threats of what he intended to do to you. I needn't go into the details."

Enid got up and came to sit beside him.

"I'm sorry you've been bothered in this way. Andrew is truly despicable."

"Don't think about me. You're the one I'm concerned about. Do you think it's safe for you to remain in London?"

"I may be leaving shortly, as a matter of fact. I wanted to tell you about it. Mr. Kemble is taking a tour and has asked me to join him."

Jumping to conclusions that weren't warranted, Lord Alfred said, "Oh, a theatrical tour of the provinces! Very good. Best thing possible to get you away from London and moving about."

Enid decided to leave him with this idea. "I may not write you for a while, but you know I'll be all right."

"I'm relieved to hear of your plans. Away from London, you won't be so liable to suffer from that vile Andrew."

"I feel that way, too," she agreed. "How is Mother? Is she well?"

"She is well and worries about you," he said with a sad smile. "I worry about you, too. How is your Frenchman?"

"Armand is still in France, working at helping other noblemen escape." She refrained from mentioning his imprisonment.

"Dangerous, from all I've read. Hope he watches out for himself."

"I'm sure he will," she murmured, trying not to show her concern.

"I thought we'd have dinner downstairs," her father suggested. "They provide a very good meal."

"Fine," she said. "Are you returning to Surrey in the morning?"

"Yes," he replied, and rose with difficulty from the divan. He eyed her anxiously as she prepared to leave with him. "Those threats," he said. "I'm glad you're leaving London for a time. I'm certain he is up to no good at all, and I pray that your troubles with him will come to a satisfactory conclusion once and for all."

Enid concurred silently with her father's wishes. For too long now her sham of a marriage to Andrew had persisted, and while she was bound to him—shackled, she thought—she could entertain no hope for a complete union with Armand.

18

The evening Enid spent with her father left her in a morose state. She felt both apprehensive and depressed. He had steadfastly refused to tell her the nature of the threats Andrew had made, either because they were so diabolical or because they were not fit for her ears. She and Lord Alfred parted with her promising him that she would go down to Surrey for a visit as soon as she returned from what he believed to be a tour of the English provinces. Naturally, she had not dared to tell her father of her true plans.

She met Susie at the stage door of Drury Lane and they took a carriage home. As Enid paid the driver, her eyes strayed to the opposite side of the dark street, and she was almost certain she saw a man standing alone in the shadows. A tiny shudder ran down her spine and she found herself wondering if Susie had been right, if someone really was watching the house.

Once they were safely upstairs, with the candles lit in the studio and in the bedroom they shared, she felt less fearful. Then she sat on the edge of the bed and told her friend what she was going to do. She did not mention that it was Prince Louis Charles whom she and Kemble hoped to rescue, merely that the boy was of noble birth whom his family hoped to save.

Susie was distraught. "You and Kemble must both be mad!" she exclaimed. "Running off to France and all that horror to find a child of strangers!"

"The idea appeals to Kemble's sense of adventure," Enid said.

"It is different for him. He is a man. But to that country consumed with anarchy and chaos no woman should venture!"

"I have given my promise."

"What about me?"

"Kemble will see to it that Jenny comes to live with you until we return."

"Jenny! How can I talk to her?" Susie wondered in disgust. "She is just a pretty face with no mind!"

Enid disagreed. "I think you misjudge her. I think most people do. Because of her pretty face and quiet temperament, they come to the conclusion that she is stupid. I don't think that's true."

"She is a dreadful Ophelia!"

"But an excellent Kate! Her forte is comedy. And it takes wit to play comedy. You of all people should know that."

"You are bound to prove me wrong. I don't know what I shall do between living alone and trying to work with that awful Mrs. Siddons!"

Enid tried to comfort her. "It will probably be only for a few weeks. The time will pass quickly."

"Not for me," Susie said unhappily, rising from the bed and starting to prepare for sleep. "Why did Gustav have to leave me?" she groaned.

Enid sighed. "It seems we are all being drawn into the maw of the revolution. It has come to dominate our lives."

"I hate living in this awful, wicked age!" Susie cried as she pulled her long nightdress over her head.

Enid laughed. "I'm sure they said the same thing in Rome and Athens in ancient days!"

She followed Susie in readying herself for bed. By the time she had snuffed out the candles, Susie was already asleep and breathing heavily. Enid was glad. She knew the unhappy girl was not getting enough rest because of worrying so about her husband. Enid had no trouble understanding this, since she was just as worried about Armand.

Sir Harry Standish had said that Armand was a prisoner in a small town near the coast. Enid wanted to believe he would be safer in a small town than in a city like Paris, where the jails were overflowing with Royalist prisoners who were routinely marched out and executed without any semblance of a trial. She hoped it would be different in the country. At least it was likely that there the so-called system of justice would move at a slower pace, which might give her time to save him.

She fell asleep with this thought in her mind, but it gave her no comfort. Her slumber was filled with terrifying dreams that reached an unbearable peak when she felt unseen hands about her throat, choking her. She gasped for breath and called out, and then she awakened with a start.

She gasped again and sat up in bed with a cry of horror. The room was full of acrid smoke, and stiflingly hot. Susie still slept peacefully. Enid jumped out of bed and tugged at her arm.

"Fire!" she screamed. "Wake up! The house is all aflame!"

Susie came awake and at once went into hysterics. Enid tried to quiet her and get her out of the room at the same time. Susie seemed to be only partially aware of their predicament. She continued to sob loudly as Enid led her through the smoke-filled studio to the door leading to the stairs. When Enid opened the door, flames licked in at her and blocked her passage. She screamed, slammed the door closed, and then ran to the nearest window. Next to it was a plain chair, which she picked up and slammed against the pane. Woodwork and glass flew wildly, but now there was an avenue of escape.

Enid looked out and saw people gathering in the street below. They shouted instructions up to her, all crying out together, so that they defeated their purpose. She could not hear what they were saying.

She ran back through the blinding smoke in search of the cot. Then she dragged its coverlet off and groped her way toward the open window.

Susie was still standing there, weeping. "What shall we do?" she sobbed.

"I'll show you," Enid said, tying one end of the coverlet around her friend's waist. "Out on the sill with you! Fast!" She shoved the whimpering, resistant girl onto the windowsill. "Now I'm going to lower you," Enid went on, "and to keep yourself from swaying, I want you to touch the wall as I let you down."

Susie still held back while Enid tied the other end of the coverlet to a sturdy table leg. Then, as Susie continued to sob, Enid slowly lowered her into the waiting arms of the approving crowd. Flames were beginning to shoot up through cracks in the floor as she swung herself out of the window and clung to the makeshift rope.

A man caught her in his arms and eased her down onto the cobblestones. "Anyone else in there?" he yelled, trying to make himself heard above the loud voices of the crowd and the roaring of the fire.

"No," she yelled back.

"Best to get back! She's going to collapse!" he shouted, and he dragged her away with him.

As the crowd slowly retreated across the street, the old wooden building became racked with flames. The yellow tongues of disaster licked out of windows and through the roof, as if eager to consume the very air itself. Then there was a strange, rasping sound and the structure disintegrated before their eyes, falling in slow motion behind a screen of fire and smoke.

The man took Enid a few steps farther along to where Susie stood. She saw Enid and ran to her, pressing herself against her. "What shall we do?" she sobbed.

"There is nothing we can do," Enid said quietly.

The man stared at her. "You lost everything?"

"All we have left are the nightdresses we stand in," she replied.

"I was coming by and I saw the flames," he told her. "And I saw a man come running out of the front door and dash down the street in a flash."

"Did you get a good look at him?"

"No. I didn't see his face at all. I was about to try going in then, but your face appeared at the window."

"Whoever it was you saw coming from the house had to be the one who started the fire!" Her tone was drenched in bitterness.

"You think so?" the man gasped, amazed. Then he turned to watch the flaming ruins again.

"I told you someone was watching the house," Susie said.

"I have an idea who it was," Enid mused.

"Who?"

"Andrew, or some agent he hired, I'm certain he promised to see me in Hell and that he threatened to set the house aflame."

"That sounds like him!" her friend whimpered.

At this point a portly man came up to them and said, "I have a carriage down the street, ladies. Can I take you anywhere?"

"Yes," Enid replied, making a quick decision. "I'll thank you if you'll take us to a friend's house."

"Wherever you like," the stranger offered generously.

"To the flat of the actor Kemble." She gave him the address.

He helped them move past the remaining onlookers, past the flames and the wreckage of the old building that had housed both happy and sad times. Within a few moments they were safely installed in his carriage and on the way to Kemble's flat.

"What will he think?" Susie fretted.

"What does it matter?" Enid said. "We are in distress. He will be glad to help us."

And this proved to be true. Once they had managed to rouse the sleeping actor and Jenny, the two were quick to show their concern for the forlorn Susie and Enid. Jenny brought them brandy and prepared a sleeping place for them in the front room of the flat.

When morning came, Jenny provided the women with clothes from her own wardrobe. They were a strangely subdued group as they sat down to breakfast together.

"At least this solves the problem of housing," Kemble said. "Susie must come here to live with Jenny while we are in France."

"But what about Gustav? Suppose he returns and is not able to find me?" Susie protested.

"You can leave word with the people in the neighboring houses that you are living here," Enid suggested.

Kemble nodded his agreement. "That should take care of the matter satisfactorily."

Jenny, looking composed in a green robe the color of her eyes, moved about the table, pouring more tea. "Then you are determined to make this journey?" she asked.

"Yes," her lover said. "Enid and I have to pay a visit to someone in the government this morning and make our arrangements."

"Thank goodness I have something decent to wear, sweet Jenny." Enid gave her a warm smile. "Directly after our appointment I must do some shopping."

"I have a good deal to do myself," Susie lamented. "And all our household things went up in flames."

Jenny sat beside her and spoke in a sympathetic manner. "You mustn't worry about it all at once. Give yourself a little time to get over the shock. You can build up your stock of household goods slowly, since you'll be living here for a while."

"That is true," Susie admitted. She turned to Kemble. "Thank you for your great kindness to us, John. I won't be forgetting it quickly, you may be sure of that."

"It is nothing," the actor told her with a hint of embarrassment at her gratitude. "All of us here are close friends. Almost like a family. It is only right that we should share."

"Are you certain that your husband set the torch to your building?" Jenny asked Enid.

"He is the one whom I first suspect," she replied.

Kemble gave her a wise glance. "It could have been someone else, you know. Remember the night you rescued Armand? He and Gustav set the warehouse on fire. Couldn't Louis Esmond or some of his agents have planned to even the score, even at this late date?"

"I hadn't thought of that," Enid confessed. "It is very much a possibility."

Susie sighed. "I expect we shall never know for certain. We can only be thankful we escaped with our lives. I was a problem for Enid. I lost my nerve completely. If she hadn't taken over, I would have died up there in the flames."

"I was just as frightened, but I didn't dare show it," Enid admitted with a smile. But she knew that the crisis had proved at least one thing. She was not as shattered as she had feared she would be. In the face of danger her courage had returned to her. Now, having gone through that experience, she felt much better about the venture that lay ahead.

An hour later she and Kemble took a carriage to the address Sir Harry had given them. Susie was going out on a shopping expedition for clothes, the funds for which were provided by Kemble, with Jenny planning to keep her company. Enid was glad to see the two young women getting along better than they had in the past.

She told the actor, "I'm sure Jenny's kindness to us after the fire has made Susie regard her more highly."

"Then at least something has been gained from the disaster," he said grimly as the carriage moved through familiar streets.

She glanced at him. "No last-minute regrets?"

He stared at her in surprise. "About trying to save the life of the Dauphin?"

"Yes."

"None whatsoever. His parents are doomed, and probably his sister as well. If we can save the boy, it will give me a great deal of satisfaction."

"I know Armand would approve."

Kemble smiled in his melancholy fashion. "He would be sure to approve in principle, but I'm not certain he would be anxious to see you taking such a risk."

"I feel we shall be successful."

"So do I." He paused. "There is one thing you ought to do."

"What?"

"Work at your fencing. You may find your swordsmanship useful in France."

"Gustav is far away, so will you fence with me?"

"You're my superior."

"At least it will give me some practice."

"I shall make the sacrifice," he said genially. "Also, I must select a suitable small pistol for you to carry at all times. And a dagger."

"A dagger?"

"They are more easily concealed than a sword and are silent and generally useful. Yes, you must have a dagger!"

She laughed softly. "Then I shall surely be a cloak-and-dagger person!"

"That is what our profession will be for the next several weeks or months."

"I hope we are back sooner than that."

The imposing brick building that was their destination lay in a block of government offices. The guard first scrutinized them carefully and then turned them over to an amiable young fellow in a brown twill coat and breeches. His only consent to fashion was his neat, powdered wig.

He greeted them with a smile. "So you are the two."

Kemble looked slightly impatient with the lad's languid manner and told him somewhat sharply, "We have an appointment with Sir Harry."

The young man showed more amusement on his rather plain, narrow face. "I'm well aware of that, Mr. Kemble," he replied. "Sir

Harry has few visitors, and rarely any as illustrious as yourself. I have long admired you on the stage."

"Thank you," Kemble said, somewhat mollified.

"May I ask an impertinent question?" the young man went on, seeming in no hurry to lead them from the anteroom to Sir Harry's office.

Kemble stared at him coolly. "You may ask me anything."

"Is that fat oaf Stephen Kemble, who always has a small part in your plays, any relation to you?"

Kemble glared. "He happens to be my brother!"

"Sorry. No offense meant."

"And none taken," the actor returned. "Despite the fact that he is my brother, I know him to be an oaf and a generally poor actor."

The young official looked pleased. "May I commend you on your frankness and honesty, sir!"

"And may I ask when we are to be ushered in for our appointment?"

"Law', I clear forgot about it! Sir Harry will be angry as blazes. Follow me."

He marched them down a broad hallway with a shining hardwood floor to a huge oaken door that bore a brass plate embossed with Sir Harry's name and nothing else. He knocked on the door and a rasping voice responded from within. The youth smiled at them, and opening the door, indicated they should enter.

Enid led the way, with Kemble a step behind her. Sir Harry was seated at his desk, looking rather irritable.

"I'm sorry we're late," she said, "but there were several obstructions along the way."

He rose and bowed. "The streets are more unpleasant all the time. Aside from the crowds on foot, there is a veritable forest of carriages, wagons, and the like."

"In addition," Kemble put in, "Lady Blair was the victim of a great conflagration which destroyed the studio where she was living. She lost everything."

Sir Harry melted into sympathy. "My dear Lady Blair, what an awful business! Do sit down, and you also, Kemble." He pulled chairs forward for them and they seated themselves.

"I shall be wearing the latest styles, since now I must shop for a new wardrobe," she said with an attempt at humor.

Sir Harry went back to sit at his desk. "I wish you some enjoyment of that, at least." He paused. "Well, what is your answer to be?"

Kemble cleared his throat. "I'm speaking for Lady Blair as well as for myself. We are ready to undertake the mission."

"Commendable!" The beetle-browed man rubbed his huge hands together, his small eyes shining with delight. "I shall today make you representatives of our sovereign."

"France is a country in a state of martial law, if you can call what that rabble offers as law," Enid said. "What are we to bring with us for identification?"

"To protect us from the French authorities," Kemble added.

"Ah, yes." Sir Harry nodded. "You need not worry about that. I shall have papers prepared at once. Yours will be false, of course, and Lady Blair's will be genuine. I must falsify certain details in your credentials as her supposed father."

"It sounds as if you do this often," Kemble remarked.

"Often enough," the immense Sir Harry chuckled. "I shall immediately set the wheels in motion for your journey to Paris. It is there you will attempt to contact Father Braun and the boy."

"Are they supposedly in Paris?" Enid asked.

"That was our last word. Of course, there is constant change. They may have moved. It will be your duty to ferret out that information for us."

"Whom are we to contact?" Kemble inquired.

"There will be agents directing you from the time you land in Calais," Sir Harry replied. "A coach will be waiting there to drive you to Paris."

"And in Paris?" Enid wanted to know.

"You will be turned over to another agent, who will put you in touch with Father Braun and the Dauphin."

"So we will be largely at the mercy of these underlings in your service," Enid pointed out.

Sir Harry showed his surprise. "But surely you realize that this is the standard procedure? We have these links already set up."

"Deception is the name of the game," Kemble said wryly. "Can you give us descriptions of Father Braun and Louis Charles?"

The master spy smiled. "I can do better than that. I can show you sketches of them. I ask you to study these drawings carefully and be sure to compare them with the actual people when you meet."

He opened a desk drawer and produced a large brown envelope. It was stuffed with a bundle of material from which he pulled out two ivory sheets of paper, each covered with a pen and ink drawing.

He passed one to Enid and said, "That is Father Braun. He will be wearing the clothing of an ordinary layman. Priests are forbidden their robes and other clerical attire in this new France."

She studied the line sketch and saw a jolly, stoutish man with crinkles at the corners of his eyes and a crop of hair that seemed to be gray. "Is his hair gray?" she asked.

"Prematurely so," Sir Harry told her. "He is not an old man."

"He is rather plump."

"Yes."

"How tall is he? That is important."

The big man was pleased with her question. "He is slightly less than six feet tall. He has blue eyes, a ruddy complexion, and a starlike scar on the back of his left hand."

"That should be enough to know," she said, memorizing all that Sir Harry had told her. She passed the sketch to Kemble, and he handed her the one he had been studying.

"You can see the lad is a true Hapsburg," Kemble pointed out. "He looks intelligent, despite his placid expression and his prominent nose, which is a replica of his father's."

Enid studied the drawing of the earnest young prince and felt a pang of sympathy for him. She asked Sir Harry, "Didn't you say Louis Charles is blond?"

"Yes. His hair is a dark gold shade," he replied. "He is about seven years old and slim of build, and has, or had, a pleasant disposition."

"I cannot imagine that knowing his father, mother, and sister are in prison and are likely to be hanged would improve his state of mind."

"I have no idea, of course." Sir Harry shifted in his chair. "We would have had the boy here by now if our agents had not been killed."

"And you really believe that having the future ruler of France here in our country will be of great diplomatic value?" Kemble wanted to know.

"Absolutely," Sir Harry declared.

"Suppose there is no future king?" Enid said. "What if the revolution changes the political structure of France for all time?"

"That can never be," the big man intoned sagely. "France, like most countries, has always had a monarchical system. It is clearly unthinkable that things would be different once this present trouble is settled. There can be no question that monarchy is the best form of government for all nations."

Kemble smiled grimly. "That sentiment would not go down well in Paris at this moment."

"I am in London, sir," Sir Harry responded with dignity. "And I will stick by my prediction."

"When do you want us to leave?" Enid asked him.

"A week from today," was his reply.

"I can manage that," Kemble said.

Sir Harry glanced at her. "What about you?"

"Yes. It is all right."

Sir Harry nodded. "I like your ability to make decisions. That is also a virtue."

"There is one more important thing I wish to ask you."

"We shall have at least another short meeting before you leave," the big man assured her.

"I would like to ask this now."

"What is it, then?"

"When will you tell me the location of the prison in which Count Armand Beaufaire is being held?"

Sir Harry blinked several times before replying. "For obvious reasons, I must withhold that information until you have completed your mission."

"Why?"

"I do not want your interest divided. It is urgent that you first put all your energies toward rescuing the Dauphin. After that I will give you the details about your friend. And, as I promised, I will do all I can to see that our network of agents effects his release."

Enid regarded him with resignation. "You drive a hard bargain," she said glumly.

"I have my duty," the diplomatic officer replied pompously. "First things must come first. The main order of the day is to get that boy safely to England."

"The count may be put to death in the meanwhile!"

"I think not. You may take my word for it that while he is presently imprisoned, his life is in no immediate danger."

Then Kemble spoke up. "There is also a point, Sir Harry, which I fear you have not considered thoroughly."

The big man fixed his shrewd eyes on the actor. "And that is?"

"Lady Blair has mentioned that she is known to Esmond. And so am I, for that matter, though I will have the advantage of a changed appearance."

"Esmond, 'tis true, is at the top of their spy system," Sir Harry acknowledged, "but he takes little active part in the daily goings-on in France. When he is here in London, it is different. Over there he is bound by desk work and seldom ventures into the field. That is why I have minimized the possibility of your meeting him."

"But if I do come face to face with him, then what?" Enid implored.

"You will be a British national traveling under the full protection of your government. Your papers will attest to that. You can tell him you are searching for your missing friend. He dare not touch you."

She smiled wanly, "That sounds all very well and good. But should I meet him, don't be surprised to hear that I've been eliminated in some strange and unexpected accident."

"Now I believe you are overtaxing your imagination, my dear."

"In any event," Kemble said, "we have made our decision and will take our chances."

The big man looked pleased. "I shall call on you at your flat the night before your departure. Then I shall give you your first instructions."

Enid and Kemble left the office of Sir Harry Standish shortly afterward. When they were on the street, she asked the actor, "Well what do you think of him?"

Kemble nodded. "I know you expect me to defend him. I won't. I'll simply say he is clever enough to deal with you and me, either separately or together."

"I'm irked by his refusal to tell me where Armand is."

"But you must respect his reason for doing so. He cannot afford to have our attention diverted. It is that simple."

19

Two days later they began to practice fencing. They were using the empty hall next to Drury Lane where Kemble sometimes held rehearsals. Enid darted back and forth, her keen blade a powerful, sure weapon. Their swords met and twisted, flashed and clanged. Kemble fought hard to match her, but it was useless. She was by far the better fencer.

At last he cried out, "Enough!" and tossed his sword to the floor.

Gasping for breath, she went up to him and asked, "Did I discourage you too much?"

"You defeat me so easily that there is no point in our going on," he panted, taking out a handkerchief to mop his brow.

"Then are you satisfied?"

"You're as good as ever. And if we find ourselves in a tight spot, you must somehow make sure you wield a blade."

She smiled. "I'll remember that. What about the pistol? You promised me one."

"I have it here." He reached into his pocket and drew out an extremely tiny pistol with a mother-of-pearl handle. "It is a beauty, so see that you take care of it."

She accepted the weapon and fingered it with awe. "Are you sure it's not a toy?"

"The man who gets a bullet in his hide from it won't think so," he assured her.

She balanced it and held it at the ready. "Remarkable."

"Crafted in Prussia," he said grudgingly. "Those people have a gift for such work."

"Thank you, John. You are a dear, good man!"

He clasped her to him in a tight embrace. "Not good enough to share your bed with you, I fear!"

"We made a promise! Let us keep it!" she entreated.

Kemble brushed his lips over hers. "I shall. I won't enjoy it, but I shall keep it." Then he released her reluctantly.

• • •

On the night before they were to leave, they had an elaborate meal at Kemble's flat. The only thing marring the eating and drinking was the mood that Susie and Jenny had fallen into. Neither young woman was in a good frame of mind.

Kemble leaned over to Jenny as they sat side by side at the table, and he kissed her. "Come! Don't look so mournful! It's not my funeral I'm going to!"

Jenny seemed about to burst into tears. "Susie says it well could be!"

Kemble glanced over at Susie. "Now, I ask you, what kind of remark is that to make?"

Susie looked down at her plate. "I cannot pretend to be happy if I'm not."

"Think of the good possibilities in store," Enid urged. "We may even meet Gustav and work with him!"

"Gustav is like the two of you, drawn to the bright glow of adventure as a moth is drawn toward a flame—with probably the same result."

"You were never the melancholy one, Susie," Kemble chided her. "That was my title."

At that moment the bell over the front door jangled wildly, and Kemble jumped up from the table. "That will be Sir Harry with our final instructions. Susie and Jenny, go into the bedroom and close the door and be silent. Our visitor will want to see us alone."

"So much for him!" Susie said indignantly as she and Jenny did as they were told.

Kemble opened the door to admit Sir Harry, carrying an umbrella in his hand. The huge man nodded, came into the room, and seeing the table heaped with food and wine, showed a look of mirth on his face.

"A feast has been in progress!" he cried, beaming at Kemble from under his heavy brows. "By this time tomorrow you will be in France and on your way to Paris."

"When are we to leave?" Enid asked.

Sir Harry went over to the table and picked up one of the bottles of red wine. After filling a goblet to the brim, he quaffed half the ruby liquid in a great gulp. Then he smiled and answered her question. "Tomorrow at dawn. A carriage will be here to pick you up and take you to the *Lady Miller* at the docks."

"Will you have some food?" Kemble offered.

"No," he replied. "The wine will do nicely." Then he gave the actor a sharp glance. "You have done nothing about your appearance!"

"I shall work on it tonight," Kemble promised. "I have been leaving it until the last moment. The delightful girl who at the present holds my heart has begged me to put off donning my disguise."

Sir Harry filled the wine glass again and downed another healthy swig. He said, "I trust she is aware that this is serious business. That your neck might depend on the quality of your disguise."

"Don't worry, I shall take care of it," the actor assured him.

Sir Harry turned to Enid. "And you, my lady, are you well versed in your role?"

"I am going to France in search of Lucinda, the Duchess d'Orsay," she said. "Word has been sent to me that she is alive and in hiding."

"That is correct." Sir Harry nodded approvingly. "Just stick to that!"

"What is our first move when we land in Calais?" Kemble inquired.

"A carriage will be waiting there, driven by a trusted French agent. You will go with him and do everything he says."

"What will he look like?" Enid asked.

Sir Harry glared at his nearly empty goblet of wine. "I cannot tell you that. He will be there and will make himself known to you. As will the French authorities. You must be calm when they question you."

"Will they be difficult to manage?" Kemble wondered.

"No," Sir Harry replied. "In a small town like Calais they have little authority and less intelligence. You two will easily outsmart them." He groped under his voluminous cloak and produced two small, leather-bound booklets. "These contain your papers."

"How do we identify ourselves to our fellow agents?" Kemble prodded.

"Show them the same papers I have given you for the authorities. Among them is a page which reveals a message under heat. But always be sure the booklets are returned to you."

Enid studied hers. "It would seem we now have everything."

Sir Harry looked grimly amused. "Not yet," he said. And again he fumbled beneath his cloak and produced two very small blue envelopes, only about three inches square, and filled with some kind of powder. He gave one to each of them.

"Keep these packets with you at all times," he cautioned. "You, Kemble, might hide yours in the back of your gold pocket watch, and you, Lady Blair, could perhaps place yours in a locket which you will wear continually around your neck."

"What is the purpose of this powder?" she asked.

"Transportation," Sir Harry told her with an odd gleam in his eyes.

"I do not follow you."

He chuckled. "Simple! Swallow the powder as it is, or in a little water, and it will transport you to another world. It is a deadly poison."

"Why do we need it?" Kemble had suddenly turned pale.

"In the event of capture and torture, you may find taking it preferable to giving away state secrets. As I said, keep it handy just in case."

Enid gasped. "Are you telling us to commit suicide in the event that we are captured?"

"It is a way of escape with honor," Sir Harry replied with his usual dignity. "I so equip all my agents, but certainly in the hope that the powder may never have to be used."

"I surely hope not," Kemble said with a shudder, grimly studying the square blue envelope.

"My prayers for your victory," Sir Harry intoned piously. "May you return with the Dauphin!"

"We'll certainly make a good try at it," Kemble promised.

At the door the big man turned and addressed Enid soberly. "And good luck to you, Lady Blair. I trust your unusual beauty will be granted an unusual amount of good luck."

"Thank you, Sir Harry," she said.

Then Kemble saw him out. When the two men had gone, Susie and Jenny emerged from the adjoining room.

"So that is the general of the cloak-and-dagger army!" Susie remarked. "He is a strange fellow indeed!"

Enid smiled. "I grant you that."

"We could not make out clearly everything that was said," Jenny complained.

"It's just as well," Enid told her. And she meant it. This last interview with Sir Harry had been a sobering one. Not only had it seemed to bear out her contention that he regarded his agents as expendable pawns, but he had actually provided them with a poison that he urged them to take so that they wouldn't reveal any secrets under torture. Enid wondered whether she had been in her right mind when she had agreed to undertake this mission. After all, she had accepted it only because she hoped it would lead her to Armand. Well, she thought to herself, I must keep my wits about me at all costs.

Kemble returned, and they spent the rest of the evening transforming him into an aristocratic older gentleman. First Jenny prepared a rinse for his hair that changed its chestnut color to one of silver. Then he painted a long-lasting stain on his face that gave him a more weathered, aged appearance. His eyebrows were also bleached gray, and as a final touch he added some purplish tints to his cheeks and etched light lines about his eyes and mouth to indicate age.

At last he turned from his mirror to ask them, "Am I not impressive?"

"You look like an old man! I hate it!" Jenny cried.

The actor laughed. "That is precisely what I'm supposed to be. And I shall continue the role until we return to England."

"I'm thankful I can be myself," Enid said.

"You might regret it if we come upon Louis Esmond," he worried. "I doubt that he'd recognize me, but you are a dead giveaway. Why don't you at least change the color of your hair?"

"Would it make that much of a difference?" she asked doubtfully.

Kemble, looking like an elderly stranger, came close and examined her. "I shall have Jenny make you up a good dye of coal-black tint. A black that glistens. We shall do your hair and eyebrows. And I shall change the contours of your brows to give them an Oriental appearance. That will help to alter your entire face."

Enid was skeptical of his suggestions, but felt they might be better than if she did nothing at all to disguise herself. So with much laughter, which helped allay the tensions of the night, she allowed

Jenny and Susie to assist her in dying her long blonde tresses. She sat before the blazing coal fire until her hair was dry. Then Kemble artfully reconstructed her eyebrows to his satisfaction. And when she looked at herself in the mirror, she was astonished.

"Well, what do you think?" Kemble asked.

"At a glance I would not know it was I," she admitted.

"That is exactly what I wanted," he said. "You look quite different."

Jenny studied her. "I would say you are not as striking as when you were a blonde, but you look more intriguing."

Susie grimaced. "She looks like a Spanish or French type."

"Operation successful," Kemble proclaimed. "Now it is time for bed. We must rise before dawn."

Susie and Enid went back into the front room, which they had used as their sleeping quarters ever since the night of the fire. Susie would remain there until Kemble returned, and happily, both she and Jenny had been given parts in the forthcoming drama over which Mrs. Siddons would preside.

Susie expressed her concerns about the undertaking and finaly fell asleep. Enid lay there wide awake, thinking of Armand and wishing she had more hope of being able to aid him. But Sir Harry was a harsh master, and she knew that in order to achieve her goal, the search for Louis Charles had to be put ahead of everything else.

20

Enid and Kemble stood by the railing of the *Lady Miller* and gazed out glumly at the rough waves. The English Channel had been in a malicious mood all day, first thick with fog and then foaming with fierce insistence. They had awakened in the gray dawn to snatch a bite of food and bid hasty goodbyes. Then they had been picked up by a carriage and taken to the docks. Now, an eternity later, they were supposedly drawing near the coast of France and the docks of Calais.

There were more than two dozen people on board. Some included French representatives of the new revolution and their wives, returning from a shopping visit in England. Others were tight-faced English merchants who were still trying to maintain ties with a market that had gone quite mad.

One of these latter was a pompous, middle-aged banker named Edward Burley, a man who could have stepped out of a drawing of John Bull. Squat, overweight, and with a broad, florid face under his three-cornered hat, he was the most talkative person on the ship. From the start he had bothered Kemble and Enid, and now he approached them once again.

Kemble groaned. "Here he comes. I thought we had rid ourselves of him for the rest of the voyage."

"Be glad this is not an Atlantic crossing," she sighed. "I do not think we could bear it."

"There's always the powder in the blue packet," Kemble reminded her with a laugh.

"Please!" she begged him. "That is not funny!"

"Good afternoon, friends!" The bumptious banker greeted them with hearty cheer.

"To be properly truthful, sir," Kemble said, "it is a most unpleasant afternoon and a damnable voyage!"

The banker looked slightly taken aback for a moment, and then he laughed and poked the unhappy Kemble in the ribs. "By George, you are right! Hit the nail exactly on the head! What do you say to that, miss? Your father is a card, is he not?"

Enid played demure. "I fear he is given to rather strong statements."

"Hearts of oak and opinions of the same quality! That's we English! I think Lord Henson—that is the proper name, isn't it?"

"That is my name," Kemble allowed, in his role as her father.

"I think that is what Lord Henson means. Whatever you might say, we English have character. And character is what makes a nation!" He glanced down the deck in disgust at the group of French people who had gathered in a group. "The Frenchies never had it. Frogs, I call them! And now these 'frogs' have overturned all law and order in their country."

"It is truly that bad?" Enid asked, pretending innocence.

"Worse!" Edward Burley boomed. "I have a number of clients with large deposits in Paris banks, and they haven't been able to get out a single sou. That is why I'm making this trip. A day or two in Paris, and I hope to get some satisfaction. My clients simply can't afford to have the mob over here take their investments!" He had become so worked up on the subject that he was perspiring, and now he mopped his brow.

"My father never believed in placing any money in France," Enid remarked.

Kemble took his cue from her, saying stuffily, "I prefer to keep my assets within the shadow of the Bank of England."

"Sound thinking!" the banker exclaimed emphatically. "I only wish my rather stupid clients had been smart enough to follow that line."

"I expect they hoped to make their fortunes in France," Enid suggested.

"And now they'll likely lose everything," Burley worried. "If you have no financial interests to protect, may I inquire why you are visiting this country which, it seems, the Almighty has long ago abandoned?"

Enid raised her newly shaped eyebrows. "Didn't Father tell you?"

"No," the banker said.

Kemble pretended indignation. "My dear, must you tell everyone? Every stranger whom we meet?"

"But I am not a stranger," Burley protested. "I am a fellow Englishman."

"Of course you are," Enid agreed, enjoying the whole charade. She was beginning to understand the attraction that acting out parts held for many performers. She continued with, "I shall tell you all. We are here in search of a friend of mine, an English girl who was married to a French noble."

"That could be unpleasant for her," the Englishman observed.

"Most unpleasant, indeed. Her husband was murdered by the mob that stormed Versailles, but we believe she escaped and is in hiding. We are making this trip in the hope of finding her."

"I would say your chances are slim, my lady," the banker said, "but I surely wish you luck! English girls should be returned to England and not left abandoned in this wretched land on which we will soon set foot."

Their conversation was interrupted by the arrival of one of the ship's officers, who informed them that land was in sight. As the *Lady Miller* gradually drew nearer to the coastline, green hills and small white houses became visible. The docks were old and gray, but there was a goodly array of people and vehicles waiting there.

An old woman near Enid and Kemble began to weep when she saw the hills of her native land and broke into a babble of French.

Enid experienced a wave of misgivings as the ship approached the docks. Very soon they would be faced with their first hurdle.

At her side Kemble whispered, "Calais! It calls for courage!"

The *Lady Miller* slipped gracefully into her berth, and soon she was securely tied and her cargo removed. The captain had warned all passengers to await the arrival of the authorities. The French laws of entry insisted that everyone had to be interviewed before disembarking.

Edward Burley pointed out a villainous-looking trio of men boarding the vessel. Nervously he muttered, "Here they come!"

Kemble nodded. He and Enid stood slightly apart from the others as the threesome made the rounds of the deck. Before many minutes had gone by, an unfortunate young man was carted off by two of the police officers, despite his protestations of innocence.

Their first moment of trial was upon them. The leader of the trio presented himself with a curt nod. "I am the captain of police in Calais. What is your purpose in visiting *la belle* France?"

Enid stood there mutely, as did Kemble. She found it impossible to answer, for she was certain the officer questioning them was one of the men she had seen with Louis Esmond on the night of the warehouse fire. But how is that possible? she asked herself. Gustav and I thought we had killed the four men with Esmond, or, if not, that they had surely died in the fire. Her mind spun with confusing thoughts, but she forced herself to focus on the present situation.

It was Kemble who broke the silence. "Our papers are in order. We are here on a mission of mercy."

The man was staring at Enid all the while. At last he turned to the actor and grunted, "Let me see the documents."

Kemble produced them and passed them over. The Frenchman scanned them in a way that caused Enid to wonder whether he could read. He studied them a second time, flipping over the sheets with his dirty fingers. She thought he might be merely putting on a show. If he suspected who she was, he could easily take her and Kemble into custody, proper papers or not.

The self-dubbed captain of police scowled at the documents and returned them to Kemble. "Are you her father?"

"That is correct," the actor replied with dignity. "I am accompanying her to Paris, where we plan to seek out an English girl, a friend of my daughter's, who has been caught up in the revolution."

"We can do without any English," the man said harshly. "You're welcome to take one of them back. But you'll have a hard time getting transportation to Paris. The only stage has left. There will be none for several days."

"Is there an inn where we might wait?" Enid asked.

"Two or three," the officer told her, "but none of them's the sort a lady like you would look for."

"I can manage," she said firmly.

"Are we free to go ashore?" Kemble inquired politely.

The captain of police gave Enid another close appraisal. He turned to Kemble and nodded. "You can leave the ship. But remember, France is under martial law. We want no tricks here, no trying to help the nobility."

"We are interested only in finding my friend and taking her back home," Enid said. "There will be no trouble proving she is English."

The rough-looking man was unimpressed. "As I said, you won't like the inns here."

"Is there any alternative?" Kemble asked. "Could we find a private conveyance to take us to Paris? We had hoped one might be here to meet us."

"None has arrived." The captain of police then leaned close to Kemble and murmured, "For a suitable sum, I could arrange for a carriage to be at your disposal. But it requires an inconvenience on your part."

Kemble promptly read the man's message. He produced a small pouch from beneath his cloak and took out a five-pound note. "Would that pay you for your trouble?" he asked.

The face of the police officer brightened, and he snatched the money from Kemble's hand and stuffed it into his pocket. "No trouble, Monsieur Henson. The carriage will be waiting for you and your daughter whenever you go ashore. The driver will ask only a modest fee."

"We still have some slight packing to do, which will take us a half hour or so to complete."

"When you are ready, my men will carry your luggage from the ship to the carriage," the captain of police promised. Then he moved on to question Edward Burley.

Enid and Kemble made their way below to their cabins. The actor followed her into hers and asked, "What do you think?"

"I was terrified that he recognized me," Enid said. "He is the image of one of the men who was with Esmond in London."

Kemble frowned. "It could be the same man, I suppose. Esmond might have recruited him here before crossing the Channel."

"But if he is the same man, he couldn't have been completely sure about me. There is quite a change in my appearance, and he wouldn't have known my name anyway."

"True," Kemble agreed. "And it is unlikely he would have offered us transportation if he guessed you were a Royalist sympathizer."

"He took your bribe readily enough, but he still might be baiting a trap for us."

"You mean we might step into the carriage and find ourselves being driven straight to a dungeon in the Bastille?"

"Such things are happening all the time, aren't they?"

Kemble rubbed his chin as he considered this. "Why didn't the carriage Sir Harry promised us arrive? The driver was to be our contact here."

"That does leave us at sixes and sevens," she mused.

"Something may have happened to him. The vehicle could have broken down. It is at least a two-day trip to Paris, perhaps more if the roads aren't in good condition."

"What shall we do?"

"We can't remain on board ship."

"So we'd best take that man's offer of the carriage."

"I'm afraid we'll have to risk it," Kemble concluded. "If our contact arrives later, he'll hear that we've moved on and follow us."

"And if he doesn't?"

"We shall have to try to locate Father Braun on our own. There must be somebody in Paris who knows of him."

"It would seem we are having problems before we even begin," she sighed. "I wonder if Sir Harry is to be trusted."

Kemble gave her a grim look. "I would say we'll know soon enough. I'll go and finish my packing now."

When they were both packed and ready to disembark, the captain of police kept his word and had his men transfer them from the ship to the waiting carriage. Enid could scarcely believe her eyes. If the captain of police was a rogue, the driver of the coach seemed a veritable ogre. He walked with a loping gait, as if he had a hip out of joint, his eyes were shifty and mocking, and he was as dirty and shabby as his conveyance. He shouted instructions for the loading of the luggage, then smiled through his scraggly black beard and bowed deeply, removing the red cloth cap that had been perched precariously atop his matted black hair.

"Pierre Giraud, at your service, dear people. I shall transport you to Paris so delightfully, you'll not even know the roads are in fiendish shape." He grinned as he finished speaking, revealing yellowed, widely spaced teeth.

"Has no other carriage appeared on the docks?" Kemble asked, holding back from entering this one and looking around.

"As you can see, good sir, there are naught but country bumpkins and their carts to pick up cargo. You are lucky people that the captain found me for you!"

Enid turned to Kemble. "We have to make a decision. What now?"

The actor let out a deep sigh. "I suppose we must place ourselves in his hands, dirty and rough as they are!"

She allowed the shifty-eyed driver to help her into the coach. As her skirt lifted, displaying her well-shaped ankle and calf, the man giggled in a most ungentlemanly fashion.

Kemble followed her inside and slumped heavily beside her. In a low voice he said, "If things look grim, remember we are doing this for our sovereign!"

"Who is going mad," she whispered. "And Sir Harry himself likely isn't too far removed from madness!"

The vehicle started forward with a jolt and rumbled over the planks of the docks and onto the rocky road. The coach seemed to have little or no springs. Enid and Kemble tried not to sway against each other as the driver wildly urged the horses on. She finally agreed to Kemble's putting his arm around her, so that they jounced about in unison rather than one making a target for the other.

Soon they left all signs of the town behind them and entered the open countryside. The road became no better, but the driver slowed the vehicle from time to time, which made the ride somewhat easier.

"Do you think we shall survive two days of this?" Enid asked.

"I'm sore already," Kemble groaned. "And we've only gone a short way!"

"The driver is clearly a lunatic and probably a rogue as well!"

"Judging from his friend the captain of police, and from his appearance and behavior, I'd say he is also one of the revolutionists!"

Enid braced herself against a bad jolt, then said, "So we may still end up in a prison somewhere."

"We're in the lap of the gods," Kemble observed philosophically.

"A rougher lap I've never known!" she gasped, holding on to him as the carriage dipped and lurched this way and that.

The torture went on for several hours, until they arrived in the courtyard of a small country inn. When the driver opened the door for them to step down, their way was blocked by a huge gray goose that let out a loud cry and jumped in beside them.

The unkempt Giraud threw back his head and guffawed with laughter. "I declare, 'tis an aristocrat wanting to be delivered to the guillotine!" He reached in and grabbed the agitated goose by the neck. "Come on, my little aristocrat!" Then he dragged out the squawking bird and tossed it to the ground.

Kemble alighted and then helped Enid from the carriage. "Where are we?" he asked the driver.

"Many miles from Calais, of course. You have noticed I made excellent time!"

"We are nearly shaken to bits," Enid snapped.

His bearded face showed amusement. "It is the road, my good madam! The new government has not yet had time to repair the roads, and the nobles only worried about their own estate roads when they were in power."

"We do not need political lectures," Kemble told him curtly. "Why are we stopping here?"

"To have food and drink, why else? When we have refreshed ourselves, I shall drive you to another carefully chosen place to stay the night."

Kemble eyed the rundown inn with disgust. "Is this the best you can do?"

"A plain place, but excellent victuals, monsieur," Giraud said. "The owner is a cousin of the captain of police, whom you met on the ship in Calais."

"And are you any relation, too?" Enid asked him.

"I am his full brother," the driver replied proudly. "Why else would he have selected me for your excellencies?"

"I can't imagine," Kemble said bluntly. "Let us have some food and carry on."

They were given a chance to freshen up in two private attic chambers, and then they descended to the dark dining room. Giraud was already there, digging his teeth into a chunky meat bone. He gave them a grin of welcome as they entered.

"The customer pays for the driver," he said. "It is the law. But I'm only gnawing at this ancient soup bone. It has a good deal of meat still on it, and the landlord offers it as his cheapest fare. You have made no mistake in hiring me!" He resumed crunching on the bone like a hungry dog.

The landlord was an old man whose wife closely resembled him. They came bowing in to Enid and Kemble, uttering flowery phrases about the great honor it was to serve them.

Kemble and Enid seated themselves at the other plank table. The actor told her, "You are more proficient in the language than I, so order what you think best."

After she had managed to interrupt the elderly couple in their paeans of praise, she learned that they could provide a hearty vegetable soup and some roast duckling. She ordered both.

Giraud stood up, wiped his greasy mouth with his hand, and smiled at them in a malevolent fashion. "I go now to tend to the horses. I'm also a kind man with animals." He chuckled slyly and limped out.

Kemble had never felt less in control of a situation. "What kind of picaroon have we given ourselves over to?" he asked in despair.

"It is Sir Harry whom I would like to have here at this moment," Enid said bitterly. "Where is the fine carriage and special agent he promised?"

"He is probably feasting on fine roast beef in Whitehall, while we take what is offered in this dreary place!" the actor fumed.

"Courage, John. We shall soon reach Paris and be free of this scrounger."

"I wonder."

The landlord approached unsteadily with two bowls of hot soup, and Enid cried, "The soup smells excellent! Who knows? This modest inn may be famed for its menu!"

Kemble bridled at this. "I, my dear Enid, am a regular patron of Simpson's on the Strand—and therefore I know good food!"

But when they had finished the repast and washed it down with large glasses of red wine, he was forced to admit the food had been excellent. They paid the old couple, who scraped and bowed and were still crying out their pleasure at having served them when the carriage jolted ahead once more.

After a half hour Kemble concluded, "There mustn't be a proper road in all of France, or else this devil is purposely selecting the worst ones!"

This ride was a repetition of the dreadful earlier one, though much shorter. Enid was grateful when they once again turned into the entrance of a small inn.

"Too dangerous to drive in darkness, dear friends," Giraud told them. "This is the Gold Lamb. It will make an agreeable stop for the night, and tomorrow we shall continue to Paris!"

Kemble helped Enid alight, and then he stepped into an enormous puddle that had not yet dried. It meant ruin for his black, silver-buckled shoes. He cursed under his breath and glanced toward the lamplit doorway.

"He calls it the Gold Lamb, and I expect that means we shall be fleeced!"

"Remember, John, it was you who convinced me we should embark on this mission!"

"You should have refused," he lamented.

After a brief conversation with the proprietor, they were given rooms with comfortable-looking feather beds and blazing hearths.

Kemble shed his cloak and then joined Enid in her room to sit before the fire for a few minutes. Both were weary from the day's events; the glow of the flames mesmerized them into a companionable silence. Then Enid broke the spell.

"If we do not find Father Braun in Paris, we shall have made this trip in vain," she remarked. "Perhaps we could at least search for Armand then."

Kemble frowned. "We have no idea of where he may be held prisoner. Sir Harry wouldn't tell us. If only we could by some stroke of fortune come upon Gustav!"

"That is most unlikely, since he is among the wanted men operating the underground escape route. He is bound to keep in the shadows."

"A fine state his Majesty's secret service must be in, if this is any example," the actor muttered.

There was a gentle knock on the door. Because it was so unexpected, Enid gave a start and glanced fearfully at Kemble. Looking old and weary in his makeup, he also showed fear. The thought in both their minds was that this very well could be the moment of truth. When she opened the door, it would be to officials who would march them off to prison.

Enid finally found her voice and asked, "Who is it?"

"It's me, madam, with some extra logs for the fire," came the voice of their driver.

"Can't you leave them out there?"

"No, madam. It would be better if I bring them in."

Enid gave Kemble a questioning look, and he nodded. She went to open the door, half expecting to see the police, but standing on the threshold was only the ever-present Pierre. He was holding an armload of wood, as he had said.

"Put them by the hearth, if you will," she directed.

He limped inside and placed the logs accordingly. He nodded to Kemble in a friendly manner and then limped back to the door. Instead of leaving the chamber, he closed the door and stood with his back to it.

Enid felt a moment of panic. Kemble looked outraged and jumped to his feet.

The roguish driver smiled and removed his red cap. Then he addressed them in a voice that was both melodious and cultured. "Let me now introduce myself. I am Count Pierre Giraud, formerly of Nantes."

"Confound you!" Kemble cried in astonishment. "You are not what you seem!"

Giraud smiled again. "Like you, Mr. Kemble of London's Drury Lane, I am dutifully playing a role."

"I can't believe it!" Enid gasped. "You're a gentleman!"

The count bowed. "At least a remembrance of one. You must pardon my filthy state and my unfortunate beard. I have had to assume this identity or risk being put to death by the revolutionists. In truth, I find the alternative rather appealing. Occasionally I meet some interesting guests from England, such as yourself, Lady Blair, and Mr. Kemble."

"You know all about us, then!" the actor exclaimed. "What is your game, sir? Do you plan to blackmail us?"

The count laughed softly. "Do you still not understand, Mr. Kemble? The captain of police was your contact. And I am the second link in the chain which will see you safely installed in Paris."

"Good Lord!" Kemble's face drained of color. "And I think of myself as an actor! You played your part to perfection!"

"We were alternately disgusted with and terrified of you," Enid confessed.

Giraud grinned. "My own continual terror never allows me to drop my assumed identity for a moment. One false move and I'm finished. That is why I waited so long to reveal myself to you."

"We are greatly relieved," Enid said with a rueful smile.

"Indeed we are," Kemble agreed in a more normal tone of voice. "We were ready to believe that Sir Harry had sent us on a mad, pointless chase!"

"You are speaking of a great man," the count said with respect, "but one who is ruthless and devious when he has to be. He has a fine mind, and he has saved many noble heads from the block."

"Do you know Gustav Brideau?" she asked.

He nodded. "Also of the underground. He is in Lyons now on a delicate mission."

"And Armand Beaufaire," she continued hopefully. "What can you tell us of him?"

"He is a man of supreme integrity. He was captured some months ago by the enemy."

"We heard he was in prison. Do you know where he is?"

"Not at the moment. He had been confined outside Calais, but I understand he's been moved to Paris."

She felt her heart skip a beat. "That could be most dangerous for him, could it not?"

"There is no point in deceiving you," Giraud replied. "He could even have been executed by now. If he is still alive, he is surely in constant danger."

"Why doesn't Sir Harry do something to save him?" she cried.

"Because there are more urgent matters to attend to," Pierre answered simply.

"You mean the Dauphin?" Kemble asked.

"You two were sent here to pick him up and take him back to England. You know that as well as I do."

Enid nodded. "Of course. How is the boy? Is he still in good hands?"

"As far as we know. Things change from day to day, but supposedly he is hidden in a monastery somewhere in Paris.

Father Braun is looking out for him. You will receive the lad from the good father."

"Why couldn't you do this?" Kemble wanted to know. "Why did Sir Harry have to recruit us for this mission?"

"Because the Dauphin is too important to be moved to England through the regular channels. You will escort him there as the son of your missing English friend, and by doing it quite openly, you won't be questioned."

"I did not realize that was the plan," Enid said.

"It is all arranged. Witnesses will swear to the lad's being hers and that she died in the attack on Versailles. You have been appointed his guardian. Since he is half English and a mere boy, the authorities will not be interested in your taking him."

"But what if they find out he is Louis Charles, escaped from prison?" Kemble demanded. "What will happen to us should the truth be discovered?"

The count shrugged. "Either you'll be torn to bits by the mob, along with the prince, or you'll be captured and tortured. The same is true for all of us. It is a dangerous profession that we practice."

"Will we reach Paris by tomorrow night?" Enid asked. "I do not wish to lose any time. I want to find the Dauphin and then try to do something for Count Beaufaire."

Giraud searched her face. "Did Sir Harry give you permission to take on anything of that nature?"

"Only after we locate the prince," Kemble replied.

"Then I wouldn't consider that possibility until then," the count advised.

"I see," Enid murmured, wondering if her beloved Armand would be executed before she could do anything to facilitate his release.

"I will go now," their driver said. "We leave at dawn, and it will be another hard day's ride."

"Will you continue to play your role?" Kemble asked.

"But of course. And you must do the same. Treat me with the contempt you have shown thus far. It could mean all our necks if we don't abide by the rules. Au revoir until the morning, then." The count flashed the loose grin of his driver's disguise and departed.

Enid turned to Kemble and asked, "Don't you agree that we sorely underestimated Sir Harry?"

"Without question," he told her with a wry smile. "And now, my dearest Enid, I shall bid you good night."

Enid was then left alone to brood before the dying embers. Will I ever see Armand again? she asked herself. Will we ever know the happiness we shared—oh, so long ago!—and be as one?

The silence of the chamber was her only response.

21

They reached Paris the next evening. Enid was amazed to discover that it seemed less impressive to her now than London. It was still a relatively medieval city, with narrow, winding, muddy streets, small wooden houses, and a few splendid buildings, such as the Ecole Militaire. Apart from its lack of charm and refinement, it bore the ravages of the current upheaval and was severely overcrowded.

The trip had been slightly easier that day, perhaps because Enid and Kemble were more relaxed. They had made their contact and all was going well. Giraud took them through a series of mean streets before halting in front of a ramshackle wooden building not far from the Seine.

He opened the carriage door and said, "This is the place, good people! This is where you asked that I bring you!"

Since they hadn't asked to be taken to any particular address, Enid assumed that this was where Sir Harry intended them to stay and where they would meet their new contact.

Kemble alighted first and then eased her down onto the mud-splashed cobblestones. "Paris is not so clean a city as London," he remarked.

"I fear you are a trifle prejudiced," she replied.

Giraud lifted their luggage off the rack atop the coach and laboriously carried the cases into the house. Then a blowzy-looking woman wearing a dust cap and a shapeless coverall came out with a boy of about five or six. The child held on to her hand with a strange look in his eyes, and Enid, feeling a pang of sympathy, decided that he was probably retarded.

The woman spoke in a harsh voice. "If my useless husband wasn't running with the mob, I wouldn't be taking in lodgers. Not English folk, anyway!"

"We are delighted to avail ourselves of your hospitality, madam," Kemble told her graciously.

The coarse-faced woman sniffed at him. "There's little of that left in this country, I can tell you! And none at all for the English! If I weren't forced to take you in, I don't know where you'd go!"

"I'm sure we are grateful," Enid said as they entered the hallway. "But won't you show us to our rooms? My father and I are most weary from our long journey."

"Most weary, indeed!" the woman retorted mockingly. "Well, you had best be prepared for plain beds and plain food. I have only one girl to help me, and I have never enjoyed cooking. Any fancy food you require will be extra!"

With that the child began to cry, and she gave him a slap and sent him running toward the back of the house. Then she took them up to their rooms. The only good thing about them, it seemed, was that they were clean and adjoining. But when Enid tested her bed, she knew it would be like sleeping on a board.

The woman stood before her lodgers with arms akimbo. "It's no use your sticking your nose up. This is the best you'll get in Paris these days. All the good places are serving as headquarters for the glorious republicans." She rolled her eyes heavenward.

"We shall manage," Enid told her. "What about food?"

"There is no proper dining room. I'll send up a tray with your evening meal. And at breakfast I'll do the same."

"That will do splendidly, thank you," Kemble said. "We are very hungry. What are you serving?"

"Calves' brains," the woman replied. "And hard enough to come by!"

Kemble looked as if he might choke. "Is that the only choice?"

"I told you this isn't a regular hotel!" the landlady snapped. "You can take what I offer or leave it! It's all the same to me!" And back downstairs she went.

"What do you think?" Kemble asked Enid.

"We seem to have jumped from frying pan to fire," she sighed, "though this woman could be another agent."

"Never," he declared angrily. "We're simply stuck with an uncouth landlady, thanks to Sir Harry."

"If all goes well, we ought to make contact soon with Father Braun. Then he might find us another place to stay."

They began to unpack, feeling sorry for themselves all the while. A scrawny girl-of-all-work came upstairs shortly thereafter with a tray in her hands. She set it on a table in Enid's room and vanished. A few minutes later Kemble appeared through the adjoining doorway and sat down with Enid.

After she had sampled the food, she said, "It is really very good."

The actor grunted and began to attack his plate. To his surprise, he liked the dish better than he had expected to. "Just so long as you don't dwell on what it is," he told her.

When they finished dinner, they remained in Enid's room, waiting to see what would transpire next. Nearly a half hour had passed before the servant girl presented herself, curtsied, and said, "The owner would like to see you now." She jerked her head. "Down there."

Kemble gave the lass an impatient glance as she flounced out. "What can that woman want from us?" he asked Enid.

"She may have decided not to take English people after all. Who knows what she's up to?"

The actor rose, grumbling. "Giraud vanished while we were standing in the hallway. He was there beside me, and when I turned around, he was nowhere."

"I have an idea he didn't wish to answer more of our questions."

"We still have a few answers coming to us, and I intend to get them."

They left the chamber and made their way down the dark, rickety stairs.

Enid was ahead of him, so she went through the doorway of the parlor first but saw no one there. Only after a few moments did she notice smoke rising from behind a folding screen in a corner of the room. She knew it wasn't a fire, but someone smoking.

"What now?" Kemble muttered.

She nodded toward the screen.

He scowled. "Are you behind there, woman? What do you want with us?"

By way of an answer, the screen was suddenly folded and put aside. The sight that greeted Enid and Kemble made them both gasp. The five-year-old was smoking a clay pipe and staring at them with disgust!

In a squeaky voice he asked, "Didn't you ever see someone smoke a pipe before?"

A man was standing quietly by the smoker's side. "They aren't ones for surprises, Ramon," he said.

"Made idiots of again!" Kemble cried. "You, sir, are the landlady whom we first talked to when we arrived! And this creature smoking a pipe is not your stupid child but a midget!"

"How did you guess, Englishman?" The midget gave a sour laugh.

"Your disguises are incredibly good!" Enid exclaimed. "I would never have seen through them!"

The man came forward good-naturedly. "I am Renaud. My feminine alter ego and a five-year-old child can venture into many places where Ramon and I would otherwise attract attention."

Ramon moved toward them, pipe in hand. "I'll have you know I'm no ordinary midget. Before the revolution I was one of King Louis's secret agents."

"Then you must know Louis Esmond," Enid said.

"Esmond!" The midget uttered the name with contempt. "He is scum! Pure scum!"

Renaud explained. "Esmond had never been a secret agent until the revolutionists took over. Before that he was a soldier, an actor, and an ordinary policeman."

"I encountered him in London," Enid told them.

"Beware of the fellow!" Ramon warned her. "He is all-powerful here. A word from him, and your head won't have any need for a neck!"

"This house is shabby, but it provides an ideally safe place for our headquarters," Renaud said. "And I trust you didn't find my cooking too bad, did you?"

Enid smiled. "It was very good indeed."

"What next?" Kemble wanted to know.

Ramon gave out another of his high-pitched laughs. "The old man is champing at the bit for action!"

Kemble glared down at him. "I'm not as old as you think. You're not the only one capable of devising disguises!"

"No quarreling, gentlemen," Renaud urged softly. "We are all in this together. One large, happy family."

"What about the Dauphin?" Enid asked him.

"It is my hope that you will return here later tonight with the lad in your possession. And that by tomorrow you'll be traveling back to Calais with our mutual friend, Pierre."

"I'm not sure I'm equal to that trip again," Kemble grunted with a shake of his head.

"It's the only safe way out of Paris," Renaud told him. "And now to business. I have an address here, only about ten minutes' walk away, where you should find Father Braun and the prince."

"Why can't the good priest bring him here on his own?" Enid wondered.

"He does not know about us," the midget said sourly. "We have to try to keep every stage of our plans carefully separate. That has proved to be our best method in the past."

Kemble studied the scrap of paper Renaud had given him. "Thirteen Rue St. Anne," he murmured. "What sort of place is it?"

"It was a monastery," the French agent replied. "It's nothing now. You know the Assembly had turned against the clergy, who must submit to civil authority. The fact is, it has turned against all rule and order, and as a result, France has been set on its head. I doubt if we shall ever see things righted again."

"I shall never live with it," Ramon said sadly. "When the time comes, I shall go to Spain."

"Are we to set out at once to meet this priest?" Kemble asked.

Renaud nodded. "He will be waiting for you at the monastery. If he should be out, it will not be for long, and you should wait for him."

"And will the boy be with him?" Enid asked.

"Either at his side or well hidden somewhere in the building. So much rests on the saving of that poor lad. He will one day be the hope of France."

Kemble sighed. "I think it might be well if the lady remained here in your safekeeping. I can manage the meeting with Father Braun on my own."

"I cannot approve," Renaud said. "Sir Harry's orders are that you both should go."

"And we do not disobey Sir Harry," Renaud added, lighting his pipe again.

• • •

They wore identical gray cloaks, the only difference being that Enid had pulled her hood over her head to hide her hair. Kemble had been in an extremely cautious frame of mind before they left the house. He had buckled on his sword, borrowed one from the man at headquarters, and made her secure it on a belt tied around her waist. She had thought the precautions overdone, since they were only to meet with a priest, but she had not argued with him.

Now they moved slowly through the narrow, unfamiliar streets. This section of Paris was clearly a working-class area, judging by the rundown houses and the occasional, poorly clothed night denizens they passed along the way. Kemble had insisted that she keep close to him, and he held her arm in a grip that threatened to crush it.

"Shouldn't we be there by now?" she asked in a low voice.

"The end of this street and to the right, if the midget's directions were correct. Never can be sure, since he's a malicious little beast!"

"I rather liked him."

"You have strange tastes in people," Kemble grumbled.

"I suppose that is why I shared your bed for a while," she flared.

"Those were happier days. How I wish I were on the boards of Drury Lane right now—anywhere but in this unholy city!"

"You sought adventure, don't you remember?"

He would have answered her but for his catching sight of some sort of torch parade moving up the street toward them. Perhaps twenty or thirty torches were borne aloft by as many people. As the crowd drew nearer, an angry roar could be heard rising into the dark night.

"Stand close to the wall!" Kemble said quickly.

Enid pressed herself against the wooden frame of an old house, and Kemble did the same, just in time. The torchbearers were joined by stragglers and curious onlookers. There was much cursing and loud shouting. Now Enid could see the two pitiful creatures whom the crowd was goading on. A man and a woman, with noble features now haggard, were shackled together, their once rich clothing a tattered collection of rags.

"Down with the nobility!" an ancient crone shouted, and jabbed at the man with a stick. Her prodding caused the couple to stagger to one side.

"Stinking aristocrats!" a man on the edge of the crowd cried hoarsely.

"Liberty, fraternity, equality!" Someone clamored shrilly for justice while at the same time taking part in the humiliating spectacle.

The mob came abreast of Enid and Kemble, and they scarcely dared breathe. And old man with toothless gums smiled at Enid in passing and said, "These were owners of a fine chateau, and now they are nothing!"

"Within an hour they won't even have their heads," a woman guffawed, and there was general laughter at this sally.

The procession moved slowly on, with a cripple on crutches and some yapping mongrel dogs bringing up the rear. Enid and Kemble waited until the eerie torchlight was well past them before they emerged into the street again.

"Poor souls!" Enid murmured as they resumed walking.

"Wouldn't want to be in their places," Kemble agreed.

"I keep worrying about Armand, and how it is with him."

"Don't harp on the man who stole you from me. And don't expect me to worry about him as you do."

She gave him a shocked look. "I vow you hope he won't escape alive!"

"What I hope has nothing to do with his fate."

"But you wouldn't care, would you?"

"I have never wept over the loss of a rival," Kemble acknowledged.

"What are we doing quarreling this way?" she cried with despair.

"It was you who brought the matter up!" he reminded her.

"Only because we saw such misery at close range."

"I have a notion we shall see more before we finish."

They had come to the end of the street. "This must be where we turn," Enid said.

"That is what the accursed Ramon said, though who knows for sure?"

"Don't confuse the directions and blame that poor little creature, for heaven's sake!"

"That poor little creature is a professional in a game in which we are mere amateurs," Kemble said savagely. "I'll warrant he has killed many times his weight in men."

She halted. "Listen!"

"What is it?"

"I hear someone running toward us!"

"So do I. Quick, backs to the wall again! Better that we be unobserved!"

They repeated their former actions. The footsteps came closer. Out of the darkness ahead emerged the shadowy figure of a man being pursued swiftly, and behind him raced two others with their swords drawn. The man ran straight toward where Enid and Kemble stood in the shadows.

All at once he stumbled and fell only a yard or two away. The swordsmen approached him, and it was then that Kemble let out a roar of outrage and ran forward, his sword drawn and ready. Enid felt a burst of admiration for the melancholy actor who had so suddenly been transformed into a man of action.

He stood over the fallen man, defending him with vigorous parries. She knew his efforts could not last very long, for he was neither that skilled a swordsman nor in perfect physical condition. With one swift motion she had drawn her own sword and leaped into the fray.

It became a vicious double battle, swords clashing, angry oaths filling the air, and the four fencers dancing back and forth around the fallen man. Enid dropped to one knee as her adversary almost overcame her, but she managed to struggle into a better position again. She could not tell anything about the size or facial appearance of her opponent, but she knew he was a skilled fencer.

As she parried blades with him, she waited for the right moment and then made a lucky lunge. Her weapon found its mark and he staggered back, clutching his ribs with a loud cry of pain. His partner, who was deftly outmaneuvering Kemble, whirled around and ran to his side.

Enid tried to make another strike, but the two swordsmen were now retreating. She heard them exchange a few words, and in the next instant they had turned and run off into the same direction from which they had come.

"Don't follow them!" Kemble warned her. "They will lay wait to ambush us from some doorway."

She stood staring after them regretfully. "You are probably right, though I hate to see them get away."

"And so do I, madam," said a pleasant voice with a slight accent.

She turned and saw that the man who had been lying on the cobblestones was now on his feet. "Are you all right?" she asked.

"I have sustained a flesh wound in my left arm and some loss of blood," he told her. "I apologize for placing you both in such danger. And the gentleman is right. It would be wrong to try to follow them. They will be waiting for you and will strike before you can defend yourself."

"An old trick," Kemble muttered. "Why were you so easy a victim for them?"

"I was unarmed," the man explained. "I never carry weapons. I count on my vocation to give me protection."

"Your vocation wouldn't have helped if we hadn't shown up," Kemble observed.

Enid was immediately alerted. "May I ask what your vocation is?"

"I am a priest, madam," he replied.

"Is your church near here?"

"The monastery I belong to is. Alas, I am its only occupant at this time. The others have fled. Even men called to serve God are turning into insane beasts in this holocaust!"

"You are Father Braun, are you not?"

"You know my name!" he gasped in astonishment. "And you are English!"

"Sent to meet you," Kemble told him solemnly. "We were on our way to the monastery when we came upon you. Or rather, when you came staggering toward us."

"Come with me," the priest said at once. "Those men could return. Esmond's agents are everywhere."

"Did they belong to Esmond?" she asked as they moved quickly along the street.

"Yes. And he is the vilest of all our enemies."

"We know a good deal about him, too," Kemble said.

The priest halted. "Here, this is the monastery."

He led them into a gray stone building. To the left of the entry was a chapel, which he entered and then motioned them to follow him. After he found a candle and lit it, he made his devotions before the altar. For the first time Enid saw his face, the same ruddy, pleasant-looking face as that in the sketch Sir Harry had shown them. There was no question that this man, with his blue eyes and gray hair, was Father Braun.

When the priest had finished his prayers, she said, "Sir Harry showed us a drawing of you. I am quite satisfied."

He nodded. "And I have no doubts about you two, either. Naturally, I was informed of your coming."

"It's lucky we arrived when we did," Kemble put in.

"Thank the Lord for your timely appearance. I had been out for a little while, and I found the two men waiting for me with drawn swords when I returned. With no one here to come to my aid, I could do nothing but flee into the street."

"What about the lad, the Dauphin?" Kemble wanted to know.

"He is safe below, in one of the dungeons," Father Braun said. "We have underground cells for those wanting to offer contritions. That seemed the safest refuge, so I put him down there."

"Let us go to him now," Kemble urged.

Father Braun's expression turned solemn. "You understand that this is a moment which will be recorded in history."

"I hope so," Kemble said fervently. "There are times when I fear our only mention will be in the list of the dead."

"We are honored to have this responsibility," the priest continued. "Remember, not only are the French people determined to kill off the royal family, but the Prussians and Austrians are aware that an exchange was made, and that the Dauphin is free and about to be delivered to England's representatives. They are scouring this city for the lad."

"Does Esmond know he was released and is here?"

"Why else would his men be loitering about and trying to kill me? It has not been voiced abroad that a deaf mute has replaced Louis Charles in his prison cell, but you may be sure the head of the French secret service knows it."

"I think he must," Enid agreed.

"Well, let us get on with it," Kemble said impatiently.

"This way." Father Braun picked up the tall white candle and led them out of the chapel and across the passage to a great oaken door. He removed the heavy latch, and they proceeded down a narrow corridor that gave way to a winding staircase.

"Careful," he warned them. "The ceiling lowers here, and the last few steps are broken off."

Enid and Kemble followed the priest along another tunnel-like corridor that had a slight curve to it. The priest was well ahead of them, and the flame of the candle cast a flickering, eerie light along the gray stone walls and ceiling. Enid felt her nerves grow more taut as they neared their destination. As Father Braun had said, this could be an important moment in history.

The priest halted and then gave a loud gasp. The door before which he was standing was partially open, and the small room beyond it was empty of life.

He turned to them in a grave state of agitation. "He is gone! The Dauphin is gone!"

"What are you saying?" Kemble demanded.

The priest turned back to stare blankly into the cell. "The boy has vanished. It is evident that while I was away for a short time, they found him—despite my bringing him down here and securely locking the door!"

Kemble pointed to the stone floor. "That is what remains of your lock!"

"Broken!" Father Braun advanced into the tiny cubicle and carefully examined it. He bent down by the cot and picked up a richly illustrated volume of animal studies. "Here is the book I left with him. You see the candle by which he read is still burning."

"They cannot have taken him very long ago," Enid murmured, trying to inject some hope into her voice.

"Now I think I understand," Father Braun said. "They came and took the lad and left those two behind to finish me off. Fortunately, you arrived in time to save me."

"Had we been earlier, we might have saved the Dauphin as well," Enid lamented.

"What now?" Kemble asked quietly.

"I don't know." Father Braun shook his head. "This is a most disastrous turn of events."

"Our mission is now pointless," Enid fretted. "What do you think the chances are of getting him back?"

"With Louis Esmond as his captor, almost none," the priest replied bitterly. "He will probably be brought back to the prison from which he was originally taken, or they may put him in some other prison. In the end he will be executed with the rest of the royal family."

Kemble threw up his hands in despair. "And England will have no ace to play when the revolution fails. There will be no soverign available to put on the French throne."

Father Braun nodded sadly.

"We mustn't give up hope," Enid insisted. "Where do you think Esmond may have taken him?"

"I will have to use other agents to determine that," the priest said. "It may take only a few hours, or it may take the like number of days." A drawn look crossed his face and paled its normal ruddiness. "I have failed Sir Harry. He will not be pleased. I tried to play the game alone to ensure the utmost secrecy. I thought I could protect the boy by myself. But I ought to have had an associate or two. I should not have left him alone when I went out. That was my error, and it may have cost us his life."

Enid felt sorry for Father Braun. His bitter condemnation of himself was touching and sincere. Gently she withdrew the children's book from his hands and studied it. "May I keep this?" she asked. "It has the royal signature in it. We can at least offer it as proof to Sir Harry that we were close to our quarry."

"Take it," he said. "Now let us return upstairs to discuss what our next moves should be."

They retraced their steps through the underground labyrinth. Then the priest led them into a dining hall at the rear of the building and produced a jug of red wine and some glasses. His expression was bitter as he remarked, "We hate been stripped of property, vestments, everything. Fortunately, they missed the best of our wine cellars."

Kemble sat down at the mahogany refectory table and gazed at Enid and the priest. "We have been outsmarted and made fools of by Esmond. It is truly unthinkable."

"He is a formidable adversary," Father Braun reminded him.

"What is your plan?" Enid asked.

The priest frowned over his wine goblet. "When we leave here, I shall go directly to the house of another agent who will alert our network. We will find out where the prince is being held."

"And then?" Kemble prodded.

"If the prison is not too difficult to enter, we will work out a plan of attack. Hopefully, there may be guards whom we can bribe. We must meet this evil with wiles of our own and try to effect the boy's rescue."

"What are the two of us to do?" Enid wondered.

"For the moment, nothing," Father Braun said. "Remain where you are. As soon as I have something to report, I will get word to you. It would be wise for you to be prepared to take action on the spur of the moment. By the time I have learned where the Dauphin is, we will have to move quickly."

Kemble protested. "Surely we can be put to some use now, can't we? I did not venture on this long, dangerous journey just to fume and fret in shabby lodgings."

"You must not be impatient," Father Braun cautioned him. "You are not familiar with Paris. And the fact that you are English will draw unwanted attention to you."

"So you think it's important that we refrain from doing anything on our own until we hear from you," Enid concluded.

"It is the only way," the priest agreed. "In the meantime, you can familiarize yourself with maps of the city, and the agents with whom you are staying can give you additional advice. By the way, where is their house?"

Enid and Kemble glanced uncertainly at each other. They both remembered Ramon's statement that the priest knew nothing of him and Renaud and that it was better that way. But this was an emergency situation, and they had no choice but to reveal their present location.

"It is probably unwise for us to remain here much longer," Enid added. "Esmond's men could return with more recruits and we would be sorely outnumbered."

Father Braun smiled at her approvingly. "I can see why Sir Harry chose you for this important mission. You have a good mind, and you are also the most expert female at wielding a sword whom I have ever encountered."

"She has an extraordinary talent for fencing," Kemble agreed.

"I'm glad I was able to put it to good use," Enid said, her sloe eyes gleaming at the memory of her efforts.

"Needless to say, I'm most grateful." The priest rose from the table. "When we leave, we shall depart by a rear exit. It would be best if you left first, and then I shall follow."

"You are in charge," Kemble allowed.

"We are equals," Father Braun hastened to say, "but in certain matters it might be wise to take my advice."

They moved out of the dining hall and drew their cloaks tighter around them. The monastery was both dank and gloomy, and the single lighted taper could not dispel the shadows that loomed at them forebodingly.

"I should get back to you sometime tomorrow," the cleric informed his English accomplices. "If my work takes longer, I'll send a message to you to that effect."

The flickering candlelight revealed a short stairway that led to an arched door. Father Braun paused there with them and said, "This will take you into a narrow alley. It is much safer, and you only have to turn left at its end to find your way back to the street." He unbarred the door and held the candle aloft.

Kemble thanked him, and he and Enid stepped into the alley. Her last view of the cleric was as he stood in the doorway, the candle casting a golden glow about him. Even though he wore ordinary clothing, his mien was priestly.

They moved warily along the cobblestones. The dark alley was, thankfully, deserted. After several minutes Enid asked Kemble, "What do you make of him?"

"Steel-trap mind and nerves."

"I agree, but there is more to him than that. He is dedicated to saving the Dauphin, even though I think he may be cynical about the uses England wishes to make of the lad."

"His responsibility is to produce the boy for us, not to criticize our diplomacy. And he has failed."

"Which means we've all failed."

"For the moment," the actor amended.

She saw they were now on the route by which they had come, and she felt easier. "It didn't take Louis Esmond very long to come back into the picture," she observed.

"As the chief of the revolutionist spy service, he was never really out of it."

"I hope I look different enough now," she worried. "I'm sure you do."

"The main thing is the boy," Kemble told her firmly. "If they have taken him back to the prison from which he was rescued, the chances of freeing him again are small."

When they reached the lodging house, they found Renaud and Ramon in a back room, silent and absorbed over a game of chess. Renaud looked up as they entered, his expression one of keen anticipation.

"What is the word?" he asked eagerly.

"Bad," Kemble growled.

The midget glared at him. "You didn't let the Dauphin escape from you?" he demanded shrilly. Enid answered him. "We didn't even get a chance to see the prince. He was abducted by Louis Esmond's men before we arrived."

Kemble then told them the entire story, ending with, "So we remain here until Father Braun learns where the Dauphin is."

The midget's pale face was twisted with scorn. "I have never trusted men of the cloth. That priest is far too simplistic in his methods."

Renaud frowned at him across the table. "No need to blame Father Braun. He had proved himself a most capable agent."

"And he has failed in his most important assignment," the midget shrilled. "Sir Harry will pay us back for this. He's liable to be so angry he'll throw us all to the rabble!"

Enid spoke soothingly. "I think Father Braun did his best. And he is intelligent. There's still hope."

"I fail to see it," Ramon said in an ugly tone. "We may as well go back to playing chess!"

Both Enid and Kemble were thoroughly exhausted. They left the men to their game and went upstairs. The actor hesitated before her bedroom door, saying, "One thing, at least. We are still together."

She smiled wanly. "A small comfort."

"It could be much more," he urged softly.

"No."

He sighed. "Ah, your infernal loyalty to a man who is probably already dead!"

"I won't believe that!"

"You have seen what Paris is like. You know he was in prison when you last heard of him. Can you honestly hope he is still alive?"

"I must."

Kemble took her in his arms and held her close, stroking her hair with a light touch. The increased pounding of her heart told Enid that his embrace had stirred her. She could not forget the blissful times they had shared together, nor did she want to. They would be forever etched in her memory. She sighed and lifted her face to his. The kiss he gave her was ardent and of long duration, and before it was over she had responded almost urgently.

"I love you, Enid," he murmured.

"I know that," she replied huskily.

"We face great uncertainty here. We could be dead in a short while, murdered by enemy agents. Shouldn't we take advantage of the time we have and become lovers again? Please say yes!"

Armand's face, his lean, hard body—the very essence of the man—rose before her eyes. She gently disengaged herself from Kemble's arms and said, "I'm sorry, John, but I cannot give myself to you unless I know for certain that Armand is dead."

"I have a phantom adversary," the actor complained bitterly. "How do you dispose of a phantom?"

Her smile was sad. "You had best find that out before you ask me to bed with you again."

He shook his head in despair. "I have a beauty in Jenny. I could have almost any woman in London. And I want only you!"

"I'm glad I hold such a high esteem in your eyes, and I shall cherish that knowledge. But I will not demean myself by going back on my given word. Good night, John."

"Good night," he said resignedly. He waited until she had gone inside and bolted her door before he entered his own chamber.

Enid fell asleep almost at once, but she was plagued by disturbing nightmares. In most of them she was fencing again, battling off the mysterious attackers in the dark street. Then the face of one was revealed, and it was that of the hateful Louis Esmond, gloating over her as he managed to twist the sword from her grasp. Unarmed, she stepped back, and he lunged at her with his rapier pointed at her heart. It was at this point in the dream that she awakened and found herself bathed in perspiration.

Almost at once there was a knock on the door between her room and Kemble's. "Enid!" he demanded urgently.

"Yes?" she answered sleepily.

"Are you all right? You screamed several times!"

"A nightmare," she said, "nothing more. Please go back to bed now."

She lay on her back, staring up at the ceiling and seeing again the details of the nightmare. She shuddered and rolled over onto her stomach, clutching the clean-smelling pillows as if they could protect her from the force of Louis Esmond.

22

When Enid came downstairs the next morning, she found Kemble poring over a map of Paris that was spread out on the wooden table in the kitchen. Renaud and Ramon were wearing their mother-and-son costumes again and stood next to Kemble, explaining the map to him. Each was making a useful contribution to the actor's knowledge.

On seeing Enid attired in a fresh blue linen dress whose low-cut neckline enhanced both the curve of her bosom and the beautiful gold locket adorning it, the midget rolled his eyes and gave her a leering smile.

"I'd say Sir Harry sent you here to tempt us!" he cried. His remark was all the more ridiculous considering his child's outfit.

Kemble told him, "It will do you no good at all to make any such overtures, little man. She has already turned me down."

"People of my size have much appeal to some ladies," Ramon chuckled. "I remember, before all this business started—when I was in the king's service—I was once given the task of surveilling the wife of a Danish ambassador, and I vow I did most of my work beside her in her four-poster!"

Ramon let out a deep growl and glared at his partner. "We are here to study the map, not to listen to tales of your erotic adventures!"

"The lady might find my stories much more pleasing," Ramon suggested, still leering at her.

"I fear I'm not in the mood for pleasantries of that nature this morning," Enid declared firmly. "Has there been any word from Father Braun?"

"Not yet," Kemble said. "I'm making the most of my time by learning how to move about Paris."

She went over to the table. "That is a good idea. Do include me in on the explanations."

For the better part of an hour they labored over the map. By the time they had finished, she had memorized quite a lot of details about the city. Kemble had some difficulty with the names of the streets and grew angry at himself. His plight was not helped by the midget, who twitted him about his intelligence.

"I would fear, Mr. Kemble, that while I possess a small body and a huge mind, you are sadly blessed with a large body and a tiny mind."

"Let's have none of that, little man!" Kemble flared, showing a fist.

Enid placated the two of them. "We are not supposed to waste our time quarreling with each other. We are here to improve our knowledge and decide on a plan of action."

At that moment they heard someone moving about in the next room. The footsteps drew nearer and the four of them stood like statues. Enid feared it might be one of Esmond's agents and hoped it was Father Braun with some helpful news. It turned out to be neither. The man entering the kitchen was Pierre Giraud, in his familiar guise as the filthy, loose-mouthed driver.

Renaud withdrew his hand from under the table top, where, to both Enid's and Kemble's surprise, he had been holding a pistol aimed at the kitchen doorway.

"I wondered who had let himself in!" he exclaimed with a sigh of relief.

"So you were going to shoot me, my friend, and then question me later?" Pierre's tone was heavy with sarcasm.

Renaud stashed the pistol in a pocket of the woman's coverall he wore. "We are constantly in danger. You should not have entered without calling out first."

"In other days my servants announced me," the count said with a grim smile. "I find it difficult now to learn to announce myself."

"What is the word?" the midget asked.

"Tonight I take six souls to Calais," Giraud reported with relish. "Three noblemen, two of their wives, and the noble mistress of the third."

Kemble nodded. "The transportation continues with success, then."

"It does. And what about you?"

"We are not so well off. Thus far our mission has failed."

"Bad news for Sir Harry," Giraud said, shaking his unruly mane. "And he is someone who dislikes such news."

"You'll enjoy passing it on to him," Ramon shrilled. "You like to see us all in trouble. You work with us because it suits you, but secretly you despise us!"

"What a mindreader you are!" the count exclaimed with mock incredulity. "Talent like yours ought to be on the stage!"

"Mr. Kemble is the play actor, and doing very badly in this new endeavor, I might add." A sly smile crossed Ramon's pixie face.

"Well, I have important things to attend to, so I shall bid you adieu. And I trust we may all meet again!"

Enid smiled. "We shall not soon forget our journey with you."

"My body still aches," Kemble complained.

"I'm hardened to it," Pierre laughed. "I make the trip constantly."

Renaud saw him out, and the threesome returned to studying the map for a while longer. Then both Ramon and Renaud went out to do their daily shopping. They explained that while they were engaged in this task, they would also contact another agent. The network was most complex.

Enid and Kemble were left behind to languish in their drab lodgings, and they moved to the parlor. She occupied herself by reading the illustrated book with Louis Charles's name proudly inscribed on the flyleaf. Kemble paced about like a caged lion and occasionally peered out the sides of the shuttered front windows.

He had brought the map of Paris with him from the kitchen, but cast it restlessly aside on a small gateleg table.

"I wonder how things are back in London. I trust my sister is not ruining my company of actors."

Enid smiled at him. "She is a very popular actress, isn't she?"

"Yes, but she is mean," he said, frowning. "She has been like that from the time she was growing up."

"Such things are often a matter of personality and are not easy to change."

"I have always received a great deal of loyalty from my performers," Kemble went on, "and I'm concerned that while I'm away she will lose some of them because of her unwillingness to pay a fair wage."

Enid closed the book and put it aside. "In that case, they will rejoin the company when you return."

"I suppose so," he said gloomily.

"You wanted to do this," she reminded him. "It was you and your friend Sir Harry who talked me into it."

He shrugged. "You were in danger in London anyway."

"I'm probably in more danger here."

He stared at her. "Have you thought of Andrew at all?" he asked suddenly. "I mean, since you left London."

She smiled ruefully. "He is never entirely out of my mind. I will be able to forget him only when I'm free of him."

"Your father's lawyers are still attending to that, aren't they?"

"Yes, but with small success, I fear."

"He tried to put you in a most compromising situation at Mother Mag's so that he could claim you were immoral and fight the annulment on those grounds."

"Happily, that attempt failed."

"And with you over here, he can't invent any other tricks. You know, it is strange to think that you first saw Paris when you were here with him on your honeymoon."

"It was a different Paris then, and a different kind of honeymoon," she reflected. "I really saw only the vicomte's chateau and stately gardens, and my honeymoon was a complete mockery."

"We could have become famous for rescuing the Dauphin," Kemble complained abruptly, returning to his favorite subject once more. "Now we have lost our chance."

"I have more faith in Father Braun than you have," she chided.

Kemble made no reply to this, but he resumed his nervous pacing.

A few minutes later they were joined by a visitor—none other than the man about whom they had just been speaking. Father Braun knocked on the door and announced himself. Kemble let him in and brought him into the parlor.

As soon as Enid saw him, she asked the all-important question: "What have you found out?"

The priest seemed in a better mood today. He was relaxed and smiling. "It was Esmond and his men who broke into the monastery and abducted the Dauphin."

"We guessed that last night," Kemble said impatiently.

Father Braun nodded. "You are right. We guessed it, but we did not know it for a certainty. Now I do, so that is a step forward. Also, the fact that Esmond himself is back in Paris is most significant with regard to the fate of the prince."

"What else have you learned?" Enid pressed.

"Esmond did not take the boy to prison. Instead, he brought him to the stone mansion that formerly belonged to a nobleman and is now Esmond's own headquarters. The prince is locked up in a room in the cellar."

"I trust he'll be safer there than he was in your cellar," Kemble remarked sardonically.

"The chances are that he is more securely guarded," the priest replied, showing no anger at Kemble's offensive tone.

"Do go on," Enid begged.

"There is some other interesting information," the cleric said, "that gives us a new picture of things."

"What is it?" she asked.

"The exchange of the mute child for the Dauphin has been kept a state secret. Few know about it. The revolutionist faction does not wish to give any heart to the Royalists still at large, so nothing has been said. Esmond, naturally, is a party to the secret."

"He had to be, to come to your monastery and seize the lad," Kemble grumbled.

Father Braun did not argue the point. "But what I didn't know is that he has not so much as whispered the identity of the boy to any of his underlings. To them the boy is simply the son of a nobleman, whom the monks attempted to hide."

Enid was puzzled. "What is Esmond's purpose in this? I would expect they'd guard the lad more zealously if they knew he was the Dauphin."

Father Braun's smile held no mirth. "You miss the point, my dear. Esmond is ambitious. He is not content merely to be the head of the secret police—he wants to experience the joy of becoming one of the leaders of the Jacobins."

"Another Robespierre," Kemble suggested.

"Exactly," the priest agreed. "So he is keeping the identity of his prisoner from the others. He hopes to use the Dauphin in order to bargain for power. The prince, therefore, is not truly a captive of the revolutionists but is the personal captive of Esmond's."

"What does this mean to us?" Enid wondered.

"It might make it easier for us to rescue the lad."

"Then why don't we move at once?" Kemble demanded with his usual impatience.

The cleric's pleasant face wore a reproving look as he replied, "Because, my good man, we cannot just storm the place like children at play. Esmond would call on the military and decimate us to minute shreds." He paused. "And that cannot happen. What we must do is devise a workable strategy. We must either find someone we can bribe from within or design a plan for a small, quiet attack on the fortress. It will take a few more days to decide which is the more practical."

Kemble frowned. "More waiting?"

"I'm afraid so," Father Braun sighed. "You must learn to be patient, sir. I fear that is a quality you have too long ignored. I have had to wait my opportunity in silence many times. I did so while I waited for you and Lady Blair to arrive."

"You probably ought to have brought the prince to Calais on your own instead of waiting for us," Kemble said.

"I was on the point of doing just that when you appeared," the priest explained. "I'd only had the boy a few weeks and dared not make another move for a while. Then he was taken from us."

"Is there nothing we can do to be useful in the meanwhile?" Enid asked.

"Very little. You might try to acquaint yourselves with the location of Esmond's headquarters. I see you have a map on the table there. I will show you where the nobleman's mansion is."

He moved to the table, bent over the map, and pointed to an area on the other side of the Seine. Then, having imparted all the information he had, he gathered his cloak around him and left the lodging house.

Not too long afterward the man wearing a woman's shabby dress and the midget pretending to be a child returned. The man carried a shopping basket and the midget clutched a tiny wool toy in his hand, which he tossed away in disgust as soon as they were safely in the house. He then took up his clay pipe and proceeded to light it.

Renaud began to remove the produce he had bought, lamenting, "Every day food costs more and becomes more scarce!"

Ramon puffed on his pipe and shrilled, "I hear some people are eating rats and finding them quite delectable!"

Kemble looked appalled. His face turned a dull purple, then an ash gray. "We shall have none of that fare here!"

"I thought rats were a popular English dish," Ramon goaded.

Enid stepped between them and turned on an enraged Kemble. "You know he is teasing you, trying to upset you! He is only poking fun at you!"

"That is not my idea of a joke!" Kemble stormed.

"Don't worry," Renaud reassured him, untying the bonnet perched atop his head. "We haven't stooped to eating rats yet."

"Did you talk to the agent in the market?" Enid asked.

"Yes," Renaud said. "The big news is that some captured nobles have escaped. A dozen or more of them tunneled their way out of a prison on the fringes of Paris."

"Did they get away safely?"

"We don't know yet. At least the poor souls are no longer in a dark cell awaiting the hangman."

She turned to Kemble with a hopeful expression on her lovely face. "Perhaps Armand was among them!"

"Why should you think that?" Kemble wondered.

"Pierre said he might have been moved closer to Paris."

"That means nothing," Kemble scoffed. "There are dozens of prisons in and about Paris. What makes you believe he would be in that particular one?"

"I don't know," she replied truthfully. "Perhaps it's just a feeling I have."

Kemble addressed Renaud. "Am I not right? There are that many prisons, I'm sure."

Renaud nodded. "But fate plays strange tricks. It may be that Madam's friend is among those who escaped. Let us hope so."

"Thank you." Enid flashed him a smile. "Oh—I nearly forgot! Father Braun was here!"

"Why didn't you tell us before?" Ramon cried. "What was his news?"

She told them what the priest had said, and finished with, "So it seems we must go on waiting."

"I know the headquarters," Renaud said grimly. "It is also used as a torture chamber. Many have died there."

"It's no easy place to get into," the midget observed as he puffed on his pipe.

"We watched a half-dozen heads roll after we left the market," Renaud remarked, sinking into a nearby chair. "It is a most unnerving experience, even for us who have endured so much."

"The people love the show!" Ramon shrilled. "They come hours in advance to get good seats. The women even bring their knitting and their handiwork! It's a disgrace to the nation, but they love to see the keen blade drop and the heads fall."

"Robespierre was there with some other bigwigs," Renaud added.

"What is he like?" Enid asked.

"He's the worst of the monsters."

Ramon let out a devilish cackle of laughter. "He's not much larger than I, and not nearly as successful with the ladies!"

Renaud gave him a look of disgust. "Ramon, you tire me!" Then, to Enid and Kemble, "It is not often you find so cunning a man as Maximilien Robespierre. He is close to the top of the party council at the moment. He is also a small man and a bachelor."

"How old is he?" Enid inquired.

"Mid-thirties, more or less. He has neat, catlike features and hair that is always well combed and powdered, and his linen is spotless. He is shortsighted and wears reading glasses. And he hates the church, though he professed to believe in a supreme being. Robespierre is mostly to blame for the persecution of nuns and priests. He hates them. And though he is a bachelor, he claims that all priests should be made to marry."

"He's shifty, that Robespierre!" the midget put in. "Never able to look you in the eye!"

"He knows how to manage the masses," Renaud said with contempt. "But one day they will turn on him, and then he will suffer the same fate as other tyrants have before him. We shall look forward to that day."

•••

That evening Kemble became most obstinate in his desire to get away from the house. Enid pleaded with him not to leave, saying that important information could arrive at any time.

"You can take whatever message comes in," he said.

"But I can make no move without you," she protested.

"I'll stay out only a short while. Just enough to get some air and exercise. I'm not used to being cooped up like this."

"The streets are unsafe at night," Renaud warned him, "especially for a lone man who does not know Paris that well."

"Then you come with me," Kemble challenged him. "Who would attack a man with an elderly lady at his side?"

Renaud frowned. "You mean to go out whether I accompany you or not?"

"Yes." The actor was clearly disgruntled.

"Then I had best go with you. The lady can remain here for messages. Ramon will guard her."

The little man gave Enid one of his leering smiles. "I will even comfort her if she wishes."

"None of that!" Renaud admonished him angrily. "A word to Sir Harry and he'd soon take your rattle away!"

"I was only having a joke," Ramon said sullenly, and walked away.

Kemble glared after him. "I could do without him and his jokes!"

Renaud shrugged. "He is a good agent. He serves a purpose… Where shall we go?"

"Let us walk toward Esmond's headquarters and study the streets around it," Kemble suggested. "Then I'll feel I'm putting my time to something useful."

"Very well," Renaud agreed.

"Don't stay away too long," Enid pleaded. "I don't enjoy the prospect of being here alone, even with Ramon."

"It will be all right," Kemble assured her.

But she knew his assurance was based on his impatience to be off, and therefore didn't count for much.

The two men left soon after. Ramon was still sulking in his bedroom, so Enid went upstairs to hers. She had an odd sensation of approaching danger and put it down to frayed nerves.

Since she had only a limited amount of clothing with her, she wanted to conserve her outfits as much as possible. With a view to this, she removed her blue linen outfit and put on a yellow silk nightdress and a matching dressing gown. She had barely tied the sash around her waist when she heard the door of her chamber creaking open.

She turned in surprise and thought for a moment that the door was opening by itself. Then she saw the smiling little man with his hand on the doorknob.

"What are you doing here?" she demanded.

He came into the room. "I thought you might be feeling lonely."

The sight of him in a pair of boy's short pants with huge white buttons and a round-collared white shirt was amusing, especially when one knew he regarded himself as a Lothario. But she was in no mood to be amused.

"I'm not lonely, but I am annoyed that you have intruded on me like this. I was changing my clothes."

"I know," he said, licking his lips. "I watched you through the keyhole."

"You are a wicked creature!"

"Quite true!" he agreed heartily.

"I shall tell the others about you," she warned him.

"Why do that?" he asked in a voice meant to enchant her. He became more daring, moved closer to her, and made a grab for the front of her dressing gown.

She backed away from him quickly. "You should be ashamed of yourself! We are comrades, after all!"

"I would prefer to be your lover." His smile became more cunning.

"You're mad!" Enid clutched her robe tighter to her. Fear had replaced her former annoyance.

"Not at all. I'm a very good lover and I have delighted many ladies," he insisted, moving toward her.

She kept backing away from him. "You are contemptible as well as mad! Leave me alone, for God's sake!"

"You would not sing the same tune if you slipped between the sheets with me," he argued, undaunted.

"I will tell the others when they return," she threatened.

"Not if you truly enjoy yourself. It could be our secret. I think you are beautiful—more lovely than most English ladies!"

"I don't care to hear your opinion of me."

An ugly look crossed his face. "I can *make* you love me!"

"Don't be absurd." She edged over to the window; he was only a few steps away from her. She had nowhere to retreat.

"I have a pistol, dear lady, which I won't hesitate to use on you if you refuse to let me make love to you."

"If you kill me, you'll have some explaining to do," she pointed out.

"Then why can't you be generous with me without my risking all that?" he asked plaintively.

"Because I can't bear the thought of you touching me!" she cried, near hysteria. "You repulse me, and not just because of your size! There is so much inside you that is evil and shameful!"

Ramon seemed taken aback by her scornful tone. "So you hate me?"

"Yes!"

"Women have pleaded for my caresses!" he huffed. "I do not need the love of a sodomist's rejected slut!" And with these surprising words, delivered viciously, he turned on his heel and strode from the room.

Enid hurried to the door and bolted it, then leaned weakly against the wood frame, feeling sick to her stomach. Her head was throbbing painfully. The little man was more corrupt than she had suspected. She began to realize what a ruthless atmosphere she had been placed in; a world where spies like herself lived in constant danger, not only from the revolutionists but from agents of other countries, as well as from each other.

This last thought was the most shocking of all. She had regarded the underground network as being uniformly loyal. But now she saw that jealousies and deceits were common among those who supposedly had given their complete trust to one another. And there were others, like Kemble, who were not ideally suited to this type of work, and whose impatience and poor judgment could endanger or cause the death of still others. She was in this unhappy predicament tonight because Kemble had needlessly insisted on going out and taking Renaud with him.

She stood at the window watching for them to return. Every fiber in her body was at its peak of nervous tautness. She did not think the midget would harass her again, but she had no way of knowing what his intense sexual drive would make him do. She thought him capable of any wild, insane act.

The candle on her night table had almost burned itself out, but she dared not go downstairs for another until Kemble came back. She watched the flame flicker and grow smaller, and thus she measured the passing minutes. Her imagination was highly active now, and despite her efforts to dispel her sense of impending danger, she could not shake the feeling threatening to choke her.

She was still staring at the waning candle when she heard a strange sound, like a clump. After a short pause it came again, then a pause, then the same sort of bumping noise, a little nearer now. She turned to look at the bolted door, and once again she heard that eerie thump followed by silence.

She could not bear it. She had to see what it was. She advanced cautiously to the door and unbolted it without making a sound. Then she opened it just a crack and peered out into the hallway. What greeted her gaze was something so horrible and terrifying that for a moment she was paralyzed with fright.

The midget was crawling up the stairs, slowly and desperately trying to reach the landing. Each time he moved an inch forward, the action was accompanied by the clumping sound. His face was battered and bloody, and a river of blood streamed out from a wound in his chest. He raised his head as he reached the landing, tried to say something, coughed, and fell silent.

Enid ran forward involuntarily to see if she could help him, thinking that he must have really gone mad and inflicted this damage on himself, possibly to take revenge on her. She knelt by his ravaged little body and realized almost at once that he was dead.

23

"Good evening, Lady Blair!" The words came from the foot of the stairs.

Enid raised her eyes to see Louis Esmond, in a black cape and three-cornered hat, standing there with a twisted smile on his face.

"You!" she gasped.

"Unfortunately," Esmond jeered, his good eye fixed on her with derision. "One hates to use violence, but he was very stubborn!"

"You brute—scoundrel!"

He limped up a few steps, drew a pistol from beneath his cloak, and pointed it at her. "We are not in England now, Lady Blair, and you are not on the stage of Drury Lane, though I vow your disguise is most excellent. Personally, I preferred you as a blonde."

"Finish me as you did that poor creature!" she cried.

"That is not my plan for you, madam," he said politely. "You will come slowly down the stairs toward me. The little one is dead, so waste no pity on him."

She made no reply but did as he had bade her, shuddering as she passed Ramon's sprawled, blood-spattered body. Then she came abreast of the infamous man with the black eye patch. He seized her by the arm with his free hand and shoved her none too gently down the remaining stairs.

A hulking figure in a shabby uniform approached Esmond. "The house is empty of anyone else, Citizen," he reported. A musket dangled loosely in his hands.

Esmond nodded. "Then let us be on our way. The lady goes with us."

"The carriage is waiting outside, Citizen," the soldier said.

Esmond led her out into the cool darkness and saw her into the coach. He took his place beside her, still holding the pistol, and the carriage started off.

He gave her a mocking glance. "You did not presume to visit Paris without my making you welcome, did you? What an oversight on your part!"

"Why have you taken me prisoner?" she asked.

"Call it a whim," he replied. "I could easily have eliminated you as I did the midget."

"You can't eliminate all your enemies," she countered.

"They multiply like rodents," he agreed. "But as long as I keep them under control, I am satisfied."

"Do you really think the revolution will last long enough for you to become a party leader?"

"The revolution cannot fail," he told her. "And my power is growing daily."

It was on the tip of her tongue to taunt him about using the poor Dauphin as a power ploy, but she restrained herself. She did not want to let him know how much information she and the others possessed. It was best to say nothing, she decided.

The carriage rolled on through the night and then crossed the river to the opposite bank. After rumbling along a broad thoroughfare for several minutes, it halted at an entrance with iron gates. Two guards came forward to inspect the vehicle; on seeing Esmond, they hastily opened the gates. The carriage turned into a half-moon driveway and stopped in front of an enormous stone mansion. Its windows were shuttered, and Enid understood now why Father Braun had called it a fortress and had been reluctant to launch an assault on it. This was where she was to be a prisoner.

Esmond stepped out of the carriage and marched her to the ornate oak door, which opened at their approach. A gaunt-faced servant bowed to Esmond and moved aside as the master spy and Enid entered.

"Up the stairway," Esmond ordered.

Enid slowly ascended the curving marble stairs, Esmond right behind her. At the landing he took her by the arm and led her into a room with book-lined shelves and a wide desk cluttered with papers. Then he closed the door and locked it. The smile he offered her was not pleasant.

"Now we will come to terms. Sit down, Lady Blair," Louis Esmond ordered, slipping off his cloak.

She stood defiantly. "May I ask again why you have brought me here?"

"If you will be seated, I will talk with you. Otherwise I shall have you shut up in one of my guest rooms. I promise you they are rather dark and cold, with no windows at all. Merely a grating high in the wall for a little air to get through."

She decided she would have to humor him, and moved to a high-backed chair.

Esmond remained smiling down at her, a bizarre-looking figure with his bald head and eye patch. "Is not this room in exquisite taste?" he inquired politely.

Enid glanced at the shelves bursting with leather-bound volumes; at the mahogany sideboards whose large candelabras lighted the room softly; at the desk, also mahogany and with another show of candles; at the rich maroon carpeting and the finely upholstered furniture.

"It is surely a credit to the man you stole it from!" she remarked. "Where is he now? A victim of the executioner's block?"

"Not at all," Esmond laughed. "I'm more generous than that. He is still here in his own house. However, for almost two years he has occupied a dungeon in the cellar."

"That sounds like your type of generosity!"

He laughed again and limped to the sideboard nearest him. "Will you join me in a cognac?" he asked.

"I do not drink with your sort!" she flared, her chin held high.

His one eye regarded her with interest. "You talk like an aristocrat. But then, that is only fitting, since you *are* an aristocrat. Your name was Lady Enid Henson before you married the pervert."

"You have researched me well."

He poured himself a cognac and then moved toward the desk, resting against one edge of it as he sipped his drink. "The Duke of Aranjais has an excellent wine cellar, but I prefer his cognac. I have developed quite a taste for it."

"I suppose you share it with him," she derided.

"I offered to," Esmond replied evenly. "I went down to him a year ago, on the anniversary of Bastille Day, and I offered to drink with him to the success of the revolution. The fool wasted his drink—threw it in my face! So he has not tasted my generosity since."

"At least his honor remains intact."

Esmond smiled nastily. "That is difficult to know, for since then his mind has snapped. The man who once possessed one of the great judicial minds of the realm is now reduced to gibbering idiocy."

"Is destroying people your favorite sport?"

He nodded. "Since you mention it, I believe it is."

"And you plan to destroy me, I suppose," she said bitterly. "I assure you I'm so unimportant that I'm not worth your efforts."

"I think differently," he demurred in his suave manner. "I'm not the ideal ladies' man. You can see that for yourself. But I do admire a certain style of feminine charm—such as yours. And how interesting that you should be in dishabille!"

Enid listened grimly, striving to hide her fear under a facade of arrogance. She knew he would want her to confess what she had learned, as well as to betray the others in the network. She was determined not to talk even under torture. And she thought it ironic that changing into her dressing gown had left her weaponless. The small pistol she always carried was in a concealed pocket in her dress. Useless to her now, since her dress hung in the closet of her room. But she did have one weapon of last resort. The poison that Sir Harry had given her was hidden in the locket she wore about her neck.

"I am a British subject, visiting France on an errand of mercy. You have no right to hold me."

"Right?" he repeated. "Who cares about rights? We make our own rights in France today."

"A great nation has become a prison ruled by the mob," she said scornfully.

He put aside his empty cognac glass and studied her with amusement. "I'm charging you with being a spy. Because of that, your British citizenship offers you no immunity."

"Am I to be given a hearing on those charges?" she demanded.

"I shall pick a judge and jury for you. You will receive a perfectly legal trial. And your execution will also be legal, and swiftly carried out. I will then send a message to Sir Harry with a lock of your hair and my regrets."

"How well you have it planned!"

"Experience, my dear lady. I have looked after such matters many times before. It was reckless enough of you to throw your lot in with the aristocrat Beaufaire and help murder several of my valuable allies in London, but now you have the insolence to appear on my own French soil in order to work for Sir Harry's spy ring."

"You must prove that at your mock trial."

"I will do it. Have no fear. And if you came here hoping to rescue Armand Beaufaire, it was a waste of time. He is rotting in prison."

She smiled. "Really? I have heard that he and others made their escape only yesterday."

The bald man scowled, and her spirits rose a trifle. She was almost positive that she had hit on the truth, that Armand had been one of the fortunate escapees. She prayed that it was so.

"Nobles escape and nobles are captured again!" Esmond scoffed. "It is a cat-and-mouse game, you see. The only ones who really get away from us are the few who flee to England or to the new colonies in America."

"It is too bad you could not emulate their type of revolution!"

"But we were inspired to revolt by the American Revolution," he said with vigor. "Only we have improved on it! We are creating an entirely new order and eliminating an impossible one."

"What could a person like you know of such things? You are a tyrant without scruples or morals!"

"One moment." He raised a hand to silence her. "Let me inform you that I am a soldier with an honorable record, and I fought alongside the Americans in the war against you British!"

"I can scarcely believe it by your present conduct."

"I suffered the wounds that made me something of a cripple by fighting with Washington's army in Pennsylvania. I lost an eye, had a musket ball smash my hip, and was left for dead. But I recovered, and I have become a power in another revolution."

"And lost your honor in the process!"

"I don't think I ever noticed that loss," Louis Esmond said with a smile. "Now to other matters. How is my elderly and peculiar rival, Sir Harry?"

"I know no one by that name."

"That is a lie."

"So you say."

"And what about the good priest, Father Braun? Is he not also a companion of yours?"

Enid shook her head as if baffled. "You try to confuse me by saying names that are foreign to me."

He fixed his eyes on her in grim study. "You are not nearly as confused as you would have me think."

"You may think what you wish."

"I will," he promised. "Now to the question of your mission. Sir Harry chose you and the actor Kemble to come over here, posing as father and daughter, to steal a rare jewel and return it to England."

"You are as mad as the Lear whom Kemble portrays so well on the stage!"

"Kemble is better suited to daring roles behind the footlights than those in real life," the master spy declared. "His disguise is paper-thin, no more effective than your own. He does not have the temperament to be a secret agent."

"You are given to strange fancies," she parried.

"All that I say is established fact. And the jewel which you and Kemble were to steal is a rather important youth named Louis Charles. In short, the Dauphin!"

"Even Frenchmen know the Dauphin is in prison with his parents."

"Don't hope to deceive me on that point," Esmond said, moving away from the desk. "I know full well of the exchange that was made. I had the venal jailer who took the bribe for the deed twisted on the rack! His screams were a delight to me, and when he pleaded for death, I reminded him of the enormity of his crime. He now drags himself about the floor of his prison cell like a kind of crawling insect, mindless and without hope."

"Satan may actually deny you your proper place in his realm," Enid retorted. "He is only a fallen angel, while you are something much more monstrous."

"You have a sharp wit and a barbed tongue. I like that. A woman without spirit is nothing! As I was saying, I know all about the Dauphin's being spirited away. And I'm fully informed of the English plot to give him security in exchange for using him in a political manner. That was a stroke of genius worthy of Sir Harry."

"You weary me with your talking in riddles," she complained.

"In that case I shall try to entertain you in a more interesting manner." He seized her by the arm and dragged her from the chair toward a closed door on the other side of the room. He opened it and pushed her into an elegantly furnished chamber. Then he bolted the door behind him and began unbuttoning his waistcoat.

She stared at him. "Is it your plan to rape me?"

"If necessary," he said quietly as he removed his garment. "You could surrender pleasantly and save yourself from the guillotine tomorrow."

"You state your terms with such clarity," she mocked.

"You are no virgin. I do not need to be too gentle."

"Would you, in any case?"

"No," he said. He had removed his shirt, and she saw a livid scar across his hairy chest. "Another battle wound," he told her.

It was a moment of dreadful decision for Enid. He had presented his terms: let him take her, or he would have her head in the morning. She did not question that he meant what he had said. It was in his power to do away with her. And he was drunk with the glory of his office, close to the state of madness. One does not argue with madmen, she realized. Better to surrender to him and hope to be rescued before she could be executed.

He led her to the side of the bed. "Weighing your decision?" he asked. "Let me assure you I'm an accomplished lover."

"As you are an accomplished villain?"

"I pride myself in doing all things well," he said softly.

He untied the cord about her dressing gown and removed it from her. Then, his hands trembling ever so slightly, he undid her nightdress and lifted it off her body.

"Lovely!" he cried, reveling in her nakedness. "You are a beautiful woman, my lady. Unhappily, you are also wrong-minded."

She said nothing. He dropped his breeches to the floor and was shaking with uncontrolled passion as he drew her to him. She had not realized until this moment how eager he was for her.

His ironic comments had artfully concealed his lust. He pushed her down on the bed and was immediately astride her. She felt his hard, throbbing penetration and lay passively, closing her eyes against his use of her flesh. Again and again he violated her with ceaseless thrusts, until, at last, his desire had been quenched.

It had been an act of rough demanding on Esmond's part. He rose from her, breathing heavily, but he made no gesture of tenderness. There was no caress, no soft word of thanks, no kiss. Enid still lay unmoving, her eyes closed. She did not open them until he spoke.

He was standing a distance from the bed, fully dressed again. She was amazed at the speed with which he had accomplished this. Once again he was urbane and controlled, not the trembling, passion racked animal of a short while earlier.

"Like other men, I have my needs," Esmond said. "You gave me nothing of yourself. Yet I enjoyed your lovely body without your approval. If you do not make too much of a nuisance of yourself, I shall have you remain my guest for a few weeks, perhaps even months."

Enid sat up in bed and drew a sheet over her. "Can the executioner wait for me so long?"

He smiled at her coldly. "The executioner does my bidding. It would be well for you to remember that and do the same. Now I shall return to my desk, where urgent papers await my consideration. You may dress at your leisure and join me when you are ready. I will have one of my staff show you to your own room."

She raised an eyebrow. "No dungeon?"

"And risk destroying your beauty? That would be defeating my purpose!" He bowed low. Then he limped to the door, unlocked it, and departed.

Enid was near tears. But something within her prevented her from giving way to such craven behavior. She was a lady born, and would not give Esmond the pleasure of her grief. She glanced about, feeling helpless and degraded. Her fingers touched the locket at her throat, and she remembered the powder. At least she had that way of escape. Desperate as it was, it would help her defeat the hangman. And with any luck, Kemble and the others would find the Dauphin and get him safely back to England. As for herself, she had little to live for. Even if Armand had escaped, she knew that Louis Esmond had been right in saying that her lover would probably be captured again. And capture for a second time would mean certain death.

She dressed slowly and tried to sort out her thoughts. The only way she could hope to live long enough to be rescued was to play on Esmond's passion. His need for her was great, and she must use it as an instrument against him. Kemble and Renaud had no doubt returned to the house by now and found Ramon murdered and her missing. They would at once devise some plan of action to seek her out and rescue her. Whether such a plan would work was the all-important question. She could only hope it would and that they would also free the Dauphin from his cellar dungeon in the oppressive stone mansion.

She tied the cord of her robe carefully and arranged her hair in a neat fashion. And then, with a show of assurance she did not feel, she left the chamber and entered the library.

Louis Esmond glanced up from the paper he was studying at the desk, and a smile crossed his ugly face. "I say it again. You are a beautiful woman."

Though Enid loathed the sight of him, she decided she must act as if her former resolve were crumbling in the face of passion. "Thank you. I must say I found you more impressive in bed than out of it."

He stood up. "I will accept that as a compliment."

"Whatever you like."

"I'm going to be considerate of you," he promised. "You shall be given a fine room upstairs and will have a maid at your disposal. Your only guard will be stationed in the hallway outside your door. He will not interfere with you unless you attempt to leave the room."

"So I remain a prisoner."

He limped over to her and eyed her with a lustful interest. "I would prefer to call you my guest."

"How tactful of you."

"Who knows? You may come to like it here."

Enid made a show of looking down as she said quietly, "That will depend on you."

"I shall be attentive," he assured her. "I have many problems. My position is not an easy one. But you shall have a full share of my time."

"Any objections I would make would count for little, I suppose."

"You are quite right." He gave her another smile. "But I find your attitude improved, so I shall treat you more kindly. However, one thing I will not do is to place a sword in your hands. I have seen too much evidence of your skill in fencing."

"You admire that?"

"Only when you are not my adversary," he laughed.

He went to the library door and spoke to someone in the hallway. A moment later Enid found herself escorted to the upper region of the mansion by a stolid-faced guard. He took her to a door on the third level and opened it for her.

She went inside and watched him light several candles and start a fire in the grate. Her glance shifted around the large room, and she saw it as one of many family bedchambers in happier days. The decor of white and pink suggested that it had had a female occupant. The entire atmosphere was of ruffles and refined elegance. Esmond had kept his promise of supplying her with proper quarters.

As soon as the soldier's tasks had been completed he went out and closed the door behind him. During the time he had been there he had not looked at Enid or spoken a word.

She moved to the fire to warm herself a little, then crossed to the single large window and saw that it overlooked the front half-moon driveway. But the window offered no hope of escape. It was a great distance to the ground, and even though it had no bars and was not locked, it was useless in helping her gain her freedom.

She was still standing by the window when the door of her room opened, and a thin, elderly woman in a black dress entered.

"I have been sent to care for Madam's needs," the woman said in a tremulous voice.

"Are you to be my maid?" Enid asked.

"Yes. I have served in this house for most of my life."

Enid found this information interesting. "You were here before it was taken by the revolutionists?"

"Yes."

"Do you not find it strange under the new order? With your master and his family gone?"

The thin woman eyed Enid defiantly. "I am of the new order, madam. I support the aims of the revolution."

Enid was somewhat shocked. "And don't you feel any pity for your former master who is imprisoned here?"

"Not at all," the servant replied sternly. "Many must suffer for the good of the nation."

"I see," Enid said, realizing it was useless to question her further. She was a true revolutionist, or Esmond would not have kept her on.

"Do you need something, madam?" the woman asked.

"Yes," Enid said. "I would like to take a warm bath."

"I will have a tub and hot and cold water brought up."

Within a short time two male servants arrived, with the woman directing them as they placed a large tin bathtub and jugs of hot and cold water in the middle of the room. When they had departed, Enid enjoyed a long, luxuriant soak in the warm water. She had felt the need to cleanse herself of the slightest contamination from the repulsive Louis Esmond. She wondered how long she could pretend to be succumbing to him and whether some sort of aid would reach her in time.

24

In the morning the woman servant appeared promptly with fresh water for Enid's morning ablutions and a heaping breakfast tray. Then came a long interval of boredom. Enid paced restlessly up and down, musing on what Kemble's reaction had been to her obviously having been taken hostage. There was little likelihood that any rescue attempt would be made by day, so she would somehow have to endure the tension until nightfall.

The servant brought her meals and looked after all her other needs. But she was unfriendly and said very little. Enid saw that it was senseless to try to reason with her, so she largely ignored her. Once she opened the door to see if the guard posted outside would continually be there. He was! On seeing her, he lifted his musket and pointed the bayonet at her. She took the hint and went back inside.

It was not until around nine in the evening that Louis Esmond made his appearance. When he came limping in, Enid felt her heart sink. She was convinced that he had come for another session of lovemaking, and she was in no mood for it. But he surprised her by saying, "I have come to see that you are comfortable."

"As much as I can be and still remain a prisoner," she told him.

"That is regrettable, but I have no choice. I wish you to remain, and I know you would leave at once if there was no guard."

Enid gave him what she hoped was a coy look. "Why are you so sure of that?"

The one-eyed man moved close to her, his bald head shining as he bent over her hand to kiss it. He murmured hoarsely, "Perhaps I can return later. Then we can have a long night of rapture!"

"You are not staying now?" She feigned a slight disappointment while thinking how easy it was to play the harlot.

"Affairs of the nation," he declared importantly. "There are many decisions to be made. Changes are coming about. I want to emerge with more power rather than less."

"You enjoy politics more than love?"

"Never!" Esmond cried. "But I have certain meetings which I must attend. Is your maid satisfactory?"

"Yes. Yet I find her strange and cold in manner."

"Ah! You have noticed!"

"Yes."

Esmond smiled. "She is a staunch revolutionist. When the party took over this mansion, it was she who opened the gates and let us pour in. And when her former mistress cried out scornfully at her for doing it, the woman struck her down with a hatchet."

Enid was appalled. "She is a murderess!"

"It was an involuntary reaction," the master spy explained. "She had known years of oppression in this house, and she would take no more."

"How can you endorse such an act of violence?"

Esmond shrugged. "In a revolution many things happen, as in a war. It is much the same thing. She had proved her loyalty to the new order, and she is a good servant."

"I shall be frightened of her from now on," Enid said with a shudder.

"Just don't cross her," Esmond warned. Then he took Enid in his arms for a long, ardent kiss before leaving regretfully and promising to try to return later.

As soon as he had gone, she washed the kiss from her lips and fervently hoped that his business would detain him for the rest of the night. As time wore on she realized grimly that her hopes of being rescued were slim indeed. She sat by the hearth and stirred the logs to make the fire brighter. Then she stared into the flames, her mind a jumble of images of Kemble and the dead Ramon and her beloved Armand. Would she ever see her French count again?

Or would they be united only in death? The heat from the fire could not penetrate the chill surrounding her heart.

Eventually the embers turned to ash, but Esmond did not show himself again. Enid decided to undress for bed and blew out the candles. A harsh wind rattled the windowpanes and made it difficult for her to fall asleep. Her nerves were in a ragged state as it was, and this added annoyance only frayed them more severely.

She sighed, turning and tossing in bed, and wished that the wind would stop. Then she heard another sound from the window, which made her sit up and glance toward it. This noise was different: a kind of tapping that came regularly through and between the clatter caused by the gusts of wind.

A wild thought struck her. Maybe someone was out there! Someone bent on rescuing her—but how could that be? The distance to the ground was frightening, and she had seen no way for anyone to scale the wall. But the tapping continued.

She left her bed and advanced timorously to the window. Then she gasped, for outside, in the moonlit darkness, a head and shoulders were clearly outlined. Someone was resting on the outside ledge, attempting to get in. With a fearful glance toward the door, and a prayer that the guard wouldn't hear her, Enid slowly raised the window sash.

It was then that she received her greatest shock. For the man at the window ledge was Armand! He looked thin and haggard compared with his appearance at their last meeting, but he seemed healthy enough. He put his fingers to his lips as a signal for her to keep silent. Then he whispered, "Come!"

Stunned as she was, she hurriedly threw on her dressing gown and joined him. Elation at the prospect of escape overwhelmed any thought of how it would be managed. Not until she was out on the precarious perch of the windowsill did she begin to panic. Armand closed his fingers over her wrist for a reassuring moment, then undid the rope that had been wound about him and carefully tied it around her waist.

"Cling to the stonework for support as you're drawn up!" he told her. Then he signaled someone on the rooftop of the mansion to lift her to safety.

Enid felt a dizzying moment of being suspended in space as she left the windowsill. She was certain she would fall to the ground, but then she remembered to dig her fingers into the joins between the stonework and press her toes into the same crevices. Whoever held the other end of the rope drew her up slowly but steadily.

After what seemed an eternity but was in actuality only a few minutes, she was assisted over the low parapet, to lay gasping on the roof. The familiar face of Gustav peered above her as he began to undo the rope around her waist.

"Gustav!" she cried.

"I must get Armand up," he told her. Quickly he went to the parapet and lowered the rope.

She got to her feet, still trembling from her ordeal. The wind was sharp up here on the rooftop. Then she turned and saw that she was not alone. A hollow-cheeked, wild-eyed man whose white hair and beard were long and straggly stood a few feet away, staring at her vacantly. He made no attempt to communicate with her, for which she was grateful since his vacant gaze held a look of madness. She moved away from him to stand near Gustav. The old man did not shift his eyes or his stance. He stood as if frozen to the spot.

Gustav strained at the rope, and in a few moments Armand came clambering over the parapet. He untied himself and then, smiling, clasped Enid to him in a kiss that burned their lips.

"Darling!" he murmured. "At last!"

"How did you know I was here?" she asked, gasping for breath.

"I didn't. I came for the duke who once owned this place." He nodded to the wild-looking man.

"Esmond kept him a prisoner. His wife was murdered."

"Yes." Armand nodded grimly. "At the moment he is surely insane. Who wouldn't be, locked in a dark dungeon for almost two years? But I have seen worse cases recover with rest and the proper treatment."

"What now?" Enid wondered, still clinging to Armand as if he might evaporate into the wind.

"We get away from here as quickly as possible."

"What about the Dauphin?"

"The Dauphin?" Armand echoed sharply. "What about him?"

"He is a prisoner somewhere in this house."

"I didn't find him, and I searched all through the cellars."

"They must have moved him then."

Gustav came up to them, full of impatience. "Time for talk later. We are endangering ouselves every minute we remain here."

"How do we escape?" she asked fearfully.

"By secret passage known only to the duke and his family. I learned about it from one of his cousins. It will take us safely down to the cellar into a tunnel leading to the family cemetery. The exit is through a vault in there."

"And Esmond knows nothing about it?"

"It seems that way, or else he would have guards posted," Armand said.

Gustav took the duke by the arm to guide him, and Armand led the way with Enid. A trapdoor in the rooftop gave them entry into the attic, an unfinished area above the upper floor. At one end there was a door hidden by a joining of beams. Armand knew its location and pushed it open. A dark space yawned beyond, within whose confines was a very narrow stairway that wound around and around in a dizzying manner. Enid could imagine that it took up very little room and so had not been noticed by Louis Esmond and the new occupants.

When they reached the cellar level, the winding stairway became a tunnel, so narrow and low that they had to progress through it on their hands and knees. After a long, almost unendurable struggle through this passage, they finally emerged into a dank and dusty mausoleum.

Enid saw the murky outlines of coffins that rested on shelves flanking both sides of the vault. She shuddered involuntarily. A cobweb brushed across her face and she gasped.

"It's almost over," Armand reassured her, holding her arm as he led her up several stone steps and out into the open. Gustav and the elderly duke followed.

They moved swiftly across the windswept burial ground, looking like phantoms who had risen from their graves, as indeed they had. Once outside the cemetery, they entered a narrow street, sped along it, and darted through an alley into another street, where a closed carriage was waiting. As soon as they were inside the vehicle, it was driven off.

Enid leaned on Armand's shoulder and repeated her earlier question. "How did you know I was there?"

"We saw the light in your window and knew it was separate from the rest of the house. I assumed that the room held a prisoner, and I decided to risk going down on the rope. When I saw you there, I couldn't believe my eyes."

"I couldn't believe it was you either, though I was hoping you had escaped from prison."

"Thanks to Gustav. He made the escape of about a dozen of us possible. Now I'm back to saving others. My first assignment was to bring out the unfortunate duke."

"And you found me as well," she sighed, snuggling against him.

He stroked her hair. "Tell me, dearest, what are you doing in France? And how did you ever get into that house?"

She told him the story as briefly as she could, and he listened quietly. Soon the carriage came to a halt at a dark, modest-looking house.

"Around to the rear," Armand whispered as the four of them left the coach.

They moved swiftly in the darkness to the rear door. Armand knocked on it, using a particular signal. After a long moment it was opened by a husky man who stepped aside to allow them to enter.

"We were beginning to worry about you, Count Beaufaire," the man said.

"It took longer than I expected," Armand replied.

They went down to the cellar, which was well lighted by candles and contained a group of six men seated at a round table sipping some wine. Enid needed only to glance at them to know that they were also fleeing aristrocrats. At her appearance they stood up hastily.

"It is all right, gentlemen," Armand said happily. "This is Lady Blair from England, here under orders from the British secret service to help us."

Enid was given a warm welcome, as was the haggard Duke of Aranjais, who was then taken away to be cleaned up and looked after. Enid stood in the background as Armand proceeded to tell his comrades about his having entered Esmond's headquarters.

He ended by smiling in Enid's direction and saying, "My reward was a special prize! This lady long ago promised her heart to me!"

His friends drank to her health, then to her and Armand's future happiness. When the merriment had subsided, Enid asked Armand about her rejoining Kemble and the other members of the spy network.

"Let it wait for tomorrow," Armand decided. "I must leave for Calais in the morning with these men, to see them on their way to England. In the meantime, tonight shall be ours!"

They left the group and disappeared up the stairs to a room Armand used from time to time. Once behind the closed door, alone at long last, they could only stare mutely at each other, relishing this moment after such a lengthy separation. Enid thought that everything she had endured since their last encounter had been worth the effort and the waiting. To see Armand standing before her, very much alive, his black eyes flashing, his strong features so dear, his body leaning toward her in yearning, filled her with a deep sense of joy.

That same feeling was reflected in his eyes, for Armand had never been happier than he was at this very moment. To him it embodied all that he had been fighting for, all that he believed in. And to think that Enid had endangered herself in his own cause! Her courage and determination were rare qualities, and he felt blessed indeed to be loved by such a woman.

Such a beautiful woman, he thought. He touched her golden hair, her cheeks, the soft flesh of her shoulder beneath the silk nightdress. Gently he removed the dressing gown from her, then the undergarment, and gazed at her supple body with renewed wonder. Enid's flesh glowed under his warm eyes; her nipples grew taut with desire. She wanted to feel his lips sear her breasts, his tongue burn down the length of her until she had become a taper of flame.

Armand quickly shed his clothing and carried her to the bed. She wrapped her arms around him and ran her fingers through his hair and along the muscles of his back. He pressed his swollen maleness against her as his hungry mouth worshipped her and his caresses drove her to the peak of passion. She arched her back to receive him, responding to his thrusts with her own insistent urgings. Again and again, higher and higher, their movements crescendoed into pulsating thunderings, and they became one, whole, flesh and spirit united for eternity.

25

In each other's arms all the past and present perils had been forgotten. Their night of lovemaking had erased Enid's memory of Esmond's having so cruelly taken her. But when morning came, the grim reality of a France churning with turmoil could not be ignored.

Armand brought their breakfast tray up to the room himself. He sat on the edge of the bed, and Enid propped herself up against the pillows, to enjoy the morning meal.

After they had finished eating, Armand said, "Now tell me, what about the Dauphin?"

She told him as much as she knew, ending with, "Father Braun had definite information that the prince was a prisoner in Esmond's headquarters."

Armand looked troubled. "I swear I saw no sign of him."

"Of course, you weren't looking for him."

"I examined every cell and found only the poor duke. And you were the only one in the upper part of the house."

"Then either they moved him or he is hidden somewhere you didn't look," she decided.

"But where?"

"I have no idea. But since there is that one secret passageway, it follows that other passages could be hidden in the house."

Armand considered this. "That is true."

"Kemble will be urging the network to try to rescue me. I must get to them before they make a move that could be dangerous for them."

"I'll have a carriage take you to the lodging house. That way you'll be sure to reach Kemble safely."

"And you?"

"I must be on my way to Calais in an hour."

Enid gave him a pleading look. "When will it end, Armand?"

"A long time from now, I fear," he said sadly. "But my own usefulness is almost finished. After I complete my present assignment, I shall come back to Paris and join you. We can return to London together."

"My dearest!" She leaned forward and kissed him with delight. "And if fortune smiles on us, perhaps we will save the Dauphin and take him along!"

"This Father Braun is obviously working with another section, for I haven't met him yet. But it seems to me he was remiss in leaving the lad alone as he did."

"He admits that."

"You might as well tell him about the secret passage," Aramand advised. "He can use it to make a further survey of the house, though I very much doubt he will find anything worthwhile."

"He will be delighted to learn there is something there that is unknown to Esmond."

"The passage is not connected with the main part of the house," Armand told her, "only with the attic and the cellar. For every other place you uncover, you must use alternate means of escape—as I did with the dropped rope to rescue you."

"I will explain it all to them," she promised.

A half hour later he kissed her goodbye and sent her off in a carriage with a trusted agent. As she proceeded to rejoin Kemble and Renaud, she fell into low spirits once more. Armand was still involved in his risky work, and she was still involved in the mission to rescue the Dauphin. Anything could happen to either of them.

She received a small measure of satisfaction at the thought of Louis Esmond's apoplexy when he found both her and the old duke gone. He would be beside himself with rage and desperate for revenge.

A feeling of excitement filled her when the carriage halted before the house that was their headquarters. The agent saw her to the door, and only when she and Kemble had thrown their arms about each other did he withdraw and return to the vehicle.

"I can scarcely believe my eyes!" the actor exclaimed. "I thought I would never see you alive again!"

"I was beginning to think the same. Did you find Ramon?"

"Dead as mutton!" Kemble said indignantly. "The poor little man was stabbed and battered as well!"

"I know." She glanced up the stairway and trembled with remembered fear. "It was Esmond who killed him and took me away."

"How did you manage to elude the scoundrel?"

"Where is Renaud?" she asked. "It will save my repeating the story if I tell you both at the same time."

"In the kitchen," Kemble replied. "In fact, Father Braun is here, and we were just holding a council of war on how to release you."

They made their way to the kitchen, where Father Braun and the man who had posed as the midget's mother greeted her. Enid noticed that Renaud was no longer wearing women's clothing.

Kemble saw her glance and said, "Our friend Renaud thinks it's not necessary to dress as a mother with his son gone."

Renaud was disgusted. "Esmond is onto us! It's too late for such charades!"

Father Braun seated her at the table, his expression grave. "Now, let us hear all about your capture and escape."

She told them everything that had happened. "The secret passage will take you to the cellar level of the house," she concluded.

Father Braun's ruddy face showed his concern. "I wonder if it is even worthwhile. Your Count Armand claimed there was no one else imprisoned down there."

"Maybe the prince is being kept somewhere else in the house. A hidden room, perhaps?" Enid suggested.

The priest stared at her. "You think I should venture there?"

"I do," she said. "If you don't believe you can find your way, I shall go with you."

"I can manage by following your directions," he assured her. "This is a task best looked after by one man."

"When will you go?" Kemble asked.

"Tonight," the cleric replied. "Just as soon as it is dark."

Father Braun and Renaud left soon afterward, and Enid and Kemble were alone in the house. He grumbled, "Your being taken hostage and Ramon's murder have halted everything."

"Now we can start again."

He frowned. "What do you think the chances are that the Dauphin is still alive?"

"I think they are good."

"Why? Esmond and his ilk are determined to wipe out the royal family along with the nobles."

"It will suit Esmond to keep the boy alive," she said, pouring them both some tea she had made earlier.

"Why?"

"There is a battle for supremacy among the leaders of the masses, and Esmond plans to use young Louis Charles to bolster his ambition to become a party leader."

"You're saying he'll keep the boy alive for purely selfish reasons?"

"Yes."

"You may be right."

"Judging by what he said, I'm certain of it."

"He'll be enraged to find you and the duke gone. And don't think he won't try to do something about it."

"I doubt if he'd dare touch me again. At least I hope not. And the duke is on his way to England via Calais. He is in Armand's safekeeping."

Kemble's brown eyes flashed angrily. "While I dawdle about, painted and dyed to look like your father, and worried sick about you, you are having a tender reunion with your lover!"

"Do you begrudge me that?"

"Of course I do!" he declared vehemently. "I'm sick of this business. We seem to be going in circles and getting nowhere!"

Enid laughed and placed a hand on his shoulder. "I think you are lonely for the stage and for your pretty Jenny."

"She has a sweet face and a mild disposition—certainly better than yours!" the actor retorted.

"I have always said she was meant for you."

"And I've always hoped that Armand would vanish and never be seen again!"

"I doubt if your wish will be fulfilled. He told me this morning that this will be his last mission."

"What then?"

"He will make England his permanent home."

"And you his wife?"

"If I'm ever able to be free of Andrew, yes." She sipped her tea and grew reflective.

Kemble gave a deep sigh. "And I'm not even sure I'll have a company to return to. My tight-fisted sister has probably alienated everyone by now."

"Not Jenny and Susie," Enid said. "They will fight back if Mrs. Siddons tries any tricks on them."

"I suppose so. Lord, how I rue the day I met Sir Harry!"

"But think of the possibilities." Enid tried to inject a bright note in her voice. "If the Dauphin is rescued by us and taken back to England, we shall be history-book heroes!"

"The way things are going, I wouldn't give a lead shilling for my place in history," Kemble groaned in typical melancholic fashion.

• • •

That night Father Braun left alone on his mission to Esmond's headquarters. Because of the importance of his errand, they had agreed to wait up for his return. If he found the Dauphin and brought him back, their goal would be accomplished and they could return to London immediately.

Renaud had found some beef that Kemble had insisted was horsemeat, but which, with suitable sauces, had made a delicious dinner for the three of them. Now they sat drinking some of the fine red wine Father Braun had brought them from the monastery.

Kemble got up from the table and began to pace slowly back and forth. "Waiting again," he muttered. "It seems I have been constantly waiting since I arrived in France."

"He should return soon if he isn't captured," Enid said hopefully. "I gave him a complete picture of the tunnel and the vault."

Renaud nodded. "The good father is not one to tarry. He knows what he is doing."

"Then why did he let the lad slip through his fingers in the first place?" Kemble snapped.

Renaud shrugged. "We all make errors. Some can never be avoided."

"He may have to hide for a little while before he is able to explore the place," Enid pointed out.

"He will come back as soon as he can," Renaud concluded.

Kemble made no reply but continued to pace. Enid began to think it might have been better to have sent him along, or Renaud, to stand guard at the tomb entrance on the burial ground. But Father Braun had insisted it should be a one-man operation. She recognized the priest's ability and intelligence, but she did not always understand him. There seemed to be an invisible barrier present, like a protective shield, whenever he was questioned too intently.

Her ruminations were interrupted by what sounded like a riot outside. The commotion sent them all hurrying to peek around the shuttered front windows. In the street two men were fighting, each rocking back and forth in an attempt to gain the upper hand. A ring of onlookers had circled them and was lustily urging them on in their battle.

Then one of the combatants flashed a dagger, and crouching low, began to stalk his opponent. The unarmed man retreated but could go only so far because of the people crowded about him. The man with the dagger lunged forward and almost succeeded in driving the weapon home. The threatened man waited until his adversary was struggling to regain his balance before moving in with some hard blows to the face and body. The unexpected attack stunned the knife-wielding man, and he almost dropped his weapon.

The onlookers, eager for some bloodletting, continued to encourage the pair to fight. One of the watchers held a lighted torch high so that all might better observe the melee. Suddenly the man with the dagger leaped forward, and this time he sank the gleaming blade deep into his opponent's chest. The wounded man slumped to the cobblestones and the crowd howled with glee.

The attacker removed the knife from his victim and wiped it clean on the other man's breeches. Then he put it back into its sheath and sauntered off, the delighted mob following on his heels, no doubt planning to celebrate this unexpected form of entertainment in a tavern or two. The man who had been stabbed remained motionless in the street.

"We must do something to help the poor fellow!" Enid insisted.

"Mix up in that? It could only lead to trouble," was Kemble's opinion.

Renaud turned to them. "Obviously no one cares, so no one can blame us if we try to give him some aid."

"I agree," Enid said. "Bring him inside, and I'll get some hot water ready and some clean cloths."

"From what I saw, he's more in need of a wooden box!" Kemble grumbled.

He and Renaud left the house, glanced warily about to see if anyone was near, then lifted up the fallen man and carried him inside.

After they had reached the kitchen, they laid him down on the floor. Enid brought the candle close so they could determine how seriously injured he was.

It was Renaud who first gave a cry of shock. "Look!" He pointed at the man. "See who he is!"

"Our driver!" Enid exclaimed.

"The count in disguise," Kemble murmured. "They must have got onto him."

"Or else he became involved in a street brawl and couldn't get away," Enid mused. "Is he still breathing?"

Renaud had pressed his ear to Pierre's bloodstained chest. Now he looked up and shook his head. "No use. He is dead."

"I'm so sorry," Enid said, gazing down at the immobile face with its stubble of black beard.

Kemble sighed heavily. "Another nobleman gone."

"Another link in Sir Harry's network broken," Enid added. "I wonder if they knew he was a spy."

"Hard to say." Renaud shrugged. "At any rate, he is dead."

"What will we do with him?" Enid asked.

"Put a cover over him until Father Braun returns. Then we can bury him here in the cellar. We three men can soon sink a grave in the muddy ground."

Enid found an old bedsheet and carefully covered the body of Pierre Giraud. "I'm afraid this is a bad omen," she said softly.

They resumed their vigil for Father Braun's return in an atmosphere of gloom. The sight of the body on the kitchen floor was a curt reminder that all their lives were held by a tenuous thread that could be snapped at any moment.

At last there was a single, soft rap on the rear door. Renaud rose, peered out cautiously, and then opened the door.

Father Braun came in looking exhausted. The first thing he saw was the shroud on the floor. He reacted at once. "Who is that?"

"Count Pierre Giraud," Renaud told him. "He has driven his last coach from Calais to Paris."

"Murdered?" the priest asked incredulously.

"Yes."

"But how did his body get here?"

"There was a brawl in the street, almost in front of the door," Enid explained. "He had an argument with someone, and the man drew a dagger and killed him."

"He must have been on his way here," Kemble said. "It is my opinion they discovered he was a spy."

"Poor man!" Father Braun shook his head sadly, his face reflecting his distress.

"Enough of that!" Kemble declared. "What do you have to report to us?"

"Nothing," the priest replied.

"Nothing!" Enid echoed him. "Didn't you get inside?"

"I was inside," he said grimly. "I thought for a while there I would never get out. A guard almost caught me."

"And no one was there?" Kemble wondered.

"Not in the cellars. I checked again on every cell. All of them were empty."

Enid considered this. "Esmond was afraid that the boy would be found, so he must have moved him somewhere else."

Father Braun nodded. "That has to be the answer. I swear he was not there!"

"Where can he be, then?" Kemble mused.

"Who knows?" Father Braun shrugged. "Take the map of Paris and stick a pin in it."

"There must be a better way of discovering his whereabouts," Enid observed.

"There is," the cleric agreed, "but it is not a quick way. I must begin all over again, contact the entire network. It is inevitable that gradually we'll have some word leaked as to where the boy is being held prisoner."

"And by then they'll have moved him somewhere else!" Kemble grumbled with disgust. "This game can go on forever!"

The priest gave him a reproachful look. "I do not consider it a game. It is a most serious business. The future of France may depend on the Dauphin's safe arrival in England."

"You destroyed our plan when you let them take the boy from you," Kemble retorted.

"I will accept that blame," Father Braun acknowledged bitterly. "But at the same time I beg credit for having devised the scheme by which the prince was freed in the first place."

"Recriminations will not help," Enid chided. "We must stay loyal to each other more than ever before."

Renaud nodded. "I agree."

"It looks as if we will return to London with empty hands," Kemble sighed.

"Give me half a week to redeem myself," the priest suggested. "If I find out nothing by then, I will give up as head of the mission."

"That sounds more than fair," Enid remarked.

"We can ask no more," was Renaud's opinion.

"I suppose I must go along with your scheme," Kemble said unhappily. "But I warn you, I have little confidence in it."

Father Braun's blue eyes could not conceal his contempt. "With all due regard to you, Kemble, it is obvious that you are not ideally suited to this line of endeavor. Sir Harry made an unfortunate mistake in sending you here."

"My appointed task was to pick up the Dauphin and take him back to England, nothing more!" Kemble stormed. "I do not feel I have failed in any way. It is *you* who have failed by not delivering the boy to us!"

"You are right," the priest said quietly. "And I'm sorry."

Renaud stood up and nodded toward the figure of the slain count. "If we are to dig the grave, let us get on with it before you leave, Father."

"Of course. I will be glad to help."

The next two hours were so macabre that Enid was convinced she would never forget them. While the three men labored down in the cellar to provide a grave for Giraud, she sewed the body of the slain count into the bedsheet. All the while she was doing this she worried about Armand and what he might be going through at this moment. Would the journey to Calais be smooth and uncomplicated, or would he be thwarted along the way? The same question applied to his return trip to Paris. Enid sighed heavily as she bent over her unpleasant chore. She knew that even though this undertaking marked Armand's last work for the underground, he would not be free from the tentacles of danger until he had left France for good.

Finished with their digging, the men carried the shrouded corpse down the ladder that gave access to the cellar. Enid followed them, holding a candle to light her steps. Once the body of Pierre Giraud had been placed in the shallow grave, they all stood with bowed heads as Father Braun offered brief prayers. Then the men set about filling in the makeshift plot.

The united efforts of the threesome to bury their fallen associate seemed to have fostered a new spirit of understanding. They offered a toast to the dead count with the good wine that the priest had brought from the monastery, and Enid joined them in expressing her own thoughts. As Kemble and Father Braun began to speak earnestly in low tones, she felt that their bitter dissension of earlier was now resolved.

Shortly thereafter the cleric departed, but not before he had promised to return in two or three days at the latest to report on the progress he had been able to achieve.

Once more Enid, Kemble, and Renaud settled down to another tense period of waiting.

26

The next morning Kemble unexpectedly found something with which to occupy himself. He was strolling along the riverbank with Enid and Renaud, who had suggested they go out on a shopping tour, when he came across an outdoor book market offering copies of a number of French plays. There were works by Molière, Racine, and Corneille, as well as lesser dramatists; the fine leather-bound books no doubt had been confiscated from some murdered nobleman's library. However, Kemble was not interested in where they had come from; his only concern was in their contents.

After he had selected three volumes, he showed them to Enid. "I'll find something I particularly like and do a translation of it. My time here will not be wasted."

"That's an excellent idea!" she encouraged him.

Locating quality foolscap suitable for his work and a supply of pens and ink required a more serious search, but the actor succeeded in purchasing all the necessary materials.

Enid bought a mauve silk dress with some misgivings, feeling she was robbing the dead. However, her own clothes were soiled and falling into disrepair after her longer-than-expected stay in Paris.

Renaud kept busy hunting for food. Someone sold him a mangy-looking fowl and a few brown eggs, and he carried these items proudly in his basket, as if they were a grand prize. And indeed they were, since all produce was at a premium these days in this torn city.

Back at their lodgings, Kemble announced, "I shall make a new translation of Molière's *The Misanthrope*. I have never yet found one that suited me." Happily and cheerfully, he seated himself at the kitchen table and applied pen to paper.

• • •

Two more days passed, and still Father Braun had not returned. Both Enid and Renaud were becoming restless and irritable. But Kemble, usually the most impatient of them all, was suddenly blissfully content. Full of enthusiasm for his translation efforts, he remained steadfastly at the kitchen table, writing on the long sheets of foolscap. Every so often he would laugh aloud and then tell them of a new twist of comic phrasing he had given to some of the famous lines.

Enid privately declared to Renaud, "I vow he has forgotten all about our mission here!"

The Frenchman shrugged. "As long as he doesn't pace back and forth like an angry British lion, it's all right with me."

"You're probably right," Enid said. She and Renaud were standing by the front windows, taking turns at watching the street.

"The good father promised he would be in touch with us whether he found out about the Dauphin or not. It's time we heard from him."

"He said two or three days," Enid reminded him. "We shouldn't really be too concerned until after tomorrow."

"True," Renaud agreed, shuffling his feet impatiently.

"I'm as much concerned for Armand." She sighed. "He should have returned from Calais by now, but there is no sign of him."

"It is a time of trial and agitation, and patience is not easy to maintain in light of all our problems. Nothing is certain any more."

Enid's reunion with Armand had been so blissful that she could not think of facing life without him. Yet she knew, as Renaud had just said, that the future was extremely uncertain. She could never count on anything until her beloved was at her side again.

A sudden pandemonium erupted outside, drawing the attention of herself and Renaud back to the windows. The sight that greeted them was both familiar and sorry. Two proud-looking men, wearing fine brocade waistcoats and white-powdered wigs, were being led along the street like cattle, heavy ropes tied about their necks. As they marched along, heads erect, pale faces expressionless, the ragged crowd clustering around and behind them jeered loudly and spat at the pair repeatedly.

Renaud gritted his teeth. "On their way to the guillotine, madam."

"What a madhouse this Paris has become!" Enid lamented.

• • •

Another night of waiting had elapsed without the appearance of Father Braun. Enid began to worry in private but said nothing. Renaud was also reserved and quiet. Only Kemble was in a good humor. He could barely wait for the day to begin so that he could resume work on the comedy.

"I shall have a prize when we return to England," he told his companions at breakfast.

Enid gave him a wise look. "But not, I fear, the prize for which we came."

He became red-faced and apologetic. "Sorry! I had forgotten for a moment!"

"Thinking about our problem does little to solve it," Renaud observed.

After breakfast the Frenchman elected to go food shopping again. "We shall be needing supplies for four or maybe five people, if Father Braun returns with the Dauphin."

"*If* he does," Enid said with meaning.

"You yourself said we must not give up hope," Renaud reminded her.

She sighed. "You are right, of course. And I'll go shopping with you. I'd like to get some air and sunshine."

Renaud turned to Kemble, who was already busy at the table. "And you, Monsieur Kemble?"

"Thank you, no," the actor said with a sheepish smile. "I'm trying to finish the third act before Father Braun returns. Besides, someone ought to remain here to greet him or take a message."

It was a pleasant autumn day, and in spite of her apprehensions, Enid felt better once she was outdoors. The warmth of the sun was comforting after the dank chill of the old house. They headed toward the food market and joined the bustling throngs. She wandered along at her own pace as Renaud occasionally halted to haggle with some farmer over a bit of produce.

She was a short distance away from him when two police officers emerged from the crowd and approached her with hostile expressions on their faces. As they each seized her by an arm, one of them told her, "Lady Blair, we are arresting you in the name of the Council."

"You're making a mistake!" she protested.

"We have our orders," the officer insisted, and he and his associate began to pull her away from the market.

She cried out, "Renaud! Help!" But her friend was lost in the crowd. She was vaguely aware of abuses being shouted at her and of a sea of sullen faces glaring in her direction. Then the two policemen shoved her into a carriage and they drove off quickly.

Fifteen minutes later she found herself in the library that Louis Esmond used as his office. He was standing next to the desk, his face dark with fury.

"Why have you brought me back here?" she demanded.

He limped over to her. "Didn't you forget to say goodbye?"

"What do you hope to gain from me this time?"

Hatred glittered in the single eye focused on her. "Where is he? Where is the Dauphin?" Esmond snarled.

"You are the one holding him!"

"I *was* the one!" he cried angrily. He limped toward the opposite wall and pressed a small knob. A panel slid back to reveal an opening into a small, cell-like room. "He was in there!"

Enid stared through the doorway of the secret chamber, lit by candlelight, saw an empty, rumpled cot and a bench. Otherwise the room was empty. "So that is where you had him!"

"Don't pretend you didn't know about it!" Esmond said, bringing a fist crashing down on the sideboard next to him. *"Where is he?"*

"I know nothing of his whereabouts," she replied haughtily.

He thrust his rage-filled face into hers and spoke scathingly. "You were sent here from England with that actor Kemble to have the Dauphin delivered to you and to see him safely back to London. Do you deny that?"

"No."

"Then tell me where he is!"

"You managed to get him away from Father Braun, so he could not deliver the prince to us. Louis Charles was last here as your prisoner. In that room—so you say!" Enid stepped back a few paces. The nearness of Esmond was makking her dizzy with nausea.

"And he was stolen from this house on the very night you and the duke vanished. I don't know by what black magic you escaped, but I am convinced that you took the boy with you!"

"No!"

"He is gone!" Esmond shouted angrily.

"I can swear he didn't leave with us. Count Beaufaire, who rescued the duke and me, didn't even know that the lad was here. Nor did he know of that secret room—any more than I did until you revealed it to me just now!"

The French master spy beamed his one eye on her. "You are clever, Lady Blair. You speak with a serpent's tongue. Sweet words of innocence which I do not believe! It is too much of a coincidence that the prince disappeared on the same night and at the same time as you did, without your being a party to it."

"You can believe what you like. I have told you the truth." She tossed her head defiantly.

"This time it is going to be different," Esmond warned her. "This time you have until tomorrow morning to tell me where that boy is. If you refuse, your head goes on the block!"

Enid smiled grimly. "You no longer want me as a bed companion? Did I not please you?"

"I've heard all that before," he told her sharply. "I could revel in your body. But I have more pressing problems. I have placed myself in a difficult position with Robespierre and the Council."

"Really?"

He came close to her again and said in a low, tense voice, "Robespierre wants to destroy me, to see me ruined! They have used me, and now they refuse to give me the equality I'm asking for. With the Dauphin to use in a trade with them, I could insist that they elevate me to the Council. But now I have lost him— and all my hopes as well!"

"I'm afriad you became too ambitious, Citizen Esmond."

"You say almost the same words as Robespierre, you vixen!" he stormed.

"Do not expect me to feel any deep sympathy for you."

"All right," he said softly. "You have my word. Tell me where you're hiding that boy or you will die on the guillotine tomorrow."

"I cannot tell what I do not know."

"I shall give you time to reconsider. As the hours shorten, you will change your mind."

"That is not possible."

"In the meanwhile, your prison shall be the very room the Dauphin occupied. You'll even have his bed." Esmond grabbed her by the arm and forcibly shoved her through the entrance to the secret room.

Enid turned to him. "This will do you no good!"

"We shall see," he said, and as he gazed at her, she saw the look of lust return to his cruel face. He pressed another small knob and the panel slid closed, leaving them alone together in a candlelit intimacy. In this room there was neither day nor night. Without windows it was always the same.

"What do you plan to do now?" she asked.

Esmond was taking off his uniform jacket. "I have changed my mind," he told her. "It would be a sheer waste to send you to the blade without once again sampling your body!"

"I do not wish to have you do that again!" she protested sharply.

He was now naked to the waist. "It is not what you wish, Lady Blair, but what I desire!"

Enid glanced away from him and noticed a crystal wine decanter and several goblets placed near one edge of the bench. She looked at Esmond again and murmured, "Very well, if you must. But may I prepare myself first with some wine?"

"Why not?" he said, his voice unsteady with mounting passion.

She smiled. "And will you join me?"

"Bring me a glass," he ordered. "And then we shall engage in the most delightful business of the bed!"

27

Enid approached the bench, her heart pounding fiercely as the fingers of her right hand fumbled with the locket at her neck. She managed to extricate the blue packet of lethal powder, and then, bending over to pour the wine, squeezed the tiny grains into one of the glasses. She had only a matter of seconds to accomplish this, and she prayed that the waiting Esmond had not noticed what she had done.

The blue packet was still crumpled in the palm of her right hand, but she concealed it by the way she held the wine goblet. She walked slowly across the room to the head of the French secret service and handed him the glass of wine into which she had emptied the poison. She was relieved to see that all traces of it had vanished in the ruby liquid.

He took the glass from her and touched hers with it. "To our union. May it not be a final one."

She watched him nervously and hoped she would not betray her fear. "Isn't that up to you?" she replied in an attempt at coyness.

"No, Lady Blair," he said firmly. "It is up to you and your memory!"

"I see." She sipped some of her wine and waited for him to do the same.

The glass of wine remained untouched in his hand. "We would make a perfect couple," he mused. "Give me the information I need, and my place on the Council will be assured. And you will be my consort!"

"Aren't you going to drink to us?" she asked softly.

He favored her with a grim smile. "I hope your lovely head will still grace your equally lovely shoulders this time tomorrow!"

He lifted the goblet to his lips and downed the wine. Then he tossed the glass aside, to splinter on the hardwood floor. "Come!" he urged, and none too gently led Enid to the bed in which the Dauphin had slept.

She could not speak, could only stand transfixed as Esmond slowly unbuttoned her dress and slipped it from her shoulders. Then he stripped her of her undergarments and leaned forward to flick his tongue lightly over her bared nipples. He straightened up and was about to remove his breeches when a strange expression crossed his face.

He stared at her in perplexity, then put a hand to his throat. He tried to say something but couldn't get the words out. Brushing roughly by her, he staggered to the opposite wall and clutched at it—to stop himself from swaying wildly to and fro.

Enid had not moved a muscle nor said a word. She could only gaze at him with a mounting repulsion mixed with horror.

Esmond turned to her as a choking sound welled up deep in his throat. In the next moment he had slumped to the floor, inert and lifeless.

Enid stood there shivering, the feel of his wet tongue still on her nipples. She feared she would be ill. She turned rigidly away and moved toward the bench as if in a trance, then lifted the decanter to her lips and took several huge swallows of wine.

The liquid burned its way down her throat and gradually revived her. She picked up her clothes, and keeping her eyes averted from the dead man, dressed as hastily as she could. Then she made several frantic attempts to locate the knob that would move the panel. At last she found it, and the panel slid open as it had before. Warily she entered the library, thinking that somehow she had to get to the cellar. From down there she could find the tunnel that would bring her outside to the burial ground.

Desperation gave Enid the courage to try a brave ploy. She opened the library door, and looking back over her shoulder and smiling, she said loudly, "Thank you, Louis. I shall return when you have finished your work."

The guard in the corridor stood impassively as Enid conducted her imaginary conversation. Then, very coolly, she shut the door after her and walked by the soldier at a leisurely pace. She did not quicken her steps until she was around the corner and out of sight. Then she shot down another corridor to the stairs leading to the attic.

Once she was alone in the protective darkness, she found her way to the hidden winding staircase and then to the tunnel. She was on her hands and knees, crawling along the passage, when all at once she heard something that struck her with terror.

Ahead of her came the sounds of someone moving straight toward her. Nothing could prevent their meeting, except her turning back, and Enid did not dare do that. She hesitated, staring into the dark shadows from which the sounds emanated and not knowing what to do.

Her panic mounted to a near-breaking point as the cloaked figure reached within a foot or two of her. And then she heard Armand's deep voice mutter tensely, "Whoever you are, my pistol covers you!"

"Armand!" she gasped.

"Enid, is that you?" His tone was incredulous.

"Yes!"

"I was coming to try to rescue you."

"I've only just managed to escape."

"I'll go back and you follow me," he said tautly.

They made their way along the tunnel. When they reached the mausoleum area, he helped her to her feet and they scrambled out into the open. Enid noticed that darkness had fallen. Neither she nor Armand attempted to speak until they were well away from the cemetery.

Armand explained, "When I returned a few hours ago, Renaud told me you had been taken away. I decided at once to go in search of you."

"I didn't know whether help would come or not," she said, trembling now.

He pulled her closer to him. "Tell me what happened after the police took you."

She related the events quickly, adding in a choked voice, "The poison worked! He died before my eyes!"

"He deserved an even worse fate," Armand grunted. "He was a monster. A mass murderer."

"I know. And the strangest part of it is that he didn't even have the Dauphin. The boy was somehow removed from the secret room where Esmond had held him prisoner. It happened the night you rescued me. Esmond was positive I knew all about it."

"We must assume, in that case, that Father Braun has the prince."

"That doesn't seem to fit, but perhaps you are right. I hope so. Then we can all leave for London as soon as possible."

After skirting the main streets and sticking to secluded alleyways, they crossed the river and reached the house a few minutes later. Kemble, Gustav, and Renaud kissed her, and there was much rejoicing. Everyone was relieved to see her returned safely.

When the excitement of her arrival had died down, Enid asked, "What about Father Braun and the boy?"

There was an uneasy silence from the three men as both she and Armand waited for a reply. Then Armand demanded, "Well, tell us!"

Gustav looked embarrassed. "I got here just shortly before you did. I fear I brought some bad news."

"Bad news?" Enid repeated.

"Is the Dauphin dead?" Armand suggested.

"Was Father Braun captured and guillotined?" Enid wondered.

Kemble looked grim. "Nothing like that!"

"What, then?" Armand prodded impatiently.

"You tell them." Kemble addressed himself to Gustav. "It is your bit of news."

Gustav exchanged a glance with Renaud, who looked equally glum, and then he cleared his throat nervously. "It appears we've been outmatched."

"The French have the Dauphin again?" Enid ventured.

"No," Gustav said. "As a matter of fact, the Austrians have him. They took him over the border two days ago."

"What of Father Braun?" Enid cried. "Did the Austrians murder him to get the boy?"

"No," Gustav said, and seemed unwilling to go on.

It was Kemble who picked up the account with a touch of scathing sarcasm. "We were hoodwinked, dear Enid."

"Hoodwinked?" she echoed blankly.

"By the good Father Braun. It is now known that he was a double agent, his first loyalty being to Austria. They have the Dauphin now and will use him when the time is ripe."

"What will Sir Harry say?" she wondered.

"Very little, I should expect," Kemble told her, "since he is the one who decided Father Braun would head his network over here."

Renaud shook his head. "I can hardly believe it."

"Well, one thing is certain," Armand put in with a smile. "You no longer need to remain in France. The mission is over."

"Heaven be thanked for that!" Kemble sighed. "And at least I have a new translation for a play out of it!"

"We shall never be listed as heroes in the history books," Enid said plaintively. "The priest has stolen our niche."

Kemble shrugged. "I care little as long as my name graces the placards for Drury Lane in the present. Let the future take care of itself."

"Well said." Armand clapped him on the shoulder. "I shall make arrangements with the network for us to sail from Calais the day after tomorrow."

Renaud stared at them despondently. "So it is over and we have failed. You will all be leaving. And I have nothing to look forward to but to carry on here and wait for the guillotine to catch up with me!"

Kemble went over to him, slapped him heartily on the back, and declared in a magnanimous tone, "Not so, old chum! We have been through too many dangers together. I have been watching you closely, and I see in you the makings of an excellent property man. You will return to England with us and work for me at Drury Lane!"

"Providing Mrs. Siddons hasn't lost the theater for you!" Enid reminded him.

"Did you have to mention that?" Kemble grumbled.

The group burst into laughter at the actor's expression, and Kemble had the grace to enjoy the merriment of his friends at his own expense.

28

On a foggy morning two days later the five of them were rowed from the Calais shore to the waiting vessel that would bring them to the security of England.

After they were safely on board, Armand stood by the bow with his arm around Enid and stared through the mist at his beloved homeland.

"My poor France!" he murmured. "What will happen to her?"

"Many things, I fear; none of them good," she said. "Let us be thankful to be leaving together."

"Yes," he agreed quietly. "We must be thankful."

The journey across the Channel was tiring but uneventful. In London everything appeared much the same. Despite Kemble's fears, his sister had operated extremely successfully during his absence. In any case, he was more than happy to be able to take over the reins of Drury Lane again.

Armand and Enid were privileged to witness the joyful reunion between Gustav and Susie at Kemble's flat. The small actress threw her arms about her husband and sobbed, "I was never so happy as now!"

Kemble, who was also watching them, remarked, "May Heaven spare us from your sorrow!" And with that he proceeded to embrace his own smiling Jenny.

A message was waiting for Enid from her father. He asked her to come down to the country at the earliest moment. There was a tone about the brief note that worried her.

She told Armand, "We shall go down together as soon as Kemble and I have reported to Sir Harry."

"Do you think your parents will welcome me again?" Armand asked.

"Of course they will," she assured him. "They liked you on your last visit."

"There is still your husband to consider."

"That may be what my father wants to see me about."

Susie told Enid about a vacant flat across the street from Kemble. The fist thing Enid did was to inspect the furnished premises, and finding them to her liking, she rented the rooms for herself and Armand.

Kemble rushed off to the theater, taking Renaud with him, since he had promised to introduce the Frenchman to his new duties immediately. It was a day crowded with events, this first day on British soil in many long weeks.

That evening Mrs. Siddons was giving her closing performance as Constance in *King John*. She invited her brother and all his friends to sit in special boxes and join the cast for a party onstage following the final curtain. So Enid found herself once more attending a gala theatrical feast, and this time she had the pleasure of Armand's presence at her side.

Mrs. Siddons gave a fine tragic performance as Constance, and everyone stood to applaud her at the end of the play.

"Penny pincher she may be, but she is my sister and a woman of talent!" Kemble observed.

Then they went backstage to congratulate the players. The banquet table was set up onstage, and soon much food was consumed and many toasts were offered.

During the party Kemble took Enid aside. "I just had a message from Sir Harry. We are to be in his office at ten in the morning."

"I'll be glad to get it over with," she said. "I'm most anxious to go to Surrey and see my parents."

"Well, I expect we cannot avoid the meeting and a stern reprimand." He sighed deeply. "Despite all our high hopes, things went awry."

"It wasn't entirely our fault, remember."

"True." Kemble glanced around him. "It is difficult not to be happy on a night like this. I plan to do my translation of the Molière comedy very soon."

"I'm glad you were kind enough to employ Renaud."

The actor smiled. "You do approve of me at times."

"You are probably my best friend."

His eyes twinkled. "And Armand is your true love!"

"Does that matter?"

"Not any more. My coming back to Jenny has made me more aware of her good qualities. And Susie says she has made some progress in coaching her stage work. I think Jenny and I will do very well."

"I knew that from the start," Enid laughed. "She is the nice, placid sort you need for balance."

"And you are not?"

"Never!"

"You're right," he admitted. "We've been through a lot together, I must say. And to think that Esmond attended the last party we had on this stage!"

Enid's face shadowed. "Don't remind me! His death throes still haunt me!"

"You did humanity a favor with that act of desperation."

A smiling Armand joined them then and asked, "What are you two conspiring about? I vow I feel a fit of jealousy coming on!"

"No need," Kemble proclaimed in grand fashion. "She is yours!"

• • •

The next morning Enid and Kemble traveled together to Sir Harry's office. Kemble asked the carriage driver to wait, and they went inside. Enid felt even stranger here than she had before. In the interim between her first visit and this one she had learned much about the secret service operations of both England and France.

The clerk greeted them as warmly as he had the other time and told Kemble, "I was at Drury Lane last night, Mr. Kemble."

"Ah!" The actor twinkled. "Then you saw a most magnificent performance!"

"I was about to say that, sir," the young man agreed. "I have only lately come to enjoy your sister's work. Last night was a high point."

"I shall pass your comment on to her."

"Thank you. I trust you will soon grace the boards in London again, sir?"

"We open next week with *Hamlet*. To be followed shortly by my own version of a play by Molière."

"I shall look forward to it," the clerk said. "You may go straight in, sir. Sir Harry is waiting for you."

As they went toward the inner office, Kemble grumbled, "You'd never guess he was waiting, considering the chatter of that lad before he let us through."

Sir Harry was seated at his desk, staring out the window. Enid remembered that he had been in this exact position when they had arrived before; she surmised that he probably spent a great deal of time gazing out the window.

The massive man turned and eyed them rather coldly. "So you are back. Both of you are alive and safe."

"We saw some comrades who weren't so fortunate along the way," Kemble said.

"Yes, quite." Sir Harry cleared his throat. "Do sit down!" He waved at two chairs placed before his desk.

"We are sorry we failed you," Enid faltered.

Sir Harry nodded. "So am I. The Austrians have the Dauphin, as you know. At least his life is saved. And in the end they won't know how to use him properly. For all their cleverness, the Austrians lack finesse in diplomacy."

"We could not guess that Father Braun was an adversary," Kemble put in. "You had made him the chief of the network over there."

"He had the talent for it," the big man said. "Unfortunately, he felt he owed his first allegiance to the opposition. In matters of espionage this is a common occurrence."

"So you are not too disappointed in us?" Enid murmured.

He surprised her by smiling suddenly. "I'm not at all disappointed. You poisoned Esmond and rid us of one of our most devious enemies. Our work in France will go on much more favorably with him out of the picture."

"All the credit must go to Lady Blair," Kemble said. "She was magnificent throughout."

"That is most generous of you," Sir Harry stated. "I'm sure you did your part as well. None of us will be noted for changing the course of history, but let us hope we may have steered it in a slightly different direction. We shall bear our anonymity with dignity."

"I feel very much the same way," Enid agreed.

Sir Harry coughed discreetly. "There is something about which I must warn you, Lady Blair."

"Yes?" she said.

"Your husband. He is daily becoming more a topic of gossip. He has broken with the vicomte and now has an Italian lad living with him. Needless to say, he is back in London."

She sighed. "I fear he will never change."

"His gambling persists, of course," Sir Harry continued. "And most distressing of all, he keeps sullying your name and linking it with those of Mr. Kemble and Count Beaufaire. To hear him tell it, you have a male harem catering to your whims!"

"The fellow must be silenced!" Kemble exclaimed.

"I didn't want you to encounter any unpleasant scandal without knowing where it came from, Lady Blair," the government man said. "Since he is still legally your husband, it is a very difficult situation."

"I know. I'm going to Surrey, and I hope my father may have a few suggestions or will be able to report some progress in the efforts to secure my freedom."

Sir Harry rose, signifying the end of their talk. "I truly hope so. Thank you both. You have done his Majesty a singular service. If I have my say, there may be a knighthood in the offing for you, Mr. Kemble."

"I expect no such honor," the actor said. "I'm repaid simply by knowing we saved a few lives over there."

As he escorted Enid back to the waiting carriage, Kemble observed, "It wasn't so very bad after all."

"He actually seemed pleased with us!"

"So he did," Kemble agreed happily. "The only shadow over us is that villain of a husband of yours! He must be prevented from ruining all our names."

"I shall leave for my father's home in a few hours," Enid said. "I'm sure he'll know how to deal with this."

• • •

She and Armand took the afternoon stage to Surrey and arrived at the Hensons' country estate in the early evening. Enid's parents greeted them warmly, and after a hearty supper of roast fowl and plum pudding, she and her father discussed the problem that was on everyone's mind.

Lord Alfred told his daughter, "My lawyers claim that your husband is slandering you in the foulest way."

"To take the spotlight away from his own debaucheries," she said bitterly.

"Without question."

"Have the lawyers made no headway at all with the annulment?"

"Very little," Lord Alfred admitted. "Andrew is fighting it every step of the way."

"Not because of love, but because of hatred."

"We have tried to make that point, but without too much success. He is doing everything to make it impossible for you to show your face in London society. In short, he is attempting to destroy any chance you may have for happiness."

"I'm not afraid of him," Enid said. "He has done his most dastardly to me, and I have survived."

"Naturally, I learned of the ordeal he made you suffer in that disgusting brothel." Lord Alfred's face flushed with indignation. "If I were a younger man, I would seek satisfaction from him!"

Armand, who had been listening quietly, spoke up now. "I, sir, am a younger man—and an interested party as well!"

Enid was immediately opposed to this suggestion. "No, no!" she protested. "We will simply ignore Andrew and his scandalous talk."

"I hope you both will be able to," Lord Alfred remarked.

And on this grim note the Hensons retired for the night.

• • •

A half hour later Enid slipped into Armand's chamber. Beams of silver moonlight filtered through the window and over his naked body, which quickly locked with hers in a feverish embrace atop the rumpled bed covers. Encouraged by the secrecy of their surroundings, the lovers succumbed to a desperate need to throw all caution to the winds and hungrily sought release in each other's burning flesh. Again and again the flames of passion consumed them, carrying them aloft to exalted heights, until, shortly before dawn had streaked across the horizon, their desires had been satiated and their souls purified.

The days at Henson House were spent strolling in the woods and going for long horseback rides. Some of the neighboring families presented Enid with several gala parties, at which Armand proved to be a popular favorite. When a week had passed, Enid thought they should make their farewells and return to London. She was determined to forge a place for them there in spite of Andrew's deviousness.

• • •

As soon as she and Armand arrived at the flat, she found an invitation from Sir James and Lady Evelyn Drake to one of their lavish soirees. Waving the gilt-edged vellum happily at Armand, she exclaimed, "This most assuredly will be a stunning affair!"

He gave her a keen look. "Will Andrew be there?" he asked.

She hesitated before replying, "Yes, he might be. He is an old friend of the Drakes'."

"In that case, should we attend? I mean, would it be wise?"

"We can't allow him to frighten us away from every social event."

"I shall leave it up to you. We will do whatever you wish."

"We will attend!" she decreed.

• • •

On the night of the party Enid decided to wear a low-cut satin gown of dark crimson. She graced her throat and bared upper chest with a heart-shaped gold locket that Armand had given her to replace the pendant in which she had kept the poison. Since Esmond's gruesome death, she had been strangely adverse to its feel against her skin. Armand's gift—a really fine antique piece—was one of the few family heirlooms he had been able to bring with him out of France.

At Enid's prompting, he dressed for the evening's festivities in a smart black waistcoat of the style currently very popular with London gentlemen. His bearing had always been impressive, and tonight he cut a handsome figure indeed.

Gay laughter and a welter of confusion greeted them as they threaded their way through the Drakes' crowded drawing room. Sir James and Lady Evelyn received them warmly, and after pleasantries had been exchanged, Enid introduced Armand to several friends whom she had not seen in months.

It was the gala affair that Enid had predicted, and someone even whispered that the prince himself and many of his circle were in attendance. Enid suggested to Armand that they join the dancers in the ballroom, and no sooner had they moved in that direction than they came face to face with a smiling, dissolute-looking Andrew Blair.

Eyeing them brazenly, Andrew waved a hand and cried, "If it isn't my charming wife and her equally charming lover!"

Armand's reply was swift and harsh. He slapped Andrew full across the face and bellowed for all to hear, "I demand satisfaction!"

Andrew did not expect such an immediate reaction. Or perhaps he had talked so loosely in their absence that he presumed he could do the same to their faces. In any event, he was quite perturbed at the obvious insult. But too many people had seen and heard the encounter for him to ignore it. Within a few hours the delicious scandal would be bubbling on everyone's lips.

Andrew straightened his waistcoat. "You shall have your satisfaction, sir," he promised.

"My second will call on yours," the count told him. "This time the duel will be with swords, not with cards."

A shaken Andrew attempted a brave smile. "How appropriate!" he declared weakly.

Armand and Enid left the party shortly afterward. She knew that Andrew had gone beyond himself and would now be trying to think of some way to avoid the duel. Despite the danger for Armand, she knew it must be carried out. It was the one hope they had of silencing her husband once and for all; perhaps it might even lead him to release her from their marriage vows.

The next morning Kemble came over to the flat she and Armand were sharing. He spoke without preamble. "I ask that I be allowed to be your second, Armand. And Gustav insists on being one also."

"I shall be honored to have both of you," Armand replied warmly.

Later in the day Kemble returned and announced, "Dawn tomorrow, St. James's Wood."

Armand nodded. "Excellent," he said. "I am looking forward to this match, believe me!"

That evening, while Enid and Armand were having an early dinner, he collapsed suddenly at the table. She hurriedly sent for the same doctor who regularly attended Kemble. Within minutes the physician appeared, the actor on his heels.

The two men carried Armand, who was in a semiconscious state, into the bedchamber and placed him gently on the bed. Then the doctor began his examination. Enid wrung her hands nervously and prayed that the attack would not be fatal. Kemble paced the room like a caged tiger.

At last the doctor left his patient's side and motioned Enid and Kemble toward the parlor.

"He has been stricken by some sort of obscure fever," the physician told them. "I have seen at least a dozen cases like this recently, and all the victims were French refugees. The disease is one that apparently they contracted over there."

"Will he get well?" Enid asked fearfully.

"He will be perfectly fit within a week or ten days," the doctor assured her. "In the meanwhile, he must have plenty of rest and good nursing care. I shall send over a woman who has handled these cases in the past."

After he had left the flat, Enid and Kemble stared blankly at each other. Then Kemble murmured, "But what about the duel?"

"We must call it off, of course!" Enid replied.

"Andrew will claim that Armand is craven, and you can be sure he'll make the most of that lie," Kemble warned her.

"But Armand is ill! You heard the doctor's diagnosis yourself!"

"Yes, but you know what Andrew is like."

"What can we do?" she moaned.

"Someone must stand in for Armand," Kemble declared. "As one of his seconds, I shall consider it my duty and an honor!"

"No, I will not allow you to do such a thing! You might be killed! After all, Andrew is not an indifferent swordsman."

"I shall manage," Kemble insisted. "I may not be your equal, but I'm as good as many others."

His words gave her a sudden inspiration. "Wait! I have an idea. Tell Andrew that Armand is ill, but that my wish is for the match to take place. And that a masked swordsman will fence in his stead."

"Masked swordsman?" Kemble echoed, puzzled.

Her eyes glinted fiercely. "Let me create a precedent. I shall be at St. James's Wood tomorrow at dawn to defend my own honor!"

"You wouldn't dare!" Kemble protested, aghast at her scheme.

"But I would! I'm probably the only one capable of taking Armand's place and closing Andrew's hateful mouth. When I defeat him on the field of honor, I'll remove my mask and show him my face. Then let him boast about the duel!"

"Diabolical!" Kemble declared, his shock turning to admiration. "It should both silence him and complete his dishonor!" Then a look of doubt crossed his face. "What if by some freak of fate he should break your defense and maim or kill you?"

Enid smiled grimly. "You have fenced with me. Do you think that is likely?"

"No, of course not."

"Then please go to him and present my offer."

Her friend returned to her within the hour. "It is all arranged to your satisfaction," he reported with delight.

"Andrew will fence the masked stranger?"

"Yes. He walked straight into the trap. I could tell he thinks Armand's stand-in will be Gustav."

"Of course," she agreed. "Gustav has been a fencing instructor, and he is one of my close friends."

"Obviously Andrew considers himself a more expert swordsman."

"That is quite possible."

"So he agreed to the match at once." Kemble chuckled. "I can't wait to see his face when he realizes that Gustav is one of your seconds. It will be a picture to enjoy!"

"The moment of his defeat will be even better," Enid vowed.

She spent the rest of the night at Armand's bedside, watching the nurse minister to him and doing whatever she could to assist her. Seeing his feverish twisting and tossing, and hearing his repeated moans, she voiced aloud her anxiety that the doctor might have been too optimistic in his pronouncement of Armand's condition.

The nurse comforted her by saying, "It is always the same in these cases. The fever must run its course. The first few days and nights are the difficult ones, but I assure you he will improve afterward."

Enid went to bed very late and slept fitfully. As a consequence, she felt little like fencing when she rose before dawn the next morning. As she kissed a sleeping Armand farewell, she could not help but wonder whether chance might not be on Andrew's side this morning. If so, he could kill her—after all, people did die on the field of honor—and she would never see Armand again.

Susie and Jenny arrived to see to her disguise as a young man.

"Much will depend on your cloak," Susie said. "Do not remove it until the last moment."

"That's right," Jenny agreed. "You are far too shapely, and he would see through the ruse at once."

Enid donned the mask they had brought. "I promise to be silent and to move in a mannish fashion. I also promise to cling to the cloak until the moment before the duel is to begin."

Susie kissed her and said, "I wish we could be there, but Kemble will not allow us to go."

"It is not proper for females to attend such events," Enid told them. "Besides, the sight of the two of you might make Andrew overly suspicious. We dare not chance it."

Kemble and Gustav came to pick her up and expressed their admiration at her outfit. Then they left by carriage for St. James's Wood. This site was a favorite meeting place for duelists, since it was within the city limits but was remote enough to ensure against any outside interference.

A thin mist hung in the air, making the clearing amid the tall trees appear even more desolate. Andrew and his second were already present. When he saw that Gustav was one of her seconds and not the swordsman, he went into a frantic huddle with his man.

Sir Drake, host of the party where the incident had taken place, had been chosen to preside over the match. He discussed the details with the seconds, who then reported back to Andrew and Enid, respectively. Then a hush fell over those assembled as the moment arrived for the duel to begin. Enid discarded her cloak and sprang forward at the ready.

She could never be sure whether it was belated panic or sheer courage that made her wicked husband respond so well. He was more than a worthy adversary. And so she and the man who hated her and whom she hated with equal fury darted back and forth in the gray mist, parrying rapidly in interplay, their swords ringing out harshly in the eerie silence.

Andrew was fencing in a most aggressive manner, and Enid soon realized that if the match lasted much longer, he might very well defeat her. He had the advantage of being able to pit his masculine strength against her weaker female frame. But her advantage lay in being in better condition than he, and she had more skill as well.

She began to wonder grimly if skill was enough. He backed her up a distance, while she frantically wielded her blade to try to protect herself. He used every trick he knew to succeed in disarming her, and she feared that in the end he might just do that. Would he then be satisfied, or would he run his weapon through her slender body and drain the life out of her?

These thoughts haunted her as she battled on in silence, breathing heavily and growing more weary with every passing moment. Then, unaccountably, Andrew lost his footing on the wet grass. Just as unaccountably, she was unable to give way, and as a result she plunged forward and drove her sword through his left side.

She had not intended to strike him. She had meant only to disarm him, or perhaps to nick his arm. But Andrew lay motionless on the ground, blood spurting from the wound and turning the grass a dark red. Sir James hurried forward to attend to him. Enid stood frozen to the spot.

Gustav and Kemble ran to her side.

"It was a freak moment. You could not avoid what happened," the actor murmured.

"I cannot look at him," she gasped, turning her back. "Tell me, is he badly hurt?"

Kemble nodded and went to kneel by Sir James. He remained there for several minutes before he approached her again. She knew at once that the situation was grave.

"He is dying," Kemble told her frankly. "The blade pierced his heart. He asks that he be allowed to congratulate you on your victory."

"No!" she cried, her eyes blurred with tears.

"It is his dying wish," Kemble pointed out.

Enid hesitated for a moment. Gustav and the actor put an arm through hers and guided her to where Andrew lay. Sir Drake was still trying to offer assistance. She knelt close to Andrew. His face was deathly pale; blood was flowing freely from the wound. The blood that could not be staunched.

Weeping, she removed her mask and sobbed, "I did not mean to harm you!"

Andrew smiled faintly. "I knew it was you…the moment you discarded the cloak. I meant to kill you…I tried to!"

"It doesn't matter now," she whispered.

"I have been…less than fair …" Andrew's voice grew weaker. "Less than fair …" Then he choked on the blood rising up in his throat and closed his eyes forever.

The carriage ride back to the flat was endured in silence by Enid and her friends. She felt numb, lifeless, as if she were moving among gray shadows that were part of a nether world.

When they reached her building, Kemble eased her out of the coach and saw her to the door.

"It will be all right," he said tenderly, kissing her on the cheek.

She was too filled with grief to reply. She merely nodded and went inside. Upstairs in the apartment she found the nurse bathing Armand's head with cool water. His eyes were open and focused, and as she approached his bedside, they lit up from within with a black fire.

"So very beautiful!" he whispered, grasping her hand.

"You must rest, my love. Go back to sleep now."

His grip tightened and his eyes burned into hers. "Tomorrow morning will settle it! We shall have a new life for ourselves!"

"Yes," Enid said softly. "A new life for ourselves."

As she bent down to brush her lips against his, the sun broke clearly through the mist and lighted the chamber. She glanced up and smiled to herself. Yes, we shall have a new life for ourselves, she thought, and it has begun this very day.